The Last Soldier of Nava

The Last Soldier of Nava

Yejin Suh

MAGPIE

Magpie Books
An imprint of HarperCollins*Publishers* Ltd
1 London Bridge Street,
London SE1 9GF
www.harpercollins.co.uk

HarperCollins*Publishers*
Macken House,
39/40 Mayor Street Upper,
Dublin 1
D01 C9W8
Ireland

First published by HarperCollins*Publishers* Ltd 2025
1

Copyright © Yejin Suh 2025
Chapter header and part title illustrations © Jason Lyon/Brilliant Artists

Yejin Suh asserts the moral right to
be identified as the author of this work.

A catalogue record for this book is available from the British Library.

ISBN: 978-0-00-868338-2 (HB)
ISBN: 978-0-00-868339-9 (TPB)

This novel is entirely a work of fiction.
The names, characters and incidents portrayed in it are
the work of the author's imagination. Any resemblance to
actual persons, living or dead, events or localities is
entirely coincidental.

Set in Sabon LT Std by Palimpsest Book Production Limited,
Falkirk, Stirlingshire

Printed and bound in the UK using 100% Renewable Electricity by
CPI Group (UK) Ltd

All rights reserved. No part of this publication may be
reproduced, stored in a retrieval system, or transmitted,
in any form or by any means, electronic, mechanical,
photocopying, recording or otherwise, without the prior
written permission of the publishers.

Without limiting the author's and publisher's exclusive rights, any unauthorised use
of this publication to train generative artificial intelligence (AI) technologies is
expressly prohibited. HarperCollins also exercise their rights under Article 4(3)
of the Digital Single Market Directive 2019/790 and expressly reserve this
publication from the text and data mining exception.

MIX
Paper | Supporting
responsible forestry
FSC
www.fsc.org
FSC™ C007454

This book contains FSC™ certified paper and other controlled sources
to ensure responsible forest management.

For more information visit: www.harpercollins.co.uk/green

To my parents

According to legend, the Soldier once drowned entire kingdoms in darkness.

A thousand years ago, the city of Nava – The Ninth City; the eternal city – flourished in the land today known as Ik-Song. It was ruled in tandem by the Bearer of the Moon and Bringer of the Dawn, kept in balance by the Dragons of East and West.

Until the Moon Bearer slaughtered the Dragon of the East in his search for power, and the City fell as consequence. The Dawn Bringer was never to be seen again.

This is when the storms began; deadzones appeared. The land warped and changed.

But the most dangerous effect of all was a new weapon that rose from the spilled blood – a mercenary known as the Soldier . . .

Prologue

One Year Ago

The unnerving part was that she woke with no blood on her hands.

She examined them carefully, trembling, turning over the knuckles double-bound in wrapping that extended all the way up to her forearms. Spotless. Perfect. As if they had never touched anything before.

Breaths coming short, her hands slammed down roughly on the ground behind her, holding herself up. Gravel gritted against the underside of her palms. The right side of her face felt like it would split in two, from eye to lip; blood ran hot in the pocket of her mouth; cold, dank cavern air seeped into her clothing.

And the body lay cooling mere paces away.

I'm sorry, she wanted to say, but her voice wouldn't return. Not yet. She'd only awakened minutes ago, but this time felt different – this time felt like she'd risen out of the ground itself, compact dirt and slabbed stone somehow colliding underground to form her body, impossibly, like a red-rusted canyon:

limbs heavy as stone, vision muddled as an eroding river. This time felt slower, weightier, harder than all the other times.

'Can you stand?' echoed a voice suddenly.

She startled, scrambling back against the wall, hitting it with a hard slam. Usually she was quieter than this, stealthier; now, the maw-dark cellar loomed in front of her like the jaws of a beast, and she squinted into them.

Panting sharply, she couldn't reply.

In the moments that followed, a foot came into view under the sliver of moonlight striping through. Bare, sandalled. Wrinkled. An old woman's foot, tough and leathery skin appearing from nowhere.

What was an old woman doing here? She tipped her head back against the wall, eyes darting from the body and back. There was no way to explain. She wouldn't be believed. She – an unkempt, dirtied, unbloodied killer – beside the corpse of a saint. Facedown on the ground, long brown hair tangled around her arms.

She waited for the inevitable screaming, the panicking. But the old woman came into view, and she did neither. Her eyes remained unalarmed, demeanour calm. 'I asked if you could stand,' she said, not without some irritation. 'Don't you hear me, girl?'

She stilled. Searched this old woman's face for some familiarity. Horror at the scene, or curiosity, even. But it stayed stagnant and closed.

And she felt immeasurable relief at this unreadable face, a face that withheld answers.

So, she stood.

One hand braced against the stone, the other dangling as her legs folded up beneath her. Shaky. The rest of her body worked perfectly well – only the pain in her face made her want to pass out.

The Last Soldier of Nava

Who are you? she wanted to ask the old woman, who only stared dispassionately. *Aren't you afraid of me?*

'My name is Sae,' the old woman announced, already turning her back. 'And you'll come with me.'

After a long moment, she followed. Then the two figures – both somewhat hunched and crooked – made their way out of the underground. And the moonlight around them seemed somehow warmer – stronger, effusive, more golden. Later, she would wonder if it had been a trick of the light.

Part 1:
백열 White Heat

Nine is the auspicious number.
It closes the circle, though the circle has no close.

– Record Annals of Nava

Chapter 1

Shadow came back to herself over a steaming stone pot of ox bone broth.

The earthy aroma reminded her sharply of where she was: the busy town markets of the capital city, Yosae, wedged in a narrow alleyway.

It had been the sand, she thought, that had unmoored her for a moment. Kicked up, maybe, by one of the ritual performers during their Mourning Day dance in the public square. It swept up a cresting wave of brilliant orange that had glittered right in front of her eyes before the wind scattered it in her face – already covered thickly by a black veil – and her body had simply frozen. Shut down. The soft impact of it had trailed like ghostly fingers across her eyes, making her hands clench into fists, the line of her back rigid. The right side of her face ached with phantom pains.

Willing her tight grip on the wooden slats of the stall next to her to loosen and release, Shadow tried to slow her breathing, looking around inconspicuously to see if anyone had caught her slip.

But it was far too busy for that. To honour the martyr Saint

Desert Rose, the market proved a thriving world of its own this afternoon, a sea of dark heads and reed paerangi hats, the rustle of hemp *hanbok* sleeves and the ruckus of haggling bargainers once again filtering back into her hearing. Enormous white Lei cattle-pulled carts carrying steep terracotta pots dragged their way across the narrow roads, barely giving her room, as townsfolk branched off into smaller interweaving footpaths. Under grass-thatch roofs the smell of fermented cabbage wafted beside clusters of fresh enoki mushrooms, seedless black grapes and buckets of watercress.

Smoked blood sausage and pig's trotters were strung up and laid out on hay, curiously examined by flighty children while they chewed on small grilled smelt fish skewered on sticks. A seller across from her – a man with his hands clasped behind his back – stood behind a low-lying table of colourfully bound books. The slap of sandalled servants labouring cargo, vendors' shrill voices, and mothers with crying babies bundled across their backs intensified the cacophony. Mock bamboo puppets of the Dragons of East and West whisked past her, carried by performers. The Dragons were kindhearted water-dwellers, and local legend had it that they kept the old world in balance, rising only on the flower moon – though their paper imitations did not nearly do them justice, and true flower blood moons came by only rarely.

In the midst of it, moved roughly along by the crowd, Shadow enjoyed her invisibility more than she probably should have. Discomforting, yes, but a small thrill still ran through her at this close contact with so many people, in a city still unfamiliar to her.

At night, the Yosae markets would transform into a place shrouded in smoke and fog, a raucous affair of workers and sellers on break disappearing into establishments where they could kick off their shoes on bamboo-woven floors and sit cross-legged around low tables to indulge in domed bowls of rice and cool barley tea – glass bottles strewn across the surfaces, a relaxed ambience.

At least, that was what she imagined the markets to be like at night; she'd never actually been. That was too risky – she couldn't stay out so long, not with the Moonbearer's people roaming around looking for her. The false ruler of Ik-Song.

The crowd moved in front of her like silver-stream fish, too fast to bother pausing for a glance, to parse her out. She was invisible – a widow, maybe, or a servant. She rejoined the masses smoothly, situating herself beside a nondescript stand, pretending to browse through trinkets. A few paces beside her a lithe, dark-haired boy with a farmer's hat milled around, silently examining the tables. She hadn't noticed him until now, which was surprising – usually she was quick to pick up on her surroundings. There was something off about his stance, tense, like he was waiting for something.

'Git,' sniped a voice from behind. A middle-aged woman, hair plaited back, swatted a schoolboy's hands away from where she moulded sweet rice cakes across a powder-strewn surface.

'I have coin,' the boy protested.

'Sure,' she said, 'and I've a palace.'

Shadow recognized the boy – he always haunted the carts on Sundays, trying to sweet-talk his way into treats, bare-handed. She smiled briefly to herself. Hair mussed and fingers sticky, he was still trying to covertly sneak something behind his angled back.

Shadow moved along the stall, curious at the myriad of small goods. A squatting, beer-bellied man with a long beard and topknot eyed her cloaked form with mild suspicion as she approached. Packed on his tables were jackets lined with animal fur, cotton-wadded boots, wool scarves, palm-sized sacks of black beans to warm over a fire and pamphlets on how to maintain fire with nothing but forest wood. Shipping these sources of warmth and fur was needlessly expensive, especially to their island nation of Ik-Song where temperatures stayed high all-year round and the humid sun ruled the days.

Yet, it was all here. And more importantly, it was all selling. Temperatures here hadn't plummeted since the neighbouring nation of Asanai had attacked Ik-Song nearly a decade ago in the White Ice Invasion. But with encroaching deadzones swallowing entire forests and the threat of another invasion with the coming flower moon, it was no surprise that people were nervously stockpiling.

Beside all the winter gear lay jewellery. Carefully, she fingered the jade-inlaid earrings, opal and spinel gems. A stunning piece caught her eye: a small, elliptical handheld mirror with the carvings of vines curling around its edges, culminating in a flowering rosebud handle.

She picked it up, looking into the reflection: her veiled face. The schoolboy's laughter echoing behind her, she imagined for a moment that she was looking at herself uncovered and sweating in the sun. She was no stranger. She was just a girl sent to the markets to fetch scallion and lotus root for her grandmother, whom she would merrily skip home to at the end of the day, after wasting a coin or two on something she wasn't supposed to indulge in – like ginger candies, buns filled with red bean paste, or glutinous rice cakes of buckwheat jelly. She would've swiped them like the schoolboy, swift and excited. And her most pressing problem would be the scolding on these small divergences, a slap on the wrist when she returned home, before she started to prepare dinner. Then a good night's sleep. A sunrise.

In another life.

'A mirror of faith,' the man with the topknot said, the

prospect of a sale warring and winning over his suspicion. 'Dedicated to the Desert Rose. When you look into it, you look into Her memory.'

The man was trying to peer past her veil. Despite the packed crowds and close proximity, so close that you could see tiny beads of sweat across foreheads, people watched one another carefully. Everyone was on edge, and it was hardly because of a smuggling schoolboy. Mourning Day, Shadow thought, was less about grieving Ik-Song's lost saint, the Desert Rose, and more about what they thought had killed her. Her hand fell a pace with the mirror. Slowly, it dawned on her that nearly all of the ornaments on the table were adorned with the same rose carvings.

She wasn't a schoolgirl sent by her grandmother. Her face burned, fingers clutching the mirror tightly. It was time to head back. She'd already risked herself by staying out so long; she'd only wanted to feel the beat of the sun against her, but not for the first time that day, she thought about how she shouldn't have come.

'Five hundred *won* for the mirror. You'd best have it before the flower moon. And furs, if you're interested.' The vendor said, scanning her rather heavy outfit. 'Though you don't seem to be in any shortage of layers.'

At her silence, the man looked irritated, but he didn't continue his pitch – he was distracted, instead, by a Guard moving near his stand, examining both of them. He sat back with a wary eye, and she stilled, too. In her peripheral she caught the Moonbearer's symbol across the Guard's chest – the thin, curving crescent insignia – over intricately scaled black armour, inlaid with gold, gleaming like it had been scrubbed by a thousand hands. His helmet bore the same sign, curving over his head, showing off the telltale white section of hair that all the Moonbearer's remades sported.

A few weeks ago, he may have been just another peddler in Yosae, bustling around like the rest of them. Now, having been taken to the palace and gifted power, the crowds parted for the moon on his chest.

Shadow kept her back turned, pretending to be absorbed in the goods. After a few tense moments, the subtle relaxing of the seller's stature signalled that the Guard had moved on.

She finally moved to return the mirror when something in it caught her eye.

Someone – behind her. A figure that looked familiar. It was the farm boy behind her that she had noticed before, browsing. But why hadn't he moved on? He lingered near the stall, unspeaking. Staying beside her, instead of moving with the crowd.

She angled the mirror slightly and watched, eyes narrowed. Over the course of a few moments – in quick succession, so subtle it was almost unnoticeable – he stole surreptitious glances over at her.

Shadow put the mirror down. His hawkish gaze was trained at the goods, and he looked about her age – although he couldn't see her face, she looked directly at him.

He looked back.

She turned and plunged into the crowd without hesitation, a cold sense of control settling into her.

Shadow didn't need to look back to know that he was hot on her heels. She wove between stalls and narrowly missed a stand weighed down with fruit as she ran towards the main road. Curse these heavy clothes – she needed to shed them. She leapt nimbly over a stream of water as waste sloshed out of an emptied bucket, charging past an oxen-cart and desperately squeezing into a claustrophobic alley. She discarded parts of her clothing as she went: first the long, robe-like *hanbok* skirt, revealing thin pants underneath, followed by her cloak.

The Last Soldier of Nava

She tried to keep her veil over her face as passers-by shot her curious glances, though the crowd remained mostly directionless. Pressing through people, harried footsteps sounded behind her.

They grew more distant as she forged on. But if her pursuer was really one of the Moonbearer's men, he would know Yosae better than her. She had only been in the capital for a year, after all – one precious year of being awake again in this changed world.

Leaving the busy markets and crowded city behind, she plunged into the winding residential streets. The hilly roads gave no respite as she climbed and skidded at intervals, trying to hurtle down as many different corners as she could.

But the footsteps – light, steady – gave no hint of letting up.

By the *Dal*, how to lose him? The edges of roofs blurred by quickly overhead, tiled and sloping – and she realized her plan.

Thinking quickly, she folded herself into yet another gap between two storied houses and swung onto the piping of one, hoisting herself up quietly until she grasped the edge of the roof. She pulled herself up and over, crouching down low on top of the home, close to the edge.

She waited.

A few moments passed before the footsteps rounded the corner.

The sweep of sparkling sand that struck up over the roof would have paralysed her again, if she wasn't prepared for it. The wind of it pitched her backwards, nearly knocking her off her feet, and she flung an arm up to shield her eyes against the gusting blow. Shadow regained balance halfway across the roof, dislodging one ancient tile, and faced down her opponent.

'He said you'd seek height,' said the boy. He had landed on the roof first, fingers simmering with heat. A Guard: a dark-haired youth who stared her down determinedly, jaw jutting out. How long had he been following her back there, flicking dirt with skilled hands and gauging her reactions? He carelessly flung his fake farmer's cap to the side, shedding all pretence, revealing the white in his hair.

'My name is Crow. You'll come with me without resistance, or risk death,' he said bluntly.

A hundred moves played out in her head. Shadow could try to knock him off with a well-placed strike, but the fall from the roof could be fatal to an unprotected head. She needed to get him off her tail as efficiently as possible, because if she ran, something told her he wouldn't give up. He seemed to take her inaction for nervousness, and slowly straightened with confidence.

'I know what you are,' Crow continued. 'A *sakasa*.'

She was silent.

He continued: 'I'm here to ask for your help.'

Help? she stopped short. Impossible. The Moonbearer didn't ask for her 'help'. She had known him long enough to understand that. He wanted her helpless, in bindings, at his mercy. He wanted to take her by force and issue his commands, as he always had. The Moonbearer did not give people a choice; especially not her.

'You know that the flower moon approaches,' Crow said, lunging on her hesitation, 'and Asanai will invade us again. Your ability could prove useful for the Stronghold. The Moonbearer is offering you a proposition.'

That caught her off-guard. She felt – suddenly, surprisingly – a sick satisfaction: that even after all this time, the Moonbearer thought her powerful enough to send undercover Guards after, to drag her back to his palace. What kind of new ruse was this? These days, she was only a half-scarred girl, a girl who panicked at mundane reminders like sand and woke up most nights drenched in sweat, twisting around her blankets. And he wanted . . .

She almost laughed. Crow looked fight-ready and sharp. But still, anxiety thrummed beneath his skin – he didn't know what to expect, not really. *Sakasa* were the stuff of dark legend, manipulators of darkness. Both of them were winded from the chase, but her breaths slowed down, calmed.

His own were rapid; when she didn't talk, he filled the silence himself. 'There hasn't been a *sakasa* in a long time.' He didn't even name it: the Soldier. *Since the Soldier walked a thousand years ago.* It was strange that all this time later, she was no longer a real person, not a girl – only a myth. 'We need you.'

And then: 'But I can just bring you in forcefully, too.'

She decided to test it: she raised a hand, as if to attack.

His reaction – wide eyes, a startled flinch – told her everything she needed to know.

In the end, Shadow did nothing but throw up a churning mirage, a dark wall that hid her departure for only a few moments. She slid down the gables and piping, taking off on the ground. The shadows would churn viscerally for only seconds before fading away, Crow watching with an open-mouthed stare. And then she ran, making her way back to the house.

She would meet the Moonbearer on her own terms; or not at all.

Before going inside, she circled the street three times to make sure the pursuit was well and truly over, that no strangers lurked in the daytime. But no one lingered or watched.

Shadow slid the wood door gently shut behind her. The house was shot through with light and humid air clambering through the back. Vines curled along its edges and the unbolted windows. An open home like this would be a sniper's dream, and, in theory, her own worst nightmare: totally unprotected, exposed, and vulnerable.

And yet – stepping inside gave her the impression that nothing could ever reach her again. Not the Moonbearer, nor the neighbouring country of Asanai, nor the freak weather rumoured to be tearing through the south with unprecedented hunger. None of it was real; all of it melted away in the face of this simple sliding door. Her shoulders loosened; her eyes shut briefly in relief.

'You smell of sweat,' came the sharp, familiar voice. 'That was a close call, girl.'

She startled. And turned to Sae, cross-legged on a mat against the wall, having assumed a strange meditative position with one eye cracked open. Her fine white hair was tied behind her head; her brown, wrinkled face giving the illusion of serenity. The eye closed again. Around her sat a half-circle of small bowls of water.

'Why are you sitting so close to the door?' Shadow asked. 'And why the . . . water?'

'You left your mirrors uncovered in the morning, girl.'

The mirrors covered at night, bathroom door closed, bedroom door open. Shadow could hardly keep track of all the superstitious antics of the old woman. 'I forgot to cover them.'

'You barely escaped your pursuers.'

Unnerved by her insight, Shadow paused. 'They were hardly pursuers. It was just – a boy. They sent a child after me.' Never mind the 'child' was the same age as her.

Sae made a noise that said she clearly didn't believe her.

Shadow might've caught onto the spying if the markets hadn't been so crowded. And they'd been crowded because . . . 'You didn't tell me today was Mourning Day,' she said stiffly.

'Why would that be of importance?'

'It's . . . not. It only seemed like a big deal for the town.'

'There would have been more Guards than usual patrolling today.'

'I was covered from head to toe, you couldn't see any part of me. The Guard just got lucky. He happened to be nearby.'

'Guard?' Sae said archly. 'And here I thought it was just a boy.'

Shadow was silenced. The movements of Sae's hands over the water bowls grew fast, a dance of their own. 'You're bound to get hurt. You are a green frog, girl.' An old folktale, about a frog who never obeyed his mother until her death. 'When I die, you'll bury me on the riverbank.'

'There's no riverbank near us, Sae.' Indeed, the closest water was the Seochon Sea.

Even as they talked, Shadow chanced a glance down at herself: now that the adrenaline wore off, tiredness inched forward, making itself known. One of her feet throbbed, and she felt a gash on her leg – maybe she'd scraped it climbing up to the roof. She looked back up. 'I don't think you should be on the floor like that. It's bad for your joints.'

'Wise words from one chased out of Mourning Day,' Sae scoffed.

'It was hectic – people were lining up for furs and things. You need some, too. Next time, I can bring some back.'

'I don't need those.'

'You're not prepared for a winter. Not even a week-long one.'

'There won't be a winter,' Sae said.

'A decade ago, there was. You were there, weren't you?' Shadow said, exasperated at her stubbornness. 'Who's to say it won't happen again?'

A long silence. And then: 'It's too dangerous for you to keep going into town.'

Shadow paused. This, she couldn't refute. This, she knew with dread mounting day by day.

Sae had never forbidden her – and never would forbid her – from leaving the house; she'd never forced her to stay hidden, chastised her, or accused her of endangering them both. But it was dangerous all the same. Shadow only prolonged the inevitable.

Against the wide backdrop of the house, Sae looked small.

'I'll start preparing dinner,' was all Shadow said as she stepped away towards the back of the home, bare feet padding softly over the bamboo floors. The small yard greeted her enthusiastically: the lilting tunes of songbirds, clucking of spotted hens stomping around the wild garden. Some patches of the dirt had been disturbed where Sae might have pulled vegetables up, but otherwise remained intact. Beside the garden was a small koi pond under the sun, sparkling green with long algae so the fish looked like they were grazing across an open field, a soft meadow of water grass. Emersed plants curled out of the water towards her, climbing up the roots of the small persimmon tree that centred the space.

She plucked a persimmon and sat, the flesh sinewy under her teeth. The hens approached curiously. She liked to sit here for hours on end, beaten by light and watching the hefty fish circle, the gently swaying leaves. The sun would soon sink in the sky, and she would wash jasmine rice, slice radishes at the root. They would eat at the low table – Sae, slowly, and her, rapidly, as if it would all disappear – and retire to bed, settling comfortably on the floor. The lull of night, the cooing of hens would put her to sleep. And she might have a nightmare, or she might not – but if she did, she would sit up and assess the surroundings – and always, cool relief would flood her, seeing this house. And she might come out to the garden to stare back at the great white eye in the night sky with her own, where she could recall stories about the great Moon Rabbit *Daltokki* and Fire Dogs, *bulgae*. She could even imagine seeing the Rabbit up there, its colossal white ears turning while a great red eye opened up at her.

Sae knew that Shadow was a fugitive. She had found her half-dead in an alley, after all. But she never asked questions. She didn't even seem to care. Still, Shadow shouldn't have risked endangering her by going out today. On Mourning Day, of all days, and straight into a chase. The prospect of Guards trailing her back here, appearing at the door to invade the old woman's space – it made Shadow see red. What would they do to Sae, if they found her harbouring a criminal? What would they do to this small garden, its many inhabitants, the persimmon tree? They would take Sae away somewhere and throw Shadow in front of the Moonbearer.

All Shadow wanted to do was to stay here for eternity, resting and eating and watching the pond day by day. She could have a lifetime of it, and it still wouldn't be enough. But with each passing day, it grew more dangerous to stay. The Moonbearer persisted in his search, drawing closer. She couldn't risk Sae's safety.

'Ik-Song grows nervous,' said a voice behind her. Shadow startled again. All her own years training for stealth, and it was baffling how quietly the old woman moved. 'But that is the ebb and flow, isn't it? War breaks and wanes like the moon; nations fragment and become new. It doesn't concern us.'

It occurred to Shadow that she had no idea how old Sae was. To her, maybe it was just a changing of hands, be it Guards or Asanai, the monsoon or dry season. But the Moonbearer was different. The Moonbearer was ancient.

'At the markets today, all anyone was talking about were

the deadzones. Are they actually real?' Whispers of woodland in the South growing strange; unassuming villagers wandering in and disappearing for days, sometimes never coming back out. Peculiar trees.

'It doesn't concern us.'

'Of course it concerns us.' She looked at the gentle garden, imagined it destroyed. Sae tended to it preciously day after day; how could she not care?

'We aren't dynasts or emperors. Those already exist, in a faraway place. We're just an old woman and a girl, you and me. What can we do?'

Nothing, really. 'I know. You're right.'

'Of course I'm right. You'll learn in your later years, girl. Things come to me in dreams. Wisdom assaults me.'

'Well, I'm sorry you're plagued by all this knowledge,' Shadow said dryly.

'Yes, it's hard.'

Shadow turned, then, to really look at her. Sae was slightly hunched, but still managed to be the same height as her. She wanted to say many things: *Thank you for everything you've done.* She wanted to say: *Thank you for saving my life.* But she didn't say any of those things; she was too cowardly. Instead, she said, haltingly: 'Dinner will be ready soon.'

Because Shadow had already decided: she would leave tonight, after they ate. Sae would never throw her to the wolves, and Shadow had already taken enough. She wasn't sure where she would go; she would take nothing, leave nothing. She would go out on her own; she would manage. Somehow.

Because some things, Shadow could never forget.

She could not forget being the Soldier. She could not forget the Moonbearer's commands, fragments of what she had done. The cold floor of the cellar and how the Desert Rose lay

The Last Soldier of Nava

lifeless beside her. She did not want the long nightmare to continue. She needed to leave this place far behind: she would rather have the entire world forget her, than risk Sae.

So she would have Sae forget her, too.

Chapter 2

Shadow pulled watercress and cabbage by hand in the garden, rinsing through the rice. Occasionally she dropped a bundle on the ground, and rinsed off the dirt, fine tremors running through her hands. The textures of things like silken tofu were too soft and slippery, reminding her of the tender skin of a neck's jugular: delicate, vulnerable. There was a violence to preparing food that she indulged in: the shredding of leaves, the knifing, the hot piping steam of fire-powered pots. She watched Sae take out a hen in the back to twist its neck sharply, sitting for a moment to honour it.

The walls here breathed with the summer heat. Sae's traditional hanok home was made entirely of the natural material that surrounded it, walls of wood and tree pulp and straw. Its life cycle would end by simply collapsing and becoming one with the ground again, like it was supposed to. The garden might overtake the house quickly, spreading from its centre to overtake it all, building the start of a new forest, the koi multiplying.

When Shadow had first woken in the home, battered and cold, she could hardly speak. Sae left her bone broth and plain rice porridge in the morning with chestnuts and soy sauce. She thought it was a sort of trick at first, meant to detain her here until she confessed.

But over time, she began to talk more, to get used to her own voice. Her power eventually returned to her – even though her memories had not – and she played with it by creating shadow figures across the walls like a child. Sometimes the old woman would let her sit at the corner window and discreetly watch passers-by on the street. And when she got stronger, she would stand in the middle of the garden and gather her darkness within herself, closing her eyes, doing nothing but staying still and breathing.

'You are a shadow when you do that,' Sae had said once. 'An apparition.'

She took the name desperately. It was something to hold on to now, when before, she had always just been an imprint of something else, something more real. Like she might have faded away at any moment.

Their relationship was somewhat unusual, she knew. In Ik-Song, one was to bow to their elders, to address them by formal speak. But she didn't do that with Sae. It always seemed futile. And Sae was no ordinary elder, either. Sometimes Shadow wondered what Sae was hiding in her past, perhaps trying to seek redemption; there was no other reason, after all, why she would take a girl under her wing that she'd found half-dead on the ground at the site of the killing of a saint, no less.

But she never asked. She did know, however, that Sae was, ironically, an avid believer of Nava, the Ninth City. She hoarded piles and piles of books. Most of Ik-Song knew little about the magic, the ancient civilization that had supposedly birthed the Moonbearer and his ways. But Sae held onto the tales, the *Daltokki,* Moon Rabbit, and massive waterfalls and rulers of light and dark. It had been a different world then, but all of it lost now. Shadow traced the pictures, wondered if Sae believed in the Soldier, too. But she didn't like to look at them much.

It was an old story. About how the city was kept in balance by the Dragons of East and West, until civil war broke out between its rulers, the Moonbearer and the Dawnbringer, and the Moonbearer created the Soldier to turn the tide. The Dawnbringer had been forced to use all of the light of Nava to defeat the Soldier, destroying the city in the process.

But Sae wouldn't know any of the truth. After all, Nava was gone; the Dawnbringer, too. The Moonbearer remained, and no one knew what he had done. What he had created. The darkness he had unleashed into the world. Shadow remembered the early months in Sae's house, her first trip to the markets. How she had seen the gleaming crescent moon insignia from every corner, jumping out at her. In the time she was gone, he had completely overtaken the city – hailed as a saviour for emerging victorious in the White Ice, fending off the vicious Asani invasion under the greedy Bloodbird Emperor a decade ago.

Shadow would clean tonight after dinner, trimming the garden herbs and scattering handfuls of seeds out. Sweep the house, throw buckets of water down the front. Clean her room – sparsely decorated, with almost no belongings – and arrange her floormat bed, smoothing out the sheets in clean lines. Afterwards, it would look like nobody had ever lived there at all.

She tore another cabbage leaf in two. She sensed that Sae stood behind her, coming out to watch her work. Shadow remained silent, continuing in her quiet routine.

'You're leaving soon.'

Her hands paused mid-air. She turned. 'How could you possibly—'

The Last Soldier of Nava

'I can sense it.'

No use in trying to evade now. 'It's dangerous for me to stay here,' Shadow said. 'You know this. They'll find me eventually, and then you.'

'What does that matter? Ik-Song will be underwater in a few months' time, or under siege by Asanai. Either way, the nation will die.'

This plain admission shocked her. Sae had never spoken so bleakly about the future. 'I thought you didn't believe Asanai would attack.' Briefly, she considered telling Sae about what had really happened today – what the Guards had offered her. But she couldn't – it opened up a ridiculous possibility, a dangerously impossible notion that lingered in her mind, this small chance, maybe, at revenge—

But no. She was a coward. She would run. 'I've overstayed,' she continued. 'I won't be a burden on you any longer. Once I go, you'll be safer.'

She didn't expect Sae to protest. That wasn't her way. Instead, she turned back to her preparations and waited for the old woman to think.

After a long moment: 'When you leave, where will you go?'

Shadow considered. 'I'm not sure.'

Yosae was a coastal city. South would bring her to the rural countryside of Ik-Song and vast plains. She'd be less likely to run into any Guards around those verdant, sloping hills. But she'd also be less likely to find any help, and superstition ran more wildly down there against powers like hers. And on the off-chance she ran across pockets of deadzones, heavily guarded, or burgeoning storms – it would result in immediate capture, or worse, being eaten by the elements.

West only led to barren land.

East: the Seochon Sea, and the nearest nation an ocean away.

And north – north was a death sentence. North had always seemed a whirlwind of tension, one she knew little about, with the Queen Dynast situated on one corner and the Moonbearer's Stronghold on the other, every village in between fraught with phantom pains of the White Ice and under constant watch of opposing forces that wanted the island nation for themselves.

'South, maybe,' Shadow murmured.

'South,' Sae considered behind her. 'Perhaps. Or perhaps north.'

North? Shadow turned, but Sae was already returning back inside. Was she that angry with her, then? Condemning her to death in the north?

Or did Sae believe something was waiting for her in the north?

And then suddenly she felt it: an icy draught blowing against her bare arm, like a shard in summer heat.

Goosebumps pricked up. It was gone as quickly as it came, and for a moment she dismissed it as a night gale, a trick of her mind – but no.

Unmistakable. A cold, polar wind.

Shadow hurried inside. Was it her mind, or had the interior grown chillier? 'Sae,' she said urgently. 'Did you feel that?'

Inside, Sae sliced up a squash across a board, impassive. She nodded.

'What is it?' Shadow asked, though they both knew. The sun would set soon, and she moved to the front sliding door, placing her fingers on the surface.

'It can't be,' Shadow said, mostly to herself, dread rising in her gut. 'It can't be an attack, it's too early, the boy on the roof – he said until the flower moon . . .' Ik-Song would not be prepared. Yosae would not be prepared.

'It's dangerous out there,' Sae said warningly.

The winds were unmistakable now. Immediately Shadow

darted around the house, closing the open windows, stuffing stray blankets into any cracks. Insulation, fire, shelter. She cursed herself – she should've bought furs at the market. It was upon them, and they needed to take cover. And yet, now that it was here, all she could think about was running out the door, headfirst into the cold. Her fingers itched to do so.

Shouting outside. Alarmed screaming, movement, the high-pitched whistling of wind picking up. There were hundreds of stalls in the markets, crowds milling about. Children. Everyone would be unprotected.

She had to help, somehow. She found herself at the door. 'I'm going to go,' she said. 'I'll bring back furs and supplies. There might be people in the market in danger.'

'Haenyeongsan,' Sae replied.

It was the name of a mountain range near them, famous for its jutting stone and intricately pressed red canyon layers. 'What?'

'A century ago, they say the devout found its composition so unnatural they ordered all travellers to cover their eyes when crossing by the foothills.'

Impatience gripped her. This was no time for a proverb. 'Sae – I'm going. I will be back.' She meant it.

'But perhaps, you will see the mountains up close now.'

Shadow opened the door. 'Please stay inside.'

'If you go, you may not be able to return. So, take this.' And something was pressed into her palm – a stone, perhaps, or a jewel. Already halfway out, Shadow didn't stop to look at it – only pocketed it close and pushed out onto the streets, wind biting at her cheeks.

It was not like any cold Shadow had ever felt before. Not the snapping seawater of a chilly morning dive along the coast; not nighttime fog that rolled in during the wet season. It was a kind of cold that seeped inside unnaturally and awakened the underside of Shadow's skin.

Shadow welcomed it. She ran back to the markets, streets emptying around her as people disappeared within their homes, boarded up their windows. A mother holding her daughter by the hand brushed past, *hanbok* skirts trailing behind her; a crying teenage boy tugged on people's sleeves, asking for the whereabouts of his brother. Most ran against her, to the opposite direction, while she forged forwards. A few brave souls cleared a path to the markets brandishing tools like axes and blades, though these would be futile against any Asani Bone Warriors, the huge half man, half skeletal guards of the Asani Emperor

And where were the Guards? Nowhere to be seen.

Was that a flicker of snow, or the light changing? Shadow heard prayers in the streets, murmurs, but overwhelming them was the snarling air, homes rattling in their wake as the wind picked up.

As she reached the outer edge of the market, it seemed like she approached the epicentre, the force of it clear. But there were no Bone Warriors and their icy plumes, no signs of battle anywhere: only this incessant cold, without a source. She cast her gaze upwards.

She had to find out what was going on.

But *furs*. She was here to get furs. Frustrated with herself, she tore her gaze from the rooftops, tried to reorient her direction, before she realized—

Cold air stayed low to the ground. It sank. But higher ground would give her a vantage point, and relieve her of the chill, if only for a moment. She once again hooked onto a nearby house, climbing up onto its roof.

She clambered onto her feet. Looked out over the city.

She could oversee the entire market from here, but still, she saw no attackers, nothing. Only people taking cover. Was the enemy hiding? Had the Stronghold not been alerted yet?

Shadow folded one leg under herself, crouched, ready to push off and leap to the next rooftop, and froze.

At the same height as her – another roof, in the distance – stood a cloaked figure. Maybe they had had the same idea as her, trying to see farther. She squinted, trying to make out the silhouette, and raised her arms, preparing to yell out—

Before registering, with shock, the fluid motions of the figure's arms, their hands. Not tall enough to be a Bone Warrior, but it was as if – as if they were *controlling* these winds.

She began to run towards them.

Feet drumming hard on the tiles underneath, it didn't take long for the figure to notice her. When they did, she threw out a hand, willing her feet to move faster, and shouted at him to stop.

Momentarily interrupted, the figure stopped moving, and all the wind around them died. They began to run.

Then: a shrill scream, from down below.

Along the outskirts of the stalls, a woman stood gesturing frantically outside a low-lying house that looked like it was about to keel over. The side of it was punched in – the wind had dragged down a spiny tree that now threatened to cave it in. The woman screamed again, and Shadow realized: there was someone stuck inside the beaming. A child.

She cursed. The mysterious figure was already far ahead – too far to catch up to. She slid down to the ground and her feet moved, carrying her closer to the scene.

The child – she recognized him as the schoolboy from the markets. Eyes wide, he desperately tried to tug his leg free from underneath a beam as the roof slowly caved in towards him, as if it was malleable. It would crush him whole – bury him under a mountain, and she would have to watch him, helpless where she stood.

Shadow didn't think about what she was doing until she'd already started – as the slab finally collapsed above them all, a mountain of rubble descending towards the boy, the woman falling to her knees – Shadow pulsed forward, pushing between two bystanders, landing on her feet, and sending – without hesitation – a vast arc of darkness towards the structure.

It collided with the skeleton house, pushing the entire roof clean off the rest of its framework and forcing it to slide backwards into the street behind, before dissolving. Part of it cracked and sailed to the side, thudding against the wall of a neighbouring house. It was like a glacier slowly backsliding into water, huge and immoveable.

Already she was running into the remnants of the house, which lay like a flayed, open thing, reaching the boy and offering one hand.

This would only be the first – there would be countless more flimsy buildings, people in danger. She needed to hurry. Quickly she devised her plan: to clear a perimeter around the market itself, search for civilians under an already-heaping destruction. She looked down at the boy . . .

. . . who only stared back, eyes wide.

Belatedly, she remembered her uncovered face, her power. 'It's all right,' she tried. 'You're safe.'

After a long moment, the boy blinked and began to reach out his hand tentatively. His fingers came up slowly to meet hers, almost there, grabbing—

'A *sakasa*,' snarled a voice behind her. 'Stay away from her!'

She whirled. A crowd had gathered, witnessing the destruction: and in the front, Crow pointing to her from the centre. Shocked and frightened murmurs rippled through the people.

She turned back to the boy. He'd snatched his hand back, just as quickly, moving to scramble away from her.

Crow approached slowly. Voice low: 'Knew we'd flush you out.'

Curse these Guards. With a single word, he had turned an entire crowd against her. He glared at her, willing her to submit. Now that the winds had abruptly ended, everyone was coming out of their homes, desperately trying to find out what had happened, who was responsible. And she stood here in the open like a nightmare come to life. Trapped on all sides but behind. No – she refused to be taken like this, exposed. She wouldn't go back.

So, she took off again. Shooting through the ruined house and weaving through the growing mass of disoriented people, she was once again pursued, though this time passers-by openly stared, and she was no longer invisible, just another person swept up in the town.

She threw quick glances over her shoulder, trying to gauge how close Crow was.

Shadow was again preoccupied with her pursuers, which was why she didn't notice, really, what was going on around her. The odd behaviour of the people. She didn't notice Yosaeans slowly turning to face the same direction, stopping in their tracks, clearing the way. Falling rapidly to the ground on their knees, like leaves from a tree. Their muted surprise and disbelief, attentions entirely focused. She only continued through them, stepping deftly between and over, thoughts drifting – *who was the figure on the rooftop?* – and as she craned her neck one last time to glance back for the Guards, she collided with something large and immoveable in her way.

She was pitched to the floor, catching herself by the palms.

What first met her sight – making her reel back – was a great, black, dewy nose. Round and extremely close. Attached to a snout and two enormous lashed eyes, pitch-black on either side, too dark for any light to escape. Its mouth parted for a quick moment, revealing a pink tongue. Large, elegant antlers wound out from the crown of its head, beside ears that flattened down while examining her. Around this *Feng* deer's head lay a thin golden circlet with a sun symbol in its centre, the image repeated across its brown harness again and again. It was tall, taller than a horse, towering above the crowd.

The symbol of light was shocking to behold: like a long-forgotten artefact thrust in her face. The Dawnbringer's.

The sun blazed low behind the brown deer, so that for a fleeting moment she couldn't discern the rider sitting on top – only a dark silhouette. It was only when the rider tugged gently at the reins and the deer circled away a bit – blocking the sun – that she saw the polished riding shoes, slanted up slightly at the toe. The spotless, white-plated armour layering up the arms and neck, underlaid with crimson as if a thin layer of blood wept out from under each scale. The uniform was intricate and must have taken a long time to make, because it wasn't overtly held together by visible buckles or straps or wrappings, so the workings must be thin, hidden, strong underneath: the markings of great wealth.

Dazed, Shadow studied the armour for a moment before it finally occurred to her to look up and when she did, she stared straight into the face of the Desert Rose – the same one she had murdered a year ago.

Chapter 3

Shadow scrabbled back on the ground, heart crescendoing. The Desert Rose was dead. She had *killed* her a year ago, her lifeless face against the ground, slack-jawed with a mouth full of sand, rivulets of it pouring down the sides. How?

She blinked frantically, trying to get her bearings. This wasn't her. It couldn't be. Her face was so similar, but it wasn't her. This girl was younger, for one – she looked around Shadow's age.

And her expression. It was of arrogant boredom, of distaste. Most people avoided looking directly at Shadow's face – this girl looked down straight at her from her high-saddle seat, lip sneered, as if she were scum on the ground.

The Desert Rose never had – and never could – look like that.

Shadow began to stand, slowly, not breaking her gaze even against the harsh glare of the sun. In the deathly silence around them, people dropped to the ground, lowering themselves to a bow, fear like a live and pulsing presence. She rose above them all – even as her peripheral caught Guards moving towards her like red blurs, dismounting, stark uniforms shining brilliantly. Hands grabbed her neck and arms, forcing her to the ground, pushing her head down face-first into the dirt. She resisted, muscles cording tensely along her back.

'You will show respect to the Royal Keeper,' a Guard snarled from behind.

The words sent a chill down her spine. *Royal Keeper? Who was this girl?* Unable to control herself, Shadow again looked up.

She'd seen that sort of expression before – on the faces of patrolling Guards, the occasional passing *yangban* nobles who cast cursory glances over the city through the windows of their carriages. It said everything without needing to speak. And it was all the more repulsive on this girl's face – not just because of her resemblance to the Desert Rose, but because she was beautiful.

Her blue-black hair bore none of the white of the remades. It was pinned back in a complex arrangement of pearls and sundrop pins, circuitously braided; her circlet much like her deer's but redder, a slash of blood across her forehead. Shadow was all too aware of her own raggedly cut hair, the way the broad daylight must illuminate every contour and groove of her scarred face, leaving nothing to the imagination. Her clothing, ripped and dirty. Everyone around them was prostrated now, no one daring to reassume a standing position.

A knee to Shadow's back made her see stars as she was forced into a mock bowing position. Instinctively, she twisted in protest and was met with a sharp kick to her side.

'Skittish, aren't we?' came the voice – mocking and smooth, amused. It grated on Shadow's ears.

Then the girl must've made some dismissive gesture, for the hand on Shadow's neck was removed. She found that the world had quickly narrowed down to this figure; everything else was muted. The girl circled her magnificent buck once again, eyes drifting lazily over the scene, before settling again on Shadow. Under the high collar, a pale sliver of skin was visible; Shadow watched the unmoving column of her neck.

The girl dismounted in one swift motion. She wasn't extraordinarily tall, but among the low crowd, she seemed so. The tension mounted; two Guards exchanged looks.

Shadow eyed her, wondered if she might be able to overtake her momentarily to escape. Despite the intricate armour, this girl didn't seem to have ability and looked like she'd never been in so much as a street brawl, much less won one. She wouldn't be quick in a chase, not with that ornamental uniform. Yet Shadow also knew better than to assume on appearance only; she couldn't stop studying her face, wondering where she'd come from.

She had the peculiar feeling that she couldn't run, even if she tried.

'Why don't you bow?' the girl said. 'Not impressed by the sight of your Keeper?'

Keeper. Shadow blinked.

'Mute?'

She didn't respond.

'Deaf?' And then a tilt of the head. 'Or maybe you don't speak the language?'

For her third bout of silence, Shadow received a stunning backhand from the Guard to her left. She felt the burn of this girl's eyes roaming slowly over her and fought the urge to shrink into herself.

'I speak it,' she said finally, face smarting. 'I just don't know who you are. . .' *Your Highness?* Was that the proper address?

All this time, the girl had been glancing over at the Guards, only half-focused on the conversation at hand. But at Shadow's admission, she barked, 'Hold her face up,' and a Guard gripped her chin roughly. The girl stared into her face – really stared – and Shadow felt that she was somehow approaching a cliff drop. Mentally, she braced herself for comments about the scarring across the side of her face – belatedly considering that maybe she shouldn't have claimed ignorance about her own country's royalty while on her knees.

'If you don't know who I am, then you're not from Ik-Song, outsider,' the Keeper said. 'Yet you're in *our* capital, in *our* clothing, in the centre of an attack that ended right as you fell. And you're looking at me like *I* am the one out of place?'

She was right. Slowly, the severity of the situation dawned on Shadow; no one would come to her rescue now.

'So, you are either a treasonous instigator,' the Keeper continued, 'or a terrorist. Either way, you must be weeded out.'

'I'm neither of those things,' Shadow tried. 'I'm not from around here. I'm from the South.'

'I was born in the South,' the Keeper said, already turning away. 'There's a lilt in the tone that gives it away, you know. But I can't seem to hear anything in yours.' Her attention seemed stretched far past its span, prone to wandering; she was already zeroing in on another point in the crowd somewhere in the distance. She remounted her deer with uncaring flourish, gesturing to a Guard. 'If that's all . . .'

The Guard unsheathed a silver-thin blade. They wouldn't even bother using ability on her – a simple sword would suffice.

'I was curious as to what Mourning Day would look like here,' the Keeper was saying, bored, looking around at the collapsed buildings. 'I can't say my sister has been honoured very well.'

Shadow's mind reeled with shock.

The Desert Rose had a *sister*. A younger sister. And she was royalty, parading around with Stronghold Guards.

The Last Soldier of Nava

The Moonbearer's Guards.

Was this his new prodigy?

She clearly didn't recognize Shadow as her sister's killer – how would she? No one knew what Shadow had done, or who she was. And there was nothing Shadow could say to prove her innocence right now, save from revealing herself as either a fugitive or the Soldier, neither of which would save her fate. Was this really how she would die? At the hand of a girl who didn't even know the Moonbearer wanted to kill her, who would do it anyway?

Shadow readied herself, eyes closing, still uselessly trying to shift free—

When a distinct voice cleaved through the crowd.

'Out of the way,' it yelled. 'Out of the way!'

She opened her eyes and was momentarily let up. She turned towards the sound, and then wished she hadn't: Crow, the boy, was pushing through the ring of Guards. He slowed when he caught sight of them, the townsfolk, eyes widening—

'Scarlet?'

Scarlet.

The higher up you were in the Stronghold hierarchy, the more syllables in the name. This girl had no trace of white in her hair, yet she had a remade name. *Scar-let*. Unusual and two-syllabled, like *Sha-dow*.

The Keeper looked back at Crow as if discovering a small nuisance, like a moth-eaten hole in her sleeve.

'What are you doing in Yosae?' Crow hissed. 'You're not supposed to be out of the Stronghold.'

The Keeper's red Guards – at least, the few Shadow could see from her vantage point – watched Crow with moderate malice, which was eagerly returned.

Why the hostility? Didn't they all hail from the same palace?

'I can't decide whether to remind you that nothing is ever

any of your business,' Scarlet replied, 'or that the celebrations here have some personal relevance to me.'

'You aren't supposed to be in town.'

'I gathered that,' she said dryly.

'Then—'

'Child,' she enunciated clearly, though they looked the same age. Crow bristled. 'I'm here on Mourning Day for my sister with half my personal guard. You're here in nondescript civvies alone. The correct path for you to take would be to explain your own presence here now.'

Crow's eyes narrowed. 'The Moonbearer sent me.'

'Yes. I also gathered that.'

'I was in pursuit of a fugitive.' His gaze swivelled to Shadow. 'In pursuit of *her*.'

'So not only do you come bumbling in demanding to know my business, but I've finished your own job for you, where you failed. The Moonbearer will be pleased to hear that.'

'I didn't fail.'

The Keeper only looked pointedly at Shadow, her own Guards holding her down.

'I didn't,' Crow insisted. 'I was in pursuit of her earlier, but I was caught off-guard, it's not like we've ever fought a—'

He cut off abruptly.

His companion stepped forward in warning.

But it was too late. Now, the Keeper's interest was well and truly piqued. 'Fought a *what*?'

Crow didn't answer.

She brought her buck closer, whose ear flicked. 'What, Crow? Spit it out.'

'A *sakasa*,' he spat. 'She has ability. Half the town saw her use it.'

Silence. Crow stared back with a combination of irritation and nervousness. Shadow wasn't sure if his timely appearance had helped or worsened her situation. Now her fate was delayed, but she was more exposed.

'You're lying,' said the Keeper.

Shadow turned to her.

This – she hadn't expected. That expression on her face. The Keeper watched her now not with horror or disgust, but with something else – something that darkened her eyes, awakened a barely contained fervour.

It gave Shadow a funny twinge in her stomach.

'I'm not lying,' Crow snapped, oblivious to her transformation. 'I—'

'Quiet.'

At the dawning realization that her death was delayed, Shadow's heart sank.

The Keeper's undivided attention was somehow worse than her disinterested order to kill. Suddenly she was plunged into a cold place – what was the Keeper thinking? What did she want? The uncertainty was paralysing. Shadow inclined her head forcefully, averted her gaze.

'I submit to my fate. I— I won't resist.' She wished for that cool press of blade against her neck, hard-edged, though she knew now – without doubt – that it would not come.

The Keeper scoffed. '*Now* you obey. When it's futile.'

Shadow shut her eyes.

'A *sakasa*. Are you really?'

Shadow shook her head uselessly.

'Suddenly,' said the Keeper with relish, smiling coldly, 'you prove an invaluable prospect.' *An invaluable prospect?* 'Bind her,' she announced. 'Let us depart. We've stayed long enough.'

A flurry of protests. 'You can't just take a fugitive back to the Stronghold,' Crow said.

'The Moonbearer must've ordered you to bring her back alive. Didn't he?'

His mouth opened, then closed.

'What you mean is, you don't want *me* taking her back. Well – if only you'd got to her first.'

Some commotion rose around them; the murmuring of Guards, villagers coming out to catch a view of the scene. Shadow's wrists were gathered behind her back and fastened. She truly considered escape now, when Scarlet and Crow distracted each other with petty squabble, but she was caged in by crimson, shuffling boots against the dirt.

'Where is your home?' the Keeper asked her suddenly. 'Do you have one, or are you a beggar?'

Sae. She had thought she was prepared to never see Sae again – but reality hit her forcefully.

'I don't have one,' Shadow replied immediately.

'She's lying,' Crow interjected. 'I know where it is.'

'I don't live with anyone but an old lady,' she snapped. 'She's harmless. You can't do anything to her.'

The Keeper raised an eyebrow. 'Do you think you're in a position to make demands?'

If they tried to hurt Sae, she wouldn't be able to overpower all of them – but she could certainly take out a few Guards. She could leave a mark.

After a long moment, she stood on two shaky legs, arms bound. And slowly, she began to move forward – through and away from the crowd, who, after all this time, still remained dutifully down: children with their foreheads pressed to their arms, men hunched awkwardly over. She was grateful that their heads were all bowed, unable to see her walking like a prisoner. In silence, they went.

The markets were a way from the house, but not too far – and judging by her dry mouth and sweating palms, far too short. They left the busier town area, moving closer to the residential parts, winding through the familiar hilly roads of hanok homes, Sae's in sight. Here, the people were more cautious, most still boarded up inside; the few stragglers venturing out looked shocked at the royal procession. One young woman bowed to her waist, seeming to recognize Scarlet, crying out, 'Our Keeper, the Light!'

Why anyone would call her *the Light* was beyond Shadow; nothing in the Keeper's countenance suggested any qualities associated with light, like warmth or joy.

Sae's home looked the same as it always was. Undisturbed.

'Make haste,' a Guard said, and Shadow kept her pace. As they walked up, she thought of warm hands balancing bowls of porridge; pulling up scallion by the root; wrapping rice and pork rinds inside perilla leaves, the deft fingers closing toothed corner by corner to make bundles. Hands illuminated in stripes by the light that streamed and cut through the rooms. Bossing her around, making her clean and dice and cover her mirrors at night. The old woman liked to circle her finger in the pond and let the koi try to swallow her nail with their gaping mouths.

The windows were closed, as Shadow had left them. She wondered if Sae was watching them approach.

There was so much about Sae that remained mysterious to her. The old woman had no family, no friends, it seemed. She spent long hours outside in the unknown. There was much that they hadn't talked about, never broached. Desperately, she wished for a diversion – something, anything – that would stop her from sliding open the door. Attacking the Guard beside her . . .

No. It would be useless. She stood with her fists clenched.

Slowly, she pressed her palm against the door, taking a breath – and flung it open to the side, watching the quick slide.

And stopped.

A wall of vines met her.

Dark and earthy roots climbing over each other, twisting and fitting against the mould of the framework. Shadow peered into this bizarre mess and found that it continued all throughout the home, like a small, self-contained forest. It was beautiful. And it appeared, to the naked eye, like no one had ever lived here at all – as if it had been consumed and overtaken, long ago, by the plants.

Chapter 4

Like an ox waiting for the slaughter, Shadow sat silently as Yosae receded in the distance. 'Flank left,' a Guard called from behind, and the rapid procession swerved expertly at an angle to avoid a stripe of muddied land. The entire party consisted of the Keeper and her few Guards on deerback, Crow, lower-ranked soldiers, and a number of servants in sage-green and white, commandeering muscled horses smaller than the deer. Riding a deer was much higher and harder than she'd expected – when this black doe had first risen, unfolding its hind legs first, Shadow had slanted forwards, trying not to fall headfirst and break her neck. Now she focused on keeping balance, wrists still bound.

It was no secret where they were headed. The prospect of facing the Moonbearer again after so long gripped her – as if everything in the world narrowed down to a singular point, and the rest all fell away. Yet, her mind continuously circuited back not to him, but to the girl who rode at the front, who no doubt sat at the right hand of his wicked throne. It was almost laughable: here was the only person who might satisfy that role for him, the only one to rival the Soldier herself.

Upon meeting the vines crowding out the house, Shadow's wrists had been effectively double bound on the Keeper's orders. At first, they'd tried to saddle her with one of the Keeper's Guards, but he'd been uncomfortable with her positioned behind him on his deer. He'd also been uncomfortable with her positioned in front. He seemed, in general, uncomfortable with all aspects of looking at, acknowledging, or existing within a close distance of her.

'By the *Dal*—' The Keeper's annoyance had unleashed in an impressive wave.

'I'll ride with her,' a brave young maid offered, but was quickly cut off with a sharp no.

After a lull: 'Sit her with Aspis instead,' the Keeper said slowly, as if it gave her great pleasure.

Thus, Shadow's transfer to the gleaming black doe, fourth in line. *Feng* does were usually larger than the bucks, and this one kept pace aggressively, its bare head Shadow's primary view. Sitting behind her was a young woman with lighter hair braided deftly at her nape. She showed no wariness about being in close proximity to Shadow.

Shadow didn't know how far the Stronghold was from Yosae – maybe a few hours' journey. Leaving Yosae and streaming further and further out, the houses grew sparser as more meadowland and distant hills began to surround them. Occasionally a villager would be outside in the drawing twilight, dimly lit, carrying a basket on their head or washing clothes in trickling streams. Along the rugged coastline of Ik-Song, the sea was lit spuriously with colour; the deer could leap enormous distances, bounding gracefully in tandem. Occasionally a Guard up front spoke in low tones to the Keeper, but Shadow gave up on trying to hear. The grounds that blurred by underneath were dotted with myrtle flowers and white peonies, to the right, rocky shores of cerulean waters and gravelly sand. The Seochon was deceptively calm, as always, its smooth surface hiding powerful riptides.

The setting extinguished any sliver of hope that Shadow had hung onto. There was nowhere to run. Open field and dark woodland around them, neither looking particularly fruitful. These deer were unmatched in their swift movement and beauty, but it was obvious why the royalty favoured them so strongly: their stealth. Natural prey animals who could pick their way through great lengths of dense, littered detritus without making so much as a twig snap. A keen sense of smell, attuned to the most gradual changes in their environments, always on the lookout for danger. Creatures like that, trained instead for bloodscent or mere speed, would be on her in an instant.

And something else – something that she didn't dare to think, if not for Sae's voice echoing in her head. *North. Go North*. Even though everything in her logic was telling her to run, her gut pressed for patience. *Wait*. Shadow felt a cool sense of detachment, like river water, at the idea of being face-to-face with the Moonbearer.

After a while, Shadow sought to look behind at her companion. A golden crescent moon flashed in the divot of the girl's high-necked collar, her dark green uniform well-made but not ostentatious. Her hair was tied through with a red ribbon. She had a confident, composed air about her, and hadn't protested when the Keeper forced her to ride with Shadow. *Aspis*, her name was. She was wearing neither servant colours nor a Guard uniform; and didn't bear any marks of the signature white hair of the remades but had been bowed to by Crow. Which meant she had high rank – yet had been tossed behind to ride with the prisoner.

Now Aspis met Shadow's curious stare coolly. Was everyone here so dubious?

'You aren't the same status as the Keeper,' Shadow gathered. 'And you're not a Guard, or a serf.'

'I forget how little commoners know about the Stronghold. And to think I was once one myself.'

'Are you a general?' Shadow asked. Aspis's straight-backed demeanour, sure voice – it was a specific sort of neatness, the tidy dress of a militiawoman . . .

Aspis paused, almost wistfully. 'Not anymore, prisoner. Though I was once one of the Queen's best generals.'

Around them, the valleys rolled by, a crevasse of forest slanting up to their right. Its colour seemed too bright, almost, mercurial. A harsh snap of a branch drew Shadow's attention to the front, where the Keeper guided her buck with a firm hand, riding faster and more ferociously than anyone behind. She always kept at least five paces ahead, as if she were about to take off and disappear over the horizon at any moment.

'The Keeper,' Shadow ventured. 'Why is she called that? What does she "keep"?'

'The Royal Keeper of the Gates of the Stronghold,' Aspis recited. 'It's an allusion to defence, and ceremonial duties. She's the first line of defence in case of attack and the first face to greet foreigners in the palace.'

'Is her sense of self so inflated that she equates herself to the sun?' *To the Dawnbringer herself?* The symbol was everywhere: her head, within her uniforms, even the saddle of her buck.

The Moonbearer would've paid attention to such detail, the disregarding of his own mark. It was strange how the Keeper rode alongside them as if she was just another Guard, no carriage, no palanquin.

Aspis laughed sharply again. 'You really don't know, do you? It's like you aren't even from this world.' Shadow only stared back, bewildered. The way Aspis looked at her gave Shadow once again the impression of being examined like a prize animal, a hog belly-up. 'In a few days' time, even the furthest reaches of Asanai will have heard about you.'

Shadow didn't have a chance to respond – the rider in front of them came to an abrupt stop, and they followed, a Guard from behind shouting.

Shadow had been so swept up in the conversation that she hadn't noticed the changing scenery around her: the dense underbrush that slowly closed in, inch by inch, threatening to surround; the air changing, slightly – reminding her of the unnatural draught in Sae's home, even though it wasn't cold anymore. There was hardly any wind. Around them, deer tapped nervously at the ground, and the doe Shadow sat on even made to turn around, stopped only by Aspis's swift kick to her side.

The Keeper remained unmoving up ahead.

Craning her neck, Shadow tried to find out what had stopped them. A tangled burst of forest, perhaps; poisonous brush, rogue bandits?

Then came the hushed murmurs travelling up and down the procession. Quiet, anxious.

'What's going on?' Shadow asked.

Aspis had stilled, watching the forest closely. 'One of the cavalry is missing.'

Missing? How could one of them have gone missing during the ride, simply plucked out of the air? Where had his steed gone? 'What do you mean, missing?'

A short caw erupted from the trees, startling Shadow immensely – a three-legged crow took off from the branches, its wings midnight-sleek and vast. It glided over the sky for a bit before disappearing back into the woods. She hardly ever saw them in person, though she knew that they thrived in Ik-Song, omens of good fortune. She exhaled in amusement at her own dramatic reaction.

She looked back down and realized half the cavalry had arrows readied at the sky. The Keeper's personal Guards held their hands steadied in defensive positions, prepared to attack.

And that was when she felt it, belatedly. A feeling of strangeness. A whiplash of sensation.

'More like *taken*,' Aspis said behind her.

Everyone was combat-ready, with no enemy in sight. At front, the Keeper held up a fist, signalling, *Wait*. Guards stared towards the forest around them, as if trying to look into their depths, some at the spot where the crow had taken flight. The air crackled, warping strangely around them, and as Shadow too peered into the trees, trying to glimpse the attackers, it occurred to her—

'A deadzone,' Shadow realized. 'We're in a deadzone.'

'Orders, Keeper,' a front Guard said.

'Hold,' the Keeper replied. Shadow grew suddenly curious; this was her first encounter with a deadzone.

'This is the same path I took to Yosae,' Crow said frustratedly. 'How could we have strayed into one now after following north exactly?'

'It's grown,' Aspis said, stiffening behind her. 'And quickly.'

'I thought they would look more . . . dead,' Shadow commented.

Deadzones had first started to appear centuries ago. Farm animals would disappear into woodland beyond grazing pens and then never return. The three-legged crow migration patterns grew erratic and time-sensitive, as if they were avoiding certain parts of the land, had no homes to return to or leave from. The deadzones were merely pockets, until they weren't. They grew, and grew, and swallowed. She'd come to imagine bark festering off wilting trees, rotting grounds, bird bones circling fungi rings. But this patch of forest looked perfectly normal. 'And I thought they were only in the south.'

'They used to be,' Aspis replied. 'But they've spread. We've never encountered this one before.' She sat up straighter on the doe, pushed forward. 'I can send a courier to the Stronghold for reinforcements,' she announced to everyone.

'There's no time for that,' the Keeper said. 'I'm going in.'

Protest erupted down the line.

'You weren't even supposed to be in Yosae, much less charging into a zone,' Crow snapped. The deer were growing antsier. And was Shadow imagining it, or had the forest closed in a little more? The Keeper was already dismounting, caressing her buck's flank before picking her way through the knee-high grasses, towards the woods.

'Stop her,' Crow ordered, but no one moved. Despite the protests, it seemed that this was some shade of an inevitable development – the Keeper, perhaps, was their only hope.

Some Guards dismounted as well – either out of fear or respect: everyone watched the Keeper approach the forest edge.

She stepped into the thick growth . . .

And disappeared.

Shadow was astonished. She hardly had time to react before she felt a tugging at her legs: Crow knifing through her bindings.

'Dismount,' he ordered.

Shadow obeyed.

'We'll send her in as bait,' he announced. 'It'll buy time for Scarlet, in case.' He grabbed her by the arm roughly and pushed her towards the same edge.

She began to walk slowly. Shadow knew she should protest, object in outrage, but her feet moved of their own accord. The deadzone fascinated her, and she didn't even look back, didn't hear the worries of the strangers behind her. She felt a strange pull towards it. Everything behind her, the cacophony, fell away swiftly.

Shadow stepped in.

As soon as she was inside, she knew there would be nothing behind her but endless trees and foliage. A thin stream ran across the ground by her feet. Kneeling down, she watched it suddenly change current, running the other direction. Sunlight glinted off dew drops across ground saplings, but the leaves cast no shadows, creating strange, dappled patterns across the forest. A peculiar feeling of wrongness, of disorientation hit her. Her hand came down on the soft earth to steady herself.

'What are you doing in here?' snapped the figure above her. The Keeper stood out against the eerie backdrop like something more visceral, a warm and breathing thing against the pallor.

'Crow pushed me in,' Shadow said, looking up. *As bait.*

The Keeper looked intensely irritated. 'Don't touch the water.' And then turned back, though she kept a wary eye on her. Below, the stream changed current again.

*Dead*zone made sense. It was unnaturally, deathly quiet, devoid of even insect buzz. Although the plants brightened and sparkled, it looked fake, too colourful in the twilight, as if someone had sewn this place like a tapestry. A weak imitation. It felt wrong . . . but almost familiar. Like a caricature of a place she'd already been long ago, standing not behind this girl but someone older and stronger. Her memories were flimsy, buried, but some of them rose within her at times, unbidden, triggered by the strangest things. Like when the Soldier had first awakened, thrust into an unfamiliar world by an unfamiliar handler.

The Keeper watched precariously as if waiting for something.

The Last Soldier of Nava

Shadow stood, carefully. 'What are you looking for?'

The Keeper turned and stared. Shadow was taken aback, until she realized she wasn't looking directly at her. 'Behind you – slowly.'

Shadow froze. Turned her head steadily to the side, followed by a shoulder, chancing a look.

There was nothing but a snarl of knotted vine, vegetation. It was only after a few moments that it jumped out, what had been there all along: a pointed snout between the leaves, russet-brown fur—

A lynx. Looking directly at her.

She tried not to show her surprise. It was incredibly close, ears tapered, pinning her with its hard gaze as she stared back, hypnotized. The eyes caught her. They weren't the characteristic yellow slit-pupils of a cats, but different – disconcertingly so, darker, rounder, not animal-like at all, almost human, almost as if—

A loud thump behind her; followed by a sharp rustling sound. The Keeper had beaten the palm of her hand against the trunk, startling the lynx. It turned tail and disappeared.

When Shadow turned, the other girl was already stepping towards her. Around them, the forest seemed to warp again and recede.

'We need to leave. Now.'

'But the rider,' Shadow said weakly. 'We still have to find . . .' At the Keeper's knowing look, she trailed off.

Reluctantly, Shadow looked towards the endless forest. Instinctively she knew they were still close enough to the outside world that they could leave this place easily, but at the same time, she didn't want to. It was as familiar as it was strange. She could run away right now, plunge into the depths of the woods. But there was no telling what lay in store for her inside, where she might end up. It was just a false lure.

Wasn't it? A few more moments to take it in, to linger between the leaves . . .

'It's this way.' She pointed west.

'How do you know?' the Keeper asked behind her.

Just follow me, Shadow thought. 'I can feel it.' She stepped forward.

They emerged back out of the underbrush.

The rest of the ride to the Stronghold was fast, urgent, sailing over the riverbeds and fields. Shadow nearly fell off her doe when it vaulted nimbly over a pebbled stream, clutching the saddle hard. The front riders kept a silent, steadfast pace while the back delved into intense whispering and speculation, which she only heard snippets of. But Shadow didn't need to hear to understand: a new deadzone was danger, and the deadzones were spreading. Consuming the land. She thought of the market gossip back in Yosae about the abnormal weather savaging the southern towns, the unparalleled destruction left behind by stem-shredding typhoons and cloud-high tsunamis, that many northerners thought a hoax.

Shadow could guess the cause of all of it. A magic older than any of them even knew, seeping through the island nation, trying to enclose it within its grasp like fingers rising from the ground, capturing in its palm. She had felt it before; she was probably the only one alive, besides the Moonbearer, who could feel it now still. And yet, what would the Stronghold care, until it came closer to them?

But all her thoughts about it momentarily fled at the sight of the Stronghold over the horizon before her.

It was magnificent.

Against the backdrop of the foaming Seochon and lilac-orange sunset stood an impenetrable beauty, measuring over fifty *kan* across. Completely lacquered in black like a sculpture of obsidian ice, high-storied hip-and-gable roofs tapering down at the edges, thin golden lines etched into the mosaics depicting scenes of curling dragons, leaping deer, Moon Rabbits. Small statues of three-legged crows perched on the roof corners, though some were surely real. Along some sections were tiles of crimson and silver – colours that she thought held meaning, though she wasn't yet sure how.

In every crack and crevice, the Moonbearer's mark shone through palpably. Beholding the size and grandeur, she wondered what the Queen Dynast's palace looked like – if it could even compare to this. But even if it did, it would be nothing more than a prop. The Stronghold was where real power lay.

'Do you remember it?' Aspis asked. 'How fitting that you return now.'

Of course – this was where every ordinary man or woman was remade into a Guard under the Moonbearer's hand – where the Keeper, Crow, everyone all lived and fought. Given new names, stripped of their old ones.

The palace sat on the edge of a cliff high above the rocky coastline. As they approached, the ground seemed to slope down strangely before them, and she realized why: a steep half-circle moat. That should've been impossible so high up from the ground, but it was there, nevertheless. Their party stopped right before it, and in seconds she heard a huge torrent of water rush in.

Aspis inched the doe forward, and Shadow was able to look in over the sheer drop. The water level had risen in a matter of seconds, though it was unclear what caused this; white gulls dragged their beaks along the soupy surface, sparkling flying fish occasionally flipping out of the water in foaming whorls. On small boats below Guards waited, working frantically to match the water force.

But she wasn't prepared for what rose out of the water next: at the sound of a Guard's bone whistle, something vast, smooth, grey, and round – like an enormous, buoyant rock – began to surface. A moment later, it went back under.

'Don't drag on,' the Keeper called out. She was unhinged, Shadow thought, talking to the moat like that. Regardless, she leaned forward, wrists pulled taut, trying to see.

Saltwater sprayed generously in her face. The momentous rock rose fully from the water, and it wasn't a rock at all, but the head of a mountainous catfish turned parallel to the moat side, its body half the width of the channel itself.

A huge yellow eye fixed them. Great slippery whiskers dragged along the surface, gills flapping in tandem. Across its sides slung, incredibly, a harness dotted with barnacle clusters and suckerfish, leading to a huge and low saddle fitted behind the sailing curve of its dorsal fin.

And it stayed above, waiting, floating beside the edge, body undulating with the waves, tail occasionally flickering up.

The journey across the back of the catfish lasted but all of a few seconds, so close to the water Shadow could've skimmed it with her fingertips. Two servants beside her grumbled every time they were intermittently splashed. As soon as they disembarked in front of the main palace gates, a flurry of servants and stable hands immediately attended to them all after quick bows – guiding animals away by the reins, receiving heavy armour pieces shed by Guards.

Three servants came forward – a young girl and boy, and an older woman – who bowed low to Aspis.

'Welcome back, Master of the Hunt,' the woman greeted. On Shadow, they cast curious, chilly gazes, taking in her state.

Shadow started. *Master of the Hunt.* This girl – Aspis – was part of the royal Court. Ex-general. A hunter. Unlike the Keeper, her title bore no ambiguity.

The Last Soldier of Nava

'We were caught in a new deadzone an hour out to Yosae,' Aspis said. 'It's imperative the Court be alerted immediately.' She was met with nods, hasty descensions.

'The . . . prisoner?' a servant asked.

'I want her less filthy. Prepare her,' the Keeper announced ahead of them, 'to be presented to the Moonbearer.'

Chapter 5

The head servant, Balam, ordered Shadow to take her clothes off, voice laced with annoyance. 'All who are presented to the Moonbearer must be made ready,' Balam said sternly. Beside her stood a willowy boy, Min, who agreed silently. For evidence, she gestured to the other side of the rooms, where a middle-aged man was also being prepared. Unlike Shadow, he offered no protest or difficulty. The baths were like miniature oceans, tinted turquoise and billowing with steam. The separate pools alternated between hot and cold, the ceiling printed with faded cranes and lotus flowers. 'You're to be prepared on the Keeper's orders.'

Sweat beaded Shadow's brow uncomfortably; she would submit to the heat before the Moonbearer ever laid a hand on her. And to think the man in the far corner was regarding this as a religious experience. No wonder guests were compelled here before presentation; it would render any man too fatigued to even put up a fight. Min was stronger than he looked, she could tell from his grip – he fixed her with a glare that said, *don't try anything* – and held her down as he loosened the linens from her, fingers moving quickly. The top of her robe was pushed off her shoulders, revealing only her underclothes, falling behind to where it bundled around her elbows.

Only hours ago, she'd been slicing radishes in the garden under the watchful eye of Sae. Now, she was stripped half-naked in the bathhouse of the Stronghold, with the Moonbearer only a few floors above her. It was almost too difficult to believe. She was in the heart of Ik-Song's power, perhaps the only place in the entire world she shouldn't be near.

Did he know of her presence yet, she wondered. Surely, he did. Yet it also seemed unlikely that the Keeper would divulge him that information, not with the sort of bewildering possessiveness she'd shown over Shadow. Which brought her back to her most pressing question – why the Keeper wanted her here at all?

'I'm going to release your bindings momentarily,' Min said. 'Do not attack me, or I'll cut the other half of your face.' He pushed her sharply into the shallow pool, stepping in after her. The water began as edging on too hot, starting an itch along her skin, but it quickly cooled. The cleaning was quick and efficient, her thoughts disappearing into the hazy air.

After the bath, her hair sat damp on her shoulders.

The Guards stationed at each exit wore nondescript, navy blue uniforms, awaiting her approach. It was there that she finally saw the man from the baths up close: he was old enough that were they not two strangers on equal footing in the Stronghold, she would've bowed formally to him in greeting. They were both handed off from the stationed men to new Guards, two of them in the Moonbearer's black. The man was led first with Shadow following, a four-person procession. As they weaved and ascended through the cavernous pathways, noises from upstairs grew louder, sounds of a busy and bustling palace.

The man's voice was almost inaudible when he spoke. 'I wish you well in your remaking.'

Dread pooled in her gut as she took in his merchant drab. He hadn't seen her wrists – as if she would ever willingly allow the Moonbearer to corrupt her. 'I'm not here to be remade. I'm a prisoner.'

A pause. 'Then I wish you a painless execution.'

'Where are you from?'

'Yosae. My name is Ki-Young.'

'I'm Shadow.'

His back stiffened as his face turned slightly. 'You grant yourself a new name without even being remade?'

The louder pitch of his voice earned a sharp reprimand from the Guard up front, who ordered him to face front.

'If you're from Yosae, you know what the Guards are like. Do you really want to become one?'

'I've come for an opportunity,' he said.

'How do you know you'll be given what you're promised?' How could she make him see? That nothing here was as it had been? Nava had thrived because of its understanding of the world. It had been built for and along nature, not against. Its people had mastered wind and water, weathered the storms and angry seas, honed the art over centuries – a far more powerful and complex form that had since been lost; now reduced to the watered down, cheap imitations that the Moonbearer bestowed on people. Now the Dawnbringer was long-dead, and the Moonbearer had devolved into something unnatural, insipid. The same thing that Shadow had in her bones.

'The Moonbearer is our saviour,' he said. 'I'm nothing but a poor merchant in Yosae, by the *Dal*, I've nothing to my name. My family awaits my return. I'm strong enough to be remade. And when I am, they'll be rewarded.'

The Last Soldier of Nava

This time, the Guards threatened physical intervention if they didn't quiet. Shadow dropped back, silent, as they neared the main doors. She thought suddenly of the schoolboy who hung around the Yosae markets – his tricky fingers, the hems of his uniform always filmy with dust. Always thoughtfully bemused the way only a child could be; still running hungry as only a child could.

'Up,' the Guard behind ordered as they ascended a final flight of stairs to a gleaming set of doors. 'You'll show proper respect in the throne room. A full bow to the floor, and use proper titles: the Councillor, the Keeper, his Highness the Crown Prince, and Advisors of the Court.'

Crown Prince? she nearly said aloud. The *Crown Prince* of Ik-Song? Why would the Crown Prince be here in the Stronghold, and not with the Queen?

They came around to gag her. Her breaths came hard against the cloth. She didn't dare think a moment ahead – about the figure who would be soon before her – open and exposed, so close she could reach out to him.

The doors opened.

The throne room.

That feeling of certain impossibility, when she'd slid open Sae's door into a wall of vines – it returned like a tidal wave. What first caught her eyes and refused to let go was the vast, high ceiling that filtered light brilliantly through its concavity; hidden crescent moons glanced out at her from everywhere: the arms of chairs, the lining of floors. A room that could fit almost everyone in the palace, probably. And it all led down to . . .

. . . a wall of darkness, at the front.

It churned like a living thing. Three high thrones were centred in the room, and around them, curving in a semicircle, was an array of faces, everyone armoured. Military generals.

The only member she recognized among the Advisors, and the only woman among them, was Aspis.

The centremost throne of the Councillor, the largest, the one that was *his* seat, it had to be – was empty. There was no Moonbearer in sight – only that wall of darkness, a vacancy.

And for the first time ever, she couldn't sense his presence. How did he seal himself off so well, even after all this time?

To her own surprise, she felt a tingling sense of disappointment – even as her palms became wet and mouth went dry.

To the right of the centre throne was a smaller one, atop which sat a young man she had never seen before: his hair shockingly stark white, features lovely. His silver-grey plated armour encircled him up to his wrists and neck, a white hemp *gat* hat strapped behind him that dangled to the side. He sat with good posture but wasn't rigid, shoulders slightly stooped as he fiddled his fingers. His eyes flickered from Shadow to Ki-Young, expression stricken, unable to hide his surprise at her face, her presence. He was captivating.

And to the centre throne's left: the Keeper sat inattentively, an arm slung over the backing – looking as neat and polished as ever, as if they hadn't all spent the better part of the day verbally sparring and running from deadzones. She stared Shadow down.

Shadow was beginning to see, for the first time, what the Moonbearer had built here. How she stood on the other side of it, a prisoner with nothing but the clothes on her back. He had taken Nava, everything he had, for granted. He had lost it all. Now, he had built a new sort of empire. Somehow he had even convinced the Crown Prince to play a role in it. She wanted the wall to drop. The darkness to recede, for him to face her and remember all that he had done to her. Even when she was *so close*, her reach was muddled and unsure; her eyes roamed the wall uselessly as if she could pinpoint his heartbeat within it, know his reasons.

'O Councillor,' gasped Ki-Young in front of her, already bowing, reduced to stuttering and open disbelief. The Moonbearer wasn't even visible, but Ki-Young was caught by the hypnotic void of nothingness that greeted them, the cold faces that looked down on them. Shadow forced herself to bow.

One of the Advisors stood. A tall, broad-shouldered man with a long grey beard and traditional black thimble *samo* hat, golden beads framing his face. He looked bored.

'I am White Crane, the head Advisor of the Court,' he said. A remade, then. 'Today, you are presented before the Councillor, the great Moonbearer; his Highness Crown Prince Yo-han; and the Royal Keeper of the Gates. Before you sit the Advisors, who will oversee the proceedings.'

Yo-han: so he had been able to keep his original name.

There was no fanfare, no strange rituals of incense and chanting, no prayer. There were only a few curt words about the nature of the 'ceremony', how it was a great honour to be remade in the Moonbearer's way, granted unimaginable gifts of wind or water – or something rarer. Sand, light. Darkness. Shadow studied the Court, throughout; Aspis gave nothing away, taking her duties seriously. From the way they'd ridden back to the Stronghold, she'd thought the Court might be up in arms about the encroaching deadzones, frantic for solutions, just like the Yosaeans were up in arms about the looming threat of Asanai and its vicious Emperor. But there was no mention of that at all – only this silent, stiff room. She studied the Prince – his hair obviously revealed that he had ability, but he didn't seem to have a remade name.

She looked to Ki-Young, who was almost frothing at the

mouth with anticipation. She couldn't parse out his intentions – whether he was really a desperate man, or a greedy one. She thought of the Guards she'd seen parading around the city, threatening townsfolk for their own amusement and leaving entire streets upended after a night of unruly drinking. Given abilities that used to be sacred in Nava, purposeful, now watered down to nothing but a cheap trick bestowed upon unworthy men for their own greed.

There was no saving him now. Shadow could only hope that he was, indeed, strong enough – that the 'test' was no test at all. After all, everyone here had already passed. The Moonbearer only wanted more soldiers, more fighters, more followers. More remades for his army. He already had ironclad control over the north, between the Stronghold and the Queen's guards – nothing but a puppet army for him – and countless patrols reinforcing down to the south. Still, it was not enough.

Ki-Young bent to one knee. The Court watched impassively. Prince Yo-han looked towards the ground, hands tight on his armrests.

And the Keeper watched Shadow directly. Head tilted, blasé. Shadow stared back, trying uselessly to glean answers, to understand. She knew why the Moonbearer wanted Ki-Young. Why Crow had pursued her. What did the Keeper want? Why did she interfere so brashly?

'You,' White Crane said, 'will now be remade.'

A long, strung-out moment of absolute silence as they waited. Nothing happened. Shadow expected the Moonbearer to emerge from the wall, to come forth. But he didn't.

It was like he was mocking her. For the first time ever, she wasn't walking with him following; she was waiting, and he was nowhere to be found. She could hardly make sense of it.

Instead of him, a tendril of darkness unfurled from the wall.

The Last Soldier of Nava

It flowed out – slowly, tentatively – towards Ki-Young. It moved like a kind of animal sniffing its prey out, like an arm detached from its owner, curling around the floor, and nearing the man. Everyone watched the darkness come closer, until finally it shot out towards him, and seemed to overtake him like a hand brushing his forehead – entering him, overwhelming the warm cocoon of his body, form tightening like he was possessed. It went on for blistering, strange moments until pained grunts started to escape him.

Shadow didn't want to watch.

The ordeal continued until – finally, just as it seemed he would reach his breaking point – the darkness dissipated.

Ki-Young collapsed to the ground in a heap.

He was absolutely still.

Until he twitched back to life.

Shadow hissed out a breath. The man rose slowly, with trembling limbs, but clearly alive. Was it just her own hope, or did he look more vibrant, alive? He looked around shakily, meeting her own stricken gaze, and burst into smile. Brightness lingered in his eyes. He flexed his hands into fists, took a step forward.

'The Moonbearer has remade me,' he cried joyously, out of breath, throwing his hands into the air. 'Great Councillor, thank you, thank you—' And he dissolved into tears and gratitude, clasped hands rising as he kneeled once again.

A lightness came to her own face as she sagged slightly in relief. They were in this strange place with strange people, but at least, for now, Ki-Young would live.

And she was comforted by this, until she saw the rest of the Court: expressionless. The Prince: knuckles whitening on his chair.

And this was when the man began to shake – to stop abruptly in his praises and tremble like he would fall apart.

She felt it before she saw it – so quietly and quickly that she could hardly react – one moment he quivered, and the next, fell to the ground, stiff as a board.

His face went slack, convulsing as if poison had pressed itself into his very bones. His body slumped awkwardly sideways on the bamboo surface. It was only when he was turned to the side by two Guards, flat onto his back, that she saw the absence of his face. Nothing remained but a shadow void, mirroring the wall, blood and darkness alike seeping out onto the ground, mingling like breaths in cold air.

Chapter 6

The long silence that ensued as the body was carried away didn't seem to strike anyone else in the room as particularly painful. Except perhaps the Prince, who tried and failed tremendously to hide his discomfort, fidgeting on his throne and regarding Shadow with some dread. In fact, he could hardly look away from her. Some of the Advisors examined their nails, stretched, muttered lowly.

She thought of the schoolboy, waiting and waiting around the stalls.

White Crane wasted no time moving on to the next topic. 'The Keeper disregards the Court's time. She comes and goes as she pleases. And – allegedly – has brought a living *sakasa* who stands before you now.'

Stillness in the Court – and all eyes on Shadow.

She tried not to squirm under the attention. In only a second, their worlds had rearranged: the Moonbearer was supposed to be the only master of darkness, burdened by this terrible and so-called heroic fate. Her presence diluted him, of course. Her presence was unnatural. Her presence evoked someone they had all thought gone. A litany of discussion started.

'Impossible,' another said. 'Never has a *sakasa* been remade in the Stronghold.'

Crow was subsequently called forth to recount a summary of the day's events.

'A cold wind was starting up in Yosae,' he stated, 'and she was wandering around the markets. I pursued her and chased her out.'

'Don't leave out the rest of the story,' Scarlet interrupted. 'How you failed to capture her one-on-one, and the only reason she's here now is because she bumbled into my buck on that disorganized fumble you call a *pursuit*.'

Outrage among the Advisors – and none of it aimed at Crow.

'The Keeper off palace grounds,' White Crane scoffed. 'A mere night before the moonline banquet, and on Mourning Day itself, no less.'

'Your own Guards weren't privy to your departure?' a different Advisor raised.

A crimson Guard was forced to talk. 'We were told that the consequence of disobeying her would be . . . worse than the Court's.'

'The consequence being?' White Crane said impatiently.

'I think,' Aspis interrupted, 'I know why she was pursued. To use her against the Asani.' Silence. 'Normally, a rogue would prove nothing more than a burden for the Stronghold, but this prisoner – a reformed one, a powerful one – could prove extremely useful.' She looked down at Crow again. 'Am I right in my suspicions?'

'A nonsensical idea,' White Crane said. 'A prisoner can't be so easily trusted. Especially a powerful one; how dangerous might such a betrayal be? Clearly, she escaped the Stronghold and deserted if she was in Yosae. I'll remind you the punishment for desertion is death.' He spoke with finality, clearly ready for this to end. 'Therefore, she will be executed.'

The Last Soldier of Nava

'No,' the Keeper said swiftly. 'She's mine.' Her fingers drummed across her throne, her face cool.

'After *that* matter,' White Crane continued, 'we'll discuss *your* fate as well.'

'*Out*,' the Keeper said, standing. 'Everyone out. I want a private audience, now, with Yo-han and the Councillor.'

'Councillor,' White Crane protested, 'you'll allow this?' It was peculiar how he looked towards the black wall – how they all did – as if it would speak in return, form words. They were used to this communication, she realized.

The wall didn't reply in any capacity. Then, slowly, reluctantly, the Advisors made to obey, rising incredulously from their seats. They shuffled out of the throne room in lines, muttering amongst themselves, White Crane with a few choice words that rang around the space. Aspis walked out with clipped precision, casting Shadow a brief glance.

The Keeper waited until no one remained in the room but Guards and the Prince. Shadow's wrists itched to pull free of their bonds; she entertained the notion of running up towards that wall, slicing through it. Reaching through to the other side, where he might be waiting. Would the darkness consume her? Or would it simply become part of her again, like returning to its owner? It was the only thing they shared.

She watched the spot right ahead where Ki-Young had died. No – had been killed. The faint patch of blood was already disappearing, lightening. How many hundreds of thousands of hopefuls had passed through the Stronghold like him, kneeling in this very space where she stood – exhilarated with the thrill of the Moonbearer's touch, the prospect of power flowing through them? Submitting to the royals of the palace and then treading out to force the rest of Ik-Song to submit to them. Returning here, back to lavish rooms and purebred deer and all the servant playthings in the world. How much blood did her feet rest on now? How many bodies felled without a face? It seemed almost to seep into her from below, marking the floors as stained beyond comprehension.

And again, Scarlet's burning gaze on her, that infuriating, half-lilting smile. *Try it.* A walking temptation to induce violence.

'I brought her here,' the Keeper said simply, as if Shadow wasn't even there. 'You understand why I brought her here. She's mine.'

Despite the centremost, elevated throne being vacant, the owner's presence felt heavy and sickly in the room. It dawned on Shadow that she was witnessing the kind of conversation that perhaps no one else in the entire palace was ever allowed to witness.

'You don't know the girl, Scarlet,' the Prince said. 'You don't even know her name. She could be anyone at all.'

'It doesn't matter,' the Keeper knifed through. 'What matters is the ability.'

The ability. But what use would she have for Shadow's ability, if not militarily?

'You can't have her,' Scarlet said, no longer speaking to Yo-han. 'You can't kill her or maim her or blind her. I need her.'

No response.

'All of these followers, diplomats, remades, nobility, in and out of this place day after day. All worthless. None of them *had* it. None of them knew a thing.' A heat to her eyes – she was serious now. 'This changes everything.'

Anger thrummed through her tone. The wall didn't respond in any way, which seemed to worsen it.

'You send Crow out to do your bidding,' Scarlet continued, 'Fetching cargo, chasing fugitives. Whatever vices you hide, I don't pry. Except you never told me you'd already made what I've been looking for all this time.'

The Last Soldier of Nava

'Scarlet,' the Prince said. 'You know that you can be . . . impulsive, when it comes to these matters.'

'You didn't know either, Yo-han, did you? She's the key. The answer. I know it. And she's mine.'

'Consider the safety of those in the Stronghold, you—'

'Councillor,' Scarlet said. A long pause. Then: 'I will bargain for her.'

The Prince couldn't hide his surprise. But even more surprising was the flickering in the wall – the first signs of what lurked behind.

Characters appeared in flashing gold strokes.

LAY YOUR TERMS, it read.

Scarlet stepped back in satisfaction, and the Prince's surprise deepened.

Shadow stared.

Where was he?

Reveal yourself, she thought.

'This *sakasa* – here, in the Stronghold, under my supervision, for however long I need her,' Scarlet said. 'And in return, my obedience.'

The characters had faded.

'Neither the girl nor I will make trouble. I'll assimilate her into the Stronghold as need be. I will no longer leave the Stronghold – at all – or threaten my personal guard into allowing me to. I won't question you. I won't heckle the Court.'

At that, Yo-han scoffed.

'I'll heckle the Court *less*,' she amended. 'And I'll also attend all of the meaningless, head-dragging parades and dinners and celebrations and every other useless arrangement you require of me. I'll cooperate by all these terms and come and stand, always, wherever you'd like me to stand, as silently as you'd like. These are my terms.'

'Generous terms,' the Prince commented.

'Accept them,' Scarlet said to the wall.

A moment. Then:

ON ONE CONDITION, came the answer.

DISCARD HER WHEN FINISHED.

'Deal,' said Scarlet immediately.

WELCOME.

This final word disappeared in smoke.

Shadow was to be trapped here, in the Stronghold – the heart of enemy territory – for who knows how long, subject to every whim of the insane, spoiled brat who ate from the Moonbearer's hand. The brat who had, perhaps, the most reason to care about the Soldier's kills. The Moonbearer wanted her here in this palace, unable to do a thing, only to watch him through an impenetrable wall as he rose further in power. It was a slow kind of torture.

And yet – all of that fell away in the face of this fact:

That she was closer than she'd ever been. The only opportunity she might ever have to be so close.

That somewhere in this palace, he waited, alive and well, cloaked in the very stuff that had made her.

The world shifted and rearranged itself around her, slowly but surely. Gone were the stealthy blades of battle and midnight assassinations. Ancient beasts and falling cities, dreamlike in her memory. Only three thrones and a Court. The world had collapsed into just one sizeable room within one palace within one nation, once a great dynasty. This centre brimmed with barely unchecked power. And this was how it was, now.

Even from mere etched characters on a wall, she could sense his thinking: *You will not last long in a place like this.* He had so much more than she'd ever expected: a formidable army, the sister of the Desert Rose, even a Crown Prince, through which ran his legitimacy. To reach him, to breach this thick border, to strike him down, would be to wade through endless layer after layer of trick and deception, strangeness unbounded, a litany of reminders she had tried so sincerely to bury and kill.

But she was here now.

She knew things that even his closest confidants would never know.

He was powerful, yes. But he was also mortal, and all dark power had a finite burn.

Welcome. She took this for the challenge it was, a resolve hardening around her heart. She had once been the Soldier. She wanted to forget, but he wouldn't let her. So be it. Sae had told her to go north. She was north now; in the heart of it all. And regardless of Asanai, the deadzones, the storms, everything she had ever really wanted to hurt was right here.

In the end, she said nothing at all, even as the busy Court resumed, Guards flooding in and flanking her exit. She didn't tear her eyes from the dark as she was escorted out. *You'll regret leaving me alive, Father,* she thought. *Leaving a weapon unchecked.*

She was escorted down corridor after corridor, up at least seven flights of stairs, an endless labyrinth that seemed to reshape itself around her at every moment. Along the way, she tried to memorize its layout, peer into the rooms and get a sense of what was where – but it all blended together. Every palace wall was exquisitely carved and surprisingly open, some sections of wall entirely punched out right to the sea. A somewhat sinister design choice. Down a slightly more austere hallway on the upmost level, they'd stopped in front of a sliding panelled door, opened by one of the Guards. Beside the door stood an incredible jade fountain, its base carved with scenes of phoenixes in flight and circling koi. The fountain was extraordinarily busy with the movement of real birds, flycatchers and magpies, which she watched in fascination. They flew in through the window cracks and bathed leisurely in what she was sure was saltwater, though they didn't seem to mind. In the corner of the hall was a three-legged crow who watched her from afar, looking like it knew far too much for its own good. She looked away.

She peered into the room – well-furnished quarters, belonging to an Advisor, perhaps – that was empty. 'Who am I to be presented to now?' she asked tiredly. Neither Guard flanking her answered, only shoving her in and shutting the door behind her.

After a long moment, she realized, with shock, that these were her own quarters.

Left alone, she saw only the stone bed, eyeing it like a starving beggar. It heated deliciously beneath her palms. It would be stupid, amateurish, to throw herself into a dead sleep now – in the heart of a hostile palace, the Moonbearer and his cronies lurking right around the corners. Two Guards flanked outside who could slip in at a moment's notice. Already she heard the low murmur of their conversation, coarse snippets catching on her ears, on the Inner, mundane matters.

She should be crouched with one ear to the door – trying to glean more information about her new environment, as quickly as possible. She should be pondering over Aspis, combing through their conversation, gauging her intentions; creating a plan to navigate tomorrow's banquet, trying to find out more about it before she inevitably stumbled into some disastrous affair. She should be standing, vigilant. But the stone was a brown granite sanded over, smooth, earthy, and warm, so warm, beside her face. Unyielding and comfortable in its hardness. She curled up on the surface and something poked painfully in her front – it was only then she remembered what was hidden there. What Sae had handed her as she left.

She dug it out. A small stone. How had it stayed with her, throughout the long, winding ride to the palace, the wash of the baths? Impossible. It was obsidian black, smooth, nearly weightless but still a presence beside her. It seemed almost to fit into the curve of her, as if it was just a piece taken from her skin.

Sae and her talismans. It was the only tangible reminder of her, but Shadow tried not to think about that too much. Through her window came the lull of crashing waves, the muted clamour of a busy palace, a rushing of water that must be the moat, where the shadow of the enormous catfish would pass by again and again. Amidst the noise, she drifted into sleep, the stone clutched in one hand.

Chapter 7

The Soldier remembered her birth.

She woke for the first time in the dirt and peered into the sloping water of a past night's rainfall, to see a girl's face. She grazed her face with her fingertips, watching the girl in the water do the same.

There was a heeled boot by her face. She looked up to a man, nothing but a silhouette, and although they did not exchange any words, she understood. Her creator, her father. Above his shoulders he bore the moon.

She remembered an enormous, dark and craggy mountain in the distance, a mountain that twitched, how it was no mountain, but really a dead thing.

Her body itched with something so fierce, something that would not be sated with anything but blood. Her hands were deft. They blended into darkness, as naturally as closing one's eyes to sleep. Only he knew how to calm the fire in her chest. It gave her satisfaction to do what needed to be done, to do what her handler asked.

First a hand, then a man, a village, a kingdom, all disappearing under the blanket of her night sky like the small things they were, the shadows pumping slow and sturdy through her blood. The Soldier could not be stopped. The Soldier was no girl, no person, no soft body, only a weapon, a razing force. The Soldier was the ultimate warrior, one that would not be weighed down by petty allegiance. She was simply guided along a path set by him, which hurtled down. She remembered others, soldiers he commanded and saw, the way they cowered at her, unnerved. And what did it matter whether they were afraid or not? They were useless to her.

But the Soldier . . .

The Soldier remembered differently, at times.

She remembered beautiful things. Things that had burned down, cities that changed shape, mountains of limestone and powdered frost. She remembered the Moon Rabbit, Daltokki, settling slowly among the stars. She remembered breaking down the door to a room with nothing inside, but a mother and her child huddled against one corner, foreheads smeared with goat's blood to ward against evil. They had been eating remnants of what they could to survive.

She remembered walking quickly and deftly along the edges of the shadows in such a home, as they trembled in fear, and she watched them, ready to strike. But she only watched and could not strike. For some reason, she left them there, those helpless lambs. She was not sure why.

Once, she left and she began to walk, and walk, and walk. Once, she walked for three nights and two days on a mission without realizing, only coming to a stop before a great pine forest where the trees stood as needle-thin and tall as the moon. The Soldier was two hundred *li* off-base from her destination, straying far and wide. Because she was thinking of blood smearing down foreheads.

Of a roaring summer, endless wells, working a roughened

hoe in the fields. Of lakes that went on forever, diving deep, deep down, great whales crying out in the soundless abyss of the oceans. Her own reflection, soft and blurred, in the rainwater.

Chapter 8

Shadow woke to the feather-light touch of an assailant, the soft sliding of her door.

In moments, she had the intruder pinned to the wall by their neck, face pressed against it with one arm twisted around their back. It was only a long moment later that she realized the person under her hands was a girl, slight and small – too weak to resist, much less attack her. In servant's wear.

She let go immediately. 'I'm sorry,' she said. 'I thought you were . . .' an attacker. There *had* been attackers . . . hadn't there? But she had dreamt . . .

The visions dawned on her slowly, shockingly. She had dreamt impossible things, things she shouldn't have been able to remember with such startling clarity. So strangely vivid. It always came back in bits and fragments, not like this. With a start, she remembered that she'd fallen asleep with the stone in her hand – it glinted at her now from her bed, black and oblivious. Was it possible that Sae's stone was really spiritual? Had pulled these memories from her mind? It was like they had risen up from the deep underbelly of the Stronghold.

An impressive array of servants had gathered in her quarters in a half-circle, as if watching a performance; she recognized only Min and Balam from the baths. Golden light flooded in through the windows. It was nearly sunset – she had slept through an entire night and most of the day. She rubbed her eyes, trying to muster up the words for a reasonable apology, standing half-dressed.

'At least *bind* her,' the girl pleaded to the nearest Guard, wringing her hands.

'No need for that,' came another voice, knife-like, from the entry.

The Keeper. The servant girl gasped in surprise and quickly kneeled to the floor, with the practised grace of someone who'd done it a thousand times before. The others all followed suit, foreheads pressing to bamboo, until Shadow remained the only one left standing. Somewhere in her sleep-addled mind it occurred to her, faintly, that she should bow, too, and avert her gaze – but her knees didn't give.

Flanked by two crimson Guards, Scarlet's hair was again swept back from her face, gathered at the nape of her neck, and the single garment she wore was unlike anything Shadow had ever seen. It was like a robe made of paper, thin and parchment-coloured, with wide sleeves that cut off at her wrists. It draped over her, sheathing the white underlayer, the soft sinew and jutting collarbone of her neck disappearing into the triangular collar. Tiny pearls twinkled at her ears.

It was very sheer – borderline see-through. Shadow had never seen such clothing on anyone, royal or not. Her face began to feel a little heated.

'You stare like a dog,' said Scarlet, one eyebrow raised.

What Shadow meant to do was to say, *I apologize, Keeper*, and lower to the floor. Instead, what came out of her mouth was: 'Can such a garment invite anything but staring?'

The Last Soldier of Nava

From the stifled noises of the servants, she knew she should've kept her mouth shut.

Scarlet didn't miss a beat, sneering. 'You insinuate that a woman's clothing determines her desire to be looked at?'

'No,' she replied. 'Just you.'

'And you're not going to bow,' Scarlet continued. A sigh. Scarlet's eyes dropped deliberately to study Shadow's body – as between them, the flurry of activity continued – and made no move to hide her lingering gaze over the scars. Shadow hadn't even realized they were on display – the stripey knife wounds, her body a pockmarked expanse. 'Do they hurt?'

Ahead of her, Scarlet indeed stood like a real gatekeeper, one who defended a beautiful and impenetrable fortress, mouth like a thing on the verge of trigger – things like fire and matchlock gunpowder, ready for wicked games. How utterly unlike the Desert Rose she was. How the entire palace didn't ruminate over the stark difference day and night was incredible. Shadow could hardly believe they were related at all if it weren't for their faces. But where the Rose had give and softness, Scarlet had a growing hardness. It was a shame she looked so sour, Shadow thought. She would be quite pretty if she really smiled.

When Shadow didn't answer, Scarlet continued. 'Tonight, we celebrate the moonlines,' she said. Moonlines were the spiritual paths that the dead were thought to take in the afterlife – streaking across the night sky under the film of stars, in lines forged of moondust, hence moonlines. Sunlines, then, were the paths of the living. It was commonly said in Yosae; one might hear friends part with, *May our sunlines cross again.*

'Any celebration of faith is bolstered by fear and threat. In this way, your presence will be very much appreciated. I'll leave you to preparations,' the Keeper addressed the servants, turning to leave . . . 'You won't bow at my departure?'

'Unlike you, I haven't rolled over and willingly signed away my freedom,' Shadow needled.

A lull of silence, in which Scarlet said nothing. And then: 'Are you sure those don't hurt?' Eyeing the scars. She pointed to a servant boy. 'You – press on them. Go on. That one, on her shoulder.'

The servant approached Shadow warily, taking two fingers to the old knife wound on her shoulder and pressed. His touch was so light she could barely feel it. The fact didn't escape Scarlet.

'Harder, come now,' she said.

Not wanting to risk the consequences of disobeying again, the boy pressed once more, this time not holding back. Despite her best efforts, Shadow full body flinched, teeth gritted, and the boy leapt back like she was a wild animal.

'Tonight,' Scarlet said, satisfied, 'we will be our truest selves.'

Shadow was left standing with her fists clenched and shirt bared half-open. The servants openly stared.

'I've never seen anyone taunt the Keeper and live,' one of them said, a bit awestruck.

'It's impossible not to,' Shadow muttered. 'Why does that wench—' At Balam's warning glance, she corrected, '—*the Keeper*, want me there?'

Min answered, shrugging. 'You could stand to be more grateful, honestly. A feast of those proportions is beyond your imagining.'

'And you'll get to see all the delegations,' another servant, a girl, clapped her hands excitedly.

'*I* heard that there would be a musical performance by Pak-Hwon's prostitutes,' someone else joined in gamely, and from there launched animated discussions about the existence and nature of such a performance.

'And the Councillor will be there?' Shadow interrupted.

There was a hush at the mention of the Moonbearer.

'Quiet. What if he's listening?' Min said.

'That's impossible,' the girl said. Her tone was confident, but she looked uncertain.

'It's not.' Min looked at Shadow, seeming to decide whether to impart something. 'Sometimes,' he said, 'at night, when the whole palace is asleep, and it's too dark to see, we think he roams around the palace like a ghost. Incorporeal. Not even the Asani Emperor could do that.'

'How would you know what the Emperor could do?' someone said.

'Why doesn't the Moonbearer show his face?' Shadow asked.

Min shrugged again. 'He's saving his energy. He only really meets with Prince Yo-han, or the Advisors – Inner circle.'

Saving his energy?

'Forget that,' A-ri interrupted. 'Is it true that you're a *sakasa*? And you're here to fight against the Asani?'

Deathly silence. Shadow knew what everyone was thinking: *there hasn't been a* sakasa *since the Soldier*. But she was spared from answering by a courier arriving at the door holding something that Balam received. 'Uniform.'

'Uniform?' Shadow froze. The clothing – she could tell, even from there – was being arranged across her bed, its different parts.

She already knew what it was. After it was laid out on the stone bed like the flanks of a dead animal, all of the servants peered down over her bed, heads bowed in observation. Someone inhaled.

'How would the tailor have had time to make something custom fit for her?' Min said. 'She arrived only a day ago and never even took measurements. Maybe the Keeper sent it.'

But Shadow knew that no Keeper, nor tailor, had sent this. This was a gift from the Moonbearer. This was his reminder that he had not forgotten.

Tonight, she would once again don the uniform of the Soldier.

Shadow wasn't prepared for the light when she entered the banquet.

The full force of a sunset streamed in from the west windows, shining directly into her eyes. Long, low tables that stretched out ahead of her, parallel to one another, exquisitely embroidered floor cushions seating close to a hundred or more guests; all eyes on her. Halfway down to the elevated thrones, a circular mat raised from the floor – the stage. At the far end, a table that didn't run parallel to the others but instead faced her horizontally. It was the only one with chairs instead of floor mats – it must be where the Inner would sit. The hall walls were finely painted with hunting scenes, armored Ik-Songans in chase, tapering antlers blending into corners; imagery of great animals of the past, an enormous bird with trailing feathers like ribbons and contrails of fog, spinning through clouds. She and the Moonbearer were the only ones here that would remember them. They'd both stayed suspended in time, caught between the waves of it, while the rest of the world had moved and aged and died, across centuries, as she slept, and he hatched. And now he wanted her to play the part again? Perhaps he was just a man after all, fuelled by ego.

The roof was indeed uncovered to a night sky. Most Ik-Songans knew their constellations; cycles like the flower moon were closely kept. In the island, visible stars were as abundant as leaves. She spied formations like the Flying Fish and the Snake's Head, ignoring instructions not to look up.

Shadow walked.

The Last Soldier of Nava

Mist flooded the room, if only slightly. The faces that stared up at her blended together into a shapeless mass. Her armour, her *costume*, fit her so perfectly, even the dark wrappings around her arms, the collar pushing up. Her hair only skimmed her brow now. She was clean, bathed. In her peripheral vision she saw rows of Guards passing, men and ladies in formal *hanboks*, the *gat* hat feathers signalling diplomats, even archer's uniforms.

She passed the stage and pressed forward. It was only as she neared the end that she remembered her seat. She had been told to look for a black flag. Passing her eyes over the tables, she saw no flag tied anywhere. Until she realized – the centre table, where the Inner would sit. There: a strip tied to the corner of one chair.

As she ascended the short steps to take her seat, low triumphant fanfare invaded the room behind her, and she released a breath she didn't know she'd been holding as attention diverted from her to the door again. Servants filed in sideways in the background, inconspicuously against the walls. From here, what lay beyond the door was indeed only darkness – a clever trick of angling.

And then the darkness was shattered through with light.

Shadow flinched and stilled, halfway to sitting down – so sudden and violent was this light, nothing like the sun's gentle touch. The streams sliced through the dim, hypnotizingly fading out, culminating into nothing but a single, standing, illuminated figure, who stepped forward and lowered their hand until all that was left was Scarlet in the door.

Applause through the hall as guests bowed respectfully. Scarlet made her way down with no difference in her blasé manner, face half-hidden by her red-lacquered decorative *ayam* cap. She wore white-scaled armour similar to the one from Yosae but somewhat more decorated. The sun circlet glinted off her forehead. Behind and around walked her personal Guards, heading straight towards the Inner's table – towards Shadow.

It was only as they ascended the stairs that Shadow realized she was still hovering above her seat, and finally sat.

A servant pulled Scarlet's seat out – three down from her own – and she paused over it, finally noticing Shadow from under her jewelled veil. 'No bow, as per usual.'

'You have ability,' Shadow said inadvertently, disbelief lacing her voice.

'Your skills of observation are phenomenal. I wonder what you'll tell me next. That my hair is black?'

'You are as rare as I.' All this time, she hadn't thought to dwell on whether the Keeper even had ability. *She equates herself to the sun*, she'd told Aspis, stupidly. The sun was not just a self-inflating symbol. White Crane had called her *your Light*, mockingly, in the throne room. It was no wonder the Moonbearer treasured her, had made her his new implement after losing the Desert Rose.

'Rarer, actually. Seeing as how there is one of me,' Scarlet looked to the front, 'and two of you.'

After a long moment, Shadow glanced irritatedly around the table. She knew that the rank, status, identities of every guest was denoted by the colours they wore, but the sheer number of them made it impossible to discern. The only group she could probably pinpoint with certainty were the eunuchs in the corner wearing *kasaya* robes, though this wasn't a great feat. Directly outside the north window, which she faced, stood two tall, spindly, twinning willow trees. They were the strangest trees she'd ever seen. Willows were cultivated for their long, blanketing beauty, but these seemed almost curiously deformed, both gnarled. She wondered why they had been kept in the gardens at all.

The Last Soldier of Nava

The display went on. The Stronghold was a so-called military body, for all intents and purposes, and the pretence showed in the Guards' dress. It was like they'd taken war armour and made it as frilly and showy as possible while still deeming it usable on a technicality. The weaponry slung at hips and over backs gleamed purposefully, any ritualistic manoeuvres strict and dry.

Various Court Advisors followed in order, and Aspis was middle in the mix. Heads turned at the Prince – donning his usual silver and grey, white head bare of any hat, a circlet glinting off his head. Noble ladies turned to each other to comment. With shock, she noticed that the closest personal Guard to Prince Yo-han's left was—

'I didn't know Crow was in the Prince's Guard,' she said, expecting her comment to go ignored.

But Scarlet answered vaguely, 'Oh, that and more.'

The Inner's table grew more crowded as time went on. There were the Advisors; noblemen and women, including a loud potbellied man who sat directly in front of her; younger guests bearing faces heavy with rouge, unusual in a time when the fashion was to stray away from sumptuous make-up. Everyone at first sent wary glances her way, but upon realizing that she was silent and not actually all that interesting, and otherwise seated so close to the Keeper herself, quickly lost interest. No one conversed about deadzones, Asanai, or the storms; everyone seemed inclined to make small talk on petty matters, none of which she had any idea how to decipher.

Prince Yo-han had paused on the round stage. He parted from his Guards momentarily and stood alone on the large slab; everyone watched in anticipation. He bowed at his waist, a sign of humility. A girl seated nearby turned to a friend.

'Tonight,' he announced, as the crowds quieted. 'Tonight,

we welcome you to the Stronghold. The beating heart of Ik-Song.'

And then – in a single melodic movement – he threw up an enormous, curling wave of water that stretched high above their heads and up towards the ceiling, rushing out from the edges of the platform. As soon as it reached the open sky, it froze from the top-down into a perfect arch of seafoam blue and icy white.

The response was immediate: chatter started up and down the hall, eliciting gasps and clapping. Yo-han was *inside* the wave itself, vaguely visible, a light shadow behind its solid walls.

As quickly as the water was frozen, it thawed. He crashed it back down around him, disappearing and seeping out of the edges of the stage, until nothing remained at all. And he bowed shortly, to the thunderous applause.

'A shame he's so powerful,' said a voice to her left. Shadow turned to two women she didn't recognize in the throes of gossip.

'Why is it a shame?' Shadow asked, before she could stop herself.

Instantly the girls looked at her like she had said something outrageous; Shadow had forgotten she was only supposed to be eavesdropping. For a moment she thought they would both ignore her, but then one said matter-of-factly, 'Because everyone knows he's a bastard.'

The casual slander was appalling.

'Only a rumour,' someone said sharply behind them. The girls instantly looked away; Shadow turned.

Aspis. She sat, unbothered by Shadow staring. 'That he's half-Asani. All because he's skilled at windstorms . . . he can conjure what you might call a winter storm in the middle of summer.'

The Last Soldier of Nava

Suddenly, the servants' protectiveness and doting seemed like less of an indulgence and more of a necessity. Rumours of a bastard heritage were bad enough, but half-Asani was worse.

'How would the Queen Dynast have even been able to sustain an affair with an Asani?' Shadow asked.

'Relations between Ik-Song and Asanai are as fickle as the wind. Only decades ago, their representatives were welcome here. In fact, there used to be meetings of all state heads, I'm told – much grander and more splendid than this flimsy banquet. Even the Asani Emperor himself would attend.'

Chills ran up her spine at the mention of the Emperor, the Bloodbird King. Aspis, evidently not as impressed, only side-eyed her.

'I didn't think you would live to see this banquet,' Aspis continued. Every inch of her uniform was polished flawlessly, not a flick of lint or debris visible, her hair bound in a single whipping braid in that swath of red ribbon. Shadow hadn't seen her since the throne room.

'Disappointed?'

'Glad, actually. You're our new weapon of war – we won't be wasting any time. You're starting training tomorrow.'

'*Tomorrow*?' Shadow was exhausted. The pace of the Stronghold gave her whiplash. '*Training*?'

Aspis only smirked in response.

Dinner would commence with a traditional tea ceremony: delicate porcelain sets of blue dragons and jade glazing were carefully set out on the table. Servants came around to pour steaming tea into the pots, tapping them with small silver spoons. The tapping was to assess the pots for quality and sturdiness; if it produced an acceptable musical note, it was ready. All across the hall rang the small clinking of hundreds of spoons to teapots, a short-lived melody. The tea was then poured onto a tea pet in front of her, a sitting deer turned white by the scalding liquid poured onto it. The cup was warm in her hands.

'I'll give you a word of advice,' Aspis said. 'You should be cautious here. Assume that everyone has an ulterior motive. Don't trust too easily.'

Including you? she wondered.

'But I might yet be able to whip you into shape,' Aspis continued.

Right. '*Master of the Hunt.* That's a fancy title. Should I be bowing?'

Aspis only looked at her, said nothing – and abruptly turned away.

Shadow stared back, puzzled. It was only a few moments later that she realized the Keeper stood directly behind them.

Chapter 9

'My Keeper,' Aspis stood, bowing.

'Aspis.' Scarlet recited her name like an ancient curse unearthed. Vaguely, the entrance of the Queen stirred up guests in the background, fanfare proceeding as Guards and noble ladies in red *hanboks* preceded her welcome. But most of Shadow's field of vision was occupied by a close-up view of this white, textured armour; the gloved hand resting menacingly on the back of her chair, devoid of any jewellery. Several Advisors and ladies around them glanced over warily at this encounter, ultimately choosing to resume their conversations without any noticeable hitches.

'You'll be pleased to observe the feast tonight,' Aspis said, not maintaining eye contact out of respect. 'This week's hunt has proved plentiful. The main dishes are ring-necked pheasant and wild boar; and we slaughtered fifteen cattle alone yesterday at dawn for the guests. The fish is delectable, too – fresh halibut and red snapper caught straight from the Seochon. Only the best cuts for you.'

'Incredible,' Scarlet replied without missing a beat, eyes narrowing with a hostility that Shadow didn't understand.

'Perhaps at the next occasion you'll have salted and prepared my riding deer as well?'

'I would never think of it, Keeper.'

Shadow was undoubtedly impressed by Aspis's ability to maintain a polite – if not outright friendly – demeanour towards the brat. Aspis was probably over five years Scarlet's senior but endured it with grace that seemed neither fake nor strained. She seemed to take genuine pride in providing for the Stronghold and feeding so many mouths. Shadow could probably learn a thing or two.

'Move,' said Scarlet. 'I'd like your seat.' The hand drummed on the chair. A servant came on Shadow's left, laying out spoons, chopstick rests, and countless *banchan* dishes set down with rapid precision.

Aspis looked over in Prince Yo-han's direction. Scarlet immediately put herself in this line of sight. 'Why do you look to them? I gave you a clear order.'

'Keeper—'

She enunciated each word very slowly and clearly, like she was speaking to a child: '*Get. Out. Of. My. Seat.* You serpentine wench.'

Aspis stood abruptly and stepped away.

The servant had slowed in her plate arrangement. Scarlet's insult was somewhat lost around the table as the Queen finally took her seat across from them: she wore a *hanbok* with deep cerulean satin skirts that trailed behind her like lapping waves, the top half a gold-embroidered cream with wide sleeves. Her dark hair was pinned through with an enormous enamelled golden pin like a shard of bone. Even from here, the resemblance between her and Yo-han was palpable, though her face was tired, aged.

The seating was rearranged. Prince Yo-han had stood to greet his mother with a bow; Scarlet settled in her new seat, leaning forward on her elbows with tea still cupped between her hands. 'Finally,' she said. 'We can delve to know each other.'

Shadow stared at her.

Around the table, guests were trying to stand to pay respects to the Queen, but a true bow wasn't possible in the tight space – many were forced to settle for awkward half-bows. Even the timing of her entrance was awkward – with tea having been cleared and in between courses, her arrival seemed like an interruption of the dinner. At the Queen's flinty eyes, Shadow realized this wasn't the result of poor planning. Yo-han seemed to be trying to catch her eye, but she steadfastly ignored him. Across the table, a potbellied nobleman was attempting to court the Keeper, the Prince, and the Queen at the same time by showing off his young performers in the *p'ansori* dance happening below.

'They are all of age for you, wonderful heir,' he said suggestively, pointing to each young performer and naming them in succession.

'A generous offer, but his Highness prefers men,' Scarlet said, interceding on the Prince's behalf. 'You've only boys, and girls.'

'I prefer both,' Yo-han corrected, looking affronted. 'Men and women, that is.'

'Really? This is news to me. Then why not just marry me and be done with the whole business?'

Half the table reacted. Yo-han looked faintly exasperated. Shadow understood enough to know by now that they regarded each other as siblings; not to mention that both would absolutely chafe at the prospect.

'Your Majesty,' Scarlet said loudly. 'I'd like you to meet my new guest, the only *sakasa* in existence besides the Councillor. You must've heard by now. She's an escaped fugitive from

Yosae who's evaded capture but has since been reinstated in the palace.'

The Queen looked like she was about to faint. 'Escaped fugitive?' she echoed weakly.

'She was presented only yesterday to the Councillor, but she's already become quite familiar with the Stronghold. You can see she's quite roguish, has the look of a trained fighter.' Scarlet took one of Shadow's hands and raised it high above the table, displaying it like a piece of jewellery.

Shadow fought the urge to glare and rip her hand away. Instead, she gently removed it, placing her hands flat on the table in an attempt to appear less threatening. 'Your Majesty,' she tried. 'I am honoured to meet you.'

As dinner resumed, Shadow looked around the table. Did anyone here know about the south's raging storms, or were they just feigning ignorance? The scare in Yosae? The deadzone approaching this very palace? Ik-Song was an unusually calm and uncaring nation, for a country that might fall soon. Why? Too much faith in the Moonbearer?

'Fifteen bastardly courses,' Scarlet muttered beside her, peering into her wine glass. 'You're in for a night.'

The porridge was cleared; two more courses came and went. Guests were getting progressively sloppier, louder, and prone to bursts of excitement. Shadow laid out two round slices of pickled radish atop her rice, frilly kimchi. At the start of the third, Aspis stood again at her end to address the hall.

'The true feast begins now,' she raised her glass, to general cheer. 'As tradition, the Royal Keeper of the Gates will signal our start.'

Clapping, murmurs. After Prince Yo-han's brilliant display, it only made sense that the Keeper might now take the reins. The hall doors opened to reveal a single servant rolling out a cart, atop which sat a large straw dome, a centrepiece. The dome was enormous, and it was wheeled halfway down the aisle until the stage, where it was elevated.

Down on the platform, the servant gripped the dome handle and lifted it off. A platter underneath, mostly empty, a wide expanse of silver.

In the centre sat a single, small bird.

It was undoubtedly alive, and twitching. A ring-necked pheasant, Shadow recognized, unusually small for its breed. It wasn't moving or escaping – possibly drugged to still its usually jerky movements. Its beak opened once and closed pitifully, as it slowly looked around in confusion behind ruffled brown feathers. It tried to stand but fell again to its knees.

Scarlet didn't move. Aspis continued, 'The Keeper commences in the name of the Councillor, the Stronghold, and the great nation of Ik-Song. *To our Light.*' She raised her glass.

'*To our Light,*' came the replies, raised glasses.

The anticipation of the crowd was palpable, and Scarlet was intensely focused – a sharp contrast to her usual demeanour. She stood up, pushing against her chair, and in a few sharp movements, raised her arm – bent at the elbow – straightened it towards the direction of the bird, and pointed with all her fingers but her thumb, which folded in.

In a moment so fast you would miss it if you blinked, a thin, pinpointed ray of light erupted from her fingertips and streamed down to the silver platter.

The bird collapsed. A finger of smoke curled upwards. The hall broke into cheering and applause, another round of toasts. Below, the same servant gathered up the small bird in a single hand, holding it up.

'Right through the eye,' she announced, and the applause strengthened. Squinting, Shadow could see that, indeed, both of its eyes were blackened through.

This level of precision was astonishing. To master such a manoeuvre would have meant approaching one's ability like an art form, a delicate kindling of the senses; not the brute force moves the Moonbearer had drilled into Shadow over and over again. Shadow felt a pang of jealousy at that – but it was mostly overwhelmed by awe, then curiosity. Tearing her eyes from the bird's, she turned to Scarlet – only to see that the Keeper was no longer seated. She was all the way at the south exit, barking orders at a servant, two Guards flanking her exit. As plates of scored pheasant began to line the tables and chopsticks were replaced a second time, Shadow saw the small, charred bird placed in the middle. There was so much meat she could hardly comprehend it; it looked terribly delicious, unreal, almost, diminished only by its own abundance. No one paid any attention to the Keeper's departure; perhaps they were all used to her spontaneous entrances and exits.

But Shadow wasn't. Gauging her chances, she rose from her seat. No Guards visibly reacted; no one fell into hysterics. Even the Advisors were all preoccupied with themselves, liberal with the drink. No one would notice if she left; now was the perfect time to leave and try to gather information. She followed to the same door she'd seen Scarlet leave from, to the two Guards standing on either side.

She was alone and unwatched. When else would she get this chance? If she wanted a private audience with the Moonbearer, now was the time.

'Excuse me,' she said. 'I have to accompany the Keeper.'

They exchanged glances. One of them said, 'On her ride?'

'I'm under her supervision. That's my entire arrangement here.' She tried to inject irritation into her voice, muster command. 'Ask White Crane himself, now. Or any of the Advisors. They'll say the same.'

The Last Soldier of Nava

A bluff. But it didn't matter. Their superiors were currently off-duty, flush with alcohol. The amusing image of one of the Guards tapping White Crane on the shoulder came, unbidden. The Guards shifted unsurely: invoke the wrath of their superiors by interrupting a hearty dinner with inane questions about the newcomer, or risk the irritation of the Keeper?

'Fine,' one shrugged. 'Go.'

She couldn't believe her luck. But the other seemed less eager to shirk his duties. 'If we lose her, it's our heads.'

'You think the brat'll care?'

'How could you possibly lose me?' Shadow butted in. 'To the north and east is a hundred-foot drop into the sea, the south bare woodland, and wild mountains in the west.' Any trouble she could cause – if she did cause it – would be contained to this estate.

A long pause. 'Go,' the Guard said finally.

Chapter 10

Wasting no time, Shadow hurried up to the seventh floor.

Was it really this easy? She could go anywhere in the Stronghold, now. The hall where her chambers were was basically deserted. The banquet had forced all the underpinnings of the palace downstairs, so she hardly glimpsed anyone on her way up. If she'd guessed right, the seventh – and highest – floor would contain royal-adjacent chambers, and at least one room of importance had to be situated near her room.

Shadow knew who she was hoping to find within the week. She envisioned meeting the Moonbearer again after all this time – but best not to hope too soon. It was hard to imagine what she could say to him; or even put into words. His absence in the throne room had only fuelled her growing anticipation. But right now, she needed to be quick, before anyone noticed her absence.

Shadow crept along the wall and peered around the corner, studying the Guard rotations for a few minutes. They seemed to linger longest at a door two down from her own; the frame embroidered with gold, but otherwise nondescript. The second the standing Guard's back was turned, she slipped in, silent on her feet.

Her eyes adjusted quickly. A large desk – a neat pile of books. A few elegant, curling quills and ink bottles arranged side-by-side. A bookshelf, a recliner. No one was inside, though it looked well-used and clean. It faced the east side, like her own, but it encompassed the gardens as well as the Seochon. On the opposite wall was a huge mural of the White Ice: Ik-Songans emerging from a world of white, the huge Bone Warriors defeated in the background, bodies smouldering. The Moonbearer a lone figure leading. She drew closer to the desk, read the titles and scripts. A small pocketbook on proper manners, prosperity and ritual, *hsaio*. Mundane texts on Gentian philosophy, mathematics, classical literature. And on the inside cover of a history book, in careful, cramped handwriting: 선요한. Son Yo-han.

Disappointment gripped her abdomen. This was the Prince's study room. The fact that it had no constant Guard outside perhaps already hinted at how important its contents were, but still. She briefly considered searching the room anyway, to look for anything of interest – after all, the servants had said Yo-han met with the Moonbearer often. If she couldn't have the Moonbearer, this might be the next best thing to parse out anything she could use against him.

Then, heavy footsteps and voices neared the door. Shadow cursed, looked around the room: there. A hidden corner between the shelf and the mural, that wasn't visible from the entry. She slotted herself in and waited, palms pressed flat against the wall.

Two Guards had stood at the doorway, from what she could tell, conferring on something unimportant. She willed them to leave; hoped they wouldn't randomly come in.

So caught up was she in straining to hear their voices that

she hadn't at first noticed the feeling under her hands – the uneven roughness of the mural, the patchiness of its application. Weren't murals painted directly onto the wall? But under her right hand, this one felt – textured, almost, a little bulbous, pressing out against her hand, as if . . .

There was something under it.

In the tight space, she turned. Traced the snowy background. Her hands drew down to the bottom edge of the wall, and saw the near-invisible lining, a catch. She scrabbled at it until one corner caught, and she peeled the paint free.

A small section of the wall peeled away. And something trapped underneath fell out. She caught it before it fell to the ground, shocked – a bundle of papers. A few sheafs, old and wrinkled, fluttered onto the floor.

Hidden papers? She replaced the wall, gathered them up to skim. There were at least ten, onion-thin, all handwritten in beautiful strokes. Perhaps Stronghold secrets, or encoded messages – how lucky she was to have stumbled on it.

But not now. She needed to get out of there while the Guards were gone. Folding up the papers and slipping them into the waistband of her pants, she stepped out of the corner—

—and almost walked face-first into a Guard.

She stood in shocked silence for a few seconds. And then, in the next moment, was blown against the mural by a powerful blast of wind, nearly tipping her out of the window.

Shadow clawed back in and spun into the other corner, already trying to plan out escape routes. The Guard that had attacked her was a woman clad in black, and another one – a man – stood a few paces behind her. Their faces were almost entirely hidden, the door shut behind them. Another burst of wind scattered papers all over the room and pushed her back, feet sliding across the floor. They both converged on her inelegantly; she tried a spinning kick but was caught

The Last Soldier of Nava

midair by the woman and thrown back down. As soon as she collapsed on the ground, the other Guard was ready to keep her down: one knee in her back, arms wrenched behind. Shadow thrashed, but she was sorely outnumbered – a third had joined the mix. She didn't want to – refused to – attack, to participate.

Cloth was tied tightly over her eyes. The mural faded into blue-black.

'I'm with the Keeper,' Shadow gasped desperately. 'I'm not an intruder, I—'

A quick knee to her side silenced her.

It slowly occurred to her that if these were the Moonbearer's Guards – and who else could they be? – it wouldn't matter if she was a trespasser or not. They wouldn't care. They were past that.

How incredibly stupid. She'd thought she'd snuck up here unnoticed, hot-headed and determined, to do what? She'd only handed the Moonbearer a perfect opportunity to catch her unawares and put an end to all this.

But the next words that came out of this Guard's mouth made her freeze down to her feet, made her world close in.

Small, butchered, frail words, but still undeniably present. The Guard wrenched her up so that she kneeled, and came close, breath hot on her ear.

'*Under the Yong of the East.*' A heavy pause. '*Under the Daltokki.*' A string of keywords: '*Scale.*' 비늘. '*Shard.*' 비늘. '*Nine.*' 아홉. With slow, mounting horror she realized what they were attempting; she mustered all her strength, trying to tear free – blind, flailing – but it was futile.

They were going to awaken the Soldier.

And then there was a sickening crunch; followed by the loosening of the grip on Shadow.

For a moment Shadow was too surprised to move, and

then she wrenched free, pulling at her blindfold – but it was too tightly wound. The quick sound of skin-to-skin combat and harsh breathing in front of her – there was someone *else* in the room. Someone on her side?

The fight stopped; the newcomer approached.

'Don't come any closer,' Shadow warned.

'Hold still,' came the curt reply.

She knew that voice.

The cool, flat press of a blade against her face made her tense before it swiped up, cleaving the silk in two. It fell from her eyes.

Shadow's hands wouldn't stop trembling, heart rabbiting. She took great gulps of air, trying to calm down, felt the cool breeze through the window. The code words – ones she hadn't heard in so long – echoed between her ears. *Scale.* 비늘. *Shard.* 비늘. *Nine.* 아홉. *Lost.* 죽은.

She looked up. The three Guards sprawled unconscious before her. One bled from the nose; another looked as if in deep sleep.

Behind them, Aspis: a hand on her hip, sheathing her throwing knife.

Shadow was dumbfounded.

'Not even an hour after I told you to exercise caution,' Aspis said. 'I guess I shouldn't have expected anything less. You haven't behaved from the start.'

In barely twenty seconds Aspis had dispatched three Guards; she'd had the element of surprise, but still. Shadow had listened to the soft sounds of combat – even blind, she could hear the power in the strokes, the brute force, no hesitation.

'You don't even have ability,' Shadow blurted out, gawking.

Whatever the Desert Rose had done a year ago when they'd fought, she'd burned the Soldier out of her. Shadow had been so sure. It had all ended there; all of it. She hadn't even considered the possibility it hadn't. For the Moonbearer to try? So quick and uncaring, in the Prince's own study chambers?

For some reason, the Moonbearer believed the Soldier still lay within Shadow. The thought filled her with a dread that she could barely see past.

Before Aspis could reply, there were footsteps behind the door.

It slid open to reveal none other than Prince Yo-han.

By some small mercy of the Moon Rabbit, he was alone. For the first few seconds as he entered the room, eyes on the floor, he didn't even notice the scene. Until he looked up and met their eyes.

Three unconscious Guards, his room in a state of catastrophe. A long silence prevailed. He could only blink, gaping slightly, eyes round with shock.

Aspis wasted no time in leaving, only casting Yo-han an unimpressed look. 'Lucky I was here,' she said before she left, leaving Shadow alone to mitigate.

'Your Highness,' a voice called from the hallway, and Shadow realized others were waiting outside – servants.

He quickly turned – 'Just a moment, please' – and slid his door shut.

'Do I need to call my personal Guards?' he asked. But he didn't sound afraid, or even wary. Just curious.

'No,' Shadow said, 'I wasn't here to attack you – I swear. I just—'

But Prince Yo-han wasn't alarmed; in fact, he looked rather grim, examining the twitching bodies on the floor.

He approached the closest one warily, kneeling down to roll him over. He uncovered the face with tentative fingers.

'He's . . . not one of mine,' the Prince said, rising again.

'Oh,' was all she could think to say, feigning surprise. He was so calm. Oddly unbothered.

'It is a good thing Aspis was here.' He exhaled. 'I admit I was more or less expecting this. Newcomers here always endure a few surprises. Especially for you, your arrival's been contentious. I just didn't know they would try it in *my* room.'

'Who is "they"?'

'Court, company. Anyone, really.' He waved a hand. 'Though seeing how unsuccessful this was, I doubt they'll be likely to try again anytime soon. In the meantime, you aren't supposed to wander around the palace alone.'

She nodded, slowly. 'I understand.' A hundred questions came to mind. It was strange – it was like he trusted her. Why? Did he simply just not care, or did she seem as meek as she felt? 'I apologize. I just wanted a break from the banquet for a bit, so I went to look around the palace, and I came up and this room caught my eye.' Her gaze was drawn unconsciously to the mural. 'Your Guards must have thought I was an intruder, they . . .'

She was babbling, unsure, but he wasn't even looking at her anymore. He had followed her gaze and was looking at the mural intensely, as if seeing it for the first time. 'It's beautiful, right?'

Something told her he wasn't talking about the artistic quality. Could a war scene be beautiful? 'It's grand,' she replied, looking at the Bone Warriors in the corner. Their bodies could be pulverized by fire, eventually, if one burned them long enough. 'It's the White Ice, right?'

He looked shocked. 'You don't recognize it?'

She shook her head.

'It's a famous scene.' He swept his hand over it. 'A reproduction.'

'I don't know much about the White Ice,' she admitted.

The Last Soldier of Nava

'Asanai took us by complete surprise,' he replied. 'The north of Ik-Song, the coasts, we all woke to a world of white. People barricaded and lit fires to survive.' He traced the wall almost tenderly. 'It seemed hopeless until the Councillor rose. He beat the Bone Warriors back with his ragtag army of remades.'

He spoke as if the Councillor was a heroic underdog, a powerless and courageous champion.

'We were victorious, but still – so many died. And Asanai wants revenge.' His voice was bitter. 'This time, we won't be so weak.'

He didn't elaborate. His gaze swivelled to her; she straightened involuntarily.

To her surprise, he laughed out loud. 'Sorry – enough about the White Ice. Tonight is supposed to be a festivity.'

A knock on the door startled them.

'Leave now,' he said. 'I'll have them clean this up. Return straight back to the banquet, or at least find an escort.' A pause. 'Any Guards you're given aren't to protect the rest of the Stronghold from you, you know. It's for your own protection.'

'Thank you,' she managed, making for the door.

She slid it open to a gaggle of shocked servants, who said nothing as she exited. It was halfway down the hall that she remembered the hidden papers in her waistband and felt a pang of guilt at having stolen them.

The gardens were the safest bet.

Sticking by the Keeper tonight was her safest best.

Yet, upon arriving, said Keeper was nowhere to be seen. Instead, Shadow slid outside and was immediately transfixed by the warm and humid night; the backdrop of rolling hills on the far western side of the palace; the roiling breeze, blowing easterly from the Seochon, whipping her hair about her face. The ocean at night under the craggy rock cliffs was unlike anything she'd seen before – an inky pool of darkness, as if one could step into nothingness. The moon illuminated it in slivering, white beats. It was only after a few minutes in the garden that she realized she had no idea where she was. Every topiary looked the same. She stifled a sigh. The willow trees acted as the centre guide, but what side of it was she on? The south, facing the entrance? The north – the palace?

'Aren't *sakasa* supposed to be able to see in the dark?' said a voice from behind.

She startled. Turned. Stepping forward – angular face illuminated by lantern – stood Crow, still in silver-blue uniform.

'Why are you out here?' she asked. 'You *followed* me?'

'Did you really think you'd just be allowed to wander around the Stronghold as you please?'

He was right – she could see better in the dark. But the short range of the intensely burning lantern still gave the impression that she was trapped in a void with Crow. His dark eyes pinned her. He was the type of boy who carried his youth like a vicious weapon, reminding everyone of his power, his sharpness – not unlike the Keeper.

Who she would prefer to be cornered by in a dark garden was up for debate.

'And what have you found?' she said. 'That I've been throwing myself against the walls to escape?'

His eyes narrowed. 'A mere day ago, I was hunting you down in Yosae to bring you back as prisoner. Now you're eating at the high table alongside the Inner, and no one's allowed to touch you as long as the Keeper says. And no one seems to be concerned.'

'You sound envious.'

He laughed coldly. 'I'm going to find you out. You're dangerous. I know you are.'

The Last Soldier of Nava

'*I* don't even know what I'm here for. The Keeper won't indulge me.'

'This isn't a joke,' he snapped. 'Ik-Song approaches catastrophe. We need soldiers – *real* soldiers – to helm the war, both within and outside our borders.'

'And weren't you asking for my help just a day ago?'

'That was before I knew—'

'You sent those Guards after me, didn't you?' she said.

'Guards?' His brow furrowed, caught by surprise. 'What Guards?'

Something rustled sharply behind them.

Shadow whirled around and looked up. Scarlet, sitting on her buck, who pawed the ground impatiently. She was dishevelled – which, by her standards, meant there were a few hairs out of place, a slight flush across her wind-bitten cheeks. A few paces back from her trailed her Guards.

'Keeper,' Crow said without missing a beat. 'Your guest has free roam of the palace?'

Scarlet's gaze toggled between her and Crow, as if she couldn't decide who to be more irritated with. 'As usual, it hardly concerns you. Leave.'

He was already on his way out – leaving the two of them alone, watching each other.

'I don't think it's wise for you to leave me by myself,' Shadow said frankly.

Scarlet arched a brow. 'Did you really think you could escape from the gardens?'

'I wasn't trying to escape.'

'Hold out your left arm.'

Her palm faced the sky. She saw it then: a lurid, coloured bruise already darkening the underside of her wrist, where the Guard had gripped her tight while holding her down.

'Skirmishing, then?' Scarlet said dispassionately.

Shadow eyed the crimsons. 'Guards attacked me upstairs.'

'Don't pry. Don't fight. Don't wander. Unless I tell you to do any of those things.' Scarlet turned her buck, who exhaled hard through his nose. 'And do resist escape. If I were you, I wouldn't choose the east exit.'

'I told you,' Shadow said, 'I wasn't trying to escape.'

She was ignored.

Shadow walked quickly after Scarlet, trying to keep up with the deer's great strides, the *clop clop clop* on the ground. 'Scarlet, wait.'

Scarlet did not wait.

'Back there, in the hall – I've never seen anything like that before.'

'An astute comment,' the Keeper said, 'considering I am the only one with that particular ability.'

'It was incredible,' Shadow said honestly. 'I suspected, but now I know – you're the strongest remade in the Stronghold. Aren't you? But I saw your face afterwards.' And here, a leap of faith: 'Are you made so uncomfortable by your own strength?'

No response.

'Because I understand what that's like.' She proceeded cautiously. Scarlet was, unfortunately, a necessary ally. Scarlet could lead her right to the Moonbearer if she played her cards right. 'Crow is envious of your power, isn't he? Many must be. But I could help you.'

A long silence. Then: 'Are you going to disobey me?' the Keeper asked, though she still didn't face her.

Don't pry. Don't fight. Don't wander. 'Only if the situation calls for it.'

'You take many liberties,' Scarlet said. 'All this for a parlour trick.'

'Scarlet—'

'That's *Keeper* to you,' she said. 'Tell me again – will you disobey my orders?'

'I told you – if the situation calls for it.'

A sigh. 'I would suggest a different answer.'

'I would suggest different rules.'

'What's frustrating about you, is that you're hardly even threatened by death. Are you? I don't think burning a hole through you like I did that bird would do a thing.' She turned, made eye contact with an unfortunate crimson Guard. 'You.' She pointed. 'Come over here.'

The Guard slowly approached.

Scarlet dismounted and beckoned him to kneel, which he did. She grabbed him by the hair in one hand and raised her other palm to his forehead: hovering just above the skin. He froze, wide-eyed.

'All right,' Shadow said crossly, understanding dawning. 'There's no need for theatrics.'

To Shadow's sharp horror, Scarlet's fingers actually sparked with bright light, and the Guard jerked back.

'*Stop*,' she gasped, flinging a hand out, running forwards, falling to one knee.

The light grew.

'*Stop*! Don't – please. I'm sorry.'

Scarlet watched impassively. The light died; she released him. The silence was excruciating – other Guards and guests milling about the gardens had all stopped to watch. The crimson looked like he wanted to spear Shadow through on the spot.

Shadow could feel sweat sheening over her forehead, heart fast from the surprise of it. How quickly that light had blown in, so daringly close to a man's eyes. How quickly it had disappeared. No hesitation, nothing but callous instinct.

'You have no leverage here,' Scarlet said, calm. Suddenly

she seemed very far away, an impenetrable wall. 'You're here to serve a purpose, and nothing more. Do you understand?'

Shadow didn't respond, dazed from shock.

'*Caring*,' Scarlet muttered under her breath. 'That's a weakness beyond my comprehension.'

Pitching forward, Shadow's breaths came harshly as she held herself up by her palms. She couldn't move, not even when Scarlet drew closer, and a heeled boot stopped beside her hand. 'You want to know why I want you here?' Scarlet's voice was low and close to her ear. 'Do you know how the Desert Rose died?'

Shadow almost flinched.

Because she was there when I awakened, and I lost control.

Scarlet continued, 'There's always a story to these things. The appearance, and the reality. A year ago yesterday she was murdered in a cellar in Yosae. The killer's method was perverse. To this day, I'm not completely sure how she managed it.'

'"She?"'

'The Soldier.'

Shadow looked up slowly. Anything she could've said to that was drowned out by the blood rushing to her own head; lit lantern lights in the garden carved out the lines of Scarlet's face as she looked straight ahead, painted in honeyed stripes. It flickered over her; her fingers, banding over her wrists, her armour. There was no possible way in the world that she could know this truth.

No way at all.

From the moment the Keeper had laid eyes on her, Shadow had ruled out the possibility that she'd recognized her as her sister's killer. And despite the Moonbearer's self-amusement at dressing her up like an obvious, glaring warning, no one here suspected – simply because that would require a certain knowledge lost to the modern world, because it was impossible

The Last Soldier of Nava

to reconcile a legend – a story that had pervaded centuries, whispered between children, compounded and accelerated until it became nothing but a spinning amalgamation of mere ideas and intangible qualities – with the appearance of one unremarkable, banged-up prisoner in the Stronghold.

Even before Shadow spoke, mouth dry, she knew it was useless. 'The Soldier,' she managed, 'is not Asani. The Soldier is a figure of myth. The kind of myth alive in the ancient world, from Nava.'

'Indeed. And somehow, she came to dispose of my sister.'

'You really think the Soldier is alive, now, and out there?' But the answer was obvious.

'I don't think. I know.'

All these followers, diplomats, remades, in and out of this place day after day, she'd said to the Moonbearer. *None of them had it. This changes everything.*

'In the courtroom before, you were talking about my ability,' Shadow realized. 'You've been searching for a *sakasa* simply because the Soldier was one.'

'You are indispensable to me.'

In the same vein as a tool. 'It doesn't make sense to presume that a *sakasa* remade a thousand years later has any connection with the Soldier. Is Crow a mimic of your sister, then, since they both controlled sand?'

The Keeper shrugged, one shoulder rising elegantly.

A last ditch-effort: 'You're not in your right mind.'

Already her mind was overrun: how could she keep up this lie? Hide who she really was? Scarlet would see right through. Guilt gnawed at her. Scarlet was only looking for her sister's killer, clawing for some sense of closure.

'I could hardly care if you think I'm insane, if you think it's a myth, if you think I'm lying. In fact, I don't care whether anyone in the whole of Ik-Song thinks any of those things. I don't care, because I know the truth. I know the truth because I saw it with my own two eyes.'

That was impossible – no one else had been there except Shadow and the Rose herself, and later, Sae.

Shadow, long gone, the body waiting. Scarlet stumbling down in the late hours of the night, rolling over the corpse and finding her sister.

'Here is the deal: you will lay yourself bare to me,' Scarlet continued. A quirk of her lip. 'You're going to let me study every single shade and facet of your ability. No one in Ik-Song has ever got the chance to see a *sakasa* up close, you know. I'll come to know every detail about your power, your limits, your reach. I'll learn everything there is to know, even the things you yourself haven't discovered yet.' A pause. 'Alongside this, you're going to aid me in my search for the Soldier. Investigative duties, so to speak, to get me closer.'

Shadow could hardly believe what she was hearing. Her hands drew taut fists in the grass.

'I'm going to find her,' Scarlet concluded, 'and I'm going to kill her. The same way she killed my sister.'

Shadow had thought herself desperate for revenge – but here was someone almost fanatical.

'The Moonbearer ordered you executed after you've served your purpose,' Scarlet said.

Discard her when finished. 'But in return for your cooperation, I'll guarantee you transport back to Yosae. Official state papers forging a new identity, a thoroughbred horse, and we can even throw in a bundle of dumplings, if you'd like. You can leave and return home to your imaginary grandmother. By then, interest in you will have waned. Any Guards warranted with the task of finding you, I'll dissuade them and threaten them if they persist. Deal?'

'Deal?' Shadow said. '*Deal?*'

The Last Soldier of Nava

'I see you're overwhelmed by the wealth of information. Perhaps a few moments to mull it over.'

There was no conceivable way this would end well. Shadow's mind raced relentlessly.

'I can't possibly trust you,' she said, too aware of the irony. 'The entire palace despises you. You believe in a superstition peddled by cowards and countrymen.'

'I'm giving you an out, fool, don't you see?' Scarlet said. 'When Ik-Song is destroyed or occupied – whichever comes first, you'll already be far from here.'

'And you – you don't care *about* Ik-Song? You don't want to save it? From the deadzones, from Asanai—'

'If you have personal delusions of saving the world, then by all means, go ahead.' Her voice was flat. 'But you'll answer to me first.'

Shadow was rendered speechless. She had spent so long as the Soldier – how foolish to think that she could be free now, that she might actually be able to help, to fight for the right side. The Moonbearer wanted to awaken her. Her dreams wanted to pull her back. And Scarlet – Scarlet would whittle her down until she was something unrecognizable.

'You think I gave up my freedom in exchange for you,' Scarlet said, rising. 'But that's not true. I didn't have freedom to begin with. In return for supervising you, the Moonbearer has given you to me. Only by proximity to you can I learn how to kill the Soldier. You're my conduit to revenge.'

Chapter 11

Eventually, Shadow followed Scarlet mindlessly back into the palace. When they were about to return inside the banquet room, Scarlet turned and said, 'We still have a performance to put on together.' It took Shadow several moments to even realize Scarlet was talking to her.

'A performance,' she echoed weakly.

'I hope my offer made you feel more favourably towards me, so that we can cooperate now. We'll have to descend down to that stage, you and I, for a display.'

'A display.'

'It's simple. It's a display of the Stronghold's power, so we must work together seamlessly, see.'

She wondered what kind of 'display' it was. Secretly, she hoped it was a duel.

'It's not a duel, so don't get excited. But it's harmonious like a duel and requires a cooperative spirit.'

When they entered, drummers had already taken up position. With everyone's curious eyes burning into her, Shadow felt near-frozen, as if the truth was written plainly on her face. She couldn't do anything but obey. They descended to the small stage. It was elevated, but still dangerously close to the guests. Shadow tried not to look closely at anyone's faces.

She stepped on.

Her mind would not quiet. How might she straddle the balance between helping, and obstructing? Plenty of people might want the Soldier dead. But Scarlet didn't just want to kill the Soldier. She wanted more. She wanted the truth, the unnameable, that would transcend mere physical borders, something ancient that rested down below with the ruins of the old city. Before she destroyed, she sought to understand – and that was somehow more dangerous. *The same way she killed my sister.* By her own element, then? How would the Keeper manage that? Shadow imagined the full force of that power on her and swallowed.

That light.

Now they stood on a stage together, but there was no duel.

Scarlet subtly raised a hand. *Follow my lead,* it said.

Then she flung up the dazzling wall of light.

It had a thousand shades to it. Curling crimson at the edges, white at its core, like a fire that couldn't decide if it was a fire or not. Like a sun come down to the land. It blazed upon the closest faces; mouths opened in appreciation.

Wind, water. All far-removed from Shadow. But light was different. Light was so close to darkness, so parallel. It was volatile.

It would hurt. And it would be weightless, too, an overwhelming sensation.

She threw up her own darkness, a low-hanging void. It was hard to see in thin air, transparent, abstract. It dimmed the room where Scarlet had brightened it.

'Tonight,' the Keeper said, moving along the edges, 'we throw into light and shadow for you, the celestial movements.'

Scarlet braved an arc, splayed it out across the hall. Dissipated.

Shadow understood now. They would mimic the natural movement of sun and moon, alternating paths. She threw out her own arc, spreading out like a ray. It was as natural to her as taking a step, even as her gut reacted against using it. They circled each other like koi fish, fluid in motion. Many of the forms she recognized: the *ki*, arms straight and head tilted. The *geon*, hands tighter to the body, face up. For each sequential arch, line, brilliant, amorphous display, she countered with her own in rapid succession. It was silent except for the brief crackling and snapping of their energies – a peculiar noise, one that shouldn't have even existed.

Her feet moved deftly, body assuming position after position. Feet planted solidly on the ground, arms stretched back – moving in tandem, chasing air, pushing for stability. The patterns grew more and more complex, dappling the hall, lively and brisk rippling. Her eyes darted from floor to ceiling. A haunting dance.

Shadow was dressed as the Soldier, Scarlet as the Keeper. The sun and the moon, an ancient dance, one that the Moonbearer and the Dawnbringer might've once stepped. Yet they didn't duel. They watched each other's movements, quick and sure-footed. Scarlet was finer, more precise; but Shadow had the strength. She'd never used her ability in this way, out of combat. It required the same stamina, strategic thinking.

Time passed, though she wasn't sure how much. A faint sheen of sweat had settled on her forehead. She threw up an unshaped form, sharpened it with a flick of her hands. They brightened and dulled towards the roof, the backdrop of the sky against it.

It was exhilarating.

And then Scarlet held her next position for longer – signalling the end. They faced each other. She made a subtle gesture for Shadow to turn sideways, and worked the same manoeuvre that she had on the bird – except this time, the unbroken stream of light aimed out through the roof to the night sky, disappearing into a stray cloud as far as the eye could see.

Shadow brought her hands together. *Can I do that?* She'd never attempted it before. But if Scarlet could do it, she would too. She inhaled deeply, pointed her arm in the direction of the sky, the other back, like drawing a bow back. Focus. Focus.

And released.

It wasn't as thin as Scarlet's fine beam, but it was thickly dark, crossing paths to create an X. Her sweat, the silk feel of her clothes, the audience – it all felt so sharp and visceral, and she wondered if there'd been something in the tea.

Everything dissipated, as quickly as it had appeared.

There followed a long stretch of silence – and then the Prince himself stood up at the high table in a rare, animated display, looking down. He clapped, loud in the silence.

The applause following proved thunderous.

Shadow breathed hard from exertion, staring at Scarlet, and thought that if it did ever come down to a duel, she wasn't sure who would win.

Chapter 12

It was only the next morning, half-drowsy after being violently roused by a flood of servants in her rooms for training, that Shadow blearily remembered the letters from yesterday.

She had completely forgotten about them after last night's events. The banquet, the performance, hearing that blasted deal. After her quarters emptied, she checked that no one was near her door and took out the sheaf to look through it. She wondered what the papers could be – coded messages, perhaps. After her encounter with the Prince, she guessed they might be battle-related plans, strategies against Asanai. Would that really be of any use to her? Likely not, but anything would do.

She read the first:

To: My Spring Flower
From: Bluebird

My Spring Flower,
I dream about you.

The Last Soldier of Nava

Our willow trees grow stronger,
The ledge we once sat.

– Bluebird

She rifled through. Every single letter was similar: all addressed from 'Bluebird' to 'Spring Flower'; traditional five-seven-five syllable haikus; incredibly short. Most of them mentioned a 'willow tree', but this was the only letter that mentioned two. *Our willow glimmers like ice. Our willow, beautiful.* Some of the words were scratched out and replaced, traces of the artistic process.

These were love letters.

She almost laughed out loud in frustration. They were nothing but love poems mentioning flowers and rosebuds and occasionally, a heated fire. Why had Prince Yo-han concealed these so carefully? Were they his own? It seemed hardly likely. The handwriting didn't match Yo-han's from what she'd seen in his study books, and there was no royal seal.

Her excitement at what she'd thought to be a larger clue was dampened; she'd snuck around the room for nothing. And worse, Yo-han would know that she'd stolen from him.

At the knock on her door, she hurriedly hid them again under her bed and followed obediently, thumbing Sae's stone, which she kept safely on her person.

In the training room, Aspis was already performing some complicated spinning kick manoeuvre against the wall. She barely spared Shadow a glance when she came in.

Shadow considered asking her about the letters. 'Thanks for yesterday, by the way,' she started.

'For what?' Aspis looked over.

'Saving my life.'

Aspis shrugged, looking taken aback. 'You are a valuable

asset, you know. It would be a shame if you fell to petty Court politics.' *A valuable asset.* The only difference between Scarlet and Aspis was that Aspis actually made it sound like a good thing. 'Why were you prying in the Prince's study? There's nothing of worth there, you know. He's not particularly interesting.'

There was an undercurrent to her words that Shadow wasn't sure about.

'Actually,' Shadow said, 'I found love letters.'

Aspis raised an eyebrow. 'What?'

Shadow explained what she had read.

'"*The ledge we once sat?*"' Aspis looked contemplative – maybe they weren't love letters, then? Maybe they were code? Shadow waited curiously. 'Well – there's a rumour of sorts – that during the dinners, there was a favoured spot by the Queen that she would slip away to. A balcony that's sort of a hidden alcove.'

'That's the rumour?'

'It's that she would meet her Asani lover there.'

'Oh,' Shadow frowned. That could be the 'ledge' the letters referred to. 'But how do you know that's what they're talking about? Just a guess?'

'Because that balcony directly faces the willow trees in the gardens. The whole purpose of it is to see the tree.'

The willow trees. They were beautiful – and also invasive. She imagined a time before the White Ice, decades ago: the Asani procession arriving in droves at the Royal Palace instead of the Stronghold, filling even larger halls with laughter and dining. Glasses of plum wine, the young Queen – then crown princess – slipping away in the night as faces reddened and the cacophony worsened. Just one of many stiff-backed figures draped in jewels seeking escape, into the cooler night air. Slipping into the alcove, shedding her elaborate *hanbok* robes, the silhouette of her unknown lover awaiting her in the recesses of the plush chairs, lit only in streaks by the icy, silvery moonlight. His legs crossed; one arm draped over the back of the bench. Nestling together, hesitant at first, but slowly giving in, pressured by the confines of time. A guard or two keeping watch outside. Watching the sway of the trees.

'But like I said before, I'm positive it's just a rumour,' Aspis said impatiently. 'I think a noblewoman or even an Advisor could've got away with it, but there were too many eyes on the Princess.'

'Why would Prince Yo-han keep letters of his mother's affair?'

'I don't know,' Aspis had said, interest waning. 'But regardless, none of that is important. You know why you're here?'

'You want me to help the Stronghold fend off Asanai.'

They didn't waste any time. Aspis circled her like prey, twiddling a knife between her fingers and waiting for the next lapse in Shadow's attention. The other girl asked strange, abstract questions about combat. Compared to what Shadow had been used to, it was relatively tame so far. At the same time, unfamiliar territory did not particularly evoke feelings of comfort.

'Half of the fight is nothing but fear. It's instinctual,' Aspis was saying. 'You know what's to be done. You're the victor; your opponent is not. There's nothing else to it.'

'You make it sound too simple.'

'Because it is.' A *tch*. 'Your form is obsolete.'

Her form was obsolete, Shadow knew, because *she* was obsolete. The Moonbearer would've been able to sweep along with the times, learning anew, but she – well, she'd been asleep.

'This technique of yours was last brought back in fashion over a century ago. It would've been taught to my great-great grandfather's generation, perhaps the few most traditional sects of my father's. Not to yours.'

There was a question in there. 'I received formal training in this,' Shadow said.

Aspis lunged her with the knife, and Shadow dodged in a split second, grabbing and turning Aspis's wrist around – applying pressure with her thumb, forcing her grip to slacken. Right when she grew aware of the bone beneath the skin, she released like it was a hot iron.

'And reluctant to fight,' Aspis said, quick as a viper.

'I just defended,' Shadow retorted. 'I disarmed you.'

'And you had my wrist. Why not go further?'

'What? You want me to break your arm or something?'

'Why not?' Aspis said, and Shadow couldn't tell if she was joking. She wondered if Aspis had ever fought Scarlet before in hand-to-hand. Probably not – she couldn't imagine that ending in anything less than a state-sanctioned civil war. 'I would break yours.'

Aspis lunged again, no knife. They traded blows until Aspis slammed the length of her forearm against the flat plane of Shadow's collarbones, knocking the breath out of her.

'Who trained you?' Aspis asked.

'Street brawlers,' Shadow replied, gasping for air.

'That's a lie.'

Shadow got back up; examined the beads of sweat on her arms. 'Did the Moonbearer train you?' she asked Aspis on a whim.

Aspis stilled. It was almost disconcerting to watch her so uneasy at the mere mention of his name.

'You know what the problem with you remades is, no matter your ability?' she said. 'You can hardly separate yourself from your power. You *become* your ability. Imagine if your throwing knife became a part of your arm? It's not a weapon anymore – just a liability. You could hurt yourself with it. It's inane.'

'But I can't separate the two, like a material weapon,' Shadow protested. 'It's part of me. I would if I could.'

'That's what's interesting about you. It's like you *want* the distance. You hold your ability at arm's length, which should be impossible. I throw a knife at you, and your first instinct is to block or dodge. If I were you, that wouldn't be my first instinct.'

'What would it be, then?'

'I would simply strike out with the darkness,' Aspis said, 'and aim for the heart.'

Why was everyone in this place, Shadow thought while she dodged another blow, so eager to fight her? Couldn't she have just one friend in this vast palace?

'No hesitation?' Shadow asked, leaping back.

'Hesitation,' said Aspis, eyes darkening, 'is the same thing as fear.'

The simplicity of it unmoored Shadow. *Fear.*

'Reaction –' Aspis lunged '– is what is dangerous – is what makes *you* the danger –'

Shadow fell into a memory.

The landscape was always changing. This is what he had taught her. In between the long periods of sleep and darkness, came the moments when he awakened her for his use.

Terrain elevated and plummeted, grew damp underfoot, or as bare as ice. Creatures that skittered at sight; ones that confronted head-on. The land they stood on was very old and varied. Each expanse had its advantages and disadvantages. The rolling, flat plains were overexposed, a merciless onslaught of vision that circled her. To keep guard on all sides, she had to keep a wider field of vision; turning meant shifting her feet in the ground, disturbing the wheat stalks, changing the landscape. Disruptive work. But it meant there was nothing in the way. It meant total and complete obliteration across incredible distances. To succeed, she had to change and be changed. It was the only way. The barren, yellow dust desert; ephemeral, a constantly changing ground where she could not even find steady purchase in standing. The heat like a mace, slicing up the limbs decisively. The rocky shore cliffs, evenings that brought windstorms and precarious footholds.

Darkness is only an element, he had taught her. Inanimate, lifeless. Nothing. It was only when it was imbued with certain qualities that it grew twice its size, became hunger, became *changed,* that was true strength. She knew of these certain qualities. The spike in circulation, the heartbeat; the breathing, quickened; the body, alert. Such qualities did not occur often in the Soldier, because the only one who could evoke them in her was him.

Pain was nothing, a survival response whose only purpose was to warn against danger. *But when there is no danger,* he said, *when you are the danger, there is no more use for it.* He trailed her across the plains, the desert, between the underbrush. He followed, and he changed her, and she changed the landscape for it. Under sky and darkness and wind and rain, he followed. When she raised her arms, his hand gripped her wrist, though whether this was real or a phantom sensation, the Soldier could not say. The Soldier only knew to abide.

'Feel,' he said, and the grip tightened, and certain qualities were evoked, after which it was like the body had disappeared and become nothing at all, replaced by a storm wherein she was unable to tell where her form ended and where the landscape began.

She knew the word for it now: *Fear.*

Shadow returned to the training room the next day. And the next. On the fourth, they fell back to small forms, side-by-side. She started to lose herself in the routine formation and strokes, how good it felt to work her muscles correctly, feel the air split around her kicks. The Moonbearer's training largely consisted of throwing her into battle. Of letting her run her thumb across a blade, feel its wet edge. Of teaching her fear so startling it ripped the sheer power out of her. Here, there was no true immediacy, no threat for now – just a room full of breathing. Their usual routine consisted of Aspis reminding her to focus while she tried to throw her off with questions like, *Who's your least favourite Advisor*, until Aspis conceded reluctantly.

After a while of sparring, with no decisive end in sight, there were footsteps at the door – so soft as to be almost unnoticeable, if Shadow weren't paying attention for it – and she turned to a new figure in the doorway.

She almost said *Keeper* out loud until the white head of hair met her like a shock. For her momentary lapse, she received a smattering blow just below the neck from Aspis and slid back, coughing profusely.

Yo-han looked faintly amused. He wore loose-fitting training clothes though he didn't look like he'd started yet. She hadn't seen him since she'd broken into his study and destroyed half his room. Where had he been? Where had he come from? Should she be bowing right now?

'You lost focus,' Aspis said.

'I can't fight in front of him,' Shadow said.

Aspis cast a glance back at Yo-han. 'Why not?'

'I can't stay long,' he said, approaching. 'I was just curious.'

Shadow shifted slightly away.

Aspis raised a brow and looked at Yo-han. 'She isn't actually deficient in hand-to-hand combat, like she led me to believe. I think it's sort of a mental block.'

'When did I lead you to believe—'

'Does she actually need training?' Yo-han said.

'It's hard to say.'

I'm right here, she thought irritatedly.

She wasn't expecting him to look at her, drop into a sudden fighting stance, and raise his arms. 'Duel me, then,' he said.

'What?' she said incredulously, looking at Aspis, who only shrugged. 'I mean – sorry, your Highness?'

'Come on. With ability. I want to see how you fight.'

'I can't attack a *prince*.'

'Why not?' he said. 'Aspis certainly has no problems with it.'

'Well, I'm not Aspis.'

'You probably didn't even know Ik-Song had a prince until you came to the Stronghold,' Aspis said.

'I did know,' she retorted crossly. Vaguely. She straightened up and looked at him. 'I can't duel you. Your Highness. I'm sorry.'

Before he had a chance to reply, all three of them turned at the sound of a page clearing his throat. Yo-han left as abruptly as he'd come, without another word.

She watched his back as he departed. When he had challenged her, a certain fire had flashed before his eyes – like he'd been transformed. Like suddenly the meekness was gone in the moment, no longer as distant, but replaced by something unfamiliar. At least Aspis's desires were written clearly along her face, so obvious in her movements – his were harder to discern.

Shadow turned back to Aspis and awaited her next instructions.

Shadow did not ask after the Keeper's whereabouts. The prospect of asking would imply that she cared where Scarlet was off to or what she was doing, and she did not. For all her dramatic monologuing about being attached at the hip, slaving day and night for vengeance, et cetera, Scarlet was nowhere to be found. But that was fine. That was good, even, because then Shadow could focus on more important and pressing matters.

Yet right when she'd started to let herself forget about the banquet, Scarlet showed up.

Shadow turned to her at the door during a training session, and Aspis bowed obediently. Scarlet didn't say a thing, only turning again to leave, but it was clear that Shadow was supposed to follow her. She exchanged a glance with Aspis before going.

They walked in complete silence until Shadow grew irritated. 'Where have you been? All that talk about using me, and then you just disappear for a week. Not –' she added, '– that I've been waiting around for you. I've been busy training.'

'I wasn't made aware,' Scarlet said, 'that Aspis was training you.'

'She's incredible. Her reflexes are—'

'I didn't ask.'

Shadow rolled her eyes. They began to descend down to a lower level. 'Well, is there a problem with her training me?'

'Aspis has specific regimens. I find some of it disagreeable.'

'You find everything disagreeable. Who else would be training me, if not her?'

'Under normal circumstances, you would be training with the Guards. That's where I'm taking you now.'

'The Guards?' Shadow pondered that. It would be less isolated. And she'd never run out of sparring partners. Scarlet's crimsons, the ones she'd seen in Yosae; the Councillor's; and the Prince's too. 'Crow's a Guard. Isn't he?'

Scarlet looked back at her, unimpressed.

'I don't want to work with him.'

'I don't care,' Scarlet said, 'what it is you want.'

Two floors below the first training room, they approached a large door. From inside the room echoed sounds of rough-housing, male voices, some unidentifiable slapping, and loud chatter.

Scarlet wasn't even flanked by any Guards in these vacant halls. Scarlet, she thought, was a highly unusual royal. The Prince remained mainly out of sight until dinnertime, keeping to the upper levels and his own chambers, probably spending his days privately training with Inner mentors, drawing milky lavender baths, and studying his princely books, or whatever princes did in their free time. He didn't roam around the palace, coming all the way down to even the servants' quarters, seeking people out. He didn't vanish in the late nights and mornings for rides out on palace grounds or travel an hour out to Yosae to parade around against the Court's wishes. Which is why no one in the palace constantly scrambled to keep up with the Prince, to obey his summons and keep him out of trouble. All things considered, neither the Prince nor the Councillor nor any Advisor sought anyone out; *they* were the ones sought after; if you desired an audience with them, you'd have to wait and suffer through an endless chain of command and formality to reach it. If you wanted an audience with the Keeper, she would probably already have been standing behind you, having listened to your private grievances for the past hour. No wonder the Stronghold remained on edge with her. She was so unlike the rest of them. They didn't know what to do with someone like this. Shadow didn't know either.

Scarlet probably felt trapped within the confines of the palace. Shadow knew what that was like. Like wearing another skin over your own, feeling completely separate from everything else. Strange and indescribable.

But what did she care about the Keeper's feelings? She could hardly feel sympathy for the girl – she lived like a true princess yet deigned to make the lives of everyone around her as difficult as possible. She'd threatened her own crimson guard, men who had pledged their lives for her safety. And from what Shadow could see, the only people in the palace loyal to her were the Prince and the Councillor.

'It won't take long,' Scarlet said.

Before she could ask what that meant, the door slid open.

Hot air blasted in her face, and the ruckus grew exponentially louder. It was a training room like upstairs, but much larger, and equipped with rows of baskets and benches beside a low-lying arena packed with a white sand ground.

Guards everywhere in various stages of undress, lounging around; sweat curling into napes; shuffling on mats halted upon seeing the Keeper. One young boy almost crashed head-first into a wall trying to put his pants back on. The room went comically silent at their entrance. It was obvious that this was a part of the Stronghold that anyone of the Inner rarely ventured down to.

'Keeper.' It was the same Guard whom Scarlet had threatened to blow to bits, and he watched Shadow warily. Out of uniform, he looked surprisingly young. 'We weren't expecting you.'

'Or your companion,' said another voice, emerging from behind. Crow, half-dressed in gear, looking predatory.

'The most civilized Guards learn by watching duels,' said Scarlet. 'So come watch, and learn, from a duel between her –' she looked at Shadow '– and one of our best.' Scarlet pointed at Crow. 'Come here.' All eyes swivelled to Shadow, who cast her gaze skyward.

For once in his life, Crow didn't protest the Keeper's order.

Shadow wondered if they'd planned this in advance – but no. Crow looked too thrilled at this surprise. They were going to duel. Right here, right now?

'Scarlet,' she tried through gritted teeth. Anyone but him, please. The memory of sand flicking across her face was heat-fresh in her mind. Why was she doing this? Just to toy with her, still? 'You can't be serious.'

No response.

Crow had already taken his place on the arena.

'If you lose,' Scarlet said to Crow loudly, 'you'll be booted from Yo-han's guard. Start with the *ly* form.'

'*What?*' Shadow said incredulously. 'Scarlet—'

Crow shattered something he had been holding in his hand: a granite rock. It cracked into smaller and smaller pieces in front of him, hypnotizingly, until a blanket of sharpened sand hovered above.

And in the next moment, he began his assault by throwing it.

Shadow wasn't even *in the arena* yet. She cursed and dived onto the sand. She dodged and once again threw up the blanket of darkness to counter, running to a better vantage point. Their audience watched intensely.

Thankfully, Crow was again momentarily unnerved and distracted by her ability, unused to it. He had to have battled countless remades in here, maybe even Scarlet, but never a *sakasa*. It threw him off-guard. She would dodge, kill time, tire him out.

The Last Soldier of Nava

But he wasn't one of the Stronghold's best for nothing. He recovered quickly, and to her own dismay, she realized that Scarlet and Crow were working together for the first time, and it was deadly.

'Try the fish scale,' Scarlet called out.

Fish scale? Crow launched a consecutive attack of diamond-hard rock shards from both his left and right, culminating in a centrepiece that aimed right at her heart. The formation was so rapid that she could only twist and weave to miss, unable to breathe between them, much less counter.

Crow panted heavily before her, already gearing up for the next. What peculiar moves.

And then it hit her.

The fish scale, the broken-down *ly* sand.

She'd encountered those before.

Was Scarlet . . . trying to *recreate* the battle between the Soldier and the Desert Rose? It wasn't a stretch to guess that Scarlet knew her sister's fighting style, her moves. What she would've attempted against the Soldier.

Why, though? What did Scarlet hope to gain? It wouldn't give any insight into her sister.

'The Keeper is almost unparalleled in combat,' Crow said. 'Luckily, so am I.'

They circled each other. Shadow watched the quick movement of Crow's feet – feather-light, just like they had been in their first-ever pursuit across the rooftops of Yosae.

'Don't you know she's bluffing?' she said. 'You don't actually have to beat me.'

'Oh,' Crow said. 'I know.'

'We don't have to fight, you know.'

'If you don't fight back, it's all the better for me,' he said. And then he continued with relish. Round after round of relentless assault unleashed onto her; slabs slamming down on the floor, sandstorms whirling past. He moved with the sturdy pace of his craft, not even close to tiring.

'My sister was especially skilled in her craft. Crow has followed in her teachings.' Scarlet was close enough for them to hear, but out of earshot of the audience that ringed back.

Shadow tried another wall of darkness, but he'd learned by now that it was just a mirror trick. He slashed through with a roundhouse kick.

'First, there was a series of quick blows to the throat, no ability,' Scarlet said.

Crow did as she said. It caught Shadow off-guard, parrying only hand-to-hand blows, blinking loose sand out of her eyes. She started to feel sick.

'And then another slam-down.' Scarlet wasn't even trying to hide it anymore. She was really doing this.

'Scarlet,' Shadow said. 'Whatever you think you're doing—'

His material reformed into huge slabs, which he brought down again and again. Shadow dodged the first, but was caught halfway under the second, and after that was history. The rock sank down slowly like the jaws of a trap. Her arms strained with the effort, muscles burning.

'And then – she pitched her to the wall.'

Shadow was indeed thrown back, vision starting to blur. She opened her eyes and was no longer in a training room, but the dull ruins of a city, as faint as a dream. She was watching her face in the water beside her father's dulled boot. She was looking up at a ring of skulls; beholding a mother and daughter marked with blood.

She blinked and she was back, Crow only a few paces away from her.

Irritation welled at her vision; a sheen of panic, and then anger.

The Last Soldier of Nava

'This will be over soon,' Crow said. He looked smug – like he had already won. His footwork had slowed, buoyed by the close reach of victory.

'Don't come any closer,' Shadow said. Only after she spoke did she realize how different her voice sounded, in the moment – hard, steely. The rancour of the room, all of the Guards watching, filtered out.

Crow paused.

'A direct slice to the face,' came Scarlet's voice then. It was all Shadow heard, and suddenly she was in a dim place, somewhere else, far away, and the face of the Desert Rose stared back at her, the crest of her neck glinting.

'You forget yourself,' Shadow said.

'How?' Crow said.

'You have never really fought a *sakasa* before.'

'*Crow*,' Scarlet's voice came again. Insistent.

'So?' Crow said. Uncertainty flashed across his face.

'So you don't know what I'm capable of.'

He tilted his head briefly, as if considering it for a second.

'This is your last chance,' Shadow said.

'I'll take my chances,' he said. His arms came up so quickly it was like lightning. He was coming closer, and the Desert Rose was curving her arms into the air, bringing them down with crippling finality – Shadow couldn't remember where she was, what she was doing. The arms coming down were like the long hands of a clock, slowing everything down, warping the world around them.

To her muted, distant surprise, the stone against her shirt pocket buzzed warmly against herself, as if reminding her of its presence. It seemed to call to her, urging her to come back to herself. But it wasn't enough in the moment to pull her from the memory. She remembered blinding pain like a thousand, tiny crystals embedded into her face, the razor-feel of a burn, the right side of her face exploding in pain. She remembered light in a dark place, and she didn't want to fight, but this time she would, this time she'd win cleanly, and Crow had closed in, and the Desert Rose snapped, and she was arcing down, down, down.

Chapter 13

Wrists rubbed raw from tugging at her bindings, Shadow slumped to the side in defeat, keeping tired eyes open.

'Don't bother.' The door, already ajar, slid open the rest of the way to reveal White Crane, two courtiers, and another Advisor that she recognized as Ji-hu. It closed behind them. 'They're doubly reinforced with Shizingan silk.'

'Is he all right?' Shadow asked, sitting upright again.

'He'll live,' Ji-hu said vaguely.

'It's that severe?'

'Not that you should be privy to that information, but he'll be on rest for the next day or two.'

Sharp relief flooded her. A day or two – that wasn't bad, certainly not dire. He'd be bruised up, at most – not unlike herself, except the difference was that she was not particularly sure what she'd done to him.

Amidst the worry and exhaustion, something else unfurled. 'The Keeper,' Shadow said, trying to steady her voice. No way was Scarlet emerging from this unscathed. 'I'd like to see her.'

'You're strapped to the ground in wrist bindings, and you

think yourself in a position to give orders?' White Crane said, unimpressed.

'It's a plea, not an order. Please. Let me see her.'

'Why?' Ji-hu prodded. 'So you can weasel your way into injuring yet another Guard?' He clucked his tongue. 'Crow is one of our most promising, you realize. Our only one with that particular ability.'

'One would think she'd attempt to preserve such skill, seeing as her sister was one,' White Crane muttered, no longer addressing Shadow.

'One would think many things.'

'The Keeper did this to me,' Shadow said. 'She forced me to fight Crow.'

'Regardless,' White Crane said. 'You incapacitated him.'

'I warned him,' she said. 'I warned him not to come any closer, and he did.'

'You're not allowed anywhere near Crow,' said White Crane. 'I, for one, relish the day the Stronghold is rid of guests like you.'

There was a long, meaningless silence, in which she looked around the small, spare room. A silent Guard stood in each of the front two corners.

Apparently, she'd reacted at the last second in the duel. Nearly obliterated half the arena. Sparked a small fire, burning off half her clothes. And tossed Crow across the room straight into a wall. Not that she remembered any of it.

She was going to wring Scarlet's neck with her bare hands.

'Advisors,' a muffled voice called from behind the door. 'A message.' The courtier came in, eyes flickered between the three of them before speaking. 'She is to be released.'

'Released,' White Crane said incredulously. 'On what grounds?'

'Unacceptable,' Ji-hu added. 'Is the Councillor aware that she attacked one of the Prince's own personal guard?'

The Last Soldier of Nava

'He bends to his *Light's* will, always. He endangers us all.' The Advisors exchanged knowing, implicit glances – clearly, this was far from the first time such complaints had been voiced.

'The decree isn't from the Councillor,' the courier said. 'It comes from Prince Yo-han.'

'*Yo-han?*' It was her own turn to be surprised. What reason would he have to pardon her? 'Why?'

The courier didn't answer, only looking to White Crane and Ji-hu, who both displayed the same surprise.

'I should like an audience with His Highness,' White Crane said.

'I'm afraid he's indisposed at the moment.'

'Very well. You're dismissed.'

The courier bowed once and slid the door shut behind him. The Advisors looked at each other, and it was clear that she was no longer the largest issue in the room.

'A ruler who gives in to a whelp's every whim,' White Crane said with venom, 'and a bastard prince who can hardly hold his own. This is the state of our great dynasty?'

It was the first time she'd heard the Advisors openly insult the ruling.

'If not for us, Ik-Song would've long fallen apart,' Ji-hu agreed. 'But it matters not – things are changing.'

They both looked dispassionately down at Shadow, still kneeling on the ground. 'I suppose you have grand ideas of running back to the Keeper and telling her all about our treasons,' White Crane said, amused.

'I have no interest in whatever Court politics you're talking about.'

'You should. It concerns you,' Crane said. 'The Moonbearer wanted you here, did he not?'

Crow chasing her down on the rooftop seemed ages ago now. 'Does it matter? I can't even get an audience with him.'

'Even us Advisors haven't had an audience with the Moonbearer in months,' White Crane said. 'What makes you think you would be first in line?'

Shadow glanced up in shock, but the Advisors weren't even looking at her, unconcerned. *In months?* Was that normal? Where was he? Why was he hiding away in his own palace?

'What do you mean?' she said. 'Is he even in the palace?'

'Why does it matter to you?' he said.

'I've stayed in the Stronghold in the hopes of meeting the Moonbearer,' she said, point-blank. 'If he isn't here, there's no reason for me to be here.'

The Advisors looked down at her. Ji-hu said, 'What business have you with him? I wasn't aware you were some kind of fanatic.'

'I'm no fanatic,' she said.

'Does it matter what she wants?' White Crane said. 'Every visitor here arrives with some delusion of consorting with the Councillor.'

'Then is he here or not?' she asked.

'It doesn't concern you,' White Crane said, exchanging a glance with Ji-hu.

They didn't know, she realized. They were not sure themselves. No wonder they were so comfortable talking amongst themselves about it all. Perhaps no one was ever listening.

But if he was not here, where could he be? Asanai? The Queen's palace? Hidden away in some grand estate in Yosae?

In the throne room, she'd looked into the Moonbearer's failed remaking and vowed to end his reign, once and for all.

But she was just a girl. She had thought she could remain in the palace long enough to find him, to confront him – but she was no closer than the first night she had been brought here. If he wasn't even in the Stronghold – if his own Advisors couldn't get to him, how could she?

And Scarlet was too dangerous. She had backed her into corners she couldn't get out of. Crow was only an early casualty — there would be more. He had already faced her once, in Yosae, and he was tensile enough to hold up against whatever Scarlet had drawn out of Shadow — but others wouldn't be as familiar, as resistant. The longer Shadow stayed, the more of a danger she would pose to everyone.

She flexed her hands, frustration building. Mere days in the Stronghold, and she'd already had enough of being caged, made to strike. In training with Aspis, this duel with Crow. Forced into murderous shapes like a dog in a pit.

'I'm a prisoner of the Keeper,' Shadow said. 'She forced me to come here. But I'm not prisoner to the Stronghold, am I?'

'What do you mean, child?' White Crane said apathetically. *I, for one, relish the day the Stronghold is rid of guests like you.* '"Prisoner" implies that whoever is doing the imprisoning *desires* their prisoner confined. The Court desires no such thing.'

The Advisors' interest had been piqued. 'The Court does not,' agreed White Crane.

'I think only the Keeper might be displeased, then, if anything were to happen to her prisoner.'

'I see,' White Crane said. 'Then it would be a shame, indeed, if — at this very moment — you fought viciously out of your bonds, overwhelmed us in battle, and fled the palace, never to be seen again.'

'Exactly,' she said. 'Tell me the way out of here, and you'll never have to lay eyes on me again.'

'Leave the palace east-side,' Ji-hu said smoothly. 'There are hidden tunnels there, watched by Guards who belong to the Court. They won't stop you.'

East? It sounded familiar. She mapped it out in her head. What steps she would take, what route, as soon as the door opened. She knew the Stronghold roughly enough by now to know the quickest way east. She'd duck her head low, walk rapidly. The Guards moving aside. The bright air that would greet her outside, the faintly churning sea. Maybe a quick detour to the stables, too, to nick a deer for herself—

No. No detours. Hopefully she would return to Yosae, and find Sae – or was that too dangerous? Either way, she had a mission: to escape. And she couldn't get waylaid. If she couldn't have vengeance, she could at least have her freedom.

'Release her from the bindings.' White Crane then nodded at one of the Guards, gesturing towards her. Upon drawing nearer, he then muttered something into the Guard's ear, too low for her to hear.

The Guard approached, mechanically unsheathing a small dagger blade from his belt and running it through the silk. She'd stretched the knot so tight that it would be impossible to untie.

'Do not return,' said Ji-hu.

'Aren't we supposed to fake a fight, though?' Shadow said to the backs of the Advisors as they left. 'Perhaps I should strike both of you once, to look as if I overpowered you.'

'Don't even think about it,' White Crane snapped without turning around. Finally, the door was slid open and left open.

There was no one left inside the room but her and the two Guards in the corners. She eyed them; they stared straight ahead. Head bowed low, arms held tight behind her back, she studied the tatami flooring.

Shadow's hair was curled to her temples with sweat from the fight; her right sleeve had been torn through, so that her arm showed through the cloth. Using so much power had exhausted her, but at the same time, a buzz of electrifying current ran underneath her skin. As soon as Crow had closed in, she had felt that buzz.

'Out,' came the sharp, familiar voice.

Shadow froze.

She didn't have to look up. She heard the Guards obediently leaving the room, the slide of the door shutting. A drop of sweat fell from her brow to the mat below her; she watched the water seep in.

'*You're* here?' Shadow said. *Why are you here?*

'A prisoner summoning the Keeper,' came Scarlet's voice. 'You've never requested to see me before.'

A request?

Of course the Advisors wouldn't make her escape so easy.

Shadow looked up, then. Scarlet looked the same as she had in the arena – unaffected, looking down at her. Shadow was reminded of their first meeting, in Yosae: the sun a bright blaze behind this silhouetted rider, the delicious gleam of well-kept armour.

'Pitting Crow against me,' Shadow said. 'Did you get what you wanted?'

'Not particularly, no,' Scarlet said. 'You had the wrong reaction.'

'The wrong *reaction*?'

Scarlet knelt down in front of her, awfully close. Shadow felt her eyes taking her in – dropping to her torn clothing, her arms behind her back.

'I was surprised,' Scarlet said, sounding amused. 'I didn't think you would attack him like that. I didn't know you had it in you.'

'I felt impassioned enough,' Shadow said. She felt the slide of silk between her fingers. 'I do now, too.'

'Then it's a shame your hands are tied.'

Shadow wanted to wipe that smug look off her face; her fingers twitched. Scarlet only reached forward, and – to her shock – tugged at her torn sleeve. The burnt, loose seam at its start fell apart instantly, exposing her collarbone to the cold air.

'Too close.'

'I'm just looking,' Scarlet smirked. And indeed, she was looking – studying her neck as if there was something particularly interesting there, and then her eyes began to rove lower. 'Why did you summon me here, prisoner?'

'To tell you something,' Shadow said.

'What?'

Now, her head said. Scarlet had already bent one knee to gloat, unbalanced, and Shadow was quick. She shot out and yanked her by the arm, forcing her down to the ground and pinning her on her back. Scarlet's surprise was overshadowed quickly by the light sparking from her left hand, but Shadow grabbed it and sent darkness coursing through her palm – making Scarlet's grip slacken and her eyes widen. She pinned her hands to her sides.

It was a quick tussle, but they were both left winded. 'Clever,' Scarlet said.

'I'm finished with you,' Shadow said, looming over her. 'And the Stronghold, and this "deal" we made. I didn't ask to be a tool for you. You're a spoiled brat. And you're not going to find out what you want this way, anyway. You're impossible, and a disgrace. To the entire palace and all of Ik-Song. You just *toy* with everyone. With me. I won't have it.'

'Finished?' Scarlet asked dryly.

'I won't be helping you anymore. No duels, no combat, nothing even related to my ability,' she said. 'I'm done.'

'So you've summoned me here – why? To do me in?'

'I did no such thing,' Shadow said. 'The Advisors did.'

It was obvious that Scarlet had no intention of fighting back. She was just lying there limply, thoughtfully. Probably to provoke Shadow further, but it was working.

Shadow released Scarlet's hands, tossing them to the floor. She stood and moved to the door, not turning her back to the other girl. Shadow would turn and walk straight out of this palace afterwards, and by the time Scarlet had thought she'd regained the upper hand, she'd be miles from the Stronghold and gone forever.

'I'll make you a new deal,' Scarlet said. 'You don't have to fight.'

Shadow paused. 'What do you mean?'

'I mean, you don't have to fight.'

'But I'm here to fight.'

'You only need to investigate with me. Help me with my research, and I won't make you fight anymore.'

'Research?'

'On the Soldier.'

Shadow waited long moments for the next backhanded comments, the catch. But there was nothing. No smirk, no cursory glance. Scarlet was serious.

If Shadow could stay without fighting, she couldn't be provoked. And if unprovoked, she wouldn't be a danger to everyone in the palace.

'Is the Moonbearer here?' Shadow asked.

A pause hung in the air.

'I'm not sure,' Scarlet said. The honesty of that answer shocked Shadow – she tried to hide her surprise. 'But I think he is.'

The Advisors had given her an out. But they were not any more trustworthy than Scarlet. If Shadow remained, the Advisors would never give her the chance again. But if she did, Scarlet would ease up, and there was still a chance for vengeance.

A slim hope, but still.

Shadow had turned to the door, but Scarlet's next words made her stop short.

'The reason I made Crow fight you is because it's impossible to die by your own element,' came the voice. 'But my sister died with sand in her lungs; she choked on the stuff.' Shadow was afraid to turn back around, to see her face. 'If you know the lore, you know it's believed that the Soldier was a thief, that she could steal ability; absorb and redirect others' power. I had a hunch that all *sakasa* could do this. But I was mistaken.'

Shadow didn't move or say anything. Scarlet could surely hear her heart pounding.

'Stay in the palace,' Scarlet said, 'or the gardens. But don't try to leave east-side. The catfish is trained to devour anyone who surfaces from the tunnels there.'

Chapter 14

Shadow would never forget the look on White Crane's face.

'He looked like he'd just found oxen shit on the bottom of his shoes,' Shadow told Aspis after recounting the recent events. She had found Aspis in the training rooms throwing daggers at the wall – seemingly her favourite activity – and cornered her into hearing the reenactment. *And here I thought you were making haste*, White Crane had said heinously, lip twitching, and she'd said, *my plans have changed. It seems I'm staying a bit longer.*

'I can't believe you would talk to him like that,' Aspis said.

'Well, *I* can't believe he tried to feed me to the catfish.'

'This is good,' Aspis said. 'With no obligations to the Keeper anymore, you'll be free to train for the invasion without interruption.'

Shadow hesitated. 'Would I even be allowed back in the arena after I destroyed half of it?'

'Possibly.' She smirked.

It was a relief having someone in the Stronghold on her side. Aspis was strait-laced – maybe too strait-laced, sometimes – and forward and honest. A long moment ensued in which

Shadow was sure Aspis would tell her to keep out of sight lest she attract unwanted attention around the palace.

'Tell me,' Aspis continued, 'were there other Advisors watching when you said all that to Crane?'

'So many,' Shadow said. 'He was bright red.'

They glanced at each other and snickered.

Later, Shadow came back to a note in her quarters. She almost missed it but caught herself by the arms right before she collapsed on top.

Sitting flat on her bed, of all places, and she knew exactly who it was from.

Two days. Beyond the throne room, the last door on the right to the lowest floor. Midnight.

During the days Shadow trained and crashed dead asleep at night. The dreams lessened; the flower moon neared. If there were still remakings or Court ultimatums going on, she was not privy to them. The only thing she was forced to attend was dinner. The dinners were excruciating – a somewhat casually extended version of the day's practical business and political talk, half of which she knew nothing about, a quarter of which she wasn't technically supposed to be privy to, and the last quarter of which generally alarmed her. And the most fascinating part of the dinners remained the food. How the palace sustained such an abundance of meat was a total mystery, surely thanks in part to Aspis's prodigial catches. Royal meals were always exquisitely prepared, entire animal heads presented on platters and stuffed in their still-gleaming skins. Pheasant, boar, chicken, oxen, and on. Raw, sliced tuna and yellowfish. It was a bit garish, sure, but it was a marker of wealth, of luxury. She had never anticipated her next meal so excitedly.

Since their encounter, Scarlet had kept true to her promise:

she didn't summon Shadow to fight for her, or to demonstrate her power. In fact, she didn't summon her for anything. She appeared unannounced at random times briefly – dropping by at dinner, watching the Guard duels for a few moments before disappearing again for days. Though Shadow knew Scarlet wasn't allowed to leave the palace, she had no idea where she went, what she did; she tried to mark a pattern to her coming and goings, but there was none. Even since their supposedly secret – was it secret? – agreement, Scarlet seemed even more of an enigma. Once, Shadow saw her with Yo-han in the gardens, their backs to her, watching crows in the distance; Yo-han said something to her, an offhand remark, and Scarlet – a hand shading her eyes from the sun – had turned to him and laughed sharply. It was the only time Shadow had ever seen her laugh genuinely. And Yo-han didn't even seem surprised. He seemed, for once, like he belonged; like his presence was purposeful. Crow was there, too, and it seemed Yo-han's presence at least temporarily mitigated the discordance between Crow and Scarlet, because neither of them were at each other's throats for once. An impressive feat, if you asked Shadow.

On the day, Shadow waited an agonizingly long time in her quarters for the countdown to midnight until she realized she couldn't wait that long. She would arrive early. Scarlet would just have to deal.

She descended to the lower floors and followed the directions vaguely in her head. *Beyond the throne room, last door on the right.* But when she drew near the throne room, there was already someone waiting there.

After a long moment, right before she turned to leave, a shadowy figure emerged at the entrance. But it wasn't who she hoped it would be.

A man, tall and imposing.
She completely stopped.
The silhouette was familiar – could it be? – could it be—
No.
The width of the shoulders was narrower, cloaked in the darkness—
Yo-han.
It was only Yo-han.
She settled for an awkward bow, slightly flustered.
'Couldn't sleep?' he asked.
She nodded.
'Me neither. I know it's strange, but . . .' he began, unprompted, looking back towards the throne room, 'sometimes, when I can't sleep, I go inside. It comforts me.'
'It's not strange,' she said. 'I understand.' Seeking relief in the dark.
'Do you?' he said – unmocking, only eager.
Shadow nodded slowly, something akin to pity rising in her chest. Yo-han looked small against the hall, almost frail; not very princely at all. He looked at her intensely, but she didn't know if she had what he was looking for.
'I know you have barely any idea who he is, but . . . the Councillor is a great leader. A powerful leader.'
'I'm sure,' she said automatically.
'He isn't as frightening as everyone makes him out to be.'
'Why doesn't he show his face?' she asked, sounding more accusatory than she intended.
He looked at her in surprise. 'He's saving his strength, for what's coming next. For Asanai.'
Saving his strength.
'And so should you,' he stepped forward, face illuminated by moonlight. He wore a nondescript dark *hanbok*, and his

hands trembled ever so slightly; for a brief moment, she wondered if she was dreaming.

'I know Aspis wants to push you, wants you to train harder. I understand why. But I believe you have the strength that it takes. I am positive that you'll succeed.'

Her surprise must have shown on her face, because his grew even more serious, as if laser-focused on convincing her. 'I *know* you can bring greatness for Ik-Song,' he said, and his tone was so sure, so committed, almost a shade desperate. 'I already know you have potential. Tell me,' he said, 'what was it like, going into that deadzone?'

It was sickening, and horrid, she should have said. *I never want to return.* Instead, she opened her mouth and said, 'It was alluring.' She didn't know why she told him the truth, and instantly wanted to take her words back. And then: 'I would return, if I could.' To the place that reeked of the Moonbearer, so familiar, like home; it would've been so easy to tip over, to give into that wordless pocket, to disappear within her own darkness. To feel nothing at all.

Shadow was afraid to look at him. But when she did, he didn't look shocked, or uneasy.

'I understand,' he said. 'I do. Without temptation, there is no true strength.'

A strange need to quell him surged through her. 'But still,' Shadow said, 'I *am* ready to fight for Ik-Song. I won't let you down.'

If you have personal delusions of saving the world, Scarlet had said. But it wasn't saving the world, so much as clearing her debts. Ensuring that the Soldier wouldn't reign any longer.

Yo-han was the true, rightful heir to the throne, the future ruler. Not the Moonbearer, who would desperately hold onto his place by pure claw and teeth, intimidating the Queen into submission, unwilling to let go. It didn't matter if Yo-han was fooled by the Moonbearer – after all, everyone else had been, too. Shadow would still fight for the Prince, even if he didn't want it. She would give him back his rightful place even if he had no idea of her motivations. Yo-han was deserving. He was untainted. She would not let the Moonbearer sink his talons into him further, too, to use him and leave him for dead, like he had done to her.

Yo-han nodded and left without another word. She faced the door.

Shadow had suspected but was now faced with a growing certainty: the Moonbearer was not in there.

Her instincts couldn't sense him. Yo-han might as well have been praying to an empty shrine.

Chapter 15

Shadow stopped in front of a dark door – the last on the right. When she opened it, a hidden set of stairs disappeared into dark nothingness, unusually spiralled and narrow, veering to the left. It looked like the kind of place one dropped their enemies into to hide them from the outside world.

Against her better judgement, she descended.

The stairs continued on for seemingly forever, until a soft light began to be visible from the bottom. Finally, an opening.

She ended mid-thought as the room came into view.

It was not so much a room as a single, giant, soaring library. They hadn't descended under the Stronghold – they'd simply taken a winding road to another part of it. Vinery, of course, crowded out the walls. Jutting into the room in the corner was a bubbling rock pool, gently waterfalling over grey slabs. The high windows were at ground level with the grass, so occasionally a grazing deer walked into view, and they were open – faint dampened trails along the walls showed where rain had last seeped in. Shelves and shelves of dusty, ancient tomes; slim-bound books; pages marked on mulberry paper, side-stitched bound, the covers tinted to repel insect wear.

It was beautiful, and completely empty except for Scarlet, who sat at one of the tables strewn with papers, along the far side. It reminded Shadow of when she'd caught her in her study, alone. Against the vast backdrop of this elaborate library, Scarlet was just a small figure: singular, lonesome. Was this where she spent all her days, whiling away?

'You're early,' Scarlet said, standing.

'I got tired of waiting,' Shadow said. She thought it was dangerous to be here with no Guards but withheld the comment. Guards would ruin the quiet sanctuary of the place, the peaceful absence of human life and the bold presence of the elements. She moved closer to the table, examining the contents of the papers, as Scarlet skimmed along a shelf, her back to Shadow.

Shadow watched her from behind. 'Tell me where the Councillor is.'

'Straight to the point.' Scarlet's hands momentarily stilled before resuming. 'I told you – I'm not sure.'

'But you must have some idea. He's not in the throne room – and the Advisors haven't seen him in months.'

'How would you know whether he's in the throne room or not?'

Because I can't sense him there. 'There aren't even Guards posted outside.'

Scarlet turned to her. 'Why do you think he's not showing his face?'

'Everyone else in the palace says he's "saving his strength",' Shadow said. 'I'm not sure what it means. The ruler of Ik-Song isn't in his own palace on the eve of a war?'

'Here is what I know,' Scarlet said. 'If all goes according

to plan, the Moonbearer will not show his face until the flower moon.'

Wait – the flower moon, meaning the *day* Asanai would invade?

Why so late?

Was this some kind of show of power, to rally morale on the day? The leader finally gracing Guards with his presence when they needed it the most?

'What plan?' Shadow said.

'Not so fast,' Scarlet said. 'You have to help me first.'

'But why—'

'No more questions,' she said, 'until you help me.' Scarlet turned around with a script – scrawled ostensibly in the ancient language, the dead language. Only royal archives would have access to records so old and well-preserved.

Until the flower moon.

Maybe she had no choice but to wait until then. But how could she get her revenge on such a day? Everyone's eyes would singularly be on him.

Perhaps in the chaos of battle, there might be an opening.

But Scarlet's next words nearly made her forget about the Moonbearer. 'The Soldier.' Scarlet gestured to the papers. 'Everything ever recorded about the Soldier – the legends, the myths, the stories. I have them all. I've mapped out claimed sightings, witnesses, oral histories passed down through generations of those who saw and survived. Not all contained to just Ik-Song, either.'

Shadow just looked, dumbfounded. She wondered if the Moonbearer knew about the sheer scale of this pursuit: if Scarlet had told him this, too, what he might've said. She looked at the texts: indeed, some were written in the more cramped linework of the Asani language.

'I thought it was a crime for anyone in Ik-Song to teach Asani,' Shadow said.

'I taught myself, so technically, no crime took place. And since when are you such a stickler for rules?'

The scope of this investigation was no small matter. Shadow swallowed nervously. 'Objectively, these are all fictional forms of storytelling, or word-of-mouth accounts.'

'No. There's also a recorded, factual mention in the Record Annals of the Dynasty. See.' Scarlet pointed at a thick volume, laid open. 'A decade ago.'

The Record Annals were official recordings of dynastic events, not mere stories. But Shadow had woken last year. Not ten years ago. Ten years ago, was the White Ice. These records were forged, or mistaken, the result of a frightened official, a search for an enemy, perhaps. But Scarlet regarded it with conviction.

Shadow had no idea how Scarlet thought she could really solve this. And yet, she also had no idea how Scarlet was so close.

'Always, the Soldier is painted as a skilled manipulator of darkness,' Scarlet paced, her hands casting a lacework of shadows across the desk. 'Always the picture of stealth, and completely unstoppable. The lore regards her as the single enemy of light. Drowning kingdoms in darkness and slitting throats without hesitation – an entity not born out of Nava, the Dawnbringer, the Moonbearer, but something else. Something older. Born seemingly with no purpose but to destroy.' A pause. 'There are only three truths we can be sure of: that the Soldier is a *sakasa,* born in the time of the Ninth, and a girl. Beyond that, nothing else. And even then, I'm not sure if she is a girl.'

'Why not?'

'Her work lacks the skill. It's simply unthought destruction.

The Last Soldier of Nava

Women destroy for understanding, for vengeance. Men destroy for blood. But she's never taken the form of a man in any story, so she must be a woman.'

Too close for comfort. How did Scarlet sense it? The Moonbearer commandeering the Soldier like a puppet, his hand stretching out, her body a vessel? 'Then that's where your knowledge ends?'

'I had several theories,' said Scarlet matter-of-factly. 'The role of the Soldier as a mantle, passed down over generations, mother to daughter. A cultish follower of the Moonbearer, who killed to pay him homage. A network of assassins, secretly upholding order under state officials.' A pause. 'But none of those work. They're complex. I don't think it's complex at all. I think she is only one person, the same person.'

'Then she would be immortal,' Shadow said dubiously, trying to instil doubt.

'Like our Councillor, yes.'

Scarlet had almost nothing to go on. It was all leaps and speculation, no real clues to track.

'But according to legend, the Dawnbringer ended the Soldier by using all of the light of Nava,' Shadow said. 'The city was destroyed, and so was the Soldier.'

No response. Shadow couldn't reveal too much, anything important. But she had to make Scarlet trust her. There was no way to navigate this palace without her. And yet, how deep did Scarlet's loyalties to the Moonbearer really run?

'At the banquet, you asked me about my identity,' Shadow said. 'The truth is, I was never remade by the Moonbearer. I was born with my power.'

Whatever reaction she had expected, it wasn't this: the smug half-smile, almost triumphant. 'I knew it.' And then Scarlet opened her palm; light flickered above it. 'So was I.'

'What?' Shadow said. 'How is that possible?'

'*You're* asking how it's possible?'

'I thought you were remade. You have a remade name.' If Scarlet was born with that power, it could only mean one thing – a magic that had survived for a long, long time, across generations. There were only three survivors in all of Nava: the Soldier, the Moonbearer and the Dawnbringer. Was it really possible? 'Then you're a direct descendant of the Dawnbringer.' A never-ending line that would've persisted across centuries.

'I saw you in the deadzone,' Scarlet said. 'On our journey to the Stronghold. You sensed the way out. You weren't scared. You recognized something in it. You're like me. You were born with ability. You were never remade by him,' Scarlet said confidently. 'Your ability is stronger, more true. Meaning you're a direct descendant of the Soldier.'

It made perfect sense, didn't it? It was what Shadow would think, if she were in Scarlet's place.

'You believe in the Ninth City,' Scarlet said suddenly.

Shadow nodded, unsure if it was a question or a statement.

'The Moonbearer, the Dawnbringer and the Soldier. The city destroyed.' This felt like when Scarlet had revealed she knew the Soldier killed her sister, pulling the rug out from under Shadow's feet. *There's always a story to these things. The appearance, and the reality. Wouldn't you agree?* 'Do you believe in that?'

'According to legend,' Shadow said, 'the Dragons kept balance. Until its end. Since then . . .' she paused. The deadzones, the freak weather, the Moonbearer's pitiful imitations of power. 'Ik-Song hasn't been in balance.'

'The deadzones,' Scarlet said, reading her mind.

'It's all from the fall. They didn't exist before Nava.'

'Something happened to the Dragons, then. One of them was hurt or killed.'

The Last Soldier of Nava

The Dragons? 'It would be incredibly difficult for someone to kill a Dragon.' But not impossible. And once they did, they would have gained unimaginable power . . . Someone who killed a Dragon would have access to power unheard of in this world. It would last for centuries. You could use it for anything.

Shadow's dream struck her like lightning: the endless lakes and wells of water. The breathless presence of something older than she imagined, grand and ancient.

The Moonbearer.

Looking up to the Moonbearer, the mountain rising in the distance that was no mountain but a dead thing.

Shadow hadn't given much thought to the Dragons before.

'That's *impossible*,' she said. Though something in her gut said it wasn't.

The Moonbearer was responsible. He had to be. For the death of a Dragon. He still subsisted on its power centuries later, and he would've used it from the start. In theory, dark power like that could be used to create *anything* – including, in theory, a perfect warrior. Something human and not, as advanced a weapon as possible.

A Soldier.

The Soldier was born from the blood of a Dragon?

Was this why the Soldier was awakened 'Under the Yong of the East'?

What did this mean? She was part *Dragon*?

'The Dragon was killed to create the Soldier,' Shadow said. Scarlet watched her as if waiting for her reaction. 'That's what you're saying.'

'Somehow,' Scarlet said. 'It should be impossible – but somehow.'

'It's impossible most of the time,' Shadow said, dread rising over her. 'But not on one day, every thousand years. The only day the Dragons are supposed to rise.'

The flower moon.

The Moonbearer had slaughtered one to create her, she knew it. Then would he slaughter the other one, too? To use its power?

'You can't bring a Dragon back from the dead to regain the world's balance,' Shadow said. All this time she had wondered how the Moonbearer might be killed, how his power might be stoppered. Had dreamed of being the one to do it. All this time, she had never considered – no, she had pushed away – the idea that the two of them were inextricably bound, made of the same stuff. She had scorned the false, dark power he wielded, regarding his skilful and deceitful use of it as monstrous. But if he was a user, she was entirely consumed. She was the darkness incarnate. She could never be separate from it, not even by choice. She was worse than him. In order for the Moonbearer and his power to die . . .

It was like a final wall coming down.

'None of this explains why the Soldier might have killed my sister, I know,' Scarlet said. 'But this isn't actually about that. The Desert Rose, you see, was more than human. None of her worshippers knew her, not really, and even they could see that. She was Nava, a light, through and through. She saw everything so differently from you and me, or anyone else, because she was destined for it. Then she met the Councillor. And I still don't understand how he drew her into his grasp, or why the Soldier took her life. But I understand that the Soldier is her opposite, her antithesis. Alien, an animal. Raised from blood that should never have been spilled, from a Dragon never meant for mortal hands to touch, used to destroy a city that should've reigned true for all of time.'

Scarlet's face had been momentarily erased of its haughty expression and Shadow had admired it for its wide-open vulnerability, its intensity. Now, it shuttered closed, quick as a blade.

Not even in the Moonbearer's death could Shadow be free.

Scarlet continued. 'You said I don't care much for the fate of Ik-Song. You're wrong. Even if I knew the circumstances, the uses, the motives of a death, it wouldn't matter. A Dragon's power is stolen, split into another body. No Asani invasion, no war, will work in restoring any kind of balance. The Soldier *has* to die. That's the only way this country will regain itself.'

Chapter 16

Time passed by in a stupor of dread after that. *Come back tomorrow*, Scarlet had told her, and Shadow was forced to agree, though the prospect of doing this night after night was painful, and now not only because of the secret she had to hide. Because—

The Soldier has to die.

It was worsened tenfold by the Stronghold, which grew startlingly alive as the date neared. She could hardly focus on training; and to make matters worse, Aspis was pushing her more and more, their sessions growing longer and more tiring, until Shadow felt stretched to her limits. Aspis showed no hesitation in taking the shot, beating her down when she was already beat, showing a remarkable lack of mercy.

'It's almost like we're not friends,' Shadow muttered one morning when Aspis kneed down on her back hard enough to bruise.

'You just don't follow through,' Aspis said, 'when I know you can. It's so frustrating. Why?'

'This may be difficult to believe, but I have no desire to hurt you.'

'Is this how you'll fight against Asanai?'

'Of course not,' Shadow replied, miffed.

'Can't you at least pretend like I'm an enemy? Do some real damage? Don't hold back.'

'No,' she said. *You sound like Scarlet,* she wanted to say. But not entirely, because now when she thought of Scarlet for some reason, she kept returning back to her sitting in the library, as still as the dusted tomes around her; looking up to meet Shadow's eyes in that split-second of veiled surprise, the only sort of moment where Shadow might be allowed a glimpse in. It replayed in her head like a dream, like if she were to go down again right now, the same suspended moment would be playing. In contrast, Aspis was like a wall in front of her.

'I've heard the servants' gossip; they think you're an assassin,' Aspis said. 'We're similar in that way. I was only sixteen, commanding the Queen's armies. A prodigy.' Aspis threw a knife to her. Shadow caught it by the handle, gingerly.

Aspis continued: 'But the difference between you and me, is that at least I own up to it. Once a killer, always a killer. At least I don't pretend otherwise.'

'It's not like you enjoyed it either.'

Aspis shrugged. 'Cut me once,' she said, 'or I'll cut you.' And then she came forward.

Their sparring did not diverge much from the usual, if a little more heated, on-edge. Aspis tried to sweep Shadow's legs out from under her, but she dodged nimbly and used the unbalanced momentum from it to pull Aspis forward. Shadow knocked the knife from her tight grip and pinned her against the wall with her own knife to the back of her neck. She considered, briefly, pressing the knife harder, leaving a mark, but cringed against it.

'See? I beat you,' Shadow said, hand dropping immediately.

Aspis turned and took the knife from her loosened grip, reclaiming it. In a matter of seconds, Shadow was the one pinned instead, and she felt the blade at the side of her arm, slicing sideways.

'I said, cut me. You didn't.'

The pain was quick but burning. Shadow didn't have to look to feel the long, red welling.

'Enough,' she snapped, trying to push the other girl off, who did not relent.

'Angry now? Spar me,' Aspis said, something unidentifiable behind her eyes. In that moment, it was like she had been replaced. Like a gulf had opened between them.

Shadow pushed her off again. This time, Aspis let her, and Shadow rolled to the side, and sat up, facing the wall, breathing heavily.

'The Keeper hates me because she hates my position, you know,' Aspis said from behind her. 'Because she doesn't understand the hunt.' A pause. 'But it's not cruel sport, not the way I see it. It's a necessary endeavour for the welfare of the palace. The hunt is as old as humanity itself.'

'We're not animals,' Shadow replied.

'Aren't we?'

After a long moment, there were receding footsteps, and Shadow knew she was gone.

Aspis was absent more and more, leaving Shadow to head down to the Guard posts, wondering where she was in the middle of the day. At least now she knew Scarlet was probably holed up in the library or riding off into the sunset with nervous servants tailing her, but Aspis was a total mystery. One night, when Shadow couldn't sleep, she stood in the hall at dawn watching the courtyard below when the hunting party returned. Aspis was covered up to her elbows in blood.

The Last Soldier of Nava

Why did she return bathed in it? Like something out of a dark fable, transformed? As if by instinct, Aspis began to look up to the palace windows, and Shadow quickly ducked back inside.

Another time, she saw her heading down to the lower levels of the palace with three servants behind her. Shadow had thought the library was the lowest, but apparently not. She almost called after her, but then decided against it, though she wasn't sure why.

That night, she dreamt about the Moonbearer.

The stillness of her room transported her back to a memory: standing barefoot in the dirt in a forest, a real forest, quieted mainly by his presence. The details kept changing. The landscape kept changing. No, she had not been barefoot. She had walked so far off-destination that he had asked her if she wanted to be put to sleep again. Buoyed by the threat, she went in where he commanded. He followed her. Her armour rain-slicked; feet aching. The Moonbearer stood behind her, out of sight, like he always did, and had her stop beside a brush.

From the small track prints lining the ground and the terrain, she was sure it was a fox den. The red fox had shed his summer coat for a dense winter one and favoured edge habitats. His bright yellow eye leapt out from behind the vegetation, and the Soldier knew instantly that this animal was slated for death.

Come back every day, he said, *to this same spot, and feed it.*

The fox was solitary, adult, too small for its age. She returned the next day and threw game in front of its den, a brown hare she had slit at the throat, but it did not come out. She waited hours. Later, she left.

She came again and again. There was only the hint of an

eye, the swishing tail. Eventually, one day, it scampered out, snarled over the prey possessively, and dragged it back to its hiding spot.

Over the weeks, the fox grew somewhat slower in its retrieval. It became lazier and fatter and less wary, until it did not even bother to hide its presence at all and waited for her appearance. He stopped dragging the game back to his den, and instead ate it in front of her, tossing her the occasional growl, but nevertheless unmoving.

It was a small animal, with thin teeth. The Soldier could kill it easily without consequence. It came out and ate in the open every day and even when she sat by the tree across, it did not move. Most of what the Soldier did was walk; walking until the body simply gave out. He was unbothered by her giving out. She looked at the red fox, at its yellow slit-pupilled eyes, and how hungry he was. How he ate without discrimination. How something in his iris resembled the moon, though she could not say why or how.

When the red fox was changed, many days later, the Moonbearer returned with her to the spot and the fox came out like a dog. He lured it himself and then grabbed it by the scruff, lightning fast, animal reflexes. She was not precisely sure what he did to it, too quick to discern; perhaps shocked it, or deadened a leg – but it whimpered and snarled, twisting out of his grip. It limped back underneath the brush, and she watched the orange blur trot away, past the brush, past the fields, far, far, far away into the distance until it disappeared over the horizon, and she knew he would not return. She knew many things, then.

See, he said, *how that thing is ruled by fear. Years and years of work can be undone by a single moment of it. Once you master this – once you give yourself over to it—*

Shadow, pressed a voice into the dark, and Shadow opened

her eyes, and it was still dark, and the Moonbearer was no longer there, and she was in the same forest but strange. Someone was grabbing her arm. Aspis. She took it back. They stood in a deadzone. *Look,* Aspis said, and pointed to a hulking mass on the floor between foliage – the body of a wild boar, dead, sinking into nothing. Lichens grew across its flank, heavy-handed lesions. Aspis wanted to take it back to the palace. *We can't,* Shadow said, *it looks diseased.* It was so close, its eye open, lolling. Its wounds were fresh, but the body years old, the bones solvent.

We always retrieve large game on my hunts, Aspis said, roping the body, *you only need to drag it.* They made their way out, and their entire party was gone. The wind had totally halted. *They're gone,* Shadow said, stilling, but Aspis did not reply. *Aspis?* She turned, but no one was there. Only rope, which trailed limply behind her, tied around nothing at all. She had the distinct feeling of being watched. The air was very, very still.

She woke, twisted in her sheets, drenched in sweat.

Her heart was so fast. She slowly sat up, spine uncurling – it was pitch-black outside; she'd only been asleep a few hours. Breathing until she matched the incessant rhythm of the sea, the cloudy sky, she looked down at her hands: curled them into fists, then released them. *I'm in the Stronghold,* she thought. *In the Stronghold.* That alone brought its own kind of terror, but the physicality grounded her.

Shadow had woken with a sickly feeling of anxiety. That memory was new – it had resurfaced for the first time, before it faded into fiction. Or was it? It was always hard to tell, if what she remembered was real or not. And she was used to nightmares, but this was different. Something was wrong.

It must've been the talisman, she thought. But when she

looked, the stone sat undisturbed beneath her bed – she hadn't even been touching it.

She was slipping out of bed towards the open window when she heard it: this low, keening noise. So, so faint it was hardly there.

Was it human? She wasn't sure. A chill ran down her arms. She stilled, straining to hear, but nothing else came.

She crept to her door. There it was again: shuffling, pained grunts. As if it was coming from within the walls of the palace itself, from somewhere distant.

She *felt* something wrong. The same peculiar feeling of unnatural wrongness that she'd felt in the deadzone, closing in around her. Something that wasn't supposed to be. Like everything around her cried for help – even the cold, inanimate walls, the floors beneath, something further down, deep down.

She slid her door open with a thud, expecting the usual Guards flanked outside her room, but the hall was quiet as she tumbled outside.

And saw Scarlet across the hall. Fully dressed, standing.

'What are you doing?' Scarlet asked, brow arched.

'What is that?' Shadow said, breaths coming harshly.

'What?'

'I can feel something.'

'Feel what?' Scarlet said.

She didn't even know how to explain.

Was Shadow going crazy? Could she no longer discern dream from reality? 'There's something wrong – there's something downstairs, there's pain downstairs, I can feel it,' she muttered. 'Like buried under this place, it's strong, it feels like the deadzone did.' She was not sure what she was saying. Scarlet would think she was absolutely, completely delusional.

Silence.

The Last Soldier of Nava

She studied her own hands, as if the whorls of them might start moving.

'Can't you feel it too?' Shadow said.

'... Shadow?' came the tentative voice.

Shadow looked up. Scarlet was very close, having closed the distance between them soundlessly. Their faces were illuminated only by weak moonlight, and Shadow suddenly became aware that she was barefoot in the hall, mussed by sleep and sweat. She felt horribly vulnerable all of a sudden, like an exposed nerve.

Scarlet looked the closest she had ever been to being alarmed. She stared at Shadow as if trying to parse out a puzzle.

'That's the first time you've called me my name,' Shadow said. She felt light-headed, confused. Like things were turning upside-down. Her palms were bare and still.

'Why are you looking at your hands like that?' Scarlet asked. She took one of her palms and drew it closer to her face, as if searching for something.

Shadow swallowed. She was so close to touching Scarlet's face that it felt like static hovered between them. In a brief, single instant, she realized she had the perfect proximity to send her power coursing through her open palm, to mar the Keeper eternally with darkness, flay open the tender skin of her cheek and her neck. She had the proximity to kill, but no desire to.

It was what the Soldier would do.

Scarlet's eyes were dark and soupy, and as if realizing the same thing instantly, she dropped Shadow's hand and moved back a step. She looked slightly unnerved, as if trying to piece Shadow together.

'Why are you dressed?' Shadow then asked, as if she hadn't just stumbled outside in the middle of the night rambling nonsense.

167

'I've been summoned,' Scarlet replied, 'for some urgent matters.'

Down the hall, one of the other doors slid open. They jumped apart. They both turned to see Yo-han round the corner, flanked by only Crow, looking harried. They glanced over in surprise.

'Actually, I guess we've all been summoned,' Scarlet said.

'What's going on? Do you know what's happening?' Yo-han asked, casting glances down the hall. Scarlet shrugged. There were noises of quick door rappings, shuffling, other figures emerging from their rooms. Something was busying the palace.

'I thought *you* called a meeting,' Crow said to Scarlet, almost accusingly.

'Why would *I* call a meeting in the middle of the night?' Scarlet said.

Immediately, Shadow thought that the Stronghold was under attack. But there were no Guards suiting up, no sounds of struggle throughout the palace.

They stared at one another in confusion.

A courier flitted down their hall, clearly striding towards a destination. Scarlet stopped him with a flick of her hand.

'You,' she said. He stopped, albeit reluctantly. 'What's going on?'

'Your presence has been requested in the courtroom by the Court,' he said shortly. 'The Soldier has been sighted in Ik-Song.'

Chapter 17

'Remove her at once,' was the greeting Shadow received upon arrival in the courtroom. Heads turned, brows raised at their entry. White Crane's face was hard, voice leaving no room for argument.

Everyone was present. Every single Advisor's seat – including the one usually left reserved for the High Diplomat, who was often abroad – was filled; every Guard and general; courtiers and even servants came to witness. Shadow caught Aspis's gaze, trying to glean clues – but the other girl appeared just as perplexed. Outside, thunder rumbled intermittently, but no rain fell yet.

The courtroom held no thrones. This was the Advisors' field. They looked down from their elevated half-circle seating, so that anyone who wished to speak to them would have to step down to the area and look up. Scarlet moved towards them now, one hand on her hip, face turned upwards. Her posture gave the impression of laxness, but Shadow knew it was a façade. Despite Crane's order, no one moved to escort Shadow out.

'She stays,' the Keeper said. 'Even the servants are privy.'

The pulsing anger, the tenseness, the *power* radiating from her was so potent that Shadow looked around, wondering how no one noticed. Or acknowledged it.

But perhaps they did, because for once, White Crane didn't argue.

The Soldier has been sighted in Ik-Song.

Would this be the exposure of her identity? The Moonbearer's idea of a joke?

No one spoke. The anticipation was palpable.

'My patience is tested,' the Keeper announced to the Court, inflectionless. 'My nerves are frail. If I'm not told the news immediately, I'm afraid I might become too excitable and burn a hole through one or two of you by accident.'

'Unbelievable,' Advisor Ji-hu said. 'Resorting to threats of death.'

'Enough,' White Crane boomed, standing. He gestured to a courier at the side, who in turn looked at two Guards standing near the east door. 'You have all been summoned because of a witness. A witness that has claimed to have been attacked by the Soldier in Ik-Song.'

The room collapsed into chaos, fervent murmurs. *A witness?* Shadow stood with her fists clenched. What kind of game was the Moonbearer playing at?

She peered towards the entry where the Guards had left – they returned a moment later, this time with a girl between them.

This girl was young – surely not older than Shadow herself – and skinny, angular. Her dark hair was tied back loosely at her neck. Her uniform was dirtied and scratched, but still recognizable: a Queensguard. Her face, in the same state of disarray. Between the walls of the Stronghold, she looked as small as a rabbit in a wide field.

Her gaze darted around, frightened by the intense attention

of an entire room on her. But when White Crane gestured for her to speak, she set a hard stare at her audience, steeling herself.

'My name is Yong,' she said tinnily. Her voice was quiet, but it didn't matter – everyone was completely silent. 'I am a footsoldier in the Queen's army.' She looked briefly at the courier, as if asking permission to continue. 'Four nights ago, I witnessed the Soldier attack in Ik-Song.'

Again, gasps throughout the room.

'How can you be sure it was the Soldier?' Aspis asked. 'Even vicious leopard or bear encounters can look like abnormal work.'

'*No* leopard, nor bear, could have done this.' Yong's tone was so certain that no one refuted her.

She was truly scared, Shadow thought. Or at least an excellent performer.

Yong spoke again, everyone rapt. 'We were on routine mission fifteen *li* east of Pangso, along the southern deadzone.' Near Pangso would be barren coastal land, sand dunes battered by strong winds and acerbic salt spray from the sea. Little grew and lived there except low-lying shrubbery and the occasional nomad. Why would the Queensguard be there?

'Why does the Queen send footsoldiers anywhere near the deadzone?' Scarlet interrupted immediately, mirroring her own thoughts. 'In such barren lands?'

Yong looked taken aback, unsure whether to directly address Scarlet. 'On a – a routine overnight patrol, your Highness.' The wrong title, but nobody bothered to correct her.

'*Patrol?* There's no strategic benefit to that,' Scarlet retorted.

'Quit interrupting,' White Crane snapped. 'We all know the Queen is paranoid in her control for power and scours what little land she can to claim obsessively. It isn't relevant.'

Yong looked like she couldn't decide if she was more

shocked by his blatant insult of the Queen, or by Scarlet's brashness. In the end, she decided to power through the rest of her story.

'We had set up camp a mile from the sea. We lit a fire, to keep warm. I think – it was attracted to our fire. Like a moth.' Her eyes shut briefly as she swallowed. 'It came from nowhere. The Soldier. We were covered in darkness, suddenly – everyone thought they'd gone blind.'

'And then?' White Crane pressed.

'And then the Soldier wreaked havoc on our camp. It killed ruthlessly. Seven out of eight of us – dead.'

'Any remades?'

'Three of us were.'

'And why were you spared?' Scarlet said.

'We scattered in different directions. I didn't make it far, but I fell into a hidden ditch by accident, covered by leaves. I stayed hidden until dawn, just to be sure. I made it back to our central base in Pangso, and then rode to the Queen's Palace.'

Hours of riding, desperate, panicked, the only survivor. Nightfall like a terrifying beast nipping at her heels. She must have been scared out of her mind.

'Did the Queen send more men to the site?' Scarlet asked.

'The bodies . . . what was left of them . . . were transported back to the Palace.'

'Let me see them,' Scarlet said to the Court. No one looked particularly surprised by this request.

'You can't,' Yong said. 'They have the festering shadow wounds, rotting from the inside. The ones I saw were already almost entirely decomposed, and that was a full day ago.' Fear trickled through the silent room. A few covert glances at Shadow.

Shadow wounds? There was no such thing. This girl was lying – or had been commanded to lie.

The Last Soldier of Nava

'Then to summarize,' Scarlet said, 'you were attacked by something you didn't see, escaped with no true witnesses, and possess no bodies as evidence.'

'There's no other evidence one might need,' White Crane said. 'The Soldier runs loose in the south. We up north will not allow anyone else to fall victim to this madness.'

'It's been a day. The Soldier could be lurking right outside the palace, for all you know.' Scarlet exaggerated, but the fear in the room was palpable.

He shook his head. 'The order to reinforce the north-south border was given three days ago, along with fortification of every port. If the Soldier passes, we'll know immediately. Even Yosae has been blocked off.'

'You knew already,' Scarlet said incredulously. 'You've known for *days*?'

Yosae had been cut off all this time. It was difficult to envision: ships halted mid-journey, visitors turned away, Guards moving into the city. And there had been no sign, no hints at all. They'd been completely oblivious to the turmoil outside.

'We received a note earlier. It pays well to be prepared,' he replied, saccharine.

She stepped back, took in all their faces. 'So, this is what you've all been doing – weaselling around the palace, going off to *business* in Yosae.' She whirled on the Prince. 'You knew, too?'

The guilt was written over his face. 'I . . . had my suspicions.'

'Relay to the Queen that I want an audience with her at her palace,' Scarlet said. 'So that I can see the evidence with my own two eyes, and hunt down the Soldier myself.'

'Absolutely not,' Ji-hu said. 'No stable hand nor carriage will permit travel from the Stronghold at the moment. This is the time to exercise caution.'

'Nothing will take off from palace grounds – not even a river canoe,' White Crane added.

'And our neighbours?' Scarlet asked.

'Shizing is in no immediate danger, unless the Soldier can scale an entire ocean before word comes through,' Aspis replied. This was said matter-of-factly, but the crowd shifted nervously – how they doubted her. How they quickly considered if such a feat was possible.

'You are too valuable to throw out to the grounds like a hound to the woods, in search of an enemy that will surely kill you,' White Crane said.

'I have many questions,' Scarlet said. 'Beginning with why the Queen sends men to scout the deadzones.'

'We don't know – but does it matter? Our priority is to guard our Stronghold, and Ik-Song. Millions of lives are at stake. We'll be closing Ik-Song and setting up an emergency state.'

The Moonbearer was shutting down the entire nation. He didn't want any interference in the coming days and weeks.

'Your solution,' Scarlet continued, voice ringing clearly throughout the room, 'is to block off Ik-Song indefinitely and forever until the Soldier is killed, which she will never be, because she's a force that none of you can understand or defeat. How long will we be terrorized by a *single* killer? How long will you people sit cowardly in your seats while an enemy is right in our hands?'

'Keeper,' Aspis said, head held high, boldly cutting through. 'This won't be solved by shipping off more Guards and bringing the fight to the Soldier. We don't know what the Soldier wants. It will be like sending lambs to the slaughter.'

'If it were up to me, Aspis,' said Scarlet, 'I would throw you into a deadzone, naked and alone, as bait for the Soldier.'

Deathly silence. Yong was open-mouthed.

The Last Soldier of Nava

'Scarlet,' Shadow said despite herself, aghast at the threat. She immediately regretted it when that gaze – and a dozen others – turned on her, but she didn't back down. Aspis trained day and night for Ik-Song, and this was how Scarlet repaid her?

'Look at your prisoner,' Ji-hu said, bemused. 'Even she warns you of your pitfalls.'

'You go too far, Keeper,' White Crane bellowed. 'Threatening the Master of the Hunt. You require discipline. Nothing between the tongue and the hands.'

'If I require discipline, let me have an audience with the Councillor,' she replied. 'He hasn't been present in months. How can a leader who doesn't show his face be the ruler of a nation?' No one openly objected to that; it was true. 'What does *he* say about the matter?'

The Advisors exchanged glances among themselves. Scarlet glared accusingly at Yo-han, who seemed to shrink in on himself.

This wasn't some emergency midnight meeting about the Soldier, then. The Advisors had already received news, debated, figured it out amongst themselves. This was to accommodate the arrival of the witness, and more importantly, to catch Scarlet unawares; to dangle the prospect tantalizingly before her face before ripping it away. To provoke.

Scarlet must know this. But it was working anyway.

'The Moonbearer decrees this, with the counsel of the Court,' White Crane started, with relish, and his voice was like a gavel coming down. 'Should you, Royal Keeper of the Gates, disobey our orders to remain in the palace, you will be stripped of your title and cast out of the Stronghold. Permanently.'

Shock rippled through the room.

Clearly, no consequence so strict had ever been imposed on the Keeper, and the satisfaction of the Advisors was palpable. Many looked smug; how long had they spent waiting for a moment like this, a slap on the wrist? Broiling over her insults and the leeway she was given? It curdled her own blood, the petty lot of them.

Scarlet's face was white-hot, her voice carefully controlled. 'I,' she said, 'came *here*, to the Stronghold, for this purpose. You know this.'

'That is not why,' White Crane countered, 'you are really here.'

Scarlet stared at him for a long moment. And then turned on her heel, storming out.

Shadow followed, skittering after her down the hall, as the courtroom devolved once again into chaos behind her and the Advisors tried to shout order over the din. No Guards followed.

Shadow called after Scarlet, watching her figure receding.

Scarlet did not wait. So Shadow ran forward until she was beside her. The outburst from Scarlet, when it came, was not unexpected.

'What are you so *persistent* for?'

'Don't go chasing after the Soldier. It's not worth exile.'

Scarlet whirled on her. 'And what do you care?'

You just can't, she thought. Something in her told her to resist, to fight against this. Shadow opened her mouth: she had a million logical things to say instead, starting with the gentle suggestion that this witness was a hoax, that all of Ik-Song could not be searched by one person, that this would throw the Stronghold into even further disarray when they were preparing for war. But all of it died on her tongue. Up close, Scarlet looked worse for wear, violent crescents smudging her under eyes, the kind of raggedness that couldn't be blurred out by make-up or an elaborate hairstyle, of which she sported neither.

'What happened?' Shadow found herself saying instead.

'What's wrong with you? You look as if you haven't slept in days.'

Scarlet reeled back, as if struck.

'You're not like the others,' she said, looking as dishevelled as Shadow had ever seen her. 'You're worse.'

'What? What are you talking about?'

Scarlet's face darkened. 'Just tell me what he promised you.'

'What are you talking about?'

Scarlet did not answer, only breathing harshly. And then her features schooled into that characteristic cold sneer. Shadow's heart sank watching it – the backslide of every moment of hard-won honesty between them.

Scarlet took a step forward, forcing Shadow to step back towards the wall. 'And what if I say I'll leave the palace? What are you going to do? Stop me? What? Will you *fight* me? Beat me in duel?'

'I don't want to fight.' Even as she said it, she knew it was partly a lie.

'I know. You never do. You're always holding back. Even when I threw you in against Crow, you wouldn't hold your own.'

'That's not fair,' she snapped. She didn't want to fight just anyone.

But Scarlet was different. Scarlet deserved it, and she could take it.

'Isn't it?' Scarlet looked bored, then. 'I may be under the thumb of idiots like Crane. But when it comes down to it, I could easily take him in duel. I can fight. Can you?'

'I'm not – would you please shut up, for once? I'm trying to help you.' *The Moonbearer is lying. The Soldier is not out there.*

'Why would you possibly want to help me?' Scarlet asked.

She had no answer to that.

'If you want to help me, then prove you're not pathetic and spineless. Prove that you can fight. Fight me. When will you bare your fangs?'

What was *wrong* with her? 'I'm not *fighting* you. I told you,' Shadow said through gritted teeth. 'I'm not—'

Scarlet threw the first hit.

Shadow barely – just barely – caught her fist a hair's breadth from the side of her face, feeling the force of it ripple through her arm, shocked.

That blow had been no bluff. It took most of her strength to hold back.

Scarlet smirked. 'That's more like it.'

And for the first time, real anger licked up Shadow's spine. Over and over again, everyone in the Stronghold had pushed her carelessly. She remembered dropping her knife from the back of Aspis's neck and regret pulsed through her. If they wanted her to strike out so badly, she would.

Scarlet drew her first back and looked at her. 'Hit me. Or I'll hit you again.'

So, she did. Shadow's blow snapped Scarlet's face to the side, and Scarlet – Scarlet looked delighted. It felt *good*, which made Shadow feel awful, which made her angrier. She had not fought in so long. They traded blows by hand only, a messy affair of jabs and elbows, with Shadow pulling back to make the other girl overextend.

Scarlet could fight. But not only could she fight, she was also inhumanly strong. And unlike Shadow, she was not reluctant. Shadow felt that split-second gap of air, weightless, before Scarlet slammed her back into the wall, one hand around her throat with her thumb pressing into the jugular. That grip was like a ring of steel enforced around the soft tendons of her neck, choking her out. That grip could break a stone in half.

The Last Soldier of Nava

So, Shadow reached up with one hand, clasped Scarlet's wrist, and sent a hard, strong lancing of darkness up her arm, a shockwave – flickering up, forcing the muscles to convulse.

Immediately Scarlet let go as if burned, cradling her wrist. Shadow took in air gratefully.

Shadow hadn't wanted to use her ability. But now that she had, it felt satisfying. Something to relish. What she imagined it was like for Scarlet, every single time.

Still so close to her, Scarlet examined her wrist absently, as if in a trance. She looked up. A bruise was already forming high on her left cheekbone, from where Shadow had hit her.

'It's cold,' she said, not with hostility – with something akin to wonder. 'Your power . . . it feels icy cold. It's the opposite of mine.'

Shadow didn't know that, having never been on the receiving end.

Scarlet continued: 'It feels exactly like what I felt that night. When I touched her body, the darkness in it – a sudden burst of cold, so cold it nearly ran hot.'

Shadow stilled.

'I think you know where the Soldier really is.' Scarlet's dark eyes were pools in the dim hall, so dark she could see her own reflection in them. 'I can see it in your face, every time I mention it. Hiding, helping her, perhaps.' A pause. 'I understand. It's your own kin.'

On the Moon Rabbit, what was Shadow supposed to say to that? 'I don't know where she is,' she said carefully. 'But I can tell you that she's not in the south, in Pangso.'

'Of course she's not there,' Scarlet said. 'She was never there.'

She was never there. And then, slowly, pieces were clicking into place in Shadow's mind.

'When you said *tell me what he promised you,* just now,'

she said. 'You're talking about the Moonbearer. You think the Moonbearer is using me against you. Is that it?'

Scarlet's eyes bored into her.

She could almost laugh. 'But you – you're his *pawn*. His right-hand. You chafe at his rules the way a child does. Because your loyalty would keep you both bound anyway.' That was what she had believed this whole time – wasn't it?

'He's a liar,' Scarlet said. 'But it seems you already know that.'

'That witness . . .'

'Is a farce. Yong, if that's even her real name, never saw the Soldier.'

Scarlet's anger in the courtroom had been so real. And yet, where was it really directed? The Keeper hidden away during the days, her animosity. Here was a girl with a façade so ridiculous one had no choice but to believe it.

'You're so alone in this vast palace,' Shadow said. 'But is that by choice?'

This close, Shadow could see the curve of Scarlet's neck into her collar, how it rose and fell with effort. It was so absurd that Shadow could trust her so suddenly after all she'd said and done. And yet – something in her gut said yes. Her mind rebelled, as it always did, but her instinct never lied. Her body never lied.

'What is he planning?' Shadow whispered. *Where is he?*

Scarlet looked at the courtroom then back towards her. 'You know the flower moon is an important date.'

'I know the Dragon rises then.'

'But that's not all. We're not preparing for an Asani attack. Ik-Song is preparing to invade Asanai.'

An invasion? Then the Moonbearer wanted to slaughter a Dragon, and use its power to invade Asanai?

The Last Soldier of Nava

'This all started with Asanai, with the White Ice,' Scarlet said. 'Everyone in the Inner knows.'

Ten years ago, a full-scale Asani invasion beaten back, the Moonbearer hailed as the saviour of Ik-Song, rewarded with a palace and army. It was indeed where everything had started; at least, in this era. 'The Moonbearer orchestrated it, didn't he?' Shadow said. It was the only possibility.

There was commotion from the courtroom, which silenced her.

'In a few days' time, you'll accompany me to Yosae,' Scarlet said.

It hit her – Yosae would be a chance to be away from prying ears, a chance to investigate.

'They're shutting Ik-Song down for war,' Shadow said, 'And you're not even allowed to leave the palace. You'll be exiled. How could you possibly—'

'They'll have to keep an eye on the capital after the storm, anyway. Yo-han can talk the Court down, he'll protect me. The Court care more about appearances than anything,' Scarlet said. 'Chastising me in front of an audience. Without it, they won't care.'

'But even if you know the truth about the White Ice, what good would it do against him? We need proof.'

'I think there's a way to get it.'

The courtroom grew louder behind them, giving Scarlet no chance to elaborate. 'And Aspis,' Scarlet said suddenly. 'If she invites you to accompany her on a hunt,' she said, 'I forbid you to accept the invitation.'

The courtroom was adjourned. Crow, turning the corner to them, was caught deftly by the arm as Scarlet forced him to stop walking. He looked up at them both in confusion and irritation.

'Who are they sending to scout the Soldier?' she asked, point-blank. 'Is it you?'

'You heard them. No one's allowed to leave the palace.'

'Crow,' Scarlet said forcefully. 'Really?'

He paused, exhaled. Looked pointedly at Shadow, who was probably not supposed to be privy to the information. 'They're not sending me. I'm needed in the palace in the coming weeks. One of the Councillor's personals is leading a party of fifteen.' He named a Guard who Shadow didn't recognize; Scarlet's eyes narrowed. 'The final picks haven't been determined yet.'

'Why even bother sending men?'

He said nothing.

Scarlet released his arm. A crackling sounded through the palace, lightning streaking the windows. Outside, the sky billowed and broke.

'Monsoon,' Scarlet muttered. 'Rains are starting.'

Chapter 18

The rains picked up into heavy-handed winds, and then into a full-blown storm that raged on for days.

It was like a beast of its own: constantly drumming at the windows, lashing out at trees around the palace, accompanying Shadow even in dreams and up to her waking in a steady rumble. It almost seemed inevitable that the Stronghold would crumble and fall under its incessant roar, but it stood. Even the twin willow trees received it with hardiness, delicate-looking as they were.

Shadow didn't know who to trust. She kept thinking of the confrontation with Scarlet. What was she leading her to in Yosae? What proof? What if it was some kind of trap?

But Scarlet had never lied to her, for all her twisted ways. She had prodded and belittled and caught her unprepared, sure, but she had never lied. The only thing she lied about was her allegiance to the Moonbearer, out of necessity: because there was no allegiance. Scarlet was not a weapon honed by him. She was trapped here. The only way she could resist him, for the time being, was to let herself be used by him. The only living proof of his once greatest enemy, the Dawnbringer, in his possession, bent again to his will.

In some ways, they were very similar.

Shadow tried not to dwell too much on all of it. There was nothing to be done right now. And guilt stabbed her when she thought of Yosae: how already the weakest houses would be trembling and collapsing, lower floors flooding. Even the Stronghold hadn't been able to keep out all the water on the lowest level. Perhaps if the rain inched its way up the Stronghold's upper levels, the Court might finally consider paying attention to the deadly weather.

In the front palace courtyard, soaked by early evening light, Scarlet quickly oversaw the harnessing of two bound deer with a nervous-looking stable hand while Shadow looked on with impatience.

There was a palpable tension in the air, like they were about to do something impossible. Scarlet was no stranger to disobeying rules – after all, it was the only reason she'd caught Shadow in Yosae. But this time seemed different. Yo-han would talk the Court down, Scarlet had said, but 'talking down' didn't seem promising. It seemed like skirting on the edges of complete and total disaster.

They had nearly finished when the rippling, ear-splitting cry of a bugle horn roared through the air. A distant rumbling, and that was when she saw it: a party coming east over the horizon, a myriad of speeding limbs and excited battle cries.

Scarlet momentarily stilled in her handiwork, which, for her, Shadow thought, was the equivalent of collapsing into hysterics.

'What is that?' Shadow asked urgently. They were too exposed to go unnoticed.

'Get on,' was all Scarlet said. Shadow obeyed, the stable hand stepped back, and they took off.

Scarlet didn't elaborate further; she didn't need to. Shadow caught the bright red flash of a familiar hair ribbon only a few moments later – Aspis. It was nearing dusk, and it was the night hunting party. Of course.

'Keep your head down,' Scarlet hissed beside her, but Shadow couldn't. She stared at the whopping, raucous party, streaming their way across the fields, Aspis leading.

Across the fields, in a single, slow moment, they saw each other. Or rather, Aspis noticed her in return, unable to hide her surprise. Shadow was unsure why the moment rankled so – why she herself felt naked, like she had been caught exposed, untethered. Why there was something peculiar and unfamiliar about the hunters under the bright light, gear gleaming, game slung over the backs of their deer, as strange as the flatness of the deadzones. She wanted to steer her own buck away, to cross over the field to Aspis and tell her it was not what it looked like. At the same time, she didn't want to go near the hunters at all. She wanted to cleave far, far away. Aspis suddenly had a different shade to her, slightly changed, and it bewildered her.

But the moment passed silently, and they continued forward uneventfully, Shadow tearing her gaze away.

She had ridden into the Stronghold a prisoner. She wasn't sure if she was riding out as one, too.

Yosae was a ghost city.

Like the aftermath of a war or pillaging, the storm had swept through and drained it of its brightness, leaving behind a husk of a town. The once lively market stalls stilled to a stop, streets once packed with busy commuters deserted. Roofs were caved in, strewn with debris and fallen trees, slowly draining flood baths of murky water forcing several changes to their route. Faces peeked out from covered windows and birds flocked out, lamenting their fallen homes. There were still people out and about but diminished to about a quarter of a normal market weekend.

'It's gutted,' Shadow commented.

'The monsoon has taken a toll,' was all Scarlet said.

They bought headscarves from a nearby market stand. The old woman manning it eyed their outfits and held a hand out. 'One silver coin.'

'For two scarves?' Scarlet said dryly, handing over the money anyway. They tied them over their faces, and ducked into an alleyway, appearing out the other side onto a main road.

They made their way down a series of increasingly convoluted turns, both of them trying to work off the vague directions Scarlet had gleaned from one of the servants – 'Southeast corner, near a three-legged crow statue' – never mind that there were crow statues all over Ik-Song. Shadow'd never been to this part of Yosae, the famed central district, Yeok-gu: street vendors laid out stewed pork feet skewered on sticks and hot rice cakes simmered in questionable water. Young ladies and boys Shadow was sure were prostitutes hung outside dimly lit houses, faces painted, fingers of smoke curling out. The streets were so narrow that she constantly had to avoid bumping into walls, other people, or large puddles, remnants of the recent flooding. Scarlet suffered no such frenzy, moving through with a fluidity that Shadow envied.

Once they had moved from the busier areas, Scarlet turned around fully as they banked a sharp corner, walking backwards. 'Rumour has it,' she said lowly, 'that an old Bone Warrior has been hanging around one of the opium dens here.'

'A *Bone Warrior*?' Shadow's jaw dropped. Bone Warriors

never left the wintery peaks of Asanai, bound as they were to the Emperor for eternity. They could hardly survive in this heat-addled climate. For one to be here – not just anywhere, but Yosae, the crowded capital . . . 'What is a Bone Warrior doing here? He'll waste away in the heat.'

'My thoughts exactly.'

'If he's been here awhile, he'll already be weakened. Weak enough for us to take on if he tries to attack us,' Shadow said. Bone Warriors lived long lives, meaning if he was full-grown . . . 'He would've definitely fought during the White Ice, right?'

'I'm counting on it,' Scarlet said.

'What do you want from him, then? A confession? No – don't tell me . . .' Shadow looked at her incredulously.

'No one would believe us with just a secondhand confession,' Scarlet said, 'I want to bring him back to the Stronghold. We can knock him out if need be.'

A dangerous, half-baked plan with a thousand things that could go wrong. An Asani Bone Warrior testifying within the walls of the Stronghold? White Crane would keel over from a heart attack before anything was even said.

And yet – the plan was shocking. It was spectacle. It would rouse the palace. If this Bone Warrior was currently weak enough, he wouldn't pose a real threat to anyone in the Stronghold.

And finally, *finally*, there would be something against the Moonbearer.

'I'm on board,' Shadow said.

'I assumed you would be.'

'What's the plan? Or do you even have one?'

'I could play nice, and you can stand back looking menacing. If he keeps resisting, we can show off your power. If he resists after that, we can knock him out together.'

'*You?* Play nice?' Shadow scoffed. 'This isn't going to work.'
'Do you have a better idea?'
Shadow did not, but didn't want to admit this, and so stayed silent.

'We're here,' Scarlet said as they paused at a nondescript door. A set of sharp eyes glanced out from behind the slot.

And then it opened. Shadow was assaulted by smell: the thick, unyielding mixed stench filled her nose, nearly choking her. She could hardly see through the smoke. Peeling, dirtied walls were loosely covered up by tapestries and men sat huddled around low tables, lying on the floors, sprawled out in corners, nursing long pipes on plush recliners. Young boys sprinted around collecting coin.

The space was larger than expected: there were several floors. One man beneath them lifted the towel from his eyes, took in their faces, clearly recognized Scarlet, likely deduced that he was hallucinating, and dropped it back down.

Shadow kept close. 'I'm uncomfortable,' she muttered.

They surveyed the first floor, but there was no Bone Warrior in sight. 'You are surprisingly prudish,' Scarlet said.

'Prudish? About what?'

'Pleasures. Debauchery. Et cetera. We'll check the downstairs.' They began to descend.

'I'm not prudish. I know what those things are,' she replied defensively.

'According to Gentian fable, the great warrior Pyeong-an slaughtered ten thousand men in her lifetime and never lay with one.'

Shadow was spared from answering as they breached the lowest level.

The Bone Warrior was unmistakably here.

Less a man than a beast – a huge pole-like figure, folded up in the corner, a good three heads taller than anyone in the

The Last Soldier of Nava

entire den. Long, white skeleton-like limbs, part exposed bone, taut as if skin was stretched tightly over him, wearing the cracked skull of a bird, hiding his face. The skull's beak jutted out, catching much of the smoke he released from his pipe.

But he was nothing like the Bone Warriors depicted in battle. He was wasting away, his robes hanging loosely on him, tendons showing. In the dim light of the den, with his eyes closed and a pipe dangling from his mouth, splayed out, he was an old man.

'No one even cares about his presence,' Shadow said in disbelief. The other customers were similarly lost in their own oblivions.

'Why would they?' Scarlet said. 'He's not exactly in fighting shape.'

How much opium would an enormous man like that need to set his mind alight. How much coin? When they approached, his eyes remained closed, unalert. Shadow had never imagined that her first encounter with a Bone Warrior would be like this. Scarlet stomped her boot unceremoniously beside his thigh. 'Wake up.'

He woke with a start. Through the skull, it took a second for his eyes to focus out of their glaze, and then he sent them a repulsed look.

'I didn't ask for girls,' he said in grating, accented Ik-Songan. 'You people are too small for me.'

'We're not prostitutes,' Scarlet said without preamble. 'We're here to ask you some questions.'

'No, I won't keep growing.' His eyes closed. 'No, I don't eat bones . . .'

'An Asani in Ik-Song is a rare sighting. I'm sure you're aware that an Asani-Songan war is on the rise.'

One eye cracked open. 'Who are you girls? Villagers? You think I will betray my state, because I am here?'

'Betray your state?' Scarlet laughed then, sharply. 'It looks to me like your state's already betrayed *you*. You're rotting in a backwater den two thousand *li* from home. You aren't fit for these temperatures; you'll start to waste away.' Her eyes flickered down at his frail body. 'Oh wait.'

I could play nice? Shadow wondered if this was genuinely Scarlet's best attempt. The Bone Warrior's eyes were fully open now, trying to peer under their hoods. Shadow ducked further under hers. *Look menacing,* she told herself, but just ended up glaring into the ground.

He muttered a string of words in Asani. 'I chose to come here, stupid girl.'

Scarlet said something back in Asani. The old man's eyes widened; the sickly ammonia scent of opium was clouding Shadow's mind. Their questioning was not off to a good start. Trust Scarlet to antagonize their source of information.

'Crazy girl,' the Bone Warrior sniped.

'I'm wondering about the White Ice and about the Moonbearer.'

At the mention of his name, the Bone Warrior sat up straighter. 'The Moonbearer is a two-headed snake,' he spat.

'I doubt you've been in Ik-Song for the last decade. You only just came, meaning you must have fought in the White Ice.'

He neither confirmed nor denied this.

Scarlet pressed. 'Ten years ago, it made perfect strategic sense for Asanai to invade: the new Bloodbird Emperor ablaze in glory, while Ik-Song barely had the cooperation to muster firearms to stop an invasion, much less counter. But the Moonbearer emerges with his own army, blessed by power that Ik-Song had never seen before. Then he's hailed as a saviour, rewarded a cushy palace, and comes to rule Ik-Song in every sense of the word; you know the rest.'

The Last Soldier of Nava

The Bone Warrior was silent.

'But that's not the real story,' Scarlet continued, voice low. 'Asanai never actually launched a full-scale invasion. Your country sent *skeleton* troops, barely any men at all. And you didn't even send them to Yosae. You sent no men to the *capital*, the openly exposed sitting duck that is this city, right on the coast, the obvious starting ground for a conqueror expecting little pushback. None of this is noted in our official Record Annals. But it's true. All the villagers north to east, at every major port, can tell you it's true. Firsthand witnesses to Bone Warriors and Asani soldiers, who, yes, pushed some air around, speared a few feisty aggressors, sure, but mostly – mostly, they sat around waiting. Waiting for what? Reinforcements? Why would a painless endeavour like this be tried in waves? Why not send enough at the start?' She bent down, close to his face. 'Any oddities are written off as Asani arrogance. But you and I both know that such carelessness is not very typical of Asanai.'

Shadow watched him, expecting him to vehemently deny everything, dismiss the two of them. But he didn't. Maybe he didn't care enough to. In that case, maybe they wouldn't have to resort to violence at all – maybe he would come willingly.

Scarlet pulled back. 'The White Ice was not an entirely Asani endeavour. There was another party involved. Someone who stood to gain power.'

The Moonbearer would've promised the Emperor that his Guards would take the full brunt of the invasion, only needing a supplement of Asani. This way, the Emperor would suffer almost no casualties at all, lose basically nothing. They split the rewards fairly.

The Emperor, Shadow thought, should've known better than to trust such a deal.

She remembered the mural in Yo-han's room, the sweeping

scene of victory. He had recounted it so brilliantly, confidently. He had no idea.

After a long moment, the Bone Warrior began to laugh, slow, long, dragging, tapering off as the pipe went back in his mouth. 'Clever. I know what you want me to say,' he said. 'But the White Ice was long ago now, and it hardly matters anymore.'

'If it hardly matters, why won't you say?'

He shrugged. 'I will not bolster your nation, even to turn the tide against a man who betrayed my own. And like you said, war approaches again. Where this time, Asanai will not see defeat.' He smiled. 'Asanai possesses a new weapon. The likes of which the world has never seen before. And Ik-Song will fall under it, like *gonggi* stones.'

'A weapon?' Scarlet echoed Shadow's exact thoughts. 'What are you talking about, a new weapon?'

His gaze had slid to Shadow. 'Who is your companion? I want to see her under there.'

Shadow's cue. She lengthened and shortened the shadows around his feet momentarily – too quick for anyone else in the den to catch, but enough for him to see. His eyes tracked the ground. And then fixed on Shadow. *Look menacing, look menacing.*

'I'm from the Stronghold,' Scarlet said. 'I've access to great wealth, connections, power. I'm trying to negotiate with you, warrior. I can give you anything you'd like. I can ship you back to Asanai, the Isles, Javvi, even; wherever you'd like.'

A beat.

'Alternatively,' Scarlet continued, 'my companion can just snap your neck.'

'Ah,' he said, leaning back. 'And what you want is . . .?'

'I want you to come to the Stronghold with me and publicly testify against the Moonbearer. Say that he *planned* the White Ice and then betrayed Asanai, to take Ik-Song himself. You'll

The Last Soldier of Nava

be protected so long as I don't leave your side, which I won't. Much of the Court will fight the accusation, but many will listen, and word will spread. The citizens of Ik-Song will listen; I know they will. And,' Scarlet finished, 'I want to know about this *new weapon* you speak of.'

But the Bone Warrior only laughed again – and this time, he didn't stop. Shadow wondered what his face looked like under all that thick bone – if it was deformed, different, or perfectly human.

'Look at the gall of these demands,' he said, addressing Scarlet, but looking at Shadow. 'You do not know anything about anything, girl.'

'Don't look at her,' Scarlet snapped. 'Look at me.'

'You're right, see. Asanai struck a deal.'

'With the Moonbearer.'

'Yes,' he said, 'but also, someone else was there. Someone rather important.'

'Another party? Another state?'

'No, only one person.' He glanced at Shadow. 'A single . . . lone . . . Soldier.'

Shadow's stomach dropped to the floor.

She had been so busy watching Scarlet that she hadn't paid much attention to the ex-Warrior studying her, taking in her face, the uniform.

How could he *possibly* know her identity? She had never been to Asanai.

Right?

Something nagged at her in her head.

Scarlet reared back, frustrated, distracted. 'What?' she said. 'What are you talking about?'

'I was one of the Emperor's best,' he said. 'I was there the day he closed the deal with the Moonbearer and the Soldier. Beside the great, leaping fire of the Imperial Palace.'

Ten years ago. The White Ice. *I've never been to the Imperial Palace,* she wanted to say, ridiculously. But how would she know where she'd been or where she hadn't? Her memory was a collection of fragments, of dreams, of bodies without faces. She was helpless to them.

She stepped back. He was going to reveal her identity: right here, right now. With such unadulterated confidence. Scarlet might even scoff at first. She might even pass over it and continue her interrogation. But it would be in her mind: the possibility. And once the possibility grew and grew, it was far too easy to make the connection. She had already halfway reached it, anyway.

'You're lying,' said Scarlet, pale, distracted. 'Why would the Soldier help Asanai? Or betray it? The Soldier has no allegiance to anyone.'

His eyes flicked back to Shadow. 'She stood in front of the Emperor's throne. Face unmarked, her eyes clear.'

A great, licking fire. A ring of animal skulls gazing down at her.

'You wonder where the Soldier is. Where she is hiding. Well, I can tell you this—' Scarlet watched him intensely, and Shadow took another step back, as his mouth opened, and he stared straight at her—

—the world lurched back.

Chapter 19

Shadow was thrown halfway back across the room, feet skidding across the floor as dust kicked up all around them and the already hazy den grew positively opaque. Scarlet shouted something incoherent, and Shadow threw up her arm to prevent sand from flying into her eyes, unease curling in her stomach. Tapestries across the walls fluttered violently, their corners kicking up.

When it all settled, the sandstorm had filled the crevices of the den. Users bumbled around in confusion, coughing it out of their lungs; some even ran out, scared.

She saw the Bone Warrior's body lying slumped against his corner, long and red-raw slits across his neck and chest.

Dead.

She turned. Across the room, standing at the bottom of the stairs with both arms outstretched, stood Crow.

He was in disarray. Instinctively, she knew he'd acted on impulse. Yet his expression hardened now, arms lowering. Formal silver armour climbed around his limbs, up his neck. How long had he been following them, watching?

'Why,' he said, striding forward, ignoring Shadow and

approaching Scarlet, 'are you consorting with an Asani Bone Warrior?' His expression had morphed to real anger, disbelief.

Scarlet rounded on him with rage akin to venom. Very quickly, without a word, she stepped forward and clipped him once across the face.

Caught completely off-guard, he fell back to the ground from the force of it. He hoisted himself up into a sitting position quickly, arms braced, looking up. For the first time, she saw him look afraid.

'I,' Scarlet said, barely able to speak, 'was interrogating him. If you had working eyes and ears. You would've known that.'

Scarlet knelt down beside him; he tensed but didn't move away. 'Why do you always insist on interrupting me? I should've known you were trailing us from the start. Which one of them put you up to this?'

'No one put me up to it,' he replied sharply. 'I'm investigating of my own accord, because you're suspicious.'

'Oh?' she said dangerously. 'Do tell.'

'You – well, for one, why is *she* with you?' He pointed at Shadow.

'Why wouldn't she be? She has more skill than my entire personal guard put together.'

'She nearly killed me.'

'I let you pummel her, and she refused to fight back.' The tone was patronizing, as if reprimanding a small child. 'And might I remind you that Yo-han pardoned her?'

'He doesn't know what he's doing,' Crow hissed, standing up. 'Ever since that day when I was sent into Yosae – you've acted strangely since. You've brought her back and given her a place in the Stronghold. Even though she is a prisoner of the Stronghold, a criminal, you – you *conspire* with her! She's staying only under your orders!'

'And why does it embroil you so?'

The Last Soldier of Nava

'She roams the palace as she likes, trains with our own Guards, and is free to do as she pleases! And now, I follow you to this' – he looked around the den with some disgust – 'place, to catch you with an *Asani soldier?* What are you using her for?'

'So, what exactly,' Scarlet said, 'are you accusing me of?'

It was silent but for the heavy breathing.

'I'm going to find out what you're up to,' Crow said with finality. 'I will. I don't care what you do to me.'

Shadow could almost admire his brazenness if he wasn't so far off the mark. Relief of her identity remaining undiscovered warred with the guilt at this crude killing – the only Bone Warrior in Yosae, gone with hardly a trace.

'I was interrogating him, Crow,' Scarlet said, suddenly tired. 'Didn't you see that?'

'All Asani Bone Warriors, ex-soldier or not, in Ik-Song, must be put down on sight. They're the *enemy*.'

'He was an old man smoking. I was close to—' Her voice broke off. 'I was close to finding out.'

'Finding out what?'

'About the Soldier. I don't know why I'm telling you this. You're just going to repeat back everything I say to them.' She sighed. 'Run along.'

'You're not making any sense.'

'Go. Try to follow me again and see what happens. You may be prodigial, but so am I. And I'm better.'

Crow scowled. 'You never make any sense.' He turned to go. 'It's why you have no allies in the Stronghold. Your only ally is your prisoner, probably, who'll either betray you or die first.'

'Coming from someone whose only sway comes from hiding behind Yo-han.'

'The Stronghold would be better off without you.'

'An admirable objective,' Scarlet called after him. 'Let me know when you achieve it.'

'You're a blight on the palace. I *earned* my rank, everything I have now. Did you?' He threw back. 'You're incapable of love. You are nothing – *nothing* – but a weak imitation of the Desert Rose, and you dishonour her memory day by day.'

With that, he stormed out.

Scarlet exhaled. 'I'm in need of drink.'

The day had rocked into inky nighttime, bringing out the full flavours of Yeok-gu. Already a street performance had started outside with real fire, spun precariously by muscled men. Scarlet and Shadow slipped into a large den, hoods back over their heads, trying to appear like lithe young boys out for a daring adventure instead of a royal and her prisoner. Luckily, the abundance of coin that Scarlet presented wherever she went, whatever she did, seemed to result in a total disinterest in prying, and instead welcomed lenience on all fronts.

Scarlet sat with her back against the wall to look out for any other unwelcome guests.

'Why was there a Bone Warrior in Ik-Song?' Shadow asked as soon as they settled.

'They can be exiled. I don't know what for. We know almost nothing about the Bone Warriors, what sustains them, creates them. But they're still mortals, not gods. I suppose they make mistakes, too.'

He hadn't made any mistake in Ik-Song, she supposed, except for talking to them. Killed cleanly by Crow. She had to ask.

'Is this why Crow and White Crane didn't stop you from coming to Yosae?' Shadow asked. 'To have a go at you?'

'They trailed me last year, too, at our military parade.'

Parade? 'This happened last year?'

'I didn't notice it last year. Then again, I don't usually go around to opium dens to seek out Bone Warriors.' She lifted her small black-stone cup, rounded and patterned, up in a mock toast. 'Special occasion.'

'Then what did you do last year? After the parade.' She tracked the whorls of the wooden table.

'I drank. And then I returned at dawn.'

'You did nothing but drink until dawn? That's . . .' She trailed off when she saw the expression on Scarlet's face and exhaled quickly, annoyed. 'Oh.' Then, flatly, 'I can see you're trying not to laugh. You don't have to hide it.'

'You intrigue me,' Scarlet muttered. 'You're an innocent.'

As if assassins could be innocent. Trained for war like a dog all her life, no opportunity for the awkward tumbling that was coming of age, the rough exploration of it all. Now there was no time for any of that; there probably would never be.

Well. Except for this. She examined her own cup. 'If you weren't remade and raised in the palace, where did you come from?' Shadow asked.

'I came to the Stronghold a year ago,' Scarlet said. 'Right after my sister's death, to investigate. I showed up at the doorstep, basically, and demanded to be given a place there, to train. I said I was related to the Desert Rose and possess fantastic abilities.'

How *unbelievably* overjoyed would the Moonbearer have been to see the sister of the Rose, the Dawnbringer's last lost descendant, turn up at his own palace begging for guidance. 'And I know the reason you went.'

'In hopes of becoming strong enough to defeat the Soldier.'

'You are strong enough,' Shadow said honestly. She would know better than anyone. 'You surpass everyone in the palace.'

Scarlet was silent at that. Possibly she didn't care about Shadow's metrics of power. 'Where are you really from, then?' Shadow asked.

'A village in the south. Anje.'

If Scarlet had come only last year, then she had disrupted the entire hierarchy of power at the Stronghold. Absorbed part of Yo-han's ruling power – he would've welcomed a strong voice anyway – and became the sole voice of reign besides the Moonbearer himself, a constant and new source of vitriol for the Court to swallow. Forced to regard her opinions, her presence, her legitimacy. Forced to submit and concede. Crow would've chafed. A nothing, a nobody, a peasant from some unheard-of village in the south, given a title equal to the Prince and beloved by the people just on the basis of who her sister was.

And the Moonbearer would've played her beautifully.

When Shadow looked back up, Scarlet's head was tilted. 'And where are you *really* from?'

She deflected. 'The Bone Warrior was lying to you about the Soldier's role in the White Ice.'

After a long moment, Scarlet let it go and grabbed the bait. 'Why.'

Shadow shrugged. 'Plenty of reasons. To throw you sideways. To amuse himself. He didn't seem particularly enthusiastic to help you disprove the Moonbearer. Who knows? Don't take his word for truth.'

Truthfully, Shadow was still reeling over everything the Bone Warrior had said. A weapon? The Soldier in Asanai? That couldn't be true – she had never gone. He was lying. But why would he lie?

'If we don't talk, we'll toast.'

'Toast to what?'

'Anything you want.'

The Last Soldier of Nava

Shadow cupped her drink between her palms, looking at the clear liquid. She imagined what her reflection would look like in such a small, distorted space; whether it had changed. 'We'll toast to Anje.' Scarlet looked surprised. Shadow glanced down. 'I've never . . . done this before.'

'There isn't much to it. You just down as many as you can and hope not to become incoherent.' A pause. 'It's stupid of us to be here right now in this capacity,' Scarlet muttered. 'With snakes and spies all around, and a nation hanging in the balance. The nation always comes first. No time for pleasures and ruinous self-destructions.'

'Well, I don't count, since I'm no ruler,' Shadow said, facing down her drink. 'And you didn't really ask to be any kind of ruler either, I think.'

'The people never asked to be ruled either, is the thing.'

Shadow drank slowly, that acidic smell filling her nose and burning her throat as it went down. It was painful. She wanted it to last forever. When she finished, she set it down, and Scarlet was staring.

'What?'

'Why did you do that so slowly?'

'It seemed better than doing it quickly,' she said defensively. Scarlet snorted.

A pause. Then: 'In a few weeks, the Moonbearer will return and announce that the Soldier has been killed. Just another reason for Ik-Song to keep him, hail him as a saviour,' Scarlet said. 'And he wants a distraction, I think. The flower moon is approaching. The Dragons.'

'But he'll keep us until then. We're still alive. It means we have our uses,' Shadow said. 'Isn't there anyone who can help? Others who know the truth about him?'

'The entire Court knows. Most of them likely helped orchestrate the White Ice. The only one I trust is Yo-han, but he's even more tied down than I am. And under more scrutiny. You've heard the rumours about his heritage?'

'I snuck around his study when I first came to the Stronghold,' Shadow confessed. 'Yo-han's. I – found love letters.'

'*Love letters?*' Scarlet looked amused. 'To Crow?'

'Crow? No – I think they were between the Queen and her Asani lover. That same night, three Guards found me and attacked me in his study.' *Trying to awaken the Soldier.* 'I thought they were the Prince's personal Guards at first, dealing with an intruder, but they had to be the Moonbearer's.'

Scarlet didn't look surprised. 'I was wondering why he hadn't tried anything of that calibre yet. It seems he already had.'

'So, you knew he would try to assassinate me point-blank?' she said incredulously. 'You could have told me that earlier, you know.'

'We could've said many things to each other earlier. Possibly none of it would've been truthful.'

Shadow considered this. *You're here to serve a purpose, and nothing more,* Scarlet had told her the night of the banquet, ordering her to lie low. *Caring – a weakness beyond my comprehension.* Scarlet was hateful towards people she sought to protect, to distance. But Scarlet was also hateful towards the people she hated, just because.

'You've toyed with me. I've watched you say unspeakably rude things to every member of the palace, save Yo-han. You lie and deceive. I don't know who you truly hate or don't. Where your act starts and ends. Would you have hurt your Guard? The night of the banquet – when I talked out of line to you.' When Scarlet's hands had glowed, and for a moment – a moment – it all seemed to fall apart. When she had assumed Scarlet was afraid of her own strength – which was almost laughable, in hindsight. Scarlet wielded her power without hesitation, with surety, with relish. In fact, there was probably nothing easier for her. Shadow was the only one who struggled with that. 'Your eyes lit up, and your fingers sparked.'

'No,' Scarlet said. Her face was the same as always. 'Do you believe me?'

Shadow said nothing.

'Get up,' Scarlet said, standing easily. Shadow followed, and instantly regretted it: all the blood in her body rushed to her head. 'There's a last, important stop we have to make.'

Shadow followed her again through the streets, but this time felt different. Every lantern light seemed brighter, the darkness murkier and unsure. Some feelings were heightened, like the colours and shape of her companion, while some were more muted, like the tightness of her face. When her cheeks began to feel hot, she pressed the back of her hands over them.

In front of her, Scarlet strode with the same perfect gait. As if she had rehearsed it or something. Stupid.

'I didn't "rehearse" anything,' came her voice. 'I can hear you muttering back there.'

Time slipped away, and she hardly even noticed when they came to a stop. It was an abandoned building, dilapidated and dark, somewhat familiar. The front side was wide open, and inside was an open hatch to an underground cellar, cave-like.

It was only when they started descending down that Shadow took in the dampness, the walls.

She froze on the steps.

Scarlet continued down. 'There's nothing down here, I promise. Come.'

There was no way she could do this. Her hands clenched

and unclenched. *Curse* Scarlet. Being around her was like walking on landmines; there was no telling what she'd do, where she would lead her, so suddenly and without warning.

This is where she had woken a little over a year ago.

'Vendors use this spot to ferment persimmon wine,' Scarlet was saying. 'Technically illegal, but no one cares enough to stop them.'

The space looked as pristine as she remembered it. Smaller. No blood, nothing. That exact corner was where she had backed up against, trembling until Sae ordered her to stand. Now, rows of large jugs lined the walls, the scent of curdling wine thick in the air.

'This is where the Desert Rose was killed,' Scarlet said.

Shadow hardly had to fake her surprise. Her steps dragged; her breath seemed magnified tenfold in the dark, fogging the humid air.

Scarlet knelt down at the exact spot. 'This is where her body was. Laying facedown. There was no blood – she died by asphyxiation. Like I told you before. Her lungs were full of sand.' Scarlet paused and stood again. 'Yong said the Soldier's victims festered and deteriorated, but I know that's a lie. The Soldier doesn't really leave a mark. I've retraced it all countless times, but I still don't know why she came down here. Who came first. Why.'

I don't know why either. Shadow knew she should offer some insight, but the tone she mustered was, at worst, nauseated, and, at best, faintly disinterested. Scarlet didn't seem to notice. 'What reason would she have to come down here?'

'I don't know. Maybe the fight started up there, and she lured the Soldier down here. Risk of collateral.'

'When did she die?'

'The afternoon.'

'The Soldier wouldn't attack in the middle of the day,

outside,' Shadow said. 'Maybe the Desert Rose was lured down here.'

Scarlet considered this. 'You're right. But how? How was she lured? There was no one else down here.'

'I don't know . . .' Her own bewilderment struck her: why *had* the Desert Rose come down here? The Soldier would've awakened quietly, hidden, like all the other times at the Moonbearer's beck-and-call. There would be nothing to attract an outsider to this small space. Shadow had never ruminated much on it, never wanted to think about it. Now that she did, it didn't make sense.

'I knew you'd be useful,' Scarlet said absentmindedly, looking pleased. 'See things I couldn't.'

And then Scarlet's entire body came to attention, turning towards the entry they'd come in from.

'What?' Shadow said immediately, trying to look past her. 'What is it?'

They both stared. Shadow sensed something, though she couldn't say what – her senses still felt muddled.

'I thought I saw something there,' Scarlet said, moving closer. 'It – must've been a trick of the light.'

But they were unnerved, now. 'Let's go,' Shadow said.

And then Scarlet was engulfed by fire.

Chapter 20

For a heart-stopping, wrenching moment, the world halted.

In hindsight, Shadow didn't even remember propelling forwards, drowning the already-tight space in darkness. The adrenaline had sobered her up sharply; Scarlet was nowhere to be seen. She assumed the worst. There were at least three attackers scuffling around in the space, their shouts loud in the quiet. Fine – she could handle three.

Cutting through, Shadow grabbed a hold of one Guard's sleeve, wrenched him back. Completely clothed from head to toe, everything except the eyes – like the ones that had attacked her in the Prince's study. The Moonbearer's Guards *again*? She pinned him to the wall and reeled her fist back, preparing to cuff him and knock him out.

But something else curdled in her. Something monstrous and dark, overwhelming her mind – and before she knew it, she could feel the shadows of this cave-like place intensifying and thickening, choking them all out, threatening to swallow them whole. She felt, dimly, the Guard thrashing under her hands, furiously fighting her grip, but it didn't matter – she would raise her arms and blast a hole through him, angry, fast, blasting the walls away into bedrock, sinking the building—

'Shadow,' said a voice very close to her.

Scarlet.

Alive and unscathed.

'Oh,' Shadow said, trying to calm down. She cuffed the Guard hard, then, rendering him unconscious and drained the shadows from the walls, letting moonlight stripe them again. Scarlet was right behind her, beside her. The force of the fire had thrown her back, not consumed her.

Their opponents became visible. There were four, not three, and they all advanced on them.

'Bring it back,' Scarlet said, shifting into fighting stance. 'Make it dark again.'

Shadow's head whipped to her, confused. 'But you can't see.'

'It's worse for them than for me. Trust me.'

She obeyed. Seconds later, ahead of her, she saw a bright burst of light fire up in the dark – momentarily alighting everything around it – before it extinguished, Scarlet lashing out towards two of the Guards.

Clever. Keep them in the dark until drawing light to see, always keeping the element of surprise. Shadow would take the other two then; she saw straight through their bumbling shapes in the dark.

One of them had been the fire Guard. No one in the Stronghold possessed that, she thought, did they? But then, if not from the Stronghold, where were these remades from? Were they some of the 'gifts' the Moonbearer bestowed to the Queen?

No time to think about it. She'd sneak up from behind,

kick the fire Guard out by the legs, and incapacitate the other while he was still down.

At least, that was the plan until a hand came around her throat from behind; her arms were pinned back with iron strength. One of Scarlet's assailants had broken off.

A voice, close to her ear, male, so quiet: 'This time, it'll work.'

'*Under the Yong of the East,*' it said. '*Under the Daltokki.*' '*Scale.*' 비늘. '*Shard.*' 비늘. '*Nine.*' 아홉. '*Lost.*' 죽은.

And to her horror, something deep in her, something long and buried, began to shift.

'No,' she hissed, and thrashed wildly. She flung back her head with all her strength, hearing the satisfying crack of bone behind, the snarl. The grip, although still tight, weakened ever so slightly, and she wrenched out as hard as possible.

She circled back with a sharp kick.

He fell back, but another Guard was on her instantly: this time, a woman who drew her hands back, but stopped immediately – and collapsed to the ground.

Shadow looked down. A tiny, smoking hole between her eyes. A pinpoint of light.

Scarlet lowered her arm from across the space.

The other Guards were momentarily down but getting back up again. 'Let's go,' Scarlet said, grabbing her by the arm – and they took off at a run to reach the city streets again.

They made it out of the entrance, trying to collapse the cavern behind them, footsteps drowned out by the catastrophic noise. In this narrow section of the neighbourhood, it was nearly deserted, the muffled noises of a live district somewhere in the distance.

Scarlet let go of Shadow and they stood breathing sharply – Shadow with her hands on her knees – breaths vapour in the night air. They stared at each other for a few moments. Shadow didn't want to look at the aftermath of the cellar behind her, not even to see whether it might crumble beneath her feet.

Scarlet was looking at her with a strange expression.

'What?' she asked.

'I've never seen you actually fight with it willingly,' Scarlet replied. 'Your ability. It's—'

Scarlet stopped, eyes shifting quickly to a point behind Shadow – and that was the moment Shadow heard the crunch of a footstep, the sudden feel of heat on her back, and then something so strong it blasted her clear across the ground.

Shadow came to seconds later, ears ringing and mouth dry.

She felt hands trying to turn her over, running over her clothing, checking for injury. Someone spoke directly and urgently above her, but it was muffled. She opened her eyes, trying with extreme effort to turn over heavily on her side. The ground was cool and inviting beneath her, but she propped up on an elbow, and then her palms, trying to stand. The Soldier never lay defenceless, like a cat showing its soft underbelly. The Soldier always stood first. The Soldier sought a safer spot to lick its wounds in private, never in the moment. The Soldier – Shadow stood; hands helped her up; the world blurred momentarily. She turned to Scarlet.

'. . . more coming,' Scarlet was saying, voice muffled. 'We have to run.'

Shadow took a breath, trying not to dry-heave, and took off first. Scarlet came hot on her heels.

'Left,' she said behind her, and Shadow made the turn. They twisted down corners and alleys; she stumbled, fell to a knee once. Got up.

She should've been verging on collapse, but somehow, she

felt like she *needed* to run. Her feet took her faster and faster. The chase took them through to the busier, crowded part of Yeok-gu, attracting stares from the drunk nightgoers milling about. Shadow was vaguely aware of Scarlet unsheathing a throwing knife and hurling it behind them, at one point. Her own breaths grew sharper and sharper.

Scarlet said her name, but she couldn't respond – only kept running. She said it again.

Shadow felt her arm being grabbed sharply, and then she was pulled to the side, down a narrow alley that could barely fit the two of them.

'In here,' Scarlet said. Halfway down the alley there was an open door – the back of some establishment, dark and unsuspecting. They fit inside the room, into the tiny space. 'We got lucky – there's some commotion outside, a street performance that just started – we lost them, for now. It's unlikely they'll find this exact alley— Shadow? Shadow?'

Shadow was trying to be quiet, but her wheezing gasps were worsening. The space was too tight, no breathing room, and by the *Dal*, she needed breathing room.

'I need – I—' She slumped against the wall; one hand braced against it. Her legs threatened to buckle, and she was so, so, hot. Burning up. 'My armour – I need – off—'

Scarlet understood immediately. She deftly unbuckled the underlayer, shedding the sections easily, revealing her lighter clothing underneath, but it still brought her no relief. Her head tipped forward; her entire body felt like it was sliding out of focus. Cool fingers were on her skin, the scarf undone, bare collarbone exposed to the air.

'Where else?' Scarlet said.

'Here,' she said, pressing Scarlet's hand to her rib. That half chest-plate came off, too, and her breaths still heaved.

They were so close that their sweat almost mingled, and through a heat-stricken haze Shadow watched the dewdrops that gathered on Scarlet's furrowed brow, her eyes that creased in focus. She was beautiful, and untouchable. Shadow wanted to reach out and touch the sweat, along the brow, the face, the lip—

The plate on her left side was peeled off like a suction, and the force of it buckled her knees, sent her almost crashing to the ground, folding weakly. Scarlet caught her, holding her up.

'Why are you burning up?' Scarlet said. 'You're – fine. It's fine.'

She was going to pass out, she thought.

'You're not going to pass out. It's fine.'

Had she said that out loud?

Scarlet cursed again. 'This is my fault. Why is your skin so hot? Shadow. Shadow!' She collapsed down the wall again, dragging the other girl down with her.

'I'm – fine, I'm . . .' she murmured. There was a cool relief against her skin, her arm; she reached over and grabbed Scarlet's wrist. 'S'cold.'

'I don't know what to do.'

'No,' she said. 'I – look. S'fine.' She just needed that cold hand, the refreshing solidity of it.

Scarlet looked down at her. 'You're joking, right?'

'I've – had worse – s'fine.'

'You're slurring your words.'

'Mm, we drank, remember?'

Scarlet's incredulous face was so close that she could see herself in the dark reflection of her eyes.

Her body was going to burn to smithereens, to ashes and bits. Right in front of Scarlet's eyes. Her eyes. They were beautiful, and so familiar. They were softened, now, looking at her. If only she knew what Shadow had done. That softness would never be unsheathed again. Shadow watched her, if only to keep this expression in her mind, to remember its lines. It pointed to other things, other lives that she had never been a part of. People had lived entire lives, being looked at like this, filling the gaps of their waking days, and she wondered what it was like: to hurt and be hurt, knowing that this would not be enough to sever what was true, only a momentary setback, something that could always be mended later, was only temporary. She had only known hardness, and unmercy. So why did her body ache for that soft, unexplainable abstraction? Why did this shapeless, amorphous thing lure her like a siren? Why did she want something she could never know? The grip on her arm tightened, the dark eyes wide.

'Why are you crying, Shadow?'

Was she? Perhaps her eyes were wet; perhaps they bled. The Desert Rose had the same eyes as Scarlet. She had them even up to when Shadow killed her, even then. She hadn't looked at her with the same fear and resistance that all the others did. She looked at her like she was an animal in need of saving, and her eyes had asked, in their own way, what unkindness had shaped her killing hands, what had moulded them so deftly. And there was Scarlet, in some dark corner, probably, watching the aftermath of it unfold.

'I didn't know you saw,' Shadow said, 'I didn't.'

Who are you, Soldier?

'Saw what? What do you mean?'

What are you doing here, Soldier?

'Who are you talking to? Who do you see?'

Questions, questions, she would pass out, the Soldier needed stasis. *What do you need?* She closed her eyes and opened them again, and it was so hot, she was so tired, the drunkenness clocking her head and the taste of blood on her tongue.

Darkness enveloped her, as it always did.

Chapter 21

Shadow woke to dawn light, wind biting into her skin, the ground moving so quickly beneath her that it was a blur. She sat on something moving, rising high above and down against the horizon, again and again, the glittering cliffs of Ik-Song undulating in her vision. A deer. It was chilly with the wind, except there was warmth, all around her waist, along her back. Someone's breath tickling the back of neck, making her shiver. An arm was holding her up around the waist.

Wait.

'Don't try to stand, idiot,' Scarlet said behind her as she shot up, something colouring her voice that might've been relief. 'You're on the back of my moving buck, if you haven't noticed.'

Shadow tried to turn on the saddle, keeping balance. Scarlet looked bone-tired, like she hadn't slept in a week.

'You look—'

'You look worse,' Scarlet countered.

It hit her like a tidal wave – last night. Trying desperately to stand up, the chase that felt endless. Scarlet's hands on her shoulders, her hands pushing her forward, pulling her into that space, coming close. Unravelling her armour piece by piece. And she'd – her face began to burn with embarrassment – slumped all over Scarlet like a lapdog, leaned her entire weight on her, dragged her down. Probably muttered nonsense.

'Do you remember what happened? You took a direct hit to the back from a Guard. You passed out.' Scarlet sounded . . . eager?

'You don't have to sound that happy about it.'

'No,' Scarlet said. 'You took a direct hit to the back, but you're perfectly intact because you *absorbed* it. You stole the element, his attack. It was *inside* you. You were burning up from the inside. It took hours to dissipate after. You don't remember?'

'*What?*' Shadow said. 'That's not right. It was my armour. Or my clothes. The fire made it hot to the touch – it was suffocating me—'

'I took your armour off you. None of that material was hot; it was normal to the touch. It was only your *skin* that was burning.'

How could that be true?

But it made sense – she always survived direct attacks; had she been . . . absorbing others' power, all this time?

Then why was the most direct hit she'd ever suffered, the one to her face – she fought the urge to reach up and touch her scarring – not *absorbed* at all? It'd just left plain scars. Mutilation.

They had tried to awaken the Soldier, in the cavern. But the word sequence had never been completed. Even though it had come close.

'I was right about the *sakasa*,' Scarlet said triumphantly. 'You *can* steal ability.'

Over the horizon, the view of the Stronghold was beginning

to appear, her elation over their narrow escape quickly dissipating. A long bugle call sounded. Shadow couldn't believe they were returning as if nothing had happened.

'Don't acknowledge anything. Don't say anything. And *don't* even think about retaliation.' Scarlet set her jaw. 'Nothing happened. This is where we have to tread carefully. The flower moon is in a week now. I'll find a different way to expose him, another solution.'

She didn't say what they were probably both thinking: that for all their small victory, they still didn't know how the Moonbearer might be defeated.

But for the first time since arriving, Shadow felt different – lighter. More hopeful. She wasn't the only one with such a goal. She felt like she could run for miles on end.

'You don't have to do it all, you know,' Shadow said. 'I can help, too.'

'Face forward,' was all Scarlet said. 'Or you'll lose your balance.'

The light that breached the fields before them now looked cold and unforgiving, dappling the forests beyond. The palace looked as it always did, albeit a little emptier.

And then again – a long, unmistakable bugle call roared before them. The gates opened: several figures on horseback and deer strode out from the main entry of the Stronghold, a party of at least fifteen, complete with couriers holding flags.

And leading them, glorious in the sunrise: Aspis. Bow and arrow slung over her back, white marks painted along her face. Her deer nimble and long-legged, a bundle of frantic energy beneath her.

Dawn hunt.

Shadow leaned forward instinctually; even that small movement caught Aspis's eye. The procession did not break flank, but Aspis veered off, momentarily separating.

She came close, reining her deer back by the muzzle.

'Keeper,' she said. But for the first time, Aspis didn't bow, politely greet, or lower herself in some small way to yield to the Keeper. 'The Court was displeased to hear of your departure.'

This time, there was little pretence. This time, she sat high up on her deer, only looking down at the other girl, and Shadow was reminded of the way Scarlet had looked at *her* the first time they'd met. Her face expressionless, cold.

Aspis looked different, and dangerous.

She looked like the hunter she was.

Standing between the two of them, both unreadable: Scarlet, still, face upturned; Aspis, arrowpoints glinting, the red ribbon in her hair bright. Shadow realized she didn't want to be caught in the middle of this, certain collateral.

'Shadow,' the Master of the Hunt said carefully. She had seen them ride out at twilight; now, they returned with only one deer with obvious signs of a fight. Her eyes were carefully questioning.

'We're riding out now. Will you accompany me?' Her gaze swivelled to Shadow, burning through her. 'Or will you stay here, with the Keeper?'

They both looked at her.

Neither of them were totally sure, she realized, whom she would pick.

Whatever she chose would be permanent, and consequential.

Shadow regarded Aspis: her first ally, her first friend here. Even the day they had ridden back to the Stronghold, she had been drawn to the martinet, eager to see what was under the surface. She trusted Aspis. Aspis had helped her, supported her.

To any reasonable outsider looking in, the choice was obvious.

But instinct never lied.

'I'll stay,' Shadow said, lowering her eyes. Aspis looked resigned, like she'd expected it. Shadow wouldn't demean her with an apology. 'I wish you luck on your hunt.'

And just like that, it was done. Aspis pulled back her deer, and her face was stony. Shadow had always thought Scarlet had mastered the poker face, but Aspis's was worse.

For once, Scarlet was silent behind her. Shadow didn't want to look up – guilt furled in her gut. Was this really the right choice?

'Remember this, Shadow,' Aspis said. 'War is not won by softness, or peace, or whatever artful thing you might think. War, like a hunt, is only won by those who can kill, and keep killing. You can pretend like you can win without cruelty or death, but you can't. You can pretend to deny your true nature, but you can't. To say otherwise is to deceive yourself. Don't forget.'

With that, she left, the party thundering across towards the woods. Shadow watched them go.

What had she done?

'Playing with our hearts,' Scarlet muttered. 'Truly the way of the Stronghold.'

'If we're really to be allies now,' Shadow said, anger rattling her, 'you can't be so vague. You have to tell me more.' She paused. 'What's wrong with the hunts? Why didn't you want me to go?'

There was a long silence.

'They're not real hunts,' Scarlet replied, finally. 'At least, not in the way you're thinking.'

'What do you mean?'

Scarlet paused, considering something. 'The night that we were told about the Soldier sighting,' she said. 'You burst out of your door beforehand. You said you felt something was wrong, something underneath.'

'Yes,' she frowned. 'This sense of wrongness . . . like the deadzone.'

'It's because there *is* something wrong, underneath. There's suffering beneath this place.'

'What kind of suffering? Secret prisons?' Hidden torture chambers that the Moonbearer used?

'They are prisons,' Scarlet said, 'but not what you're imagining.' She looked towards the palace. 'I'll just show you.'

They descended into depths of the palace that Shadow hadn't known even existed through a series of tightly sealed doors.

'I thought the library was the lowest level,' Shadow said.

Scarlet didn't look back. 'This is the true bowel of the Stronghold.'

The air began to change; it smelled thickly rotten, though Shadow wasn't sure with what. She covered her nose to block it out. They arrived at a stone, dungeon-like door. Strange shuffling sounds and grunts came behind it; the same noises that she'd heard that night.

'Do you ever wonder how there's such a plentiful stock of meats in the palace?' Scarlet asked. 'It's never ending.'

Shadow *had* wondered. The animal heads lining the table, the sheer volume of it. 'I thought the woods here were just particularly fertile. And that the hunters are disciplined.'

'They are disciplined. And the woods are fertile. But even by catching ten boar every single day without fail, such a stock would still be impossible. That's why most of the supply is kept down here,' she said, resigned, and opened the door.

The first thing that hit her was the stench: rotting flesh, strong and sickly, rolling out with pungent force.

There was movement inside – many things, moving around – and her eyes adjusted in less than a second to the near-darkness.

And then she saw the glinting of silver wire bars – thin cages, stacked one on top of another – and realized this room went back incredibly far, possibly spanning the entire length of the palace. It was absolutely and completely packed to the brim with live animals. Boar, chicken, pig, even enormous cows – all confined to this dark and squalid space, each given so little room nothing could move any which way. A cacophony of low grunting, pained moans, the muted squawking of birds. Every animal was slathered in their own filth, mingling all together in mud; the pigs closest to the entrance so fattened they couldn't even stand under their own weight. One boar in front of her dragged itself around its cage with a leg bent at an unnatural angle; a bird tried desperately to spread its wings and failed in the tight space. Many birds had portions of their beaks mutilated, the tails and wings clipped, their chests grossly enlarged. Every single animal was marked by hot brands, their ears notched, printed, stamped, strings of numbers and symbols and giant X's for identification. Above them in rows hanging back as far as the eye could see hung racks and racks of raw, curing meat; huge slabs of it, still in the airless space.

Something small squirmed on the bottom of a cage near her. Nausea rose in the back of Shadow's throat. And then there were the odd animals that she couldn't recognize at all – neither mammal nor bird nor fish, mutilated, missing parts, strange eyes.

Nothing here would ever see the light of day; nothing here could walk; nothing here looked as it should. Trapped underneath the Stronghold all this time, unable to move with the natural cycles of sun and moon, day by day, as she'd slept and eaten and walked freely above, oblivious to it all. She wished, for the first time in her life, that she couldn't see so well in the dark; that she could miss the details and let it all fade into the grainy background. But it stayed so sharp and clear to her, as if saturated by the light of day, branding itself into the back of her eyes.

How could something like this exist beside the beautiful, manicured Stronghold?

The door shut in front of her, and it ended.

She pitched forward. 'Why did you close it? We have to help them. The one right inside, that was drowning in its own filth, didn't you see—'

'You have incredible night vision,' Scarlet said. 'I could probably only see a quarter of what you did, and nothing more. Everything is bred below in these dark chambers.'

Everything. Guilt pricked at her; Shadow had so thoroughly enjoyed her meals here. 'The Stronghold should know about this. You have to show them, like you showed me.'

'What makes you think everyone doesn't already know? They learn, and they forget. It's so easy to forget. I forget, most of the time. It's inevitable. You're meant to forget. That's why it's all down here, and if no one thinks about it, it hardly matters at all.'

They were just animals. She was a predator, and they were prey. That was the way things were, the way things always had been. *Eat, or be eaten.* Anything that deviated may be an unfortunate digression, but it all eventually led to the same, exact place: death and consumption. These creatures would all be slaughtered in weeks or months; whether here or tracked down in the forests, what did it matter? It was hard to imagine Aspis coming down here, watching it all with indifference.

But it wasn't so hard when she thought of everyone in the entire palace awaiting her service, her meals. They praised her, followed her hunts. They depended on it. Including Shadow. Deep down, she'd known there was something off. Yet, it was easy to forget – easy to just tear into flesh, to eat. When it was right in front of her – no one would punish her if she did. Even if she refused, a hundred mouths would take her place gladly.

Scarlet had always refused.

'Here is the truth,' Scarlet said. 'I can't stomach most meats. It has to do with the way it's prepared. If I eat something wrong, it can kill me.'

'That's a practice of Nava,' Shadow said, shocked.

Aspis oversaw all the cooking and dinery in the entire palace for almost every meal. Shadow had thought of Scarlet as ungrateful every time they ate, picking through her food like it was a puzzle. Something told her that Aspis did not cater to her diet. *Only the best cuts for you,* she'd said at the banquet to Scarlet, in front of the table. That had been a taunt, she realized. Shadow had been so bewildered by Scarlet's vitriol back. The animal heads, the eyes staring grotesquely back. The killing of the bird – spearing it through the eye – had never been a display of the Keeper's power, not to the Inner. It had always been a display of Aspis's power – bending even her highers to her will.

'Aspis thinks I'm too weak-willed for this,' Scarlet said. 'Soft. But it's not about that. She doesn't understand that it's the *principle* of the thing. To be denied instinct is to be denied life, and then after that, after this violation, there's nothing. It's all connected, it's not separate – human suffering, our relationship with what's around us. The environment we live in. It's in everyone's interests; it's not separate.'

'Aspis isn't evil,' Shadow said. She couldn't be. The same

person who mocked the Advisors with her, who explained to her the rules of the Stronghold when she was new and uncertain.

'No. It's about choice, and ignorance. It's about seeing beyond what already exists. To be trapped by the same constructs is to bring us farther and farther from the truth: and our own happiness, our natural state. It's a disregarding, a lack of appreciation, and if everyone thinks the same, it has massive implications.'

Scarlet turned to leave. Shadow didn't follow. 'You're just going to leave them there?'

'What do you think would happen if you released them all, right now? Most of them would die. Or escape to the forests, throwing them out of balance. And by the next week, it'd all be replenished, anyway.'

She was right, though Shadow didn't want to admit it. 'I saw animals in there that I didn't recognize. Strange looking ones I've never seen before.'

'Some of them are bycatch from the deadzones.'

The memory of her first encounter with a deadzone came to her, pushed into the woods by Crow, the missing foot-soldier, the lynx with human eyes. 'But that would mean—'

'It's all connected,' Scarlet said shortly. 'Now let's leave. We both need to clean up.'

And then: 'I'm going for a ride.'

Disappointment caught her. Looking at Scarlet now, Shadow became all too aware of the distance between them, like a wall in place. Scarlet had shown her entire shades of herself, glimpses. Yet she would disappear back into the mountains on her buck, and she would take everything with her inside that mind. Like a storm Shadow had been allowed to traverse suddenly changing its centre just as she found its eye, its sanctuary. She didn't want to separate in this sinister place. Scarlet's face had amalgamated back into that smooth blandness.

'All right,' Shadow said, resigned.

Scarlet's eyebrow arched. 'You're not going to accompany me?'

Chapter 22

Shadow ran a hand over the tawny, white-spotted flank. 'What's his name?'

'He doesn't have a name,' Scarlet replied.

'Why not?'

'To name an animal is to possess it. The want to possess is a human flaw.'

'You already possess it,' Shadow pointed out. 'It's your riding deer.'

'Without his harness, he's just a deer.' Scarlet tested the foothold before mounting. 'He can wander the woods as he pleases.'

Every time Shadow'd seen this buck, he had worn the sun circlet. Now his head was bare, save for the antlers. Shadow came up to his shoulder standing. 'So why does he stay here instead of the wild?'

'Because we met in our childhoods, and now we're too weak to part. Now if you're done with the questions—' Scarlet turned to Shadow. 'You can ride your own deer this time.'

'I don't know how.'

'It's not that different from a horse. Or a donkey.' Scarlet gestured to one of the does, which a stablehand guided over. It was big – bigger than Scarlet's own buck.

'She's huge,' Shadow accused.

'Does are larger and therefore sturdier,' she explained. 'She's easier to ride and control. Bucks like mine are flighty and light – you can feel every jolt of his movements.'

Shadow eyed the doe warily. She ran a hand over its pitch-black fur, coarse and beautiful, the only white spot on her forehead. Her eyes were large and dark, no light escaping them at all. She tested the foothold; swung herself over, settled quickly down on her back, lying low. The doe tapped forward on its front legs, fidgeting, but calmed quickly. She again placed her hand on its warm neck. 'Hello,' she said.

'"Hello?" Really?'

'You said I couldn't name it.' Now securely seated, Shadow tentatively nudged it forward, steering it slowly in the direction they were headed: towards the thick forest grounds, over open meadow. Scarlet followed at her side, lagging slightly. It was almost late afternoon, the light golden.

'You can do anything you want or don't want. It's merely about the creature. About how you see it. The space you make for it in the world.' Scarlet gestured at the open field, towards the palace standing tall. 'Thousands of slaves were used to build this place, after the White Ice. Backbreaking labour. Trees axed down, limestone slabbed over ground where countless things lived and breathed in a single patch. It chokes and suffocates everything underneath. And the gardens – bare imitations of real nature. Nothing can live in a manicured, sterile bed like that, filled with plants that aren't even native to this country.'

'But all of the world is built like this,' Shadow said.

'Yes,' Scarlet agreed. 'It is. And within these places and these cities, there's no space for anything other than ourselves. Can you imagine any different?' *Nava was different.* Lying never went easily for Shadow, but this one especially stuck in her throat. 'No.'

'Me neither. It's how far gone we are. How securely we've built these invisible prisons around us, these walls. Change is impossible to envision until you're living in it. But it starts with due appreciation.' The deer sped up, now; Shadow kept low until she grew familiar with the doe's movement, the way to ride with it, instead of against.

'Ik-Song used to be so beautiful,' Scarlet said. 'It still is, but we've lost so much of it, and we don't even know it.'

They had neared the edge of the forest. Shadow thought of the Stronghold, how plant life had forced its way into so many odd places, windows carefully teased open and walls caved in. 'You're responsible for how the palace looks, aren't you? All the vines inside.'

'I tried my best,' Scarlet said. 'Once it overtakes, it's impossible to weed out. It just has to take hold.'

'It's beautiful,' Shadow said, thinking of the fountain in their hall, alive with the dialogue of birds.

They rode in silence into the mouth of the forest, travelling a path that had clearly been ridden many times before. It was only wide enough for one, so they went in a line, Shadow first. She adjusted to the steep incline, the way her doe began to climb and pick her way among the scattered stones instead of just walking. The trees grew thin and tall, some dripping in strings of green moss; a crisp air surrounded them. Occasionally, their deer slowed to sniff a stray flower or the ground. Poplars and sparrows fluttered high up; insects chirped.

'I know you've named your buck, though,' said Shadow, breaking the silence. 'Haven't you?'

Scarlet rolled her eyes. 'By the *Dal*.'

'You have to call him something in your head. You don't just call him "deer".'

No answer. They passed a trickling river on their ascent. 'There are sometimes river otters here,' Scarlet said. 'And minnows.'

Then Shadow halted.

A figure was there, behind a tree. Alarmed, she began to rein her doe back. 'Someone's here,' she hissed.

'What?' Scarlet turned immediately. They both sidled out of view. Were they being followed again? So soon?

And then Scarlet relaxed. 'Oh,' she said. 'It's just Yo-han.'

Prince Yo-han? What was he doing here? Shadow looked closer. His white hair was unmistakable, but she couldn't tell what he was doing. Half-cloaked with papers in his hand – a book? Was he reading? Meditating?

'Why is he here?' *Alone?*

'The same reason I come,' Scarlet said. 'The palace is stuffy.'

It seemed awfully strange for him to be here by himself, without any Guards, no deer or horse in sight. He looked forlorn, too.

As if reading her mind, Scarlet said, 'He's always been that way.'

'What way?'

'Melancholic. Listless.'

'But he's so dutiful.'

'I know. He keeps it inside, I think – like a grief that eats away at him. I don't know exactly where it comes from; it could be any number of things.'

'Loss?'

'Maybe. A Prince doesn't have many people to turn to who aren't his subordinates, or advisors, or figures with ulterior motives. His father died when he was young; his mother disowns him. But he keeps his head high, still, for the state. And his power honed.'

'He has incredible ability.' She thought back to the crescendoing wave at the banquet, the effortless leap of it.

'Sometimes I fear that his power is what drains his psyche. The stronger it is, the more tiring.'

'If that were true, you'd be dead by now.'

Scarlet looked at her. 'Why do you say such things? Things like that. That are . . . kind.'

'I'm not trying to be kind,' Shadow said. 'I'm stating an objective fact. You're strong. The world has never seen the likes of such ability before.'

Scarlet looked like she wanted to say something but withheld. They were deeper into the hills now, higher.

'You're not a bad rider,' Scarlet settled for.

'Don't strain yourself,' Shadow said. Then, changing the conversation, 'Don't the deer ever get tired?'

'This is their natural terrain. It tires them more to be bounding across open, barren land than these hilly paths.'

Maybe it was just the altitude – but Shadow felt noticeably colder. 'Where's the farthest you've ever ridden to?'

'There's a hidden foothold at the very peak, where you can watch the sunrise.'

'Perhaps you can show me, sometime.' She wondered how many times Scarlet had ridden here through the year, trapped in the palace, watching the sun's red glow with yearning. Because the sun brightened and burned constantly, whenever it wished, which was always. Imagine such freedom.

'Perhaps I will.'

They stopped at the next point where the river reappeared, Shadow's doe pausing to lap water.

'I know what you mean, you know. What you feel,' Shadow said after a bit. 'If I try hard enough, I can sense the different winds, which seas they blow from. I can feel vibrations in the ground of burrowing creatures. I can hear the cries and calls and growths of all the living things behind me. I know what you're speaking of.'

Scarlet turned to her. 'Are we the only ones who remember the old world in this way, then?'

'Perhaps.' But that was a burden neither wanted. 'Why don't you just leave?' Shadow swept a hand over. 'All this behind. You can go anywhere you'd like.'

'You say that like leaving is easy.'

'It is, when it's necessary,' Shadow said automatically. 'You can learn to do it over and over again.'

Scarlet watched her so intensely Shadow wanted to squirm. It felt like everything in her was flayed open for the viewing. 'Sometimes, I feel like we're cut from the same mould – like we've known each other before, in another lifetime. And sometimes, I see a darkness in your eyes, the likes of which I've never seen before.' A pause. 'I'm unsure which is true.'

Shadow had no response to that.

'As long as I am Keeper, I'm entangled here,' she continued. 'I'm too far in, now. It's like the forest – if you destroy one small part, the entire system collapses. Aspis hunts the wolves here for sport, but do you know what happens when wolves are ripped from a landscape? The prey grows bold, and lazy; their diets begin to meld together. It all becomes a mess.

'Eventually, Aspis wants a future of successful domination. Stopping storms and mastering beasts and wrestling mountains into the ground. But she doesn't want to work alongside the world. She wants war. War on all fronts. I'm no longer enough to keep her in balance.' Then, Scarlet looked at her. 'I left behind everything to come here, and it was for the worse. You've left behind everything, too, it seems, but you're liberated.'

The Last Soldier of Nava

Shadow pondered this. 'I didn't leave behind much.'

'Who is waiting for you, Shadow?'

Who is waiting for me? No one at all, she thought. *Who have I left behind?* 'I had a father, once.'

'Did he love you?'

What a peculiar question. She considered not answering, but Scarlet's gaze reflected back like a spiderweb, and Shadow knew whatever she said would be caught in there without doubt. 'Sort of. I became everything he wanted me to be and he was all I knew. I did it all for him.'

Scarlet listened silently.

'But he was cold. He used me. And when finished, discarded me so easily. I realize now that I never really knew him, nor did he know me. I didn't understand him. But one day I woke up and saw everything for how it was, the part I'd played.' She exhaled, waiting for judgement, but it didn't come.

Instead: 'Is he the one who taught you how to kill?'

Shadow nodded.

'Fathers are like that, aren't they? For them, the language of love and the language of destruction are often one and the same.'

'I never knew what he wanted. Even now, I don't . . .'

What did the Moonbearer possibly want? What did he yearn for now? Nothing pure. He had had Nava, and still he wanted more. He could not escape his own greed; was too blind to see past it. He wouldn't be satisfied with a country, a palace, an army to rule. In his own twisted way, he sought truth. He was searching for something that could not be won, or stolen, or brute forced. He sought what he had already lost.

But truth had a timeline of its own. Truth could be muddled and then forever distorted. To reach a pure, original truth, the way things had been, one had to impossibly bring back the past.

The past.
The truth.
The Ninth.
And the thought became clear to her, like it was always there:
The Moonbearer wanted Nava back.
He would reach the ends of the world; he would slaughter the last Dragon to have it again. A twisted version of it.

Why else would he have taken this entire country for himself, cultivated a ground where he had sole authority? Space for his plans? Watching over these forests and coasts for a decade, where the Dragon would rise from once again? For a thousand years, while the deadzones and the weather worsened – the only option left, he must have realized, was to wait for the Dragon. He needed to raise the Dragon to bring Nava back. And in order to kill it, he needed unfettered access to Ik-Song.

Shadow looked up, about to tell Scarlet, when a sharp whirring sound and a *thunk* startled them both.

A pace from either of their heads, lodged into the trunk of a tree, was a tipped arrow.

They both eyed the arrow for several moments before Scarlet turned the reins of her deer tight. 'Follow me – and sit low.'

Thus began their descent. Hurdles of broken branches and decaying trees that the deer would usually cautiously trot around were leapt over.

'The hunters?' Shadow asked.

'Too close for comfort,' Scarlet replied, nearly flattened along the length of her buck, body streamlined.

There came the distinct sound of hooves, small noises like twigs breaking – growing louder.

'Are they *chasing* us?' Shadow asked incredulously.

Scarlet rose upright and sent a flying arc of light sparking into the air. It stuttered and shone up above before dying: a warning signal.

'I suppose you'll say this is a regular occurrence,' Shadow said dryly.

'No – for once, it isn't.' The hooves were, indeed, getting louder, like they were barrelling over the forest floor. It sounded like an entire army was after them.

'That sounds like the entire party,' Shadow said.

'They're running from something.'

They exchanged glances. From what? A rabid carnivore, a bear? But fifteen hunters could take down a single bear easily, and even if not, they wouldn't all run in the same direction. They were only halfway down the mountain by now – and was it just her, or had the air grown even chillier?

Rumbling sounded. But there was no thunder, no rain. In the distance below, she could see the opening out to the field: their exit.

And then a sudden, icy wind whipped through them.

'Why is it so cold?' Shadow asked urgently.

'Nearly there,' Scarlet said, before a world of white enveloped them.

Chapter 23

Shadow couldn't tell which way was which – all sense of orientation fled momentarily, and it felt like she'd be wading through this whiteness forever. The frozen winds battered her face painfully, tearing at her bare skin, snowfall like a pale void around her. She yelled out for Scarlet, but her voice was deafened by the howl. Faintly, she made out the outlines of trees – but they faded away into nothingness in only moments.

Her doe grunted in pain and confusion, stomping down its front legs. *It's all right, it's all right*, she kept saying, trying to stop and think. These winds were heart-stopping, but if she stilled and sensed them for long enough – they came from one general direction. West. A few seconds ago, they'd come from the east: meaning they were turned the wrong way.

'We have to turn,' she told the deer, steering cautiously. It obeyed reluctantly, facing another path of nothingness, which Shadow hoped was the right way. Patches of glacial ice were already freezing across parts of the forest floor, shiny and dangerous. One could easily fall to their death.

The Asani couldn't be here so early. It wasn't possible. It wasn't even the flower moon yet, it—

But no time to think about that. 'Let's go – slow,' she said, and her doe continued. They could only see a few paces in front of them at a time, and she tried her best to guide her in tandem, thankful for her patience even as the cold gnawed at their every limb.

Just a bit longer in this blizzard, and she'd catch frostbite. They went on for an excruciating minute – what if the wind had switched direction since the start, and she was leading them further sideways into the mountain? Her teeth chattered violently; her fingers were already turning violet – but soon, the entrance out appeared: beautiful and light.

They pushed through together, landing outside on the field.

The difference was so stark that it was like walking into another world. The meadows remained sunny and clear, a gentle breeze rustling the grass. The Stronghold in the distance. Behind her—

Behind her raged a storm of fantastic proportions, completely shrouding the mountain, the sky above it grey with charred clouds. It was a self-contained storm, like an invisible border separated the fields from it; it was monstrous. It was a sight.

Shadow dismounted, trying to shake the snow off. Her lashes were already flaked with the stuff, face red from the cold. The scarring on her face felt tight, the muscles having contracted and tightened as they lost heat.

Shadow felt warm hands searching her form, driving away the chill. Taken aback, she stepped back from Scarlet, regretting it when the cold returned to her skin.

Scarlet stepped back as well, expression shuttering quickly. Keeping her distance. 'You made it out quick.'

'We followed the winds.'

They watched the blizzard crackle above them. There was only one explanation for this – but it was impossible. She thought of the defected soldier in the opium den, wasting away, barely able to conjure a snowflake, much less a blizzard in summer. But in their prime, they were strong beyond comprehension.

'The hunters – Aspis – we have to go back in for them—'

'We're useless in there,' Scarlet said. 'We're not properly clothed, and we can barely see.' She looked towards the palace. 'We need backup.'

'The storm,' Shadow pointed. 'It's growing. Is it strong enough to take out the Stronghold?'

Indeed, it seemed to crawl towards them, an icy blur. Scarlet shook her head. 'I don't think so – it's called that for a reason. Still – we have to warn them.'

Without another word, they remounted and set off towards the palace.

They leapt back towards the building like madmen, the deer sensing their urgency, two dark dots streaming across the green vastness. The dreaded implications of the storm settled over them: winter in the middle of Ik-Song.

Just like the start of the White Ice.

They neared the Stronghold and saw that it hardly needed to be warned: everyone had already gathered outside, watching the storm with barely contained horror. The Court stood in a line, as if in ranking. As they drew close, Scarlet slowed her buck to a jog, commanding the masses.

'The blizzard is growing,' she yelled. 'The hunters are still trapped inside – we need Guards and furs. Everyone else needs to return inside, stay in the protection of the fortress.'

No one moved. Everyone just watched with horrified expressions, dismay.

Many looked resigned.

No. This inaction would get them killed.

'Didn't you hear her?' Shadow said. 'There are hunters in the mountain!'

Shocked faces looked back at her – including Scarlet's. Why wasn't anyone moving? Couldn't they see the storm? Couldn't they—

'We won't be sending anyone else in,' sliced in a cold voice. White Crane.

What was he doing? This was no time for a petty debate with the Keeper; the hunters were dying off. But he was resolute.

And then Shadow looked closely at the people. They looked afraid, terrified, yes – but many of them weren't even looking at the storm.

They were looking at the Keeper.

'What are you waiting for?' Scarlet tried. 'Do you have no sense of urgency?'

Not a single Guard had obeyed her.

'Look behind you,' Advisor Ji-hu said. 'The storm is ending.'

It was. The winds were dying down, the snow flickering away, thawing unnaturally quickly to reveal the green of the woods, as if it had never happened at all. The mountains looked almost serene in the aftermath.

And then a figure erupted from the woods, shooting out like a cannon. One lone rider on a small, antlerless buck riding towards them with urgent fury: the figure grew larger and larger, all eyes awaiting the approach.

It was one of the hunters. Shadow didn't know her name, but she was a smaller girl, lithe, which stood out more against what she was carrying: something almost half her entire size, hefty and cumbersome, tucked under one arm. Her face was white with shock, arms dotted with small cuts.

But no one was looking at her face.

Under her arm was the broken skull of a Bone Warrior.

She slid her buck to a stop and held up the enormous helmet in two hands, raising it above the crowd for everyone to see.

It was a gigantic bird's skull: half-intact, dewy with melting snow. Its lower half was cracked and missing, but it was undeniably authentic.

The skull of the Warrior they had met in the opium den.

Too tired to lift it up further, the hunter let it thud to the ground. 'A Bone Warrior,' she gasped. 'In Ik-Song.'

A shocked silence.

Impossible. He was *dead*, and even if he'd lived, he was too weak to do this. But if they admitted that they knew that – it was a confession anyway. A quick glance at Scarlet reaffirmed her thoughts – they were trapped.

It was White Crane who spoke next. 'By the power vested in the Court and the Councillor, I decree the Royal Keeper of the Gates under arrest and in bindings.'

Shock ran through Shadow.

Guards approached – but they were hesitant, standing back.

'Don't touch me,' Scarlet hissed, and they didn't. 'What are you doing, Crane? You're going to arrest me right before the flower moon? You *need* me on the front lines. What does the Councillor say about this?'

He didn't respond, only turning to the lone hunter. 'Jade,' he said. 'What happened?'

She tried to catch her breath. 'They're gone – they're *all gone*. One minute we were chasing down prey, and the next . . .'

'Did you see the Keeper and her companion in the forest?' he asked. Everyone listened raptly.

Jade nodded. 'One of our arrows hit a tree, and we heard voices – we realized they were in the forest trail below us. They started to run down. And then the blizzard hit from behind.' She halted. 'We tried to get down, too, but – the

The Last Soldier of Nava

Master died first. She was speared right through the chest with ice. She was the only one who was targeted.'

'No,' Shadow said. 'You're lying.' Aspis could not be dead.

Aspis was a soldier, a survivor, a hunter. She was unbeatable. She'd been alive only an hour earlier, disappearing into the mountains with her quiver. She wouldn't die so easily, so quietly, body hardening over in the cold. Once the Queen's best general, the Moonbearer's first Keeper. Wise enough to know when not to lead; her undying confidence that Shadow could steer them into battle.

Aspis had been the one to warn her not to trust too easily. But then she'd made Aspis trust her, and hadn't she turned around and broken it? *You're lying,* she wanted to say. The last thing she'd said to her was a betrayal. For all Aspis's hidden motives, Shadow had still cared for her.

'And then you brought down the Bone Warrior?' Crane was asking. *Prompting.* It was just like Yong and the Soldier sighting, this staged show. It was too late. Scarlet had been so confident that no one would ever truly move against her, not with Yo-han on her side, and it had left her wide open to the Court.

'All of us drew our bows at the same time – and I took his helmet.'

'Are you the sole survivor?'

'I don't know,' Jade said, but it was clear that no one else would be riding out from the mountains. No one else had lived.

Her bright, accusing eyes turned on Scarlet. 'You left us to die,' she spat at her, 'by your own doing.'

Shadow was incredulous. 'We almost died trying to escape, too—'

Scarlet held up a hand. 'Say what it is that you accuse me of,' she said to Crane.

He drew himself up with satisfaction. 'You, Keeper of the Gates, are formally accused of consorting with the Asanai Empire to commit acts of treason against the Ik-Song Dynasty. You orchestrated this weather with a Bone Warrior, and you are responsible for the murder of one of your rivals, the Master of the Hunt.'

'And your evidence?' Scarlet asked coolly.

He turned to the crowd.

Crow.

Of course. He stood near the back, tense. It was only after White Crane said his name that he slowly came forward. She had expected Crow to relish a moment like this, but he only looked grim. She tried to catch his eye, then. To plead.

'I witnessed the Keeper and her companion with this Warrior in an opium den in Yosae last night.'

You killed him on the spot. 'Then tell them, too, Crow,' Shadow said, 'how he was an old, frail defected soldier thrown out like a dog on the streets. He—'

'Enough,' White Crane silenced her.

'Then what else?' Scarlet said crassly. 'Or is that all? Your impressionable little lackey catching me in Yeok-gu interrogating some addict?'

'And,' Crane continued, 'mere days ago, at the announcement of the Soldier's resurgence, you threatened the Master of the Hunt with death.'

If it were up to me, Aspis, I would throw you into a deadzone, naked and alone, as bait for the Soldier. Everyone had heard it.

'I didn't know your threat would be made true,' White Crane said. 'If I did, I would've taken action sooner. And Aspis wouldn't have been killed at your order.'

'After all the time I've spent here insulting Aspis and every member of the Court, including you, why do I suddenly act on my words now? Why would I do what I've never done before?'

'Because you have brought a sickness into the palace,' he said, and looked directly at Shadow. 'Something you haven't had before. A co-conspirator, an ally.'

Shadow paled. This neat evisceration, this public decapitation was so practised, so clever. They had sought out a Bone Warrior to turn the palace on the Moonbearer, but instead, the palace had turned on them.

'This,' Scarlet laughed low. 'This is diabolical. Even for you lot.' It didn't matter if the evidence was tight or not. The palace had made its decision. They parted around the Keeper like a sea, a wall, a division clear as day.

'And where is our Prince? The only one with power to vouch for me?' Scarlet asked.

'Prince Yo-han is inside, being tended to,' White Crane said.

'Then let us be clear,' she said. 'Without his final word, you cannot make formal accusations against me, bind me, imprison me, or take any action whatsoever. I suppose you'll have to wait until tomorrow morning for my execution, or whatever it is you look forward to.'

Silence. No one could argue with that.

'As of now,' she finished, 'nothing has changed. I'm still Keeper, second only to Yo-han. I will roam the palace as I please and continue on with my day.' She dismounted from her deer, which parted on its own to the nearest stablehand. After a beat of hesitation, he took the buck in and began to guide it away, unclipping the harness.

Scarlet disappeared inside the palace without another word.

Up in their chambers, Scarlet had told her to stay in her room, before disappearing into her own.

But Shadow had decided.

Scarlet's door loomed in front of her in the hall.

One thing was clear: Scarlet was no longer needed. Scarlet was expendable. Shadow would likely be kept in the prisons for the war. By tomorrow morning, Scarlet would be executed. The Stronghold had never been, and was no longer, safe.

In Sae's home, Shadow had been taught how to kill a chicken with her bare hands; how to honour its body properly. The final glint of their eye before it would be gone forever in a single, careless act. Necessary and painful.

She had to twist. She had to tell Scarlet that she was the Soldier.

Scarlet wouldn't be so rash as to fight her on the spot.

At least, she hoped.

Scarlet would let her anger simmer and burn. She would save it for later.

In the meantime, she would let Scarlet awaken her.

Tell her the string of words to utter to bring the Soldier back to life – but this time, *Scarlet* would be her handler. Scarlet would direct her, use her. Shadow would let her. She *wanted* Scarlet to use her.

It was the only way. With the Soldier awakened, it might be enough to give them a fighting chance, a head start. When the Moonbearer came after Scarlet, she would have a weapon strong enough to hold him off.

Shadow inhaled sharply, spread her palm on the door, and pushed it open with finality.

The room appeared.

Darkened.

Empty.

Scarlet's rooms were empty. Why? How?

Shadow stepped inside. There were no signs of struggle or much disarray in the room; most of it was neat. She stood in the centre, turning in a circle. Stiff. Unsure.

The Last Soldier of Nava

Where would Scarlet possibly be? Surely, she wouldn't be wandering around the palace at this time, not when her life hung in this transitory limbo. Guilty or innocent. Royal or dead.

'She's not here,' said a voice behind her.

Chapter 24

Shadow's heart seized; she spun around and crashed into someone so hard that they both went sprawling onto the ground; she landed face first onto a solid weight.

She looked up.

Crow stared back, wide-eyed, propped up on his elbows.

Shadow was on him in an instant, pinning his arms to the ground. He didn't even react, much less resist.

'Tell me where she is right now,' she said, thumbs pressing into his wrists. He winced. 'Or this time, I won't hold back.'

'Scarlet is in the stables,' Crow said. 'Mounting her deer.'

Whatever Shadow was about to say next died on her lips. 'She's not with the Moonbearer?'

'No one is with the Councillor,' he said. 'No one can be.'

What? Shadow drew back and saw Crow suddenly for the first time. In her anger, she hadn't noticed it – how nervous he looked. The sheen of sweat. He looked disarrayed, unfocused.

'Shadow,' he said, and something in his voice made her stop. 'Go with her. And leave this place.' He glanced towards the door. 'I know you don't trust me,' he said. 'You have good reason not to. But you have to listen to me, now – you have to leave.'

She stared at him. 'Of course I don't trust you. You haven't trusted *me* since the start.'

'I know.' He sounded desperate. 'I haven't been on your side this entire time. But right now, I am.'

'Do you expect me to believe that? So suddenly?'

'Don't believe me, then. But go anyway. I'm not lying about where she is.' He ran a hand over his face, clutching at his hair.

'Crow?' she said.

And then, the quiet admission: 'He's gone too far.'

'What do you mean?'

Eyes serious, dark. 'I believed in him – in everything he wanted. I still do, somehow. But he *killed* Aspis. He massacred the entire party. And I helped.' His jaw clenched. 'He plans to kill more, probably. But it's not too late for me to turn.'

At any other time, she would have assumed that he was talking about the Moonbearer.

Now, she was certain that he wasn't.

Crow was silent for a moment, blinking hard. And then he looked up. 'There's something you need to see.'

Shadow stood and let him up. He took a moment to gather himself together, hands clenching and unclenching into fists, consciously schooling his expression into something calmer. For the first time since she'd met him, she thought of his likeness to his name – sharp, cunning. Birdlike.

He glanced at her once, and then began to step forwards. She followed without question. He was leading her to the throne room. Usually so heavily guarded and bustling with people, the halls were eerily quiet, vacant.

Crow could easily be leading her into a trap. But he looked

on the verge of collapse, the remorse in his voice real. Eyes distracted, frenzied.

She should've seen this sooner, she thought.

Crow went in first.

It was dark inside, the churning wall of darkness still there – crowding out every ounce of light.

She hadn't seen this wall since the first day she'd arrived. She still sensed almost nothing behind it – barely anything more than a vestige of the Moonbearer's power.

Crow walked up right to it.

And he waved his hand through the viscous fog.

Instantly, it dissipated.

It was nothing different than her own shadow wall, the harmless mirage she used to throw off opponents. Why had it looked so different to her before? Stronger, darker? Only because she had known *he* was behind it?

Behind it was nothing but a bed, within a sparse imitation of a bedchamber. And lying on the mat, halfway covered by a blanket, was someone that she hadn't seen in a thousand years. She almost fell to her knees, hand covering her mouth.

The Moonbearer was completely comatose.

Emaciated, weak, spidery black veins running up and down his near-translucent limbs, even across the thin skin of one of his eyelids. His arteries pulsed, as if this ink wanted to burst through them. You could almost mistake him for a corpse, slowly pressing down into the sinking mat. He reminded her of the animals below the palace. So far from what he'd once been. *Is he even alive?* she thought, but his chest rose ever so slowly, faintly.

This was why she hadn't been able to sense him. There was little to sense.

A sick twist of satisfaction warred with guilt in her. The desire to kneel beside him, to hold one hand between hers. All the time spent looking up at him, assuming her rightful place as the Soldier. He had taught her so much. Once, she might have thought that he had taught her strength. She knew better now.

'The Councillor,' Crow said, thinking she wouldn't recognize him.

She drew closer. She couldn't resist reaching a hand out to skim over his skin, the strangeness of it, how it felt like her fingers might pass through. They sparked, and she pulled back. Abruptly, she felt drained, as if a part of her was weakened by seeing him rendered helpless. All the rage, the fantasies of vengeance – imagining their confrontation – had fallen apart in an instant.

'How long has he been like this?'

'Almost a year now.'

'Does everyone know?'

'Most of the Inner. But not everyone, no.' A pause. 'Not Scarlet.'

His power was indisputably fading. Most likely, the fuel of Dragon slaughter wasn't sustainable; it never could be. It would eventually overwhelm the user, weaken as much as it had once strengthened. She understood, now, the urgency of the Stronghold in all of its training sessions, its preparations for war. Slaughtering the Dragon of the West was the only way to rejuvenate the Moonbearer's strength, to bring him back.

But none of this had been at the command of this near-lifeless man. It couldn't have been. It had been someone else. Someone desperate to revive him. Someone Crow would have been completely loyal to.

'Yo-han,' she said softly. 'It's always been Prince Yo-han, hasn't it? From the start.'

Slowly, the pieces slotted into place: even back on Mourning

Day, the cloaked figure controlling the winds from the rooftops of Yosae. He had run at the sight of her. That was no remade.

'You saw the blizzard just now,' Crow said. 'You've seen the extent of his true power.'

'Then it's true? He's half-Asani?'

Crow nodded. 'He's not evil – he isn't. He's misguided. But maybe he thinks he's too far in to turn back, now. I've been loyal to him, I've tried to make him see, I've tried . . .'

Yo-han must know that she was the Soldier. He'd known all along. *He'd* sent Crow after her in the markets, not the Moonbearer; would've known that she would react to sand, without telling Crow why.

The night of the banquet, when she'd wandered into his own study – he had tried to have her awakened in there, waiting for the Guards to finish their job. But he'd failed. Even after the duel with Crow, he'd pardoned her.

'But he strays farther from the truth,' Crow continued, distraught. 'He can't *see* anymore. He's so vengeful – against the Queen, against Asanai. For abandoning him and casting him aside. His anger – it consumes him. The Moonbearer is facing the consequences of using the Dragon's power. Yo-han wants to finish what he intended.'

And the snowstorm they had only just weathered, beside the Stronghold, where Yo-han had been standing beneath the trees. Still, quiet, face impassive.

Gathering a storm.

All this time, she had been so focused on the Moonbearer. She'd regarded every move as a play by him. And she had once thought Scarlet to be the sneak, so walled-off. But that white head of hair, that mellow face . . . what furious rage, what guarded ambitions did it hide? How long had it festered within him, clamouring for an out?

The Last Soldier of Nava

'He sent Guards after us in Yosae, after the parade,' Shadow said. 'At the site where the Desert Rose died.'

Crow's eyes went wide, shame flitting across his face. 'I thought he only sent me.' He turned his face to the shadow, voice hopeless. 'Perhaps he's been lying to me this entire time.'

'I'm sorry,' she said. And she meant it. 'You're preparing to slaughter the Dragon on the flower moon, aren't you? How?'

He nodded. 'Yo-han is set on using its power to conquer Asanai. To merge it with Ik-Song. And bring the Moonbearer back. It's what they planned before he was so weakened. I don't know how – I just know you're essential.'

'That's not what the Moonbearer wants,' she said with certainty. 'He doesn't care about Asanai. The Moonbearer wants to kill the Dragon, because he wants to raise the Ninth City again. And in doing so, he'll destroy Ik-Song as it stands. It's already falling apart now – the deadzones, the storms. It's nature trying to right itself.'

Crow was incredulous. '*Nava?* He wants to bring back *Nava?*'

It's what he's always wanted. She saw that now. He wouldn't conquer Asanai; he wouldn't save Ik-Song. He would regain his home by force, whatever dark and twisted version of it rose with the Dragon's blood. And he had deceived Yo-han into doing the dirty work.

'Is that what the Stronghold believes will happen? When the Dragon falls, Asanai will, too?'

'Yes – I believed that, too. All this time, I clung to that.'

'The Moonbearer himself orchestrated the White Ice,' Shadow said. 'He did it to have Ik-Song. None of this is any of our faults. This was a plan set in motion long before we were even players. Yo-han isn't the first to fall to his lies –' She glanced at the sickly state of her father '– and he won't be the last. This is a sickness – when touched by him, we can no longer discern what's right and what's not.

'You have to try to get through to Yo-han, to make him see that the Moonbearer won't give him what he wants. You can't slaughter the Dragon again. Asanai will never be his.'

'*Again?*'

Shadow exhaled. There was no use in hiding it anymore. And Crow needed to know. 'A thousand years ago, he slaughtered the *Yong* of the East.'

Crow looked puzzled. 'How do you know that?'

'Because he used it to create me.'

There was no telling how Crow would react, but a strange calmness had settled over her. It was the truth, wasn't it? No less, no more.

He stared for a long moment, uncomprehending. When it hit him, his face transformed; he staggered back. She could almost see his mind frantically working.

'I've been asleep,' she said. 'For a long time.'

Crow sounded soft-spoken. 'I can't fathom this.'

'Lately, though, I've been wondering how long it's been, whether I've woken across the ages.'

'It's you, then. You are the last Soldier of Nava. How is that possible? You . . . you . . .' He cut off, shaking his head. 'I'm not meant to be here, running with royals and gods and myths. Remnants of the old world.'

'None of us are gods,' she said. 'Especially not the Moonbearer. He's a false god. He takes and takes, and soon, there'll be nothing left to take – not even the seas or the lands. He'd build the Ninth out of bones again if it were up to him. To save the world, the Dawnbringer put me to sleep with the light of Nava, drawing out its power – destroying it in the process. It might take something as drastic as that to kill the Moonbearer, too, if he were to regain his power.'

'Scarlet knows,' he said. 'I don't know where she's going, but you can't stay here, either. You need to leave, go far away. They said you were important, that you had to be here – but I don't know why.'

'Why did they spare me, and not her? What do they plan to use me for?'

'I don't know, but don't stay to find out.' His tone was urgent. 'Go, and I wish you speed by the Moon Rabbit.' He rapidly listed off directions through the hidden tunnel exit to the stables. 'I'll delay for you as long as possible.'

After a moment, she nodded and hurried to the door. She thought of their first encounter in Yosae, Crow's powerfully launched blows, perched on the roof. Cornering her in the gardens under the willow; facing her down in the arena, swiping hot sand. A lone figure in silver in the opium den. She envied how he fought with purpose, with knowledge. And she knew little about him except that he'd been brave enough to come to her now. They might have been friends, once.

But she was tired of mourning things she'd never lost.

'Come with me,' she said. 'Leave this place behind.'

'I can't,' he said. 'I have to stay with Yo-han.'

'Vengeance changes people,' she said. 'You might die if you stay here. And it might be his hand that you die by.'

'If I die, I'll die trying to save him,' Crow said, and there was no room for argument there. 'He would do the same for me.'

She nodded. She understood. 'Then thank you, Crow,' she said. 'May our sunlines cross again.'

'And if not, our moonlines.'

Yejin Suh

She paused in the doorway when Crow called out to her.

'If you really were once the Soldier,' he said, 'I've always wondered – what was the Ninth City like?'

She smiled gravely. 'I don't remember. All of it – it's like a dream.'

Chapter 25

Shadow spotted her immediately outside as she ran to the stables – she knew which exit Scarlet would take. Scarlet didn't look at her as she approached. She was so tense that it looked painful; the motions of her harnessing, usually so gentle towards her buck, were unusually sharp. As if her body didn't know what to do with all its hurt. *The only person who I trust is Yo-han,* she had said once. She'd meant that with all her heart, but even that couldn't be true anymore.

'The Moonbearer is comatose,' Shadow said. 'Yo-han has been acting in his place.'

Scarlet's motions stilled momentarily – before starting up again, her tone acerbic: 'And where is Yo-han now?'

'I don't know. But I think Crow will stall him. At least until—'

'I'm going to Asanai.'

Around Shadow, the world shifted several paces. '*What?*'

'I want an audience with the Emperor. So don't bother with the heartwarming speeches of loyalty,' Scarlet continued. 'This is your chance, fool, don't you see? Go run. Run while you still can. You said it yourself, leaving is easy when it's necessary. You've done it before, and you can do it again.'

'Why Asanai?'

'This started with the Asani, with the White Ice. It'll end with it, too. I'm going to go find the truth. And I'm going to ask for help.'

'You lead a suicide mission,' Shadow said. 'You plan to head straight into the heart of enemy territory by yourself, with no backup, no leverage, nothing. You don't even have a plan.'

'The Bone Warrior said they have a weapon. Remember? The likes of which the world has never seen before. Perhaps this weapon is powerful enough to bring balance again.'

'Why would the Emperor help you?'

'If the Moonbearer wants Nava back, Ik-Song won't be the only state in danger,' she said. 'Whether I stay here or go there, I'll probably die either way. What army do we have to regroup? What arsenal to gather, what strategists? What *power*. At least in Asanai, I can try.'

'There's an old woman in Yosae – who I said was my grandmother before, I lied, but she helped me recover. She knows things, she could help us—'

'Go to her, then. Find her and protect her against what will come. Here's your chance for escape. Your Councillor is incapacitated; your Court, power-hungry; your prince, a traitor. You're useless. You shouldn't come. And you shouldn't trust me.'

Frustration welled. 'Why are you talking like that? As if I'm still a prisoner, just waiting for my chance to run? After everything? Stop baiting me.'

'I am ultimately selfish. I'll get what I want, regardless of the road there and the consequences of it. I don't care.'

'In the opium den, Crow said that you were incapable of love. That you dishonour your sister's memory,' Shadow said. 'And maybe it's true.'

The Last Soldier of Nava

Crow could only stall Yo-han for so long. Guards were probably on their way out of the Stronghold already.

'But I know what it's like,' Shadow continued, 'to have your identity fractured, to be robbed of something essential. Trust is so hard to give and then so easily broken. But I don't think you have to learn how to trust. And I don't think you're incapable of love. I think you just have to remember.'

Remember.

'Let's go to the Emperor together,' Shadow said, forcing down everything that she had just been planning. 'If everything you said about the White Ice was true, then the Emperor was betrayed. All he got was a slew of dead Bone Warriors while the Moonbearer became revered here. Perhaps the thought of revenge will awaken his cold heart.'

A pause.

'You're right,' Scarlet said.

'See? We're plotting together,' Shadow said. 'It's good that you didn't kill me that day in Yosae. We'd never have got the chance otherwise.'

Soon you will see that I have betrayed you the same way Yo-han has, Shadow thought. *The Emperor will recognize me on the spot.*

'I was never going to kill you, Shadow. That was just for show,' Scarlet said. 'It's all for show; you take me so seriously.' And then, sombrely: 'I don't think anyone's taken me so seriously before.'

There was definitely Guard movement now – Shadow sensed it before she heard it. The clicking of boots and commotion.

'I used to think of Asanai as the hostile territory,' Scarlet said. 'But everywhere I step is somewhere I should not be.'

She moved closer: 'I'm your ally, Scarlet. I'm not enemy land.'

Your heart will break once more.

But I am selfish.
I want this for as long as possible.
They turned at movement just outside the palace. A stray servant was fuzzily visible in the dark, stopped dead in her tracks. They had tested their time to the very limits, anyway.

Scarlet mounted and reached down a gloved hand.

Shadow grabbed it, slinging one foot on the foothold and bracing her other hand on the warm, breathing flank. There were packs already bundled behind her. In the upper windows of the Stronghold, lanterns lit up. Guards streamed out of the southside exit.

Shadow wanted to come, so badly. And yet – this time, she was the one to hesitate. 'If you knew who I really was,' Shadow said softly, 'you wouldn't have risked yourself for me.'

Scarlet pulled her forcefully up behind her, the clasp of her hand warm; Shadow's eyes traced the divot of her shoulder blade. 'I *have* seen who you really are, idiot.'

Scarlet's back was warm against her front; this close, the fine hairs of the nape of her neck were visible. Scarlet turned, bracing one hand against Shadow's leg slung over the deer – and the proximity made Shadow shiver, even in the heat, the urgency.

Scarlet nudged the buck, hurtling out into the night air, across the open fields – not to the mountains, but this time towards Yosae and its spindling side roads. Roads that would lead to the glittering sea, then straight north across blue waters that would lighten and grow cold, to the Asani Sea, and beyond the snowy shores, great rocky mountains and bone-bleached lands.

The Moonbearer would hate for their talents to go to waste in that snowy desert. Where soldiers as tall as two men waited and the Emperor sat beside his fire.

If it was true that she had been awoken before, ten years

The Last Soldier of Nava

ago, he would recognize Shadow on sight, even scarred, even after so much time. He would expose her if she didn't reveal herself first, and Scarlet would hate her for the rest of time. But that was all right. Shadow would still do her duty, help her find the truth. At whose hand she would die, she didn't know, but she would exchange her life for it all.

'We need a ship,' Shadow said dazedly. A ship bound for Asanai. The ground passed quickly behind them, distant figures on deerback giving chase.

'Quick thinking,' Scarlet said. 'It's a relief the logistics are up to me.'

And then their buck stumbled and leapt. Below, the grass began to curl insidiously with frost, entire sheets freezing over patches.

Shadow looked back.

Yo-han.

He gained on them at terrifying speed, a silvery blur on his doe, traversing the fields like an otherworldly force, so far ahead of any other Guard. He lowered even further along its back, and pure ice chased them relentlessly, forging forward across the ground, nipping at their buck's back hooves.

Around them, the world rushed by blindingly; Shadow's hair whipped around her face.

'He's catching up,' Shadow said. Scarlet did not ask who 'he' was, and only sped up.

His full armour gleamed under the moonlight; serrated knives lined his right thigh, a blade along his left arm. He drew so close that Shadow could see his eyes narrow; she didn't want to attack him, she wished she could talk to him. Ask him why.

But he had no such qualms about violence. Yo-han unclipped one of the daggers at his leg and hurled it point-blank towards her.

It came so fast that she hardly had time to clap it between her palms, body twisted around, hissing at the blade cutting into her skin. She flung it to the side and threw back her own long arc of conjured darkness that he countered quickly. He was an expert rider, and exactly as skilled with hard weapons as with ability – agile like Crow, but with more brute strength behind the blows. He aimed precisely at non-lethal points: the abdomen, shoulder, legs. Nothing she did made him lose balance, not even for a moment. And unlike Crow, Shadow knew little of his mind, his interiority.

Shadow did not want to face off against this particular opponent.

She turned back to relay this to Scarlet but saw that they neared the moat.

She cursed. 'How are we going to—' She looked back at Yo-han. 'Crossing it will take too long.'

'Trust me,' Scarlet said.

They were only seconds from the steep drop.

And then:

All of the water in the moat seemed to rise up at once, like a living thing, in one huge and undulating lift; its slow ascent made it feel like time had slowed around them.

It froze from the top-down, solidifying in seconds. A wall of ice, thick and unyielding.

They wouldn't even make it off palace grounds. Behind them, Yo-han was already slowing down, dismounting his doe, regarding his trap.

But in front of her, Scarlet reached into the folds of her clothes and fished out a small bone whistle.

Its call was short, and low.

Looking back, Shadow wasn't sure if she had been dreaming or not. There was a deafening stillness all around them, until there wasn't. Until faint tremors spliced the ground like the beginnings of an earthquake. A slight darkening under the ice, and then a shadow rising so vast behind the glacial block that it seemed to be a part of it, highlighting every groove. The shadow almost transcended it, the tangibility of it, so high up it seemed to blot out the moon. And the ice shattered in a thousand different pieces, the catfish spinning back down in a slow and momentous turn, receding under the surface with a crash, water sloshing out on all sides, soaking the ground through, thawing the frost. Their buck leapt through the collapse, hidden behind its enormous body, a single, staggering bound over the divide – and landed on the other side.

Mid-air, Shadow was still looking back at Yo-han remounting, preparing to chase, until he was tackled off from the side by another figure, fast and nimble: Crow. They tussled on the ground, and eventually Yo-han stopped struggling.

It was the last thing she saw, Crow's figure crouching over Yo-han, Yo-han looking after them – hand outstretched towards her like he would coalesce the ice once again, blocking them out with the wall, covering the view of the field, the Stronghold, everything, entirely.

Part 2:
유빙 Drift Ice

Chapter 26

Shadow had been watching the sea when Scarlet came above deck. 'They're throwing some kind of festivity, you know,' Scarlet said. 'For the holiday.'

The mornings would always see low fog settle over the water, so that you couldn't tell where the sky ended and where the sea started; beginning in the afternoon, the sun would break through with sharp, streaming brilliance.

'The holiday?' Shadow turned from where she'd been leaning on the rail, wrapped in a fur, wind whipping her hair astray. It had got progressively chillier the farther north they'd journeyed.

'The tomb-sweeping.'

Traditional tomb-sweeping cycles honoured the dead and the fallen by laying food beside their graves for their spirits to eat. Indeed, Shadow could smell the faint burn of incense. 'They're leaving food?'

Scarlet nodded. 'And maybe a drink. Or two.'

'I suppose you enjoy the thought of getting your ancestors blind drunk.'

Scarlet tried to hide her smile, settling beside Shadow to

watch the sea. The Asa was a different beast from the Seochon; a lighter blue, deep and clear, like nothing had touched the surface in aeons. Ice floes tittered by; the occasional slender-winged seabird circled overhead. They had passed countless small islands, some so tiny that only a single house might stand on the foundations, dotted with tall and skinny evergreens. In the distance lurked the shapes of glaciers and arching mountains.

It was all mostly barren of human life. Only wild creatures lived here. And it was beautiful. That was what the Ninth had looked like, sort of – one would look upon a wild forest without knowing it was really a sprawling city. Is this what the Moonbearer wanted again? This pristineness, this wild reclaim? Silence for miles?

He would kill for it, it seemed.

'. . . starting in a few hours, once they've finished up for the night,' Scarlet was saying.

'How can they tomb-sweep on the sea?' Shadow asked, turning. 'There are no graves here.'

'Most of their fathers and forefathers were sailors who probably died at sea. Perhaps the ocean, to them, is just one large grave.'

'That's morbid.'

'I see it as an exchange. They offer their lives up to the sea, and the sea becomes the medium to their ancestors.'

They'd been onboard for nearly a week. Cargo ships like this were dependable, self-manned; trade had always continued, even during the White Ice, even recently when the Moonbearer shut down Ik-Song. Nations had fought and reshaped around these ships, and they were unaffected by it all. Sailors lived in a world of their own, untouched by outside affairs. Here, there was no Court, no banquet dinners. There was only a brotherhood, oblivious to the building war out there; their weeks were not determined by the sun and moon, but rather by the coastlines that came into view over the horizon; the changing temperatures and tides of the seas. They subsisted on herring, rice wine, millet. Slept in free-swinging hammocks, chased off the occasional gull onboard. There was a certain beauty to it. Shadow wondered what they thought, what they regarded as real and not. She wondered many strange things, having settled into the calm acceptance of the lull before disaster, the certainty of death and change.

Back in Ik-Song, they'd barely made it onto the cargo ship bound for the cold country of Asanai, Scarlet with probably enough coin to buy it out. She'd wanted to bring her buck, but a ship on the high seas was no place for a deer. Scarlet had let him go at the edge of the forest, unharnessing, touching at first his neck and then the dashing spiral of his antlers. No one had seen them leave in the dark from a small shore village, except perhaps stray neighbourhood kids playing on the rocks nearby, turning over tide pools, too young to care or notice.

Disaster was certain, but they were free. Here, time was liminal. Scarlet would feel it better than anyone, she thought. Scarlet, unlike her, had already had a life before the Moonbearer trapped her. She had lived in Anje for most of it, with her sister, and maybe she had fond childhood memories. It may have been a false freedom, what they felt, but somehow, it didn't matter at the moment. It was clear from Scarlet's face that she didn't care.

'And will we be participating?' Shadow asked, turning to the other girl, who wasn't watching the sea anymore, but her.

'It depends on the tombs we intend to sweep. Whose, for you?'

'I would have three,' Shadow said. Taking a breath. 'The first, would be Aspis.' Nava had believed in reincarnation; not only spiritually, but in the literal sense, too – everything that constituted their skin and their hair had once been the stuff of dirt and stars and would return after death. In the early mornings, she eyed the white birds and wondered if any of them held Aspis within them.

'And?' Scarlet asked.

'My own,' Shadow replied. 'Or is that very dramatic?'

She smiled gently. 'You've died, then?'

'My past self – whoever I was before, whoever I am now. Who I am becoming. All different.' It was something that Sae would say, vague and esoteric. She thought of the stone in her shirt. Sae had given it to her on purpose and collapsed her own house. There were many odd things about her that she had never figured out.

'And the third?'

A bang from behind made them both turn.

'You ladies will freeze your tits off, roughing it out in the wind like that,' yelled a voice emerging from below deck. Captain Pongi, halfway up the stairs. He was a ruddy-faced, potbellied man; right now, he appeared to have already started on the spirits.

'Why don't you two come down and join the crews for a pankin'?'

'Quit bothering 'em,' came another voice. There were muffled noises, followed by something breaking.

'All right, all right, quit bothering *me*,' Pongi said, winking at them, and disappeared back down with a smile full of broken teeth. The door closed behind him with a small thud.

Shadow turned back to Scarlet, who was smirking. Shadow also couldn't stop her own smile. If anyone on the ship fit the stereotypical bill of a pirate, it was Pongi by far; she could almost imagine him as a swashbuckling figure, brandishing his rigging knife, like the Asani raiders she'd once read about.

The Last Soldier of Nava

All this time, neither of them had been able to identify his accent – an extraordinary blend of southern tones, foreign slang, and general crassness.

'"Panking"? Is that really a saying?' Scarlet said, at which she began to laugh.

'Do you think he was the first sailor to ever sail?'

'With him, the livelihood simply began.'

'To the beginning of all sailors, started by Pongi,' Shadow smiled. 'Let's join them below. I'm getting cold.'

The night was raucous, as expected – in no small part thanks to Scarlet and her easy camaraderie with the sailors. In the Stronghold, she was a prickly menace, a tantrum to the entire palace – but really, she knew how people worked. That much was clear. Like how the Desert Rose had been so attuned, made a martyr, the perfect figure for followers to use and pray to; Scarlet possessed the same kind of gift, she suspected, but she did not give hers away so generously. She was guarded, stingy with it; giving when she wanted, withholding when not. But there was no such hesitation when it came to the sailors.

The sailors were used to travelling the straits between Ik-Song and Asanai. This was no thrilling feat for them, no anxiety at the state that would soon loom over the horizon. They'd been overjoyed at the new company, two new and strange guests. They weren't put off by Shadow's appearance, because half of them were scarred themselves; even without that, there were countless other problems to account for, like decaying teeth, or sunburnt flesh. In short, her appearance was of little concern.

They didn't mind Shadow, usually quiet and prone to contemplation above deck. But they loved Scarlet, who was unafraid to quip back and could hold her own in just about anything – darts, cards, drink.

None of them were privy to their mission. There was no way to know that either of them had ability, since they had no white hair to give it away. If anyone recognized Scarlet as the Keeper – a stretch, considering their unlikely situation – no one said anything.

Now, after a hearty meal of rice and fish, they sprawled out over tables in the warm underbelly of the ship, playing dice, around the carefully supervised burn of incense, ancestral prayers muttered in between. Beside Shadow, one of the younger sailors, a lanky boy named Yi-yoon, played his violin in a lovely melody. She liked Yi-yoon. He was quiet, and often spent his time playing or sketching; she watched his fingers pluck delicately at the strings while Scarlet tried actively to goad one of the men into a knife fight to see who would win. Shadow rolled her eyes.

'You're both combat-trained,' Yi-yoon said shrewdly, looking from her to Scarlet. 'Do you happen to hail from a family of warlords?'

'Hardly,' Shadow mused. 'We just learned to fight from the same teacher.' True enough.

Pongi had taken Scarlet up on the offer. 'I would bet you coin that the Captain wins.'

'Really?' Shadow looked at him in surprise. 'You aren't expecting her to win?'

'I am,' he replied. 'My bet is a way of prayer for Pongi's safety.'

Shadow laughed. 'Smart. I don't have coin, though.' She considered. 'You don't even need it out here. There are no prices, no debts at sea.'

'No wealthy or poor.' He smiled. 'But don't be fooled – this life is not for everyone.'

They watched the commencement of the fight, the old, rusted blunt blades too flimsy to do any real damage. Scarlet twirled it expertly between her fingers. Show-off. It reminded Shadow of how purposefully Yo-han had hurled his dagger at her, how it had acted almost as an extension of him. His dagger had strained to cut her. *He* wanted to cut her, even as he needed her.

Neither of them had yet broached the subject of Yo-han. Even though the world was closing in, here, she could forget that for a moment as warmth filled her belly. In the middle of treacherous high seas, she had never felt better. She enjoyed it all. She enjoyed the loudness and the laughter, the voices fighting for attention, the racket of cups and fists slammed down on tables, ensuing uncensored yelling. The rocking of the ship and the occasional crashing wave against its hull. Her face was warm. It dawned on her that she'd never been in such a warm and crowded room like this; the last time she'd been surrounded by a number of people was the banquet, and that had been cold and vast and quiet.

So, this is what people meant by *cosy*. Lulling in its quiet, seeping din. This in-between.

After the fight concluded – Scarlet finished him at belly point, to a general uproar – and the violin ramped up to a fiddling tempo, Shadow went back up outside the quarters, to the deck. Night had fallen hard and fast; though it was hard to even tell, with the perpetual low grey cover. Here, stars twinkled brilliantly through the moving clouds; she thought of all the moonlines streaking above them, the streaming lines of everyone who had once lived. Perhaps in the skies, their lines intersected, intertwined, ran parallel; perhaps they were connected in odd ways, too far to be seen from down here. The line of Aspis. The line of Ki-Young the merchant. The lines of Nava.

Shadow found a hidden, quiet nook beside one of the masts, leaning over and watching the sea pass by. After a while, she sat down, propped up against the wood, cushioned by her fur, the water no longer in view but the spinning, constellation-studded wheel of sky above her.

The shapes of the stars felt instinctual. The water did, too. Like she had learned their patterns long before birth, imprinted under the skin of her body.

After a while, her eyes slowly began to drift closed, head tilting back. She wouldn't mind falling asleep outside, waking to a brilliant sunrise. Frost might coat her lashes, but when else would she ever have the time to enjoy the cold? She nodded off, silent in the dark, waves in her ears . . .

And was awakened by a faint rustle. She opened her eyes. Scarlet was crouching beside her, very close.

'You sleep like the dead.'

Shadow blinked, groggy. Usually, she was an incredibly light sleeper, alert and catlike. Scarlet waited for her to speak, but she only blinked some more.

'I even yelled your name,' Scarlet said, bemused.

'I . . . your hair is down.'

Shadow had never seen it unbound before. The reason it was always braided up and pulled away from her face, she realized, was because there was so much of it. Long and straight, almost down the length of her back, the edges curling against her forehead, her nape, no doubt from the heat of below. Its sway was almost hypnotizing. Without really thinking, Shadow reached out and touched a strand close to her. It was soft, thick.

Shadow realized the moment had gone on too long when she grew aware of Scarlet's eyes on her, the sleepiness subsiding. She began to draw her hand back. 'Sorry.'

But Scarlet only caught her hand and held it in place, leaning in closer. 'That's hardly worth noticing. You've been paying attention.'

The Last Soldier of Nava

Her first instinct was to deny it. She felt as exposed as a live nerve, straight out of sleep. 'It's just always up,' she said rather defensively.

'I wish yours was always up.'

'Mine?'

'So I could see more of your face,' said Scarlet, and then with her other hand, she brushed the hair out of the side of Shadow's face.

Shadow became suddenly aware of the solid ship's mast behind her, preventing her from backing up. She wished she could avert her eyes. But something was keeping her – *demanding* her from moving. 'Why do you need to see my face?'

'So I can watch you,' Scarlet said. 'The way you watch me.'

'Who says I'm watching you?' Shadow said. She felt her face growing hot, fingers growing lax in Scarlet's tight grip.

Scarlet smirked. 'Remember one of our first meetings – when I came in your quarters? And I was wearing something very sheer.'

'I remember. I had never seen anything like that before.'

Pause.

'And what were you thinking about, when you saw me?'

Shadow wasn't sure what to say to that. Her heartbeat had long stopped.

'Because,' Scarlet said, and her eyes flickered down to her lips once – and then lower – 'I can tell you what I think of when I watch you,' Scarlet said, and then she was even closer. The proximity made her heart drop low, and it was nothing she had ever experienced before. The fraughtness of a moment so delicate she was afraid that moving might shatter everything, like a pocket of air suspended outside of time. She had nothing to say.

Before either of them could do anything else, a long, sounding call ripped through the air.

They broke apart. Scarlet turned to the sea, and Shadow was left dazed, slightly out of breath, though she hadn't moved an inch.

The cloud cover had looked almost impassable, but as their ship tore cleanly through it, the fog parted, lifted.

She squinted at the hulking shapes through the grey. Dark, blurred masses, blending with the night until they weren't, until buildings materialized, cliffs came into view. The evergreens, dark thatched roofs dusted lightly with snow, lanterns lighting up the night warmly, the night port in movement.

They had arrived. Shadow turned her face away from the dim moonlight, unwilling to let Scarlet see her expression.

The deck was alive with activity, the sailors interrupted in their lull. They took inventory of stock, barked orders across the helm, and the crisp morning air snapped them all out of their reverie.

Shadow wanted to scan the docks, but no use in drawing unwanted attention. Instead, she watched Scarlet do a sweep from their vantage point for a long moment.

'How is it looking?' Shadow asked.

'I think there's some kind of festival going on,' Scarlet replied, peering out at the town. 'It looks fun.'

'I meant,' Shadow said, 'the logistics of us undocking.'

'I don't think that's up to us.'

Shadow opened her mouth to ask what that meant when the crew abruptly quieted and unease rippled through the ship. Some of them looked nervously overboard; some stilled in their unpacking.

Captain was talking to three of the men; when Shadow approached, he glanced over briefly at her. 'We're not supposed to directly interact with any Asani. Only port and back. We have a deck-checker for that.'

The Last Soldier of Nava

'Then why are they approaching?' someone muttered.
Approaching?

'It could be a random security measure,' Yoon-yi suggested. Nobody protested this, but no one agreed either. It was clear this sort of thing did not happen. Ever.

Shadow looked back and met eyes with Scarlet, who listened from the outskirts.

'We've got to arm ourselves,' one sailor said nervously. There was a flurry of outbursts, mostly objections, but a few heated agreements.

'Absolutely not,' Pongi said. 'We'll appear hostile.'

'They're already hostile!'

'What's the point of arms?' Yoon-yi said. 'One sweep of their hand and this entire ship will be half-frozen.'

'We're doomed,' said another man, and there came the moans, the panicked mutterings.

'We're not doomed,' Yoon-yi said. 'We have firepower.'

'Firepower?' Pongi said.

'Them.' He pointed at Shadow and Scarlet.

The Captain looked in disbelief. 'The girls? For what? I hope you're not suggesting we use them as scapegoats.' His brow darkened. 'That sort of thing does not fly on this ship.'

'No,' Yoon-yi said. 'They're remades.'

The crew looked at them questioningly, curiously.

'Both of them,' he continued. 'And strong ones, too, by the looks of it.'

'Is this true?' the Captain said.

Shadow didn't know how Yoon-yi knew – maybe he'd glimpsed them use ability some time, late at night when she skittered shadows along the water to entertain herself. They hadn't bothered to hide it very hard. But it didn't matter whether he knew or not, she realized. Their path was clear.

'It's true,' Shadow said to shocked murmurs. 'We are.'

Everyone turned at the harried footsteps coming up above deck. 'Captain,' one of the sailors said, stopping to catch his breath. 'They won't take no for an answer – they're insisting on coming on deck. Says it's by royal assent and everything. Want to do a sweep.'

'What for?' he asked, bewildered.

'A live cargo check,' cut another voice through the din, and the boat immediately quieted. There was a slow click of heeled boots, and then a figure appeared behind them.

An Asani port officer. He was young, uniform clean-cut and slick, gloved hands clasped behind his back. Tall despite his lean frame. Characteristic darkened grey hair – jarring against a youthful face – and the colour of his eyes made them look like they'd been fogged over, like he was blind. Unnerving. Immediately they landed on Shadow – and then Scarlet – before perusing the packages.

The crew instantly relaxed. It was only one man, and he was completely unarmed.

'We don't have live cargo,' the Captain said. 'Who are you?'

'My name is Nari,' the man replied, his accent heavy. 'Royal position. I am collecting something that belongs to the Emperor.' He smiled. 'I will do a momentary check.'

When he stepped forward and gestured behind him, they saw why he was unarmed. Behind him rose the enormous, hulking frame of a Bone Warrior – stooped low – like a white ghost appearing in the dark. When he unfolded himself onto the deck, he rose to full height, towering over both Nari and the rest of the men.

This Bone Warrior was nothing like the enfeebled exile in the opium den. He stood tall, incredibly tall, limbs like a giant's, half-skeleton, half-man; clothed in intricately sewn furs and leather, back slung with spears and knives, but with his bare arms still exposed to the cold. His breaths didn't even fog in the air. He wore a ram's skull, colossal, spiralling horns jutting out from either side, one section of the dusk-white ivory broken from past battle. Ice seemed to crackle and snap around him, as if he was colder, even, than his environment, as if he changed it as he passed through.

Despite having journeyed to Asanai so many times, clearly none of the crew had ever seen one before – they gawked, backed up and exchanged horrified glances. Shadow knew it would be best for her to back up, too, but she was entranced, fascinated by its gleaming form. Bone Warriors were not common foot soldiers; they were kept only in the vicinity of the Emperor's palace. Yet he had gone through all the trouble of sending one here.

As Nari came forward, muttering a few choice words in Asani, the Warrior trailed him. Here in the heartland, the creature seemed barely sentient, unlike the one Shadow had previously encountered. He didn't even glance around curiously, scope out the ship; only drew to where Nari directed on a tight leash.

'They're not here to attack you,' Shadow said, fighting back her uneasiness. 'They're only here for us.'

'We'll protect you, then,' Pongi said.

'No,' Shadow said. 'It's not necessary.'

The Bone Warrior approached, and Shadow tried not to back away. Unease roiled in her gut. He crouched, came close, and she looked up at his eyes, dark pits through the skull. Goosebumps ran over her arms, the air around them dropping a few degrees. After a moment, without even glancing at Scarlet, he looked back at Nari, as if confirming something.

Nari came close, right up to Shadow's face. 'What business have you in Asanai?'

'Take us to the Emperor,' she said. 'We have business with him.'

'That's suicide,' Pongi said incredulously.

The crew looked at her like she was insane. Questions abounded:

'You're venturing into the Empire?'

'Who are you?'

Nari appeared satisfied. 'Then come with me.' He turned and began to exit the ship.

'Thank you for letting us voyage with you,' Shadow said to the crew. 'I'm honoured that you would take us in.' She and Scarlet both bowed at the waist. 'May our sunlines cross again.'

Shadow turned and took a deep breath, exhaling mist into the cold air. No one replied except for Yoon-yi, whose voice she heard brush after her. 'And if not,' he said assuredly, 'our moonlines.'

Chapter 27

There was indeed, as Scarlet said, a festival under the growing moon. Although the docks were a good distance away from the inner town, Shadow could still hear the muted noise of it, the cheering and mill of people. They walked in a line across the decks and inland: Nari leading, followed by Scarlet, then Shadow, tail-ended by the Warrior. Shadow glanced back at the Bone Warrior, shivering, and pulled her hood tighter over her head.

'How did you know we were going to be on that ship?' Scarlet asked Nari. He didn't seem particularly eager to supply them with any information, choosing to lead them in complete silence. It was somehow more sinister than just boasting to them of their impending doom.

'We know who breaches Asani borders,' was all he said.

'What's the festival for?'

'Flower moon, of course.'

They drew stares from across the port, though Nari did not seem to care at all.

'You know, it kind of defeats the point of this –' Scarlet

pointed to her own hood – 'when you have a giant Warrior sulking behind us.'

Nari either ignored her or pretended not to understand. It was more or less quiet at this time of night, but still. For an alarmed moment she wondered if they would be walking like this through the crowded town, too. Thankfully, once they reached a more deserted area of the coast town, closer to the actual homes, Nari gestured towards the Bone Warrior, who loped off the path and stood to wait. They were led behind an outcrop of towering obsidian rock and needle evergreens towards a humble-looking makeshift den-cabin. It was less of a cabin, really, and more of an incredibly small enclosure that looked like it had been thrown together last minute, like a closet in the middle of the woods. The whole thing was maybe half the size of Shadow's own quarters in the Stronghold. Scarlet stepped forward and threw open the door.

There was nothing inside. Just floor and a bucket of water.

Instantly, the play became clear. No sleep, no food, just a few drawn-out hours of dread before their journey. This place would supply the bare minimum shelter needed just to make sure they didn't completely freeze to death overnight. The Emperor was toying with his prey.

The Emperor beside his great, licking fire.

'Tomorrow at dawn, we will meet back at the same dock.' Nari smiled pleasantly, in that same lilting tone. 'Understand?'

'You're just going to leave us here?' Scarlet said. 'No guards? What if we run away?'

'Did you not come to see the Emperor? Why would you run? Where would you go, back to Ik-Song?' His gaze was knowing, sure.

'What if we wreak havoc in that little town of yours?' Scarlet asked.

Nari shrugged. 'Do as you please. Tomorrow, we will be fetching you.' He smiled again and left.

Shadow watched his back as he left. This was worse than being thrown in a cell rotation beforehand. It felt like small walls were closing in on her, the reality of what they had done, what they had come here to do. *Tomorrow at dawn.* Dawn, and then nothing.

She turned and saw Scarlet watching her.

Scarlet smirked. 'You know what this means. We're going to the festival.'

'That's—' *a stupid idea,* she was going to say, but they were already way past that, weren't they?

'We can't possibly stay here.'

'There will be so many people at the festival.'

'Also,' Scarlet said, 'I've always wanted to try sea grapes.'

'*Sea grapes?*'

'Bubble algae. They're like seaweed. Pops in your mouth.'

'That sounds kind of disgusting.'

'It's an acquired taste, supposedly.'

'You don't even have Asani coin for that.'

'I'll win some, then.'

She was already following Scarlet out into the sleepless night, away from the port, towards the people.

The night was deathly frigid, but the furs Pongi had given them were insulating well. The racket of the festival grew louder and louder as they approached, stragglers passing by; they swept past residential areas within the crowd, houses with low and dark roofs, inclined so as not to accumulate snow, lit up by crackling fires inside. They talked sparsely to each other in case the language attracted attention and tried not to look too cold. The Asani wore furs, sometimes bundled all the way up to their noses; one man's eyes were the only visible part of his face through his. Scarlet hardly even bothered with her hood. Intermittently, a light dusting of snow would fall on them; Shadow ran a hand through her hair to shake off the wetness, eyeing the melting flake point on her finger. Behind them, in the distance, the ocean stretched out; a dark, calm thing. Occasionally a sharp and biting wind would rip through the festival, momentarily darkening fires, and chatter would start up again as if everyone had somehow been *rejuvenated* by the cold. She missed Ik-Song's weather.

But truthfully, she forgot all about Ik-Song when they actually breached the main square. The centrepiece of the festivities was an enormous mock ice palace, spiralling up into the sky, a real silver-rimmed clock engraved into its middle. The ice was not like anything she had ever seen before. Beautiful and translucent, lighting the entire town around it; it looked like Yo-han's, but clearer, bluer, almost supernatural – unnaturally ethereal. Their breaths fogged in the night air as she beheld the castle. Below the clock was etched a huge, intricate mural of a girl – with long, white hair, face hidden by a veil. Like a figure out of a story tale.

'Who is that?' she asked. 'A saint?'

Scarlet shrugged. 'Maybe a virgin sacrifice.'

Shadow shot her a look. They continued on. Performers spun fiery torches in blurs; ring fights broke out; roasting meats smoked deliciously. Smaller sculptures and miniature carvings of elk and evergreens surrounded them. Children hurled snow at one another and slid across the thick sheets of upraised ice. There were remnants of an earlier parade. They slowed by a circle of onlookers watching a single Asani man, shirtless, face screwed in intense concentration. He was growing a thin sheet of ice over his shoulders, like body armour; the only thing that gave him away was the occasional twitch of his fingers at his sides. It was impressive, not using the hands.

'Really leaning into the whole ice thing,' Scarlet commented. Behind him there was an impressive arsenal display of weaponry managed by an elderly woman; steel curving blades and throwing stars. Shadow couldn't tell if they were props or not. She studied one of the daggers from afar.

No matter where they stopped, Scarlet kept drawing stares. 'I think it's my hair,' she said, reaching up to touch her head.

'Definitely not,' Shadow replied. Yes, there were few heads as dark as theirs here, with most ranging along greys and silver to the occasional stark white, but that wasn't why. It was because Scarlet just stepped where she wanted to, head held high, and didn't move out of the way. 'You need to try to look more like a nobody.'

Scarlet rolled her eyes. She said something brief to the old woman in Asani, who responded promptly. 'She's charging an insane price for the knives,' Scarlet whispered to Shadow afterwards.

'Do you really need one? Besides, you don't even have Asani coin.'

Scarlet eyed one of the ring fights. '*They're* betting plenty.'

'Unless you suddenly gained new ability . . .'

'Wait, look,' Scarlet said, grabbing her by the arm. 'They're only sparring. See?'

They were. An Asani boy and girl, both lithe and spry, younger than them – wearing traditional *gi* uniforms – dived at each other with curved ice blades, forcing brilliantly high-pitched clanging noises with every encounter.

But then, as they watched, both opponents began to change their blade shapes throughout the game – widening to intercept blows, lengthening to jab, curling back so quickly it was like they were thrusting mirages towards each other; in the end, the boy reformed his back to its original shape and sliced at the girl with a well-armed blow, cutting at her arm. She stumbled back, defeated, as the crowd groaned in sympathy, and new fighters took the ring.

Shadow turned instead to the ice palace and pointed. 'Why don't we go in there?'

It took a good amount of time to push through the crowd and reach the little palace. Shadow accidentally jostled into someone and looked up to a boy's back, and his hair was white enough that for a disconcerting moment she almost wondered if it was Yo-han. But of course he turned, and his eyes were not dark, but cloudy. She quickly hid further under her hood, but it was too late – someone beside them made an alarmed comment in Asani.

Scarlet turned and snapped something back. The situation was instantly resolved.

'What did they say?' Shadow asked.

'Nothing.'

She rolled her eyes. 'You'll attract more attention doing that.'

'Doing what?'

'Insulting strangers.'

'Who said I insulted anyone?'

The sculpture was even more stunning up close. A flawless surface scrubbed down and flattened, devoid of any chips or kinks. Shadow glided her fingers over the cold exterior. There were more people around it than those actually going inside, and they made their way towards the entrance.

Inside: caverns, dim in the night. They quieted their voices so as not to echo.

'I think this is supposed to mimic the real tunnel systems underground,' Scarlet said, reading the faint etchings along the interior.

Ice shelves jutted out from the wall and there were ceiling

corners packed with stalactites that tapered down into pointed tips. The glacier caves seemed to extend into many different rooms and doors, but upon drawing closer, Shadow realized many were false openings.

They wandered the maze-like systems, occasionally stumbling upon hidden, smaller rooms. When Shadow spotted light escaping one of the entrances, she immediately drew towards it and slipped inside. The opening was small enough that she had to stoop slightly, arms nearly pressed against the narrow sides.

When inside, Shadow halted. It was clear and blue, folding and unfolding in a myriad of shapes. But what caught her attention was that it was reflective – the room seemed to expand far beyond its real size, the same patterns recurring over and over again. Patches of the floor gave way to weaker, milky ice, before reforming again into the blue. Occasionally, the floor would shift; or a shelf of ice would change shape, and the same movement would echo across the entire place.

There was no one inside. Shadow dared to take off her hood, if only for a brief moment, breath fogging in the air. Her reflection fractured into a thousand different pieces. She was unsure which one of them was real, which ephemeral, which permanent.

She watched in the mirrors as Scarlet approached from behind, her face appearing beside hers over and over again, scanning the room. Every time she walked around a corner, her reflection disappeared momentarily between the hinges and cracks, reappearing in a different space.

Shadow watched all of her own faces and wished they would all collapse and merge into one; that she could know exactly where the real one was.

'Scarlet,' she said, and the echo of her own voice sounded very far away, as if she was hearing herself from a distance. 'We're going to die tomorrow, aren't we?'

There was a moment of silence; Scarlet's face said nothing.

'We're prisoners to execution,' Shadow said. 'So, they're just letting us frolic.'

It was absurd, just wandering around a festival like a pleasant outing. Like they had no impending fates, like they had not left behind an entire country.

'I'm glad I followed you,' Shadow said. 'I had to. But—' *I'm scared,* she thought, but didn't say it.

A long silence. Then: 'I'm not sure anymore, really, who followed who,' Scarlet said.

Shadow had no answer to that.

'Are you scared of dying?' Scarlet asked.

Was Shadow scared? Yes, but not of death – she was scared of leaving behind what was unfinished. Of dying for nothing. She had done a lot of things, for nothing.

'There are worse things than death,' Shadow replied. She looked at Scarlet in the mirror, considering. If they were to die tomorrow, then today, nothing was real. Nothing counted. 'I'll tell you a story,' she said.

Scarlet barely veiled her surprise.

'Once,' Shadow started, 'long ago, there was a girl.'

'An Ik-Songan girl?'

'Yes,' she said, smiling briefly. 'And she believed in the Moon Rabbit. She sensed it very strongly despite its distance, and not only it but also the colour it imbued into the world; the silvery streaks of lakes and flat salt plains and even the fine hair on the underside of her arms, which were all the Rabbit's creations.

'But the girl was forbidden from worshipping the Rabbit. She could not look at it, nor dream of touching it. Indulging brought only pain, but so did rejecting it. The only solution was to look away, to ignore it wholly, to pretend it was impossible, to realize it as unreachable and beyond her.'

Scarlet listened silently.

'And yet,' Shadow continued, 'the girl couldn't help but wonder about the Rabbit. Even as she was made to worship other gods, smaller and lesser ones that lived underneath the ground instead of above in the sky. She thought more and more about the things she could not have, about what might await her if she ever reached the Rabbit; the beauty that would transform her, the freedom of absolution.

'So, one night, she gives into her desires, and she is buoyed by the land itself; it lifts her up all the way to the skies and the stars so that she might look up and reach out one finger to its soft white fur.'

'And then?'

'And then the story ends,' Shadow said, lowering her eyes. 'It's a famous story. Haven't you heard it before?'

Scarlet paused. 'That can't be the end.'

'It ends with a single word.' Shadow said the word in the old language.

Scarlet repeated it.

'Roughly, the closest translation is "brightness",' Shadow said. 'One finger to its fur, and then "brightness". But that's ambiguous, see. There were different meanings for light then. There is the meaning that means beautiful, silver, kind, to illuminate what is already given. And then there is the burning kind, the painful, the one that would have made the world a desolate wasteland, to destroy and make anew.' She turned away from the ice, to really look at Scarlet.

'So, the story can be read in different ways. She might have been elevated and freed, aided by the land. Or she might have twisted it for her own bidding, blind to its pain, consumed by her own mind. One is a story of temptation; the other, liberation.'

Returning to herself and turning away from Scarlet, Shadow

heard voices and footsteps approaching in symphony, intruding strangers. After a moment, she covered her face again with her hood.

The walk back was quiet. Shadow threw behind occasional glances surreptitiously to make sure no one was trailing them, but there was nothing except the slowly receding glow of the town, and ahead of them, black coastline. No one here recognized them or cared. When they reached the sparse trail and headed into the forest, it was so dark that Scarlet started a low blaze under her sleeve.

'Don't,' Shadow said. 'Someone will see. Just follow my steps.'

'The Ik-Songan girl,' Scarlet said. 'Do you think she really ended up reaching the Moon Rabbit?'

'It's only a story,' Shadow said, 'so no. I think she is suspended forever in time, just on the cusp, unable to move.'

'But it's only a story, so we can imagine it any way we want,' Scarlet said. 'We can extend it. We can say she met her god, and it was her freedom. She buried her hand in its fur and every star around her pulsed gloriously, or something like that.'

'"Pulsed"?' Shadow said. 'Poetic.'

'"Trembled"? "Combusted"? You can pick.'

Shadow almost laughed, watching the light play over Scarlet's fingers. But the true rising flower moon, the glorious and amber supermoon, gazed down at her from the sky like a giant eye, and she thought that this might be the last time she saw it.

'It's useless,' Shadow said. 'All of it. Even if the girl reached it, the force of it would be too powerful. It would burn her from the inside out.'

'Then her moonline would travel the stars for eternity, having found peace.'

Shadow turned, frustrated. 'After she burns to death?'

The Last Soldier of Nava

Instantly, she regretted turning. Scarlet's face was illuminated only by the golden fire of her light, carved out, and the intensity of her gaze was almost frightening. Shadow was reminded of the garden, when Scarlet had first looked down at her and said, *the Soldier,* before looking away. She stopped walking.

'You can't change every story,' Shadow said.

There was a long moment of silence where she thought Scarlet might just keep walking. But Scarlet only continued to look.

'Why are you looking at me like that?' Shadow asked.

'You never told me the last tomb you wanted to sweep,' Scarlet said.

'What?' she said, taken aback.

'Back on the ship.'

'Oh.' She had forgotten. 'I was going to say, my father.'

'Your father,' Scarlet said. 'The one who sort of loved you. The one you're still waiting for.'

'I'm not waiting for him anymore.' The Moonbearer wasn't dead, not yet. But wasn't he dead to her? A faint memory arose, so intangible it could have been a dream – a blade between her fingers. His eyes tracking them. Her eyes lowered. 'But that's all in the past.' He wasn't a threat anymore, even though his promises to Yo-han still were.

'And you would honour his tomb?'

A pause. 'I don't know,' she said honestly.

'Then I have to say this,' Scarlet said, and she turned fully so that they faced each other, grabbing her wrist. 'That fathers envy their daughters. And you were born to be envied. Your strength, your understanding. You surpass him, but not in any material way – just simply in being.'

'Kind words,' Shadow replied, taken aback. 'But I don't care about being envied.'

'I know,' Scarlet said. 'That's why I also have to say this: that I've never met anyone else like you, in all my life.'

Nor I, you.

'Do you remember that stupid dinner, after I levelled that bird? You chased me down outside and said you'd never seen anything like that before. That it was incredible.'

'It was.'

'But for me,' Scarlet said, 'for me, almost every moment around you has been like that. Watching you. I couldn't possibly begin to explain it to you. From the first moment we met in Yosae, the defiance in your face.' She spoke urgently, her eyes clear. 'When those Guards attacked us in the cellar, and you drowned that cave – I'd never seen you really fight before. I've never seen anything like that. Like *you*. You're so powerful that it's shocking to me. It's almost monstrous.'

Shadow flinched away at that. *Monstrous.*

Scarlet let go of her wrist, expression falling. 'I didn't mean it like that,' she said. 'I can't articulate it, I'm sorry. I only mean the strength you hold and wield.' Their breaths mingled in the air. 'If only you could see yourself through my own gaze.' Her eyes roamed Shadow's face, almost feverish in their quickness. 'If only.'

Shadow did not want to move. Not now, not ever. Slowly, as if approaching a skittish animal, Scarlet raised a hand to Shadow's face, brushing against it with the back of her knuckles. Shadow was stock-still, gaze caught, afraid even to breathe.

'Scarlet—' Shadow started, and then stopped. 'Tomorrow, everything will change.' She wanted Scarlet's gaze to break and give.

Tell me you would still have me, after you find out what I am. Tell me you would give me another chance. But this gaze was only sombre, unyielding. It showed no negotiation.

'Maybe the girl dies,' Scarlet continued, 'she burns inside out. Maybe we die, tomorrow. But it would be worth it to die two deaths, just for this. By fire or by ice, I would prefer the fire. No,' she said. 'I don't just prefer it. I want it.'

'Then say what it is you want,' Shadow replied.

Scarlet said her name. So close that every lash could be counted.

Her lips parted slightly.

'Can I?' Scarlet said, and then the kiss that followed was slow, a burning thing, long and drawn out. Shadow felt heat rise to her cheeks, a quickness grip her own breath. It was like all the cold air had gathered into one tiny, brilliant spot of heat, between their mouths, and if it was snuffed out, all of the light in the world would be extinguished, too, unendingly. Scarlet pulled back a fraction, an inch, briefly, looking at her, and then there were hands grasping her face, the grooves of her scars, and Shadow's heart rabbited ridiculously, she would pass out from the sheer ardour of it. She turned her face to the side, dazed – thankful that although she could see perfectly, Scarlet could not see her well in return.

'What's wrong?' Scarlet whispered, and Shadow could only close her eyes. *I can hardly contain it in me, the heat.* A hand trailing across the slope of her neck, her shoulder. Down her arm. Shadow was all too aware of their surroundings, the churning sea.

'Someone will see,' she said.

'I don't *care*,' Scarlet said, the grip on her wrist tightening, unyielding, 'Let them see.' So, Scarlet swept the hair back from Shadow's face and kissed her again. Shadow's hands drifted instinctually, trying to match pace, pull her closer in, and pressed against her, one long line of heat that never seemed to end.

The kiss had deepened, had plunged her into depths. Shadow

was remembering their show of light and dark, back in the Stronghold, how their forms had crashed up against one another, intertwining and battling, until it was entirely unclear who ended where, until they had fused to create something entirely new, something other. She felt it now, the forces of their own power grappling against each other. Scarlet's light should have been a repellent – instinctively, Shadow's body should have protested to the magnificent fire of it, its eternal burn, how it could destroy her in a glance. Out of anyone in this world, Scarlet was the one who could hurt her the most. Who could burn the darkness, and therefore her spirit, out of her body. She knew this inherently. She knew this like every past life of hers knew it, like their meeting was a clash of ancient, dual forces that had ravaged the world long before their births and had reincarnated in their bodies. She hadn't wanted to admit it. And now – now it was like dropping over a cliff, disappearing into this blinding light, letting herself be thrown and seared open. She would let anything happen to herself, for this. For in the mountainous empire tomorrow Scarlet may as well hold a blade to her neck and press, and Shadow would let her. She had already followed her to the abyss of this place. She had left behind everything to do so. *Wherever you go, I will always follow.* There was no choice. In another world, perhaps, another lifetime, she might have stayed behind, taken the Moonbearer, Yo-han, on her own; it would've been difficult and precarious, finding Sae, allying with Crow, awaiting the Dragon, slitting the Moonbearer's throat before he could even wake, but still possible, yes, still within the bounds of victory; and if victorious, she would have the Stronghold, the Prince, the Dynasty, its neighbours, the world – but it didn't matter. None of it did. Not as long as Scarlet was that lone figure in furs treading snow in Asanai, her reflection darting in and out of glacial ice like a ghost waiting to be caught. Then in every lifetime, Scarlet was a figure in a field of white, and in every lifetime, Shadow looked out – not east, towards the mountains, not south, nor to victory, but north, across the icy Asa channel, the channel that led to her. To Scarlet. To the Light, over and over again. The thought of an entire dynasty couldn't even sway her.

Scarlet held her so tightly; Shadow thought her own eyes must be as foggy, her lips as red. Her hands under the furs were cold, so deliciously cold, and their exhales in the night were like plumes of smoke. Shadow could not explain their wanting so precisely; like two animals circling each other, waiting.

Tomorrow, everything would change.

Chapter 28

Come dawn, Nari arrived to lead them to the shore. They stopped at the edge of the water and Scarlet stared him down.

'What,' she said, 'are we swimming to the palace?'

A call sounded. Not a bugle, but something strangely hollow and low, unfamiliar, and out of the fog, in the distance, emerged a shape in the water – several shapes. Like small black ships, but so low to the surface that Shadow couldn't make out exactly what they were. They drew closer at incredible speed, streamlining through the water in triangle formation. And here she realized two things: first, that these were not ships. They were enormous black and white orca whales, passing like shadows underwater, occasionally spouting up sky-high streams through their blowholes. Their bodies were like dunes rising above the cresting waves, their dorsal fins high and sharply pointed.

The second: they were saddled, with leathery white harnesses. Behind the fins rode—

'Bone Warriors,' Shadow breathed.

She was dead tired from the night. They had stayed up, sat

side-by-side in the small den. The low temperatures made their muscles rigid; made her scar tissue seize up, alternating between numbness and the dreadful return to feeling again, punctuated by needle-like spasms, until her entire body felt sore. And then Scarlet did something as innocuous as grabbing her wrist and the pain seemed to fall away, become other. Shadow hated it. She would rather there be no relief, so that she wouldn't remember what relief would feel like. They traded stories; or rather, Shadow asked for offerings and Scarlet conceded.

'Tell me about your hometown,' she said. Anje. *Tell me about your sister and how you lost her.* But Scarlet didn't mention her sister. She only told her about the seaside town, how it tapered into stacked rice terraces, ruins connected by old stone bridges that crossed over tidepools where you could overturn stones to find barnacle clusters and seaweed. There were many, many different types of seaweed – violet kelp, buoyant stems, sun-bleached sheets as flat as paper – but no sea grapes. Those only grew in colder climates.

Yellow *yuchae* flowers dotted the green after monsoon season. All across the town, stone steps started from the tops of high hills and then wound down all the way to the shore, into the ocean, leading to nothing, to long-sunken temples. They seemed creepy, but they weren't. The locals thought they were ancient and beautiful. Not all stairs had to lead to something. Sometimes there was no destination. There was only the high part of the journey up along the ascent, and then the lower part along the water. Bookended by the sea and the sky.

Before they left the cabin, Scarlet had apologized to her.

'Sorry for what?' Shadow had asked, but Scarlet would not say for what.

'I don't want your pity,' Shadow had said. She thought

about it now, watching the hint of an eye rise above the waves, stone-black and pinpointed. She felt pity for the Bone Warriors; she wished they could leave Asanai. But then she thought of the one in Ik-Song; how some creatures had no habitats to return to, not always.

All five Bone Warriors wore different animal skulls, their true faces a dark mystery behind them; the leading Warrior was the ram's skull from yesterday. His horns seemed even longer now, parallel to the horizon.

When they neared, they stilled in their path. The curve of orcas waited silently, the only intrusion an occasional spray of water. The leather harnesses looked thick and hard as bone. They didn't look very comfortable, but Bone Warriors didn't look like they cared. For them, comfort seemed a thing of the past.

After they were bound separately to the first two orcas, they took off immediately in a whistling of wind. Shadow tentatively felt the whale's slippery body beneath her hand, the hard ridge of its fin; because the water was too cold for her, her saddle stayed above surface. She looked up at the Bone Warrior riding behind her – her head came up barely past his waist, and she peered at the dark pits within the skull, the eyes. She wondered if she touched his skin, whether it would be ice-cold, no different from real stone.

It was achingly silent.

'Fun company,' Scarlet muttered to expected silence. From their viewpoint, the coastline of Asanai passed, a tantalizing crust.

Brown-grey rocks made up the shores, vast mountains rising in the distance like an afterthought, their triangular snow-capped peaks like claws ripping into the soft underbelly of clouds. When they reached a black sand coast, the orca breached its heavy body momentarily, where they dismounted, before disappearing back into the inky depths.

And the tapping began. The leading Bone Warrior began to tap their skulls with small bone pieces – a hard and fast tapping, this distinct rhythm echoing through the snow. The piece itself was tiny, but the noise cut effectively through.

They were calling something. A moment later, a distant rumble, like the start of an avalanche. A cacophony of thuds, hitting the ground one after the other, of snarls, short howls, panting.

The wolves had come.

They were striking. Enormous and thickly furred, large enough to seat even the Bone Warriors, yellow-eyed and red-tongued. So white it was like they'd just formed out of the snow and would soon dissipate into it again. There were five: one for each Warrior, yipping and snapping at one another, tails swishing.

When Shadow approached the wolf, she saw that up close, the fangs were like daggers, the curling lip wary. One tap of the wishbone from its master, however, silenced it in perfect, incredible harmony.

If Ik-Songan deer were swift and nimble, the Asani wolves drove forward at a breakneck, brutal speed. Lower to the ground, a creature used to stalking, to chase, tucking its limbs in and out along the straight back that ploughed through any snow. Their paws hit the ground efficiently, ears twitching, the occasional snarl or jaw-click of communication, a language of their own. The outermost coats flaked with ice crystal. Were they in the midst of a blizzard, she thought, these wolves would forge forward anyway.

*

The journey was long, but the landscape of Asanai proved neither repetitive nor bleak, not the endless world of white one might imagine it to be. Inky, craggy volcanoes smoked into the air. Ice shelves and rocky coastlines continued. Formations of rounded ice like fingers rose from the ground, a blue so otherworldly and transparent they seemed illusions. They were ascending, climbing to higher ground; the wind began to pick up, snow fell intermittently. Yes, she was cold, but it had all since faded into numbness.

They entered a hidden footpath into winding, rocky mountains and it was here the palace finally made itself known.

Nestled between the peaks, built in a place that should have been impossible and unsustainable, but held. Where the Stronghold was sloped and tiled low roofs, the Imperial Palace was jagged, protruding, mirroring the barbed natural points surrounding it, steeper to allow ice to glide off instead of accumulating and weighing down the surface. Starkly white, it almost camouflaged into the mountain snow itself.

Outside the main gates there were carved stone statues of foxes and guardian lions, animals that had never existed in Asanai. Or at least, Shadow thought so. She wondered if the skulls the Bone Warriors wore were of animals they had slaughtered themselves, whether the spoils constituted the becoming of a Warrior. Yet some skulls she couldn't identify at all; they were from animals that hadn't lived and walked here in a long, long time.

Some of the wolves departed; some lingered around the gates, settling down in the white.

Before they entered the palace, they were blindfolded by dark cloth and their wrists were bound, a Bone Warrior's enormous hand coming down around her face. Shadow was less uneasy than she had expected herself to be; instead, she was numb. She closed her eyes resignedly. They were led through a passage, silent until there was the sound of heavy doors being opened.

Shadow was pushed forward, landing on her knees. She felt heat. An intense, scorching heat. She immediately scrambled back, but there was no direct source; the intense warmth radiated through all parts of the room equally.

Her cover was taken off.

She first saw the fire. A fire so tall and great it leapt up to the ceiling of the palace, so hot it burned blue in the middle and white at its edges.

Sitting on his throne in front of this wall of fire, above a row of silently standing Bone Warriors, sat the Bloodbird King, the Emperor.

She knew he was human, but for a moment, briefly, she wondered whether he was of the Bone Warriors, somehow. Because he was immensely tall, his skin stretched tautly over his bearded face; not atrophied, but immortal, almost, unchangeable. And because he, too, wore a skull, covering one eye, ending at the cheek, and this skull was a crest she had never seen before: like a two-pronged antler, one point shorter than the other, both sloping up impossibly high. Narrow jaws like a crocodile's closing around his face. He wore white, a fur draped over his shoulders, despite the heat.

So caught up was she that she didn't notice the figure standing beside him, at first. A woman, completely hidden under a white veil from head to toe. If she wore white, she was of high status, but of her role, Shadow wasn't sure. After all, everyone knew that the Asani Emperor had no queen.

Scarlet was already standing beside her, waiting. Shadow got to her feet.

Yejin Suh

The Emperor gazed upon Shadow, and instantly, she knew that he knew. He looked slowly from the Keeper to the Soldier and smiled.

Scarlet spoke first, and Shadow felt the words in her bones. 'Emperor,' she said. 'I have come to your home, prepared to die.'

Chapter 29

Her voice echoed across the enormous interior.

It was too large for a throne room; the Emperor seemed almost small in comparison. Shadow knew why. It was because of two considerations. First: simply to intimidate guests with the prospect of their own meagre presence in all the space of this hall.

'The Royal Keeper of Ik-Song in my throne room,' he replied, in perfect, fluent Ik-Songan. 'Why have you left your country?' Beside him, the veiled figure stood like a ghost.

Second: half of the room doubled as an arena. She knew, because she had been here before. The great, leaping fire; a ring of animal skulls gazing down on her. The memories rose faintly, though she didn't want them to, threatening to split her open. Her heart pounded; mouth sandpaper dry.

Scarlet stepped in front of her, as if shielding her from his gaze.

If she had been here before, she hadn't been asleep for a thousand years. She had been woken only ten years ago, so the Moonbearer could use her to gain Ik-Song, for the White Ice. How many times had she been woken before, then? How many times had she been used again and again, without even knowing?

Shadow looked around at the strange, yet familiar palace. It was like she was outside of her own body, looking down on herself.

Then, Scarlet bowed.

The sight was shocking.

'Emperor,' Scarlet said, her voice far away. Had she ever sounded like that, so ready to please, so earnest? 'We've travelled across the sea for an audience with you. I left Ik-Song because my life was in danger there.'

'And what do you seek from me?'

'Answers,' she said, 'or your help.'

'My answers, my help. This all rings so familiarly to me.'

The Bone Warriors stood – unfeeling, still.

'The Moonbearer plans to raise and slaughter the Dragon of the West,' Scarlet said. 'When he does, he'll destroy Ik-Song with its power.'

'And what importance does that have for me?' the Emperor asked.

'Because he plans to bring back a place that has been buried for a thousand years,' Scarlet said, 'and the entire world will be thrown out of balance. He won't stop at Ik-Song. He'll move on to Asanai next. He'll raze the world down; the deadzones in our state will spread across continents, the storms will worsen.'

'And what would you like me to do?'

'Bring your army to Ik-Song. Help us defeat him. I was told that Asanai has a new weapon – the likes of which the world has never seen before.'

Silence.

'And why,' the Emperor said, patient as ever, 'would I help you?'

The Last Soldier of Nava

Shadow listened distantly. The heat of the fire closed in on her; but there was nothing she could do to move away. Dread slugged down in her stomach.

'I believe that a decade ago, you were double-crossed by the Moonbearer. He promised you our nation, and then took it for himself. Then I also believe you would want vengeance against him,' Scarlet continued. 'He's weakened now – comatose, frail. He could die ever so easily. This would be your chance, after ten years, to get the blood you're owed.'

'A decade ago, your ruler deceived me. Now, his Keeper shows up at my door, trying, perhaps, to do the same.'

'I'm not here to deceive you.'

'I could kill you now, and then kill the Moonbearer, too,' he said. 'Or I could kill you and do nothing else. It seems that whether you get what you want or not, I get what I want every time.'

To demonstrate, he flicked a single hand – a barely perceptible movement – and immediately, every Bone Warrior in the row fell to combat stance: such gigantic proportions that moved so limberly.

Scarlet did not react. 'That's why I am prepared to die.'

'And your companion?' His gaze slid to Shadow.

'My companion will not be dying. You can't kill her, or maim her, or blind her. If you do, I'll burn my heart from the inside out right now, and you'll be robbed of the chance to do anything at all to me.'

Shadow was aghast. *You're exaggerating,* she thought, but Scarlet's face was serious, and that made the guilt come in waves. She wanted to just come forward now; to expose herself to Scarlet before the Emperor did. To get it over with. To stop these declarations. The only reason she didn't was because she was frozen, and it would be over soon. She had been foolish to think there would be anything besides an ending.

The Emperor looked even more intrigued, gaining light on the situation. He passed his hand again; the Warriors fell at ease.

'But why do you pay her all the attention?' Scarlet said. 'Am I not a worthy adversary myself?'

'By yourself? With no Dynasty, nor Stronghold behind you? An exile?'

'I was never reliant on the Stronghold or the Dynasty. I've only ever been myself. And especially now, I am more powerful than you could ever imagine.' Shadow watched the line of Scarlet's back silently.

'You want your country's throne, girl?'

'I don't want any throne.'

'Then what do you want? I had thought you came here,' the Emperor said, 'to ask about your sister.' His eyes slid to Shadow; she stared back, daring him to say it. To expose her.

There could be worse endings. For all Scarlet's talk of vengeance, controlling the Soldier would be better than killing her. Who wouldn't grasp the opportunity? All that power, bound to them alone?

'Your entire nation thinks an Asani killed your Saint Rose. You don't think so, too?'

'Was it not an Asani, your Highness?' Scarlet feigned ignorance.

'No Warrior of mine was sent after her.' The Emperor looked upon her. 'After the White Ice, your people hated the Moonbearer and his Guards. They hate Asanai, too, but at least we are a familiar enemy. Our nations are centuries-old neighbours, continuously bound to each other. But the Moonbearer is unfamiliar, an alien. Until the emergence of the Saint, the people did not trust him. Then, she was the true reason for his glory. Her kindness is what won him Ik-Song, not his power.'

'Then do you propose that the Moonbearer killed my sister, Emperor?'

'In a way,' the Emperor said. 'But he used a tool to do so.'

'A tool.'

'The Soldier.'

A long moment of silence.

'And what importance,' Scarlet said, 'does the Soldier have here and now, your Highness?'

He began to laugh.

A deep, sonorous bellow that started low and then crescendoed. It echoed richly off the walls, the voice of a man who knew he would win. He looked at Shadow, then, clearly, and spoke to her. 'I recognized you the moment your face was revealed,' he said.

All Shadow could do was stare at Scarlet's back, unable to look away.

'Do you remember me?' The Emperor asked. Shadow didn't want to behold him, his face, to remember.

'You stood in that very spot, all those years ago, at his right hand, like a lapdog. Your face wasn't so mutilated yet – it was clear, and fierce – and the bottom half masked, but I remember those eyes. Those eyes so dark and blank that I thought, surely this girl cannot see anything at all. Surely, she is blind in the day, a creature of the night. Yet here you stand now, seeing me, plain as day. And do you remember me? The palace, the fire? My Warriors surrounding you in the snow?'

There was deathly silence in the room. 'Scarlet,' Shadow said, but Scarlet didn't move at all.

'I have a story to tell,' he said, 'if you will listen. A story that begins with a night like this, when my Warriors informed me that they had witnessed a strange man trekking his way through the ice and snow to my palace. With him, a ragtag team, a young girl. They wore the armours of royals, but they were no royals that I had ever heard of.

'But they did not interest me. My Warriors suspected they were from Ik-Song, so I said, "Kill them, and be done with it. I don't want intruders gallivanting on Asani land as they please." They weren't properly clothed for the climate, anyway; they would be dead before sunrise. But here is where I was paused and told that the strange man was not walking to the Empire. He was already *here*. He stood at the foot of the mountain, at the hidden trail that has not been found by a foreigner since this nation was created. And that was where the patrol had found him: standing and waiting.

'I asked, "What does he wait for?" And my scout replied: "An audience with you."'

He bellowed again with laughter.

The room was so very still.

The fire flickered.

He continued: 'I thought, "What gall this man has!" He thinks he can come to my mountain, to my palace, and demand an audience with me. He amused me. He intrigued me. So, I allowed it. I invited his party into the palace. I would listen to him, and then put him out of his misery. Better to die by the Asani sword than frostbite out in the mountains.

'He and his company came into this throne room. Most of them were freezing cold, verging on death, insignificant sufferers. But two of them caught my attention. The man himself – and his young prodigy. They both had such dark hair and eyes. You see –' He looked at Scarlet – 'Your sister was his Light. But before her, there was one as vicious as the night itself.

'Neither the man nor girl shivered from cold. They were perfectly intact, unaffected. The girl made my Bone Warriors nervous; they wouldn't stop moving, restless at her arrival.'

Shadow looked at the line of stony Warriors, imagined them nervously fidgeting. It was impossible.

'The man knelt to me and bowed proper. But the girl didn't bow,' he continued. 'She only looked ahead at nothing. I asked, "Why doesn't your whelp bow?" and he said, "She was not made for things like bowing." So, I asked, "What is she made for, then?" and he said: "To kill."'

'I laughed then, as I do now. "Then you plan to kill me," I said to him. But he denied it. He said, "Let me show you what I can do," and darkness rose from his fingers, black and roiling, heady as night itself. I was impressed. But he was just one man, after all. I said, "That is a clever trick. But is this all you've come to show me?" And then he gestured the girl forward – saying, "She is more powerful than I." And at a flick of his hand, the girl came forward to one of my Warriors and cut him clean in two.'

That couldn't have happened. She would remember.

Wouldn't she?

'They're ancient, difficult to kill, see. They can't be run through by the common sword. I was furious, and my guards rushed to attention. But the damage was already done. "That was not a threat," the man said. "That was only to prove to you the power I possess."

'Then he told me that he had come all this way to strike a deal with me. Here I saw that the people he brought with him – they were human, indeed, but they possessed ability – ability that *he* had gifted them, somehow, which they returned with utmost loyalty. There were more back home, he said. Together, we could take Ik-Song by force, and he would take the brunt of the work. He only needed a few Bone Warriors to help. I was younger, full of fantasies of conquering. I saw Asanai richened, emboldened, ruling over the island as we should have been doing all this time. He said Asanai would lose close to nothing, for the cause. He promised me plenty. And in return, he only asked for a piece of the empire, in this new age of victory.

'But such a proposition was too easy to be true. You know what happened next, dear Keeper. My men, slaughtered on the shores of Ik-Song. The Moonbearer hailed a saviour.' The Emperor sighed. 'And afterwards, the rise of the Stronghold.'

He rose from his throne. 'What shocked me most about the killing of the Bone Warrior, see, is not that she killed it. It was that the Warrior did not resist. Did not even fight back. It was *drawn* to her, like a flame. Because the Soldier and the Warriors are made of the same sort of dark power, you see – the spilled blood of ancient creatures, beautiful trophies.' He gestured to his arcing skull. 'Born of slaughter.'

And then the Bone Warrior centremost of the Emperor's throne stepped forward. The enormous limbs folded themselves together, descending, and the Bone Warrior had knelt to one knee.

Bowing down.

Bowing down to *her*.

She was rooted to the spot – she couldn't move back even if she tried. And yet a small part of her, lying in wait, was unsurprised.

'My Bone Warriors pledge loyalty to me, but really, they know no country's borders, no petty laws. Instinctually, they obey their cores, that pull towards the same darkness that sustains them. And they recognize such power when they see it.'

The Last Soldier of Nava

Beside the first Bone Warrior, the second one dropped. One by one, they began to fall to the ground, skulls rattling on their heads, knees thudding. A line all the way down.

'You came thinking the Soldier would be here?' the Emperor said. 'You brought her with you, fool. She stands beside you now.'

It was like nothing was registering, and then everything – Scarlet's back to her. A spear of guilt through her gut, so sharp it felt like her knees would buckle

Scarlet, she wanted to say. She thought of them riding away from the Stronghold in the nighttime and how free she had felt, even though her impending betrayal had hung around her neck like a noose. Now it tightened, and there was nothing she could do.

'In a way,' he said to Scarlet, 'you and I stand in the same place, amidst these games. Both wronged by beings that are not from our time. They hail from an ancient era: one that neither you nor I can fully understand, simply because it has been buried under falsity and the natural flow of years.' A pause. 'But do not worry. Now, I will take you out of your misery, make you forget. I will avenge your sister for you.' He smiled.

And then several things happened at once.

At his command, the Bone Warriors rose again, coming towards them.

Scarlet turned.

There was a split-second where their eyes met – and Shadow only stared back. There was nothing to hide behind now. No mask, no façade. *You see me for what I am.*

Scarlet came close. Her expression was unreadable as always, eyes dark pools. She grabbed Shadow by the arm, pulling her towards her.

Scarlet spun her around deftly.

And then Shadow felt the cool press of a blade against her neck. An arm around her.

She froze.

'Forgive me,' came the whisper in her ear.

The Bone Warriors stopped.

The Emperor stilled.

'Did you really think I would come without leverage?' Scarlet asked. 'Did you really think I didn't *know*?'

Her hand gripped Scarlet's wrist; the blade trembled against her bare skin.

Scarlet's voice was hard in the room. 'I know how to awaken the Soldier,' she said. 'I always have. If I do right now, she will be bound to me, under *my* control.'

Silence.

'If it's true what you've said,' Scarlet said, 'no Bone Warriors will resist her touch. I'll command her to kill every single one in this palace, and none of them will even fight back.'

The evisceration of it was thin and clean.

Scarlet had known all along, what she was. After all this, *Shadow* was going to be the one betrayed – although, after all, the lie had always been hers first.

Shadow shut her eyes. *She will be bound to me.* Shadow would let her. She wanted to run far, far from this place – but if that wasn't possible, she would let her. If she was to be awakened, she would let Scarlet be the one to do it.

In the long quiet, no one moved: the Emperor, still; the Bone Warriors, bowed. Shadow breathing hard under the knife's edge, hatred coiling in her gut, though at who exactly, she was unsure.

She sensed a tingling of something familiar, but it faded into the background, behind the disbelief and ringing in her own ears.

The Last Soldier of Nava

'You have fire,' the Emperor said finally. 'I must admit. But don't make haste. I still have other plans in mind, for your companion.' He looked to the door, then.

Where the Moonbearer stood.

Chapter 30

'Father,' Shadow gasped.

Gone were his violet undereyes, the spidery black veins. He stood tall and straight, looking more youthful than he should ever have been allowed, black hair neatened back.

No Bone Warriors even moved to entrap him.

'What is this?' Shadow said, hand falling from where it had held Scarlet's wrist. Her heart would give out, surely; she struggled to control her breathing. For a split second, she wished she were truly gone, then, an apparition – shadows along the floor and walls. For a second, she wished that everything now would reverse, for that fateful day in Yosae to turn back, to notice Crow in that rose-engraved mirror and run away, back, back, back to the arms of Sae, to the house, which she would never leave again, never even think about it. 'You were fading away – I *saw* you. Your power was completely sapped.'

'You revived me, daughter,' he said. And to her aching surprise, held out his hand. 'With your touch.'

Her touch. The fingers she had just barely skimmed over his skin, feeling the magnetic pull of the dark blood that ran through his veins, the same as hers. How was that possible? How could he be alive and well when his state had been the only thing that had given her hope? How had he risen in that palace, falling to command—

Crow. She thought of Crow. Was he even alive, still? What agreement had Yo-han and the Moonbearer come to? Was the Stronghold in chaos?

With mounting dread, she saw that the Moonbearer was not alone. There were Guards with him, throngs of them. Advisors. Hunters. *No.*

'You,' the Moonbearer said, 'are not supposed to be awake yet.'

Then why did you wake me? she wanted to scream in frustration. *Why are you here?*

'As soon as my scouts spotted you entering Asani seas, I sent word,' the Emperor said to her. 'You see, I cherish the opportunity to have the Soldier in my throne room. Because there is something I have been wanting to do for a long, long time.'

The grip on her tightened; the knife pressed closer. 'Do neither of you see what is in front of you?' Scarlet said behind her. 'Who possesses the Soldier here, and now? Who is in control?'

'You will release her,' the Moonbearer said. 'See my army?' He gestured behind him to where soldiers waited. 'Perhaps they, like you, have come prepared to die. Perhaps they have come to fight the Bone Warriors, the might of Asanai. In a battle here and now, on enemy ground, an impossible fight. They are ready to die gloriously defending the Stronghold overseas.'

'Is this your invasion, then? You want the Empire?'

He shrugged. 'I could have them fight, or I won't. It is your choice.'

'My choice,' she said. 'Do you think I care whether your Guards die or not?'

'You would let them be slaughtered?'

'*You* would? After all the time you spent remaking them, raising them?'

'It is not ideal,' he said. 'But the Emperor wants no bloodshed, either.'

The Moonbearer, the Emperor – they were not enemies so much as ringleaders of the same game.

'I should like to test the strength of Asanai,' the Emperor said. 'But why waste my Bone Warriors against Ik-Songan scum? Why hassle with battle, war?' The Emperor sat again on his throne.

'If not war, then what?' Scarlet asked.

'A duel,' he said simply.

'A duel,' Scarlet echoed. 'Between whom?'

'Our nation's champions.'

Our nation's champions.

Realization dawned.

Shadow reached up to where Scarlet cradled the knife – and embraced her hand with her own. Scarlet's fingers stilled in shock, unresisting as Shadow lowered it from her neck and let go.

She heard it clatter to the floor as she stepped forward.

The Moonbearer's eyes gleamed.

'Enough talk,' Shadow said. 'We don't need it.'

'Why not, my Soldier?' the Moonbearer replied. His knowing face – she wanted to burn it off. A thousand years of sleep had not erased the fury that burned low in her gut.

'I know what it is you want.'

'And what is that?'

'You want me to fight,' she said. 'As you always have.'

The Last Soldier of Nava

The Emperor wanted to test the Soldier's strength. He wanted to test *her*.

They had come here of their own accord, escaped; yet Shadow felt that they were only pawns on a board, inevitably moving to where hands guided them. The brilliantly arcing catfish, Crow's bravery, their journey across the sea. How utterly futile it had all been. All of it, from the start, from the first pursuit to their last.

After everything, she would still be made to fight to the death. A dog in a pit.

'Even after everything, there is a comfort to knowing,' the Moonbearer said. 'There is a comfort to doing what you are familiar with; what you have been made to do.'

'No comfort,' she said. 'Nothing familiar. This time is different.'

I've come prepared to die, Scarlet had said. And Shadow thought she'd been prepared, too. But she found that she didn't want to. Her body rebelled against it. She had ridden deer across mountain streams; slept beside the Seochon Sea. She'd weathered the high Asani seas; watched a monsoon beat against the palace walls. She had been pulled close in the dark, another face so very close, caught in a pocket of feeling that she hadn't thought possible not so long ago – and now, she realized why people hungered to live.

'Different?' he said archly.

'You have always forced my hand,' she said. 'But for the first time, I desire to fight.'

'Your bravado means nothing,' the Moonbearer said.

He would never show it, but she knew he must be caught off-guard. He knew nothing of what she had seen and known after rising from sleep again.

'No bravado,' she said. 'I'll fight Asanai's champion. I'll fight the Emperor. And after him – *you*.'

'Then it is settled,' the Moonbearer finished slowly. 'You duel, or war will begin here.'

'If Ik-Song wins, you are both free to go,' the Emperor said. 'If Asanai wins, the champion is mine.'

If Shadow won, the Moonbearer would walk away unscathed; if she lost, the Emperor would gain. If she refused, this palace would become the site of massacre for the amusement of two indifferent leaders. Any way you looked at it, they reaped the benefits.

She was tired of the fight, to be truthful.

She didn't want to die.

But she was prepared to.

She was no pawn. Not anymore.

Shadow looked up at the Emperor. 'Face me, then. We'll duel to the death.'

'Me?' he said. 'You won't be fighting me.'

She paused. What was he talking about? 'You said I would fight the champion of Asanai.'

If he wasn't the champion of Asanai, then who was?

Then he gestured to the figure at his side. The cloaked girl, who had stood silently all this time.

'Your beloved Prince back home,' he said. 'You know he has Asani blood. Did you ever wonder who his father might be? Who the man was that your Queen loved?'

She could only stare in disbelief; it was Scarlet who exhaled her shock behind her. 'Impossible.'

She thought of the love letters she had found in his room – from *Bluebird* to *Spring Flower*. Between the Queen and her Asani lover. The Bloodbird.

'Yo-han is my son,' he said.

All the mentions of the willow tree.

The twinning willow trees.

'There is no way, of course, that you would've known,'

the Emperor continued. 'That Ik-Song and Asanai are deeply bound in this way.' He gestured to the figure. 'Kura, come forth.'

The veiled figure stepped forward at his side. 'Unveil,' he commanded, and she did so.

It was a girl. An Asani girl, dressed in the same regal furs, her face beautiful, half-covered by bone – but none of this caught their attention.

It was her hair – flowing down her back, as white and glassy as snow. Shadow knew only one other person with hair like that.

'My daughter,' he introduced. 'Princess Kura of Asanai.'

The Bone Warriors bent low to her.

'There is no Asani princess,' came Scarlet's voice, incredulous. 'There is no Asani heir.'

'You see, there were two children born that night,' he said. 'Twins. One to belong to Ik-Song, and the other to me. I left out a part of my story, before. When the Moonbearer came that night to me, to propose the invasion, I did not merely take his word for it. I was granted a gift: the remaking of my daughter. She is a special one, you see. Not fully remade; not fully Bone Warrior; not fully human.' He smiled for the first time. 'And my, she has grown more powerful than anyone could ever have imagined. Much stronger than your prince, who has always been weak. Strong enough to defeat even your Soldier in battle.'

Our willow glimmers like ice.

Grows stronger.

This was the weapon that the Bone Warrior in Yosae had been speaking of.

Shadow regarded her with not just dread, but pity.

'This is a weapon I have been wanting to test for a long, long time,' the Emperor said. 'Your Soldier is not even awakened properly. This will be a quick duel.'

'But she has something that can't be recreated with training,' the Moonbearer replied. 'Time, and experience. War has settled deep in her bones.'

'I guess we will see.'

'Who says I've no experience?' Princess Kura spoke, her voice light as day. Her left eye was hidden in the depths behind bone fragment. 'Your power wanes after so many centuries, and thus weakens in the Soldier.'

She spoke as if Shadow wasn't even there.

Kura unsheathed her heavy furs and stepped down to the floor, the arena, revealing armour like nothing Shadow had ever seen before – translucent, thin slicing of bone layered around her, reflecting the walls back. She flung the fur back with a careless, sharp flick of the wrist; every movement showed her slow confidence, sure-footedness.

'I will duel the Soldier in the name of my father.' The Bone Warriors parted for her, letting her draw closer to them. Her white hair spilled down her shoulders. 'Why do we delay?'

Perhaps she was arrogant, Shadow thought. If so, she would be easy to best.

As the room waited in silence, Kura made a simple motion with her hands – closing them together, coming down, down – and from the ceiling, seemingly out of nowhere: a jagged, flashing bolt of lightning that glimmered in the air for an entire second, lighting up all of their faces, followed by rumbling thunder, the sound of cracking along the ground. The air instantly chilled; the palace floor marked by a black-smoked scar, the wood of it splitting open like a seam.

The Emperor had not been bluffing. Lightning could kill fast; it could burn, Kura could splice it cold. It was faster and deadlier than anyone could imagine.

The smoke cleared; Kura was close. Shadow saw her eyes. Her eyes held no pity, smugness, or arrogance.

They were only determined.

Kura was taking this seriously. And her confidence in her ability was not at all contrived.

For the first time, Shadow could not deny the thrill that came down to her fingertips, the match of a strong opponent. Briefly, the memory of facing off against Crow flashed back to her: *Don't come any closer.*

This is your last chance.

Shadow stepped back, and they watched each other.

This is our first meeting, Shadow thought. *But this is your last chance.*

Kura understood. She didn't waste any time. Her rapid, successive attacks lit up the room in a myriad of spinal blue lines that she could only dodge, flickering and twisting, willing herself to fade away, fighting in that liminal state between lightning striking and thunder roaring, that deafened Shadow's ears up close. Kura's first strokes started clean and tentative, like a new fighter who had just been introduced to the field, copying routine moves by memorization. Precise and careful, she did not overstep, nor come on too strongly.

Shadow couldn't help but wonder if this was her first time really fighting where it mattered. Had she ever traded blows outside of the Bone Warriors, disposable Asani guards? Or had her father just thrown her into the thick of it for his own benefit, uncaring? Shadow couldn't tell.

She wondered what it would take to unravel her. To push her to the brink and do away with the neat façade, give way to her rage. Kura didn't say a thing, but she could feel it in every hit anyway: *Fight me.*

Shadow stayed nimbly on the defensive, dodging, leaping back.

Fight me.

The princess battered at every opening, refusing to miss a single chance to close in. She aimed for the heart, for the jugular.

Shadow had to end this. There was only one way, though – and she didn't know if she could. She blocked the blows, fought back the glare threatening to blind her. Up close, Kura's face was illuminated by the glow of her own heat lightning, whiter even than the Emperor's fire. Like cold, pale marble. Shadow met her halfway, and it was like time slowed down to a single point, in that small grey area: where wind whipped around them and her body followed instincts of survival, of battle that had etched itself into her over years and years, and she still fought the urge to lie down and roll over, to let Kura strike clean through her heart until it beat too frantically to hurt anymore. Something would have to give. She wondered how long Kura had been holed up in this place, an arctic tower high up the cliffs of Asanai, spending long days training and tiring against an enemy she had never seen, never met, hardly knew about, all to follow the word of her father. Born gifted and pushed to the brink, honing her lethal electricity again and again with deft hands, and the lightning was reflected in her eyes, the white of her hair tinting blue from it.

The Princess didn't hold back in her barrage of hits, over and over again – she was good. Not only good, but healthy, unburdened. Battle-new. She knew to wear the opponent down, and she did not show mercy. Maybe her father had told her as much; maybe he'd said, *The Soldier will try to deceive you, to look weak.*

The hits, when they landed, flashed through Shadow's body, white-hot. The pain, delayed. She remembered explicitly the burn of the Desert Rose across her face: searing, flayed, as if the entire underside of her jaw had been exposed. Just on the verge of numbness, but not quite there, and the middle ground, the right-before, was agony. Shadow had wished her nerves had been obliterated, too, then. This pain was different. It was like being slammed into a wall, the curious sensation of tingling, numbness on the tongue and ringing in her ears. *Icy cold,* Scarlet had said about Shadow's power. Lightning was neither hot nor cold. It was neutral, and unfeeling, and strangely terrifying.

The Soldier will try to deceive you, to look weak.

In the end, Shadow came close. She arced one sizable blow that flung Kura across the room. Kura landed facedown, breath beaten from her lungs, slammed into the ground, and she didn't recover quickly.

So, Shadow approached and pinned her down, turned her over.

Kura struggled, but Shadow's grip was iron-strong. She prepared to split her head open; there was wetness running down Shadow's neck, and she realized her own ears were bleeding.

Kura looked up, stony. *Try to kill me,* her eyes said. *I dare you.* Shadow saw herself reflected in them, inches away, as dark as Yo-han's.

She raised her arm. All she had to do was deliver the blow.

She thought suddenly of the Soldier, the mother and daughter, goat's blood running down their foreheads. They had marked themselves with her touch, even before she had come. It was the first time the Soldier had thought about a victim – even briefly. She thought of how Kura's eyes would go slate; the fire would blaze. The Emperor would let them go; she was sure of it. He would mourn his daughter, or rather, her efficiency, and he would remain here to devise whatever he wanted next, whatever new opponent, amidst his endless supply of Bone Warriors.

Shadow raised an arm.

The Soldier would've struck without hesitation. But Shadow was no Soldier. Couldn't *anyone* here see that? *I am not the Soldier,* she thought, and it felt like she had already screamed it into the void countless times, even though she had never actually uttered the words out loud once. *I am myself, and nothing else.* Did she have to die to prove that?

She remembered her first time seeing the Moonbearer, the certainty of being for him and nothing else. She remembered Sae watching her cast shadows on the walls. Scarlet pulling her up on the deer as they left the Stronghold behind. Memory always seemed like an infallible thing, an inevitable effect of living, but memory itself could be a choice. This is what she had now, that she had not always had: a choice.

She let go.

Stood up, breathing heavily.

And Kura did not hesitate. She leapt up, too, forcing her down so gracefully it almost felt like she was being laid to rest. Kura slammed down into her again and again with brutal efficacy, striking ceaselessly, and Shadow was trapped on the ground.

The bolts grew successively stronger; shock waves tremored through her body – it was agony. Her systems would shut down. Already half-dead.

Kura made no move to back away, and instead leaned in close, her voice soft beside Shadow's ear. 'They told me I would be battling the Soldier,' she said. 'But you are no Soldier. You won't even fight back.'

With immense difficulty, Shadow rose, her arms barely holding her up. She looked ahead, not at Kura's kneeling form, but further away, at the boot, the same boot that she'd woken to so long ago, beside the water. Up to the robe, to the face of the Moonbearer, who stood watching. She had never felt as intense an anger as this at the sight of him.

He needed her; he wouldn't let her die yet. Would he? There was so much she still did not understand, even after so long. Perhaps he would steal her from the brink of death, powerless, leave to let his men be slaughtered just to buy him time, ensure his departure. Trapped and cornered in this ice palace, they would die almost immediately by the droves, under the sure hand of Kura and the Bone Warriors. Already they were moving into formation. The Emperor would barely have to lift a hand. This filled her with such rage she could hardly move, though whether it was towards the Moonbearer or at herself – the line was too blurred to tell.

War could not start here. A small slaughter at the blink of an eye, carried over to the homeland through his twisted lies, whatever falsities he would make up to rally the people. She wouldn't let it start here. Not at her expense.

'Such weakness,' Kura said, eyes narrowed, 'cannot be forgiven.'

'Nothing will come of your death,' Shadow said. 'But nothing will come of mine either.'

'It must be one or the other. You must make a choice.'

'I'll make my own choice,' she said. And she met Scarlet's eyes over the palace floor.

Scarlet knew. Had always known, maybe from the moment they collided in Yosae, and Shadow had looked up to a figure silhouetted against the sun. Every single moment they had shared, every heart-stopping close call, and Scarlet had always seen through it all, right through to the bone. *You traitor,* Shadow thought, *You brilliant, fanatical traitor.*

Your turn to help me now.

Scarlet was aware of exactly what she was thinking.

'Do it,' Shadow said, and despite it all, her voice rang loud and clear. She didn't – couldn't – move, didn't do anything but stare. She hoped Scarlet would understand.

And then Scarlet nodded, parted her lips to speak.

Chapter 31

*U*nder *the Yong of the East.* 동쪽의 용 아래.

Scarlet's mouth moved almost imperceptibly, pressing the words into existence.

Under the Daltokki. 달토끼 아래.

Shadow caught hold of the ground, dragged her feet.

Scale. 비늘. *Shard.* 비늘.

It was the same feeling as in Prince Yo-han's study when Guards had tried to wrench it out of her. The same slow rise of temptation, a return of something so familiar it was hard to know what to resist and what was already a part of her.

But this time was different. This time, she couldn't fight it. She had to let it overcome her, consume her. She could not resist.

Nine. 아홉.

This was as far as they had got, hadn't they? Over halfway, but they had not been strong. Their voices indistinguishable, weak. Handlers like that would hardly have been able to assert control.

Lost. 죽은.

But this voice was new. Scarlet's. Her gaze intense, unwavering against the Guards' grasp, palms alight. Her voice growing in volume.

Rusted. 녹슨.

I accept, Shadow thought. *I'll let you in.* For the first time, she took control by relinquishing it. And even as her body tensed up, shook in fighting to keep control, she opened her mind like prising open the jaws of something dead and heavy. *Open,* she thought, and there was a shift in the air, so small as to be unnoticeable.

But the Moonbearer noticed. She knew he would.

Through the Guards surrounding his back, he stilled.

Twilight. 어스름.

She couldn't see his expression, but knew from his slow, incredulous words that cut through the din like a knife.

'You don't know what it's like to control her,' his voice came – warning, aged. 'You don't know the incredible strain. It's nothing like you're thinking.'

Scarlet never dropped her gaze, not even until the last second.

'I assume it feels like fire,' she said. 'Like burning from the inside out.' And then, the final word hung above them like an axe swinging down:

Moon. 달.

And somewhere in the murky depths, the Soldier opened her eyes.

It was like surfacing from underwater.

This viscous liquid filling her lungs, draining out; and a lightness at the end, coming closer and closer.

The Soldier woke in the midst of battle; and this was nothing new. Vaguely she grew aware of faces and names, where she was, but these details were not relevant, and therefore not to be regarded.

The Last Soldier of Nava

What was new was her handler. Where before the presence in her head was like an overflowing thing, dark and large, threatening to overtake – this was new, smaller, lighter.

Weaker.

Instinctively, the Soldier pushed back. A presence so frail as to be indistinguishable from her own mind, not enough to contain her, not *enough*. She surrounded the force with her own mind – *Guide me. Lead me. Direct me.* Here is all of my power, it begs for a way out.

The handler was shrinking, retreating. Flimsy.

The Soldier grew frustrated. Her senses were as sharp as knives: the battle a vivid blur around her, the sound of harsh breathing and slicing, the feeling of her own hands, less-than-optimal temperatures, the condition of her body. The body was damaged; needed recuperation.

Beside her: a bystander, roughly the same size as her, backing away. Unarmed. From behind: an opponent approaching. The Soldier turned, assessed. Superior to her in size, armed heavily. Use her size to her advantage. But the opponent approached and kneeled before her. Offered its body for the taking. The Soldier stepped forward and sliced through in one sweeping motion, and the creature was cleaved in two.

Power surged through her. Instantly she looked to the next target. There were dozens, all would approach, all would sit ready for the taking, unresisting. She could have them all, with no effort—

And then the command froze her in time. There were no words, but she felt it clearly in her head. *Stop.*

Stop.

Stop.

The Soldier pushed back. There was no need to stop.

But this new handler was not so weak anymore. This handler had regained footing, was forcing her back into shape, making her back tense up and her fingers stop moving. *Listen,* the force of it said. *You will obey me.*

The presence grew in her mind, threatening to overwhelm, burning like a thousand lacerations. The presence did not relent.

And then – the warm press of something against her. The outline of a stone. It grew warmer and warmer until it burned like fire, as if imprinting into her skin. These senses worked in tandem to call her back.

The Soldier gazed upon her handler; she hated this new leash. It was better than the others, different, giving her more space to breathe – but still.

This time, it was like something reborn, the command that rang so clearly, unwilling to compromise.

Kill the fire. Like the vice of a grip around her wrist, tightening by the second. The stone buzzing.

KILL THE FIRE.

So, the Soldier obeyed.

The fire – crackling, leaping, white as snow – she stole, and then everything was plunged into darkness, flowing from her hands, effortless, enormous. It swept over everything, and she felt it blanket like a living thing, a tightening noose.

Around her, the battle stilled; confusion erupted. The subject ahead of her could not see his own hand. The Soldier saw all; it would take a matter of seconds to run through this crowd.

But the commands were still insistent. *Target,* they said. *Target.* The target on the throne, high-up and unreachable.

The Emperor.

There was a hand around her forearm, gripping. The Soldier turned. Her handler?

But no – this was not the handler. This was someone else – someone familiar, and the Soldier felt darkness course through her, a touch that she had forgotten.

His voice was in the air, in her head, everywhere around. A different voice.

'Look at me.'

A thousand lakes, a hand, a Rabbit – *Look at me.*

He saw her as clearly as she saw him, undeterred by the dark, untethered to anything. The Soldier could not quite distinguish between faces, but his was—

'Just do what is easy,' he said. 'Drown this place in darkness.'

Drown this place.

'End it all,' the voice continued. 'It can be me and you again. We can do it all. A thousand more years, what is it to us? We are not like them.' He looked around them. 'We are above them.'

Give in.

The Soldier stilled. Drown this place, yes, drown—

But she remembered him.

His presence reminded her of pain, the same as an open wound. His voice brought nothing but this hurt and something stronger, something that burned like fire within her.

Old wrongs. He was an enemy. She wanted to put him down.

But her new handler was merciless and ripped through her mind like a sword.

THE – EMPEROR.

KILL – THE – EMPEROR.

There was no way to resist.

She tore her arm from his grasp, turned. It was pitch black, but the Soldier could hit true in the dark.

Even before it was done, she felt its inevitability. After, her body threatened to give. The shadows rushed back into her, and the fire roared to life, illuminating Kura's whitening face, the Emperor slumping over, face frozen in his eternal sleep. The

Bone Warriors didn't move, like the machinery they were. The Soldier looked to the handler for guidance, but the handler had gone dark, gone quiet – was no longer there. The Soldier – Shadow's hand unfurled; her fingers went lax. Kura knelt over her father's body. The Bone Warriors still, useless without a user. Unsure what to do. Uncaring. Shadow fell into blessed darkness.

And before it all, the Soldier had woken on the damp floor of the cellar, staring up at the face of a young woman.
'The Soldier,' this young woman said, with more awe than fear. In all her lifetimes, the Soldier had never heard anyone refer to her like that. With softness in the voice, with restrained wonder instead of fear. And in all her lifetimes, no one had ever come *closer* – drawing even nearer to her, treading cautiously.
'You're awake,' she continued quietly, almost like a whisper. When she examined her face closer in the dark, her eyes widened in shock. 'You're so young.'
The Soldier did not and could not say anything. Her brain went haywire, mind short-circuiting. *Don't,* the Soldier wanted to say, and her head went, *attack attack attack* but her body felt so different, though she wasn't sure why. For the first time, she felt how her fingers ached; how her limbs rusted. How cold she was. How tender and new. The Soldier wanted to run away, to leave this place and never come back.
'Can you speak?' the girl whispered, hair falling around her face. 'Why is your face covered?'
And slowly, ever so carefully, she reached out. The Soldier knew the moment her fingers hit the mask, the way they grazed.
This was a serious breach. The subject could attack at any moment: to the jugular, the chest, every and all points of

The Last Soldier of Nava

weakness were exposed and vulnerable. Move back, move back, move back. She fought against all her instinct and senses not to move back. She was faulty. She could not obey the Moonbearer's orders here. She was caught, a fly in a spider's web. The fingers finding the edges of her mask, unfurled something ancient in her that she didn't even know existed.

'Whoever is making you do this,' she said, 'I can stop them. I'm powerful. I can help you. You see?' And she unfurled her palm, a small storm of sand conjuring in her hand. 'I'm here.' The sand dissipated, and she was taking both of her hands and reaching out and—

And here was the possibility, opened raw and new like the belly of an animal slit open. The possibility of light, of glittering desert storms, awakening things in the Soldier that she had never felt. She wanted to chase them, even as they receded in the distance. Was this possible? Every instinct in her told her no, but she wanted to resist. For the first time, she wanted to resist.

Perhaps this was too much to bear, all at once. Or perhaps it was the rolling thunder outside, the sudden noise it created, like a warning from the skies. Or the edges of her own pain, lancing through her head. Or even the girl's nearness, how the only bodies the Soldier had ever been close to were her handler and her victims. She hadn't known what could exist in the middle, between being the hunted and hunter. Clarity shot through the Soldier's head like a knife, and she pushed out against the Desert Rose with all her strength, sending an arc of darkness flying through the air. The fight was not a long fight, but it was the longest one that the Soldier had ever experienced against a single opponent. None moved so deftly and surely as this girl, who fought like she had been born to, though it clearly pained her to do it.

But all fights came to an end, and the Soldier attacked with the ruthlessness of one who aimed to kill – nothing less, nothing more. The Saint Desert Rose was disinclined to do this. She sent blows that were meant to sweep the Soldier off her feet, knock her out.

Such ruses wouldn't work on the Soldier, but this girl wouldn't know that. She was starting to learn, starting to realize what she had to do. The Soldier always hit true in the dark, but so did *she*.

In the end, the final blows brushed at the same time. Maybe, when the Saint knew she would die, she aimed purposefully at the face; maybe she had known. The Soldier wouldn't know, wouldn't remember. She only remembered how the pain was unimaginable. How she fell to her knees, hands to her face. A thousand burning cinders rushing through, her eye burning, like a single stripe of death running all the way down to her lip, her face in agony. In all her life, she had never known pain like this.

Chapter 32

She woke in a dark place.

Barely any light streamed in; Shadow waited for her eyes to adjust. It was so dark inside that even she had trouble seeing. Her mouth was dry, muscles aching. She still felt groggy, weighed down, but it was less intense now, everything felt clearer.

It was a cell. Built out of overlaid thin logs and planks, packed together to ensure nothing could seep through, sturdy and cleverly torturous. Its fashion meant that any prisoner would be victim to any onslaught of weather, be it cold or hot, with no chance of escape. She wondered where she was in the Stronghold; where this prison had been all this time. Wrists bound and one foot chained to the wall, she at first tried to peer through the thin cracks to catch anything. They had stripped her of any armour, fur, leaving her only in thin underclothes.

The journey back from Asanai had been breakneck fast. While she and Scarlet had travelled there by cumbersome cargo ship, the Moonbearer's fleet of small, fast *bigeodo* warships sailed back over the waters at double the speed.

She'd been unconscious for most of the journey, barely able to keep time by the cycles of the day.

They had kept her drugged on a concoction of mandrake extract, wolfsbane, and opium; chained to a wall, made to relieve herself in a bucket – not that she had much to relieve, having eaten nothing. Her bruises were garish and populous. Miraculously, Kura hadn't broken anything, though her insides felt rearranged.

Now, Shadow sat in this faint, dusty place. At first, she had failed to kill; and then she had failed to die. Surely this was worse.

She wondered if Scarlet was dead. The Moonbearer had always been going to kill her, anyway; he would have no reason to keep her alive now. But the thought made her want to claw her own eyes out, so she didn't think about it.

She spent the first hour heaving herself up, scouring the walls of the prison to try to look for chinks in the architecture. The floor needed a good scouring, dark and strange stains in the corners. Unkempt, but not unused. How many people had died here over the years, and why? Reaching the tips of their fingernails through the latticework of wood? Prisoners that weren't supposed to exist, in a palace that should never have been built, under a ruler who should've fallen a long time ago.

If she were stronger, she would've considered screaming out for Guards, trying to overtake them. But even then, how would she escape the Stronghold? Who would be waiting for her if she did?

She pressed a hand to one wall, eyes sliding into wetness. She didn't want to think about it. But she had to face it.

Scarlet could be dead. Even though she had betrayed her, the anger was equally matched by something else – something more devastating.

The Last Soldier of Nava

Crow was most likely dead.

Even Sae, she thought, was most likely dead. Why else would she have told her to go north, a last-ditch try? Why else had the house been consumed by vines? They flowered in the wake of her corpse. Perhaps she had already been anticipating her impending death for weeks. And the day of it, Shadow had left her there.

In the house, alone.

A sickness overcame her, a wave of nausea. Shadow tipped her head back against the wall, bone-tired, begging sleep or the drug haze to come back, but neither did. She bent a knee up and pulled it close to her.

It was only when she finally started drifting off that she heard it: a faint rustle. A footstep. Immediately, her eyes startled open. A Guard? She stilled, watching.

And then, slowly, quietly, the door to her prison opened.

Standing there: a cloaked figure.

Scarlet.

A wave of relief – and at the same time, a low fury.

'It's you,' said Shadow quietly.

Scarlet didn't say anything, only watching her gravely. 'You look awful, Shadow.' And she stepped forward, as if to reach her – but didn't come in further. Like something was holding her back. 'Are you—'

'You're a traitor,' Shadow said.

Scarlet flinched.

'You knew,' Shadow said. 'You knew I was the Soldier. That I killed your sister. When did you realize? From the start?'

There were a thousand things she wanted to say, and she wasn't sure where to start.

Scarlet didn't answer.

'The first time I saw you, I thought you were the Desert Rose,' she said. 'I thought a face had come to haunt me from the dead. But you weren't her. You weren't, but you haunted me all the same. She saw what I really was, and I repaid her by killing her. You saw me, too, and you returned the betrayal.'

'That isn't what I wanted,' Scarlet said. 'It never was. I thought I knew where we would end up. But the course of things has changed since then.'

'Regardless,' Shadow said, 'if you wanted vengeance, you succeeded. But I haven't got mine yet. As long as the Moonbearer still lives and breathes, I haven't done a thing.'

'Shadow—'

'Why have you come here? To gloat? Or to help me against him?'

'I've come—' Scarlet began, voice charged; but then she flinched, ever so slightly. 'I've come to tell you something.'

'What?'

'When we arrive back to Ik-Song, you must lure out the Dragon.'

Lure out the Dragon? How?

'Why?' she said.

'For the Moonbearer,' Scarlet said.

Shadow stared uncomprehendingly. 'The Dragon can't be raised. Ik-Song will sink. Millions will die. I can't "lure it out". I don't even know how.'

'You do,' said another voice from the dark.

Shadow froze.

She peered hard into the blackness, trying to see. There was someone else there. A lit lantern came into view, features illuminated by the honey light.

Yo-han.

Shadow flinched back from the light. She could see everything now: the grimy floor, Scarlet's stricken face, how her wrists were bound in front of her, under the cloak. The knife that Yo-han held to her back. He had heard everything.

How was he here? He must have been tailing them; he looked like he hadn't slept in days.

'You can, and you will,' he said. 'Now that you know she's alive.'

Eyes grim, weaponry strung across his armoured back.

'Go now,' he said to Scarlet.

'You have always advised me,' she said. 'You've never commanded me. Forced me. You were the only person in the Stronghold that I ever trusted.'

'As you said,' he returned, 'the course of things has changed since then.'

With a last look at him, Scarlet turned reluctantly. Guards immediately flanked her, leading her out.

The two of them were left alone.

The worst part was that he looked the same. He had not transformed into some stony, murderous villain, power-hungry and ravaging. He still looked uncomfortable; he still wore his heart on his sleeve. He hadn't changed, fit himself into some role. He was still Prince Yo-han. And he wanted this. He believed in the Moonbearer, in his promises, with his whole being. He had even killed Aspis for it.

They stared each other down. Shadow was the first to break the silence. 'Did you hurt Crow?'

He stared at her. 'Of course not.'

'Then what did you do? Imprison him? He wouldn't stand for this.'

'I don't think of you as a monster,' Yo-han said. 'Do you think of me as one?'

She was silent at that. While the Moonbearer slumbered, it was Yo-han who contrived this plot. Back then, it was Shadow who killed for him. *Monster*, they were all *monsters*.

'Your fate was decided before you were ever even born,' he said. 'Or created. Whichever one it was. I know how that feels.'

'Do you?' she said. 'A Prince is very different from a Soldier.'

'My mother could never stand to look upon her own mistake. She threw me to the Stronghold like a dog,' he said. 'You know a thing about that. I could never ascend to her throne. Nor can I rule the Stronghold, not really. All I have are false titles, questioned allegiances.' His eyes were like hard, diamond flints. 'But the Moonbearer took me in. He trained me, made me this powerful.'

'The Moonbearer orchestrated the White Ice,' she said. 'Did you know that?'

'Asanai would have attacked Ik-Song regardless of his presence. He graced our nation with military might; he made sure no one would test us for decades. Don't you understand? He's transformed the land.'

'The Moonbearer started this game a long, long time ago. I should know. He's not for you to trust. He doesn't care about Ik-Song, or Asanai, or these petty lands. He's raising the Dragon for himself.' Yo-han had to understand – couldn't he *see* what was going to happen? Couldn't he see what was right in front of him?

'He's raising it so we can finally conquer.'

'Your father, the Emperor, is dead,' she said. 'I killed him. You won't have to worry about Asanai for a long time, now. Your sister grieves alone in that ice palace.'

He was silent.

'When the Councillor raises the Dragon,' she continued, 'he'll remake the world in his vision. He is going to bring back the Ninth, and he won't care whether it breaks Ik-Song in two. The cities and forests will sink, and millions will die.'

He shook his head. 'That isn't true. You're blinded.'

'By what?'

'Your own want for revenge. He never believed you as strong as your potential. You are wounded by him.'

'As strong as my potential?' she said. 'I've surpassed my potential. I did everything he asked. I defeated the Emperor and bested your sister. I have a new handler – I am no longer bound to him.'

'Scarlet won't be your handler for long,' he said. 'The Moonbearer has offered me something I can't refuse.'

'What?'

'*You.*' He drew closer. 'All this time, I've been trying to awaken you. Since the first day you rose, one year ago, in that cellar of Yosae. I have always known you were the key – the weapon we needed – to defeat Asanai once and for all. Not just to fend them off, but to conquer. And now, after the Dragon rises, I *will* awaken you, and you'll be mine. He's given you to me.'

But this wasn't what she was thinking about. 'The Moonbearer sent you to raise me?'

Yo-han shook his head. 'He was weak. Wasting away. I thought I could accomplish what he set out to do. I thought I could awaken you.'

'And the Desert Rose found out,' she said, the shock settling in. 'You didn't know what it would take to control me. She came down into that cellar after you, and then you left her to deal with the consequences.'

You are not supposed to be awake yet.

He wouldn't have been able to control the Soldier. Not unprepared, unknowing. He would've let the Soldier run free, unable to stop what he had awakened, terrified. By the time the Desert Rose would've reached him, the last word would've fallen from his lips.

Moon.

'Awakening you wasn't . . . what I expected.'

'How do you expect to control the Soldier when you couldn't the first time?'

'I'm stronger now, under new tutelage. I'm prepared. And you've been broken in. Even your power wanes after so long.'

'You *lost control*. You—' *killed her.*

'I told her to leave,' he said, face turning to the shadows. 'I told her you were dangerous. But she didn't listen.'

'Does Scarlet know this? If her sister hadn't followed you, she wouldn't have died.'

'If you hadn't *killed* her, she wouldn't be dead.' He watched her. 'You're being given a merciful fate. Not even a real death. Be grateful for that. It's more than what you gave her.'

Guards dragged her outside.

Shadow cringed at the bright sunlight, so white in her eyes. When the world came into focus, the first thing she saw was Scarlet on her feet, still held at knifepoint. They stood just outside the palace, the day clear and bright.

The Moonbearer was on horseback.

'I suppose there's no need for any explanation,' he said. 'You'll do as I say, since you're in this precarious situation.'

They made their journey down the rocky shores, along the cliffside, deer nimbly picking their way between the ash-grey limestone trailing down. It was a large party, diverging at several points to keep watch and guard. She stared at the strange weaponry and contraptions that the Guards carried – carved and white, like nothing she'd ever seen before.

'Reinforced with the bones of sacred animals,' the Moonbearer said. 'Even from the skulls of Bone Warriors, melted down and forged into links.'

She looked away.

The walk was made mostly in silence. She didn't know if this would even really work – if she alone was enough to call forth a being so ancient.

It was only when they neared the underbrush along the

coast – the thick tangle of forest, opposite from the sea – that she paused, just for a half-fraction of a second. A bare moment of hesitation.

She could feel it. The *pull* of something, so strong as to be tugging at her, deep in her gut. *No.* Like a flow of energy she could naturally sense, not unlike the feeling of other's ability, of Scarlet's pulsing light. But unlike Scarlet's – flighty, ever-changing, young – this one was old. Lurking, waiting, in certain depths. A force that none of them could match up to, no matter how much they tried.

The Moonbearer caught it immediately. 'Where?' He dismounted his horse. '*Where?*'

Predictably, he gestured to the Guards, who wielded the blade against the nape of Scarlet's neck.

Shadow didn't want to tell him where. But she wouldn't have a choice – and a plan was forming in her head. A half-baked, reckless idea. 'I don't know.'

The Moonbearer came close, grabbed her by the arm. Exhaled. For the first time, some of his countenance deteriorated; his calm tone belied a feverish haze in his eyes.

'I'm this close. You understand, child? *This* close to having back everything that ever was. Are you so careless as to not want it, too?' He gestured to the fields, the Stronghold. 'This isn't your home. It's not even your time. It never was. I'm only setting things right.'

'Nava was destroyed *because* of you,' she spat. 'Because of your greed, your thirst for war. You're the one who threw everything out of balance.'

'I may have begun the fight, but the Dawnbringer was the one who collapsed the city to stop you. She ended it for eternity. And she was lucky – she died. I didn't. I went on for centuries in this weak, blasted world, with no one but myself.'

Shadow came close to his face, too. 'You created your own

nightmare world. You made me just to control me. Never gave me a choice, or a chance, even.' She shut her eyes briefly. The sea lapped behind her. 'I thought I could do it. I thought I could fight you, bring you down, somehow. But you don't fight, not really. Not with honour, or dignity. You cheat and steal; twist the very nature of our world to get what you want. You stole my body and made a weapon out of it. You cultivated this rat's nest of a palace' – she looked towards the Stronghold – 'and pitted everyone against each other, pulling the strings from behind, all for your own entertainment. Games. You're surrounded by a mountain of innocent corpses.'

He said nothing.

'You,' she said, 'from a city that was once so grand and glorious, beyond all this.'

A silence. And then: 'You don't know what it's like to lose everything,' he said stonily, 'because you never had anything at all.'

She staggered back as he turned her roughly by the arm. They looked together at the forest, where a deadzone played at the edges of her senses.

'Here is the truth, child,' he said. 'Look around in the new world. Do you think Nava would have survived? It was destined to fall. We only sped the inevitable. The deadzones may have started with its fall, an attempt to restore balance. But they grew, and grew, and nothing was done.'

You can no longer see what you once knew. Nava was no city; it was not physical. It was something unnameable and intangible. It was a way of life. He couldn't force it back into existence; couldn't change the ocean tides or the borders of forests. And even now, balance was possible, but he had long since lost his balance.

The sea was where life had really begun, taken its tentative first steps. Not the forests. The trees had come so much later,

The Last Soldier of Nava

standing tall over centuries and centuries of silence. Then why did the deadzones swallow only the forests? They did not target the roots, the beginnings. Only the now.

That far down the line, the world had begun to warp, and it never changed back. What was taken was never given back. And life was never regarded life as life, an impossible probability, another being, a sprawling being that encompassed millions of creatures and plants and small wonders.

And the land took revenge.

'You were always faulty,' the Moonbearer said. 'You were never a good Soldier. I gave you a chance, but you squandered it. You turned away from what could have been.'

'That's what life is,' she said. His words were like a dulled blade's edge, now. Blunt, brittle. She saw it for what it was. 'It's nothing but a chance. Chance that was given to us. I'm glad that I wasn't a good Soldier. I'm glad I could be human, and imperfect, and strange.'

'Then I'm glad you are at peace,' he said.

And he pushed her into the deadzone.

Stillness.

Shadow breathed in the smell of the forest. The Dragon would come, she was sure. And when it did, it might see this for the mirage it was, kill her out of anger. She'd be splayed out in the dirt, returned back to where she came from. Over time, the trees would change, the surging storms would overspill the sea, come erode, overtake. She could float, her spirit free. Like the sea tombs of the sailors.

Sea tombs. Watching the ice beside her, smiling. Scarlet had told her once not to touch anything here. Shadow wondered what would happen if she did. Even as she glanced away and back, the shape of the leaves seemed to have altered slightly, the composition of trunks, different. The landscape was changing. The landscape is always changing, Shadow thought. There was an intensity to it now, to the rapidity at which it hovered.

The landscape was always changing, but so was she.

You were never a good Soldier.

The Dragon would come, she was sure. But after that, what? The Moonbearer had decided the course of things for so long. But he wasn't here right now. There was no one in this deadzone but her.

Under her feet, the ground tremored slightly.

Behind her came rustling.

Shadow turned around.

'Scarlet,' she said.

'I thought,' Scarlet said, out of breath. 'I thought you might already be dead in here.'

'He pushed you in?'

She shook her head. 'I followed you in.' She came close, reaching out – as if to examine Shadow, to run her hands over her – but stopped herself.

'Why?'

'Because,' Scarlet said. 'Do I really have to say it?'

'Say what?'

'That I would follow you anywhere. I'm prepared to die at the foot of the Dragon with you.' Long pause. Then: 'I'm sorry I awakened you.'

'I'm sorry for your sister.'

'That wasn't you,' she said. 'That was the Soldier.'

'Is there a difference, really?' Shadow looked down at her hands, unfeeling. 'It felt good. It felt like being here, in a deadzone. It tempts me. I would give in so easily, gladly. You wouldn't understand.'

'I understand,' Scarlet said. 'I understand now. Have you ever seen yourself as the Soldier? There's a deadness behind your eyes. You go utterly still, not like a living thing should. Exactly like how the deadzones are. You flicker in and out intermittently, like a real shadow. Your powers, they look completely different – like something real, tangible, suffocating. And your gaze –' her breath hitched – 'your gaze was trained on nothing but *me*. Nothing but your handler, whoever you're bound to. It was the worst thing, to be looked at like that. For you to just await my next command, demand to be guided.' She stepped closer. 'But at the same time, so alluring. To have all this power at my hands, ready to do my will. It was intoxicating – like nothing I had ever felt before.

'I understand why he created you. Why he wants to hold onto you so badly. A thousand years later, he wants you by his side still. If you're no different from the Soldier, then I'm no different from him. I'm sorry. I'm sorry for everything.'

Shadow was rendered speechless. 'You're nothing like the Moonbearer.'

'You're nothing like what I ever imagined you to be. I knew who had marked you. I only wished to torment you, to learn how to destroy you.' Scarlet lowered her gaze. 'But you kept surprising me.'

The landscape was always changing, but so was Shadow. The Dragon was coming, but she wasn't the one who had wronged him. That was the Moonbearer, and he wasn't here.

Even the most hostile of creatures can be tender inside.

'I have a plan, Scarlet,' Shadow said.

Scarlet straightened. 'You do?'

'I won't give this Dragon the chance to destroy Ik-Song. It has to listen to me first.'

'Listen to you?' Scarlet said.

'I was born of a slaughtered Dragon,' she said. 'I share the same blood.'

'He may recognize you,' Scarlet said, realization dawning. 'He might see you as kin.'

Under them, the ground trembled again, this time more strongly.

Shadow stepped forward. She was no Soldier, not in that moment – but she was still the product of a great being. 'Help him see me,' she said. What she was stepping into, she didn't know. She only knew that the landscape was changing, that Scarlet was a steady force behind her, and perhaps that she could appeal to a Dragon's will. The Moonbearer was not here. It was only her and the forest. 'Let him see me with his own eyes.'

The trembling turned swiftly into a violent rumbling, both of them pitched down on their knees for balance as the ground shook. There was an energy, a living pulse, that she was sure even Scarlet could feel. The forest shook, leaves falling, a trunk even snapping.

The Dragon was coming.

Chapter 33

Impossibly, before them, the stream thinned and then widened, turning into a gaping river, swallowing the ground and trees around them, into a lake, into a sea, out of which – in one glorious, long sweep, arced out something so large it blocked out the entire sun and sky. The air itself shattered and reformed around its massive bulk, streaked through with scars of black, blue-silver scales flickering in solid increments. It was shrouded in fog, intangible, unable to be pinned with the naked human eye – parts of its body almost incorporeal, solidifying in some places and melting into mist in others. Its eruption displaced the water, hurtling it out towards them, bending over.

Shadow and Scarlet stood like two tiny figures under a huge shadow. The wave swept sideways, backwards, crashing down; beyond the filmy veil, the Dragon twisted and curled, bellowing cries like thunder come to life. It was the sea; the sky; the fog; even the mountains, its massive back cresting like crags of rock. They could do nothing but stare.

He was angry, and he was beautiful. In his roar, she heard the calls of all living things; the microcosms beneath her shoe, the great catfish tipping over, the three-legged crows perched high up on the spruces. She heard all of their anger like a great, steaming thing, and she sought to stay down on her knees and repent. But she could only stay very still and listen. She listened and felt the Dragon's grief, his pain, the blood of his brother spilled, a thousand years ago. Around them, the forest twisted and grew exponentially, trees shooting up to the clouds, vines curling around their feet, leaves growing monstrously large.

She looked at Scarlet, who looked back with the same intensity. The woods now illuminated by the violet light of the Dragon's eye, wine-dark in its iris.

Scarlet bathed the forest in her own light, blazing behind, illuminating Shadow to the Dragon. Yet in the face of his power, they saw that it was grander than anything they could build or imagine, greater than all their poor attempts. The palace of the Stronghold, the city of Yosae, all of Ik-Song seemed to fall away at this beast that the storms had sent their way, rippling across the nation.

Scarlet knelt, as if guided by an invisible force. It was tempting to kneel and fall. Fall under the Dragon, let him crumble the world, start anew.

Shadow looked up. Hair whipped around her face. Eyes closed. Around them, the ground was ripped up by hurtling debris, but the circle only surrounding them saw no such destruction, an untouched corner.

She didn't kneel. She took a step forward – and then another, and another.

The Dragon pulsed in anger.

She heard Scarlet scream her name behind her, but it was lost quickly to the wind. She met that huge eye, continuing to come forward. *Look at me,* she thought. *You know me.*

The Last Soldier of Nava

The wind almost blew her off her feet; she stumbled and fell, holding steady against the storm. She was forced to shut her eyes.

All she could do now was wait.

Perhaps wait for the Dragon to take her.

The winds howled.

But after only moments, they were slowing.

Dying down.

Light brightened behind her closed lids.

She listened to the calming whistle, the quietness emerging.

Had they died? Was this something else?

Shadow opened her eyes.

She was still in the forest, but Scarlet was no longer beside her. And directly in front of her, gazing down at her face, the Dragon.

Shadow began to rise again, cautiously. Her heart pounded in her chest. But slowly, over the roaring in her ears, she listened. This was not the same forest, the same deadzone. This forest was alive. The plants no longer looked like contrived arrangements, too vivid; they were real, rustling. Faintly, birds chattered in the background, flitting from branch to branch; small insects burrowed underfoot; flowers dotted the ground. It smelled real. It looked real.

And the *yong* watched her watching it, paused in its rage. She couldn't discern its expression.

Do you speak? she thought.

And then she realized what a stupid question this was. Of course, he did – but different animals spoke different languages.

Yet, even without language, she felt his melancholy, his sadness.

'You do recognize me,' she said, shocked. 'You sense your brother in me.'

Yejin Suh

Was the Dragon confused? The spirit of his great, world-shattering brother in the body of one weak human, this warring of energies.

She reached out a hand towards his great eye, and in it she thought she could see everything. They knew each other. The *yong* could feel it in her. It stilled in its frenetic chaos, fixing her with one eye, listening. Mollified.

She pulled her hand back. In an instant, she was back on the ground, kneeling, the forest shifting back to the deadzone.

Scarlet was clutching her shoulder.

She turned to her. 'Scarlet,' she said, 'he saw me. Look.'

The Dragon's enormous face appeared beside them, almost incorporeal, blending with the greenery.

Scarlet didn't even glance back at the Dragon. She just stared at Shadow.

Memories ran through her mind. The same memories of diving deep down into endless lakes, small creatures trailing her in her wake; the ocean's soundless abyss, the whales. It felt like she had known this Dragon her entire life, since her creation, undeniably and inextricably bound to each other in threads that surpassed the material world and into the unexplainable.

The Dragon was not really a Dragon. It was Nava. *Nava* was the one thing in the world irreplaceable, that they would forever remain desperate to imitate, exploit, tear apart the inner workings of. *Nava* was infinite and invaluable.

Scarlet saw the same.

'He understands,' Shadow said. 'He shows mercy.'

She heard Scarlet rise hesitantly beside her.

'The *yong* will be able to heal the land of its dark magic,' Shadow said. 'Strip everything unnatural of its plagues.' *Including me,* she dared to think, selfishly. Burn the Soldier out of her. 'Save everyone.'

The Last Soldier of Nava

'How do we thank you?' Scarlet asked.

He dipped his head low to them, presenting the scales across his neck, towards his back.

Shadow placed one hand on a massive scale.

'I think he's allowing you to saddle him,' Scarlet whispered. 'To touch him.'

She looked up at that great eye, the inky pool of it.

It was only within the eye's reflection that she saw the forest around them lurching, then – the fire ripping through the ground, the Moonbearer and his men edging inside; the beautiful woods crumbling in a single second to ashes and flame, the Dragon roaring in pain, in oblivion.

Chapter 34

'No,' Shadow gasped. The illusion of endless forest around them faded away, the Stronghold sliding back into view, the Seochon. Plumes of smoke, sable flames vaulting up, eating everything in its path. An unnatural black fire, the Moonbearer in brutal command. The Dragon roared in pain, resisting its end, and she forced her way towards him, but Guards surrounded her, and it was already dying, burning up, evaporating away, extinguished forever. It was fading into the ground like part of its rot, eaten alive.

A strangled sound escaped her. She pitched forwards, trying to hold on, to touch the dirt, the trees, but it all crumbled away under her touch. She snatched her hands back like they'd been burned.

The Moonbearer's growing strength was thick and pungent in the air; she almost choked on it. His veins ran dark as his body took in the Dragon's power; eyes glazing pitch black. She tried to step towards him, but Guards were every which way, stringing along like pest ants. She stood back-to-back with Scarlet, looking around at the ring closing in, wiping dirt off her face.

This is what the Dragon had got for trusting them.

The anger came hot, licking at her chest. The Moonbearer was a literal shadow, transparent; he flickered in and out, hands outstretched, relishing it. The blood of two Dragons, the East and West, sustained him.

He raised his hand to the sky. 'With this,' he said. 'I will bring back what has been lost.'

The ground began to shake again. But this time, it was no coming Dragon, no wonderful storm. This time, it was freakish. A block of earth near them jutted out of the ground and then back down; cracks appeared; the land rearranged itself abnormally. Guards lost their balance; others keeled over. There were already too many people in this deadzone.

Even with the forest ripping itself apart around them, Shadow and Scarlet were forced to kneel. Blades to necks. Outnumbered. No longer needed. The Moonbearer was already leaving, mounting his horse.

He looked back at them. 'Kill the girls,' he said, 'and behold the new dawn.'

She struggled – tried to tear free—

'*Release them*,' came a voice ringing through the clearing.

She looked up. Yo-han on his doe, who pawed the ground nervously; behind him emerged—

'Crow,' she greeted in relief. 'You're alive.'

'What are you *doing*?' Yo-han asked. His face was stricken; confused, angry. 'Let them go,' he commanded the Guards, face hard. 'Don't touch them.'

'We're under the Councillor's orders,' one said. 'Not yours.'

Yo-han's eyes went wide. He shook his head. 'Tell them that's wrong,' he said to the Moonbearer. 'Tell them – my orders go, too.'

The Moonbearer was silent. Even as Yo-han said the words, his face revealed the truth, understanding dawning in his eyes.

'Councillor?'

'Let this one go, boy,' he said, gesturing to Scarlet. 'And I'll give you her –' he jerked his head at Shadow – 'like I promised. It's what you wanted, isn't it?'

'What I wanted?' Yo-han looked between them. There was a long silence. He looked very small.

'It's almost here,' the Moonbearer said, and the ground shattered, pitching Shadow forward as she tried to keep balance.

'*What's* almost here?' Yo-han asked. 'Why is the land under my feet falling apart?'

'I told you,' Shadow said. 'He's *sinking* Ik-Song to try to bring Nava back. Everyone here will die.'

Yo-han's face was pale with shock. He had truly believed otherwise, even now. He had trusted in the lies.

'The *yong* was going to help us restore order,' she continued, vision threatening to blur, thinking of the Dragon. 'But he slaughtered it. He burned it alive.'

'I am giving you the power that you want, boy,' the Moonbearer said. 'It's so close – just in reach. All you need to do now is accept it. Accept what you have prepared for, reap the fruits of your labour.' He held out his hand.

'You promised me Asanai,' Yo-han said. 'You promised a united country.'

'This country is rotted, falling apart. Look where you stand, right now—'

'The deadzones were *your* doing,' Shadow interjected.

'You want Asanai,' Crow said, tone acerbic, and everyone turned to look at him except for Yo-han, 'you can have it. They left the Bloodbird King dead and the Bone Warriors without a leader. Nothing there but your sister, and she is too inexperienced, and now distraught, for the throne. There was nothing stopping him from taking Asanai then and there. But he's left it behind to return here – to act on his own plan. He'll never give you what you want. You may as well march up there now. It's yours for the taking.' A pause. 'It's what you wanted, right?'

The Prince looked around at the scale of the destruction, the number of Guards versus their meagre group of four. The greying sky, the death. As if he was seeing it all clearly for the first time ever. Shadow waited for him to lash out, to tell Crow he was wrong, but anger only flickered in his eyes, and she wasn't sure at what.

'I don't care what you want, though,' Crow said. 'There's only one thing you can do now. You see that, don't you?'

Yo-han stared at the Moonbearer's outstretched hand. He would take it, Shadow thought. He would take it and bring winter down on them all and they would be buried underfoot in glacial crust. She would sleep for eternity.

'Ik-Song will fall,' Scarlet said with certainty.

And then Yo-han – teeth gritted, eyes furious – raised his hands to strike, lightning-fast – not at Scarlet, but the Moonbearer.

The Moonbearer was faster, and he had centuries and Dragon blood on his side. The deadzone was pitched into inky blackness – so dark that for the first time ever, even Shadow had trouble seeing past the murky shapes. *Drown this place.* Vaguely she saw Crow and Yo-han duck for cover; Scarlet slip from the Guards' grasp; the Moonbearer mount his deer.

Shadow tried desperately to strike him, to no avail. She struck a tree instead, slicing branches clean in two. She began to suck the darkness back, willing the forest to clear again, slowly.

There was a brilliant, all-consuming light blazing through the black, casting dappled patterns across the trees, the undulating land. The Moonbearer was a silhouette bursting rapidly through the forest, disappearing from the deadzone to the outside world.

Shadow watched Scarlet run to where Crow and Yo-han were, voice low. 'We need to get out of here. Only twenty paces behind you – go – before the land changes again—'

'Where has he gone? The Moonbearer?' Shadow interrupted.

Yo-han didn't answer, breaths coming in sharp exhales, staring at the ground.

'Yo-han,' she said.

'He'll be seeking higher ground,' he said, 'towards the Stronghold.'

'I'm going to burn him like he did the Dragon,' Shadow snarled. 'He'll pay for this.'

'Wait,' Scarlet said. 'Shadow—'

Yo-han's stray deer. Shadow mounted it swiftly, limbs moving of their own accord.

She heard Scarlet running after her, but it was too late. 'Wait!'

With a final burst, she rode out, leaving the deadzone.

He had killed the Dragon. She had looked into its eyes and understood its language – if only for a brief second – and he had burned him to the ground.

He would pay.

It was only after a minute of running that she realized—

She was in another deadzone – or maybe the same one.

She dismounted the deer, who nosed her arm, as if in warning. The Stronghold had slipped out of view, and the forest seemed to grow farther and farther out around her, consuming her, overtaking her.

She cursed. The others were nowhere in sight, and neither was the palace, now. Would she grow lost in the deadzone before she even got the chance to try to fight?

She tripped over a bulging root on the ground, pitched to the floor by her palms.

Her breaths came sharply.

She looked up – and stilled. There was a figure standing a little away from her, back turned to her. With a pang, she thought at first it was Scarlet – there was light around her, golden and effusive – maybe she'd got lost, too.

But no. This figure was not tall enough. This figure was shorter, a bit hunched over.

Sae turned around.

Shadow gawked. 'You're here,' she said, in disbelief. 'How are you here?'

Sae didn't answer, only drawing closer. Yes, it was her – wearing the same irritated expression, mildly unimpressed, looking her down from head to toe.

Shadow could only scramble to her feet, staring. 'Is this – some kind of dream? A vision? Have I died?'

'Stupid girl,' Sae said. 'You're not dead.'

Well, this was no pleasant afterlife, that was for sure. 'Sae – I thought you were dead.'

'I'm not dead either,' Sae said. 'I'm helping you stop the Moonbearer from raising the Ninth.'

Shadow froze. 'The Moonbearer? Ninth? How do you even know – how would you—' She shook her head. 'I don't understand. You've come all the way here? To find me?'

'I'm not actually here,' the old woman said. 'But I have access to long-forgotten magic, girl. I see you through this.' She tapped at the right breast pocket of her shirt.

Shadow mirrored her movement. It was where she'd kept the black stone.

'Magic,' she echoed. She thought of all the times it had

seemed to come alive: every time, calling her back to herself. That had been Sae counteracting everything. Forcing her to steady; to recall.

'But it's hardly important how I came here or not. What's important is you putting an end to this nonsense.'

'How? He's so powerful now, he's unstoppable. But—' She paused. 'How do you know all of this? How do you even know who he is?'

'Look at me,' Sae said. 'Don't you know who I am?'

Shadow stared. 'Of course I do, you're Sae. What do you mean? I lived with you—'

'No. Before Yosae. Before even Ik-Song, we met. Our meeting was not long, but it was lasting.'

She stopped. Looked at her. Her face. So many familiar faces around, ones that she couldn't forget – the Moonbearer, Scarlet, Sae – and she'd attributed it to her overactive mind trying desperately to shape a home out of wherever she was, whoever she saw.

Everything seemed slowed down, in this moment.

'Perhaps this will help,' Sae said, and she turned over her palm, where a solemn flicker of light appeared above.

Shadow's breath caught. Sae's light was like Scarlet's, but different – like pure liquid gold, unfettered by time and generations of dilution. The original. It was as if they were standing not in a forest but a field, a battlefield, the Soldier, a figure she had never seen before who brought the wrath of the sun down—

'By the *Dal*,' she gasped.

Her name was Sae. *Sae-byeok. Dawn.*

'You're the Dawnbringer.' How could she have been so oblivious? In hindsight, it was obvious. All the scrolls and books of lore in her home, that vinework. Power from another time, remnants. The Dawnbringer had beheld the Soldier, her enemy, alone and trembling and cold. It would've been so easy, then, to put her down for good.

'You've known this entire time that I was the Soldier. But – you let me into your home. You nursed me back to life.'

'Of course I knew.'

'I could've hurt you,' she said, in disbelief. 'I was dangerous. I wasn't in full control of myself.'

'You couldn't have killed me,' Sae scoffed. 'I'm very powerful.'

'I thought the Moonbearer and myself were the only ones left. But all this time – how did you survive? Does that mean there are more left?'

'No. We are the only artefacts. But while the Moonbearer kept himself animated with dark power, youth, I assimilated. I aged, I lived, I started a family of my own.' Sae smiled. 'And I had resigned myself to watching the world from afar, never interfering again. Letting nature run its course. But you changed my mind, Shadow.' *War breaks and wanes like the moon; nations fragment and become new. It doesn't concern us.* 'Somehow, you broke your mould; you defied expectations. You helped me understand that I still have a role to play, even now.'

Sae had seen her in two lifetimes: the first, as the Soldier; and the second, as herself. 'Then tell me how,' Shadow said. 'Tell me how to defeat him.'

Sae reached out a hand. Shadow took it. 'A thousand years ago, I pulled all of the light out of Nava and put you to sleep with it. The life source, the energy. And don't you know where it all went?'

Where it all went.

I don't know, she wanted to say, but she did know. She knew because she'd woken up to cool dawn, riding with Scarlet; after her body had burned up, finding coolness in the expanse of her skin. Because of how the Desert Rose had died. *You can steal ability.* She was a *sakasa*, reigner of shadows, inside her a void of nothing, save for the spirit of a Dragon. It was impossible that she should have that much light within her; she was meant to hold only darkness.

'It has always been in you, all along,' Sae said, tapping at her chest.

She *was* the key to saving Ik-Song – just not in the way she'd thought.

She looked down at her own hand as if she'd never seen it before.

Sae watched her. 'Now go,' she commanded. 'We haven't got long.'

'But how do I know how to channel it?' Redirecting at the Desert Rose had been a last-minute act of instinct, something she couldn't even control. When the fire Guard had attacked her, she couldn't even let go of the heat. 'How do I release it?'

'You absorbed it as the Soldier,' Sae said. 'To release it, you must once again become the Soldier.'

It was not unexpected. Still, hearing it made her heart quicken.

Sae shook her head. 'Don't fear, Shadow. You will have help. And you will know what to do.'

Don't fear.

The forest was already sliding away from them, vines creeping out, the palace coming back into view. Shadow clutched her hand, tried to hold on. 'Wait – Sae – you have to stay safe, seek shelter—'

The old woman harrumphed. 'I'm no decrepit.'

And then the deadzone was gone.

In its place, nothing but herself – and that was enough.

And Shadow ran.

Chapter 35

She ran like she never had before, towards the Stronghold, the Moonbearer. As the world seemed to destruct and reshape around her, she pushed forwards.

At the topmost level of the Stronghold, the north-side, overlooking the sea, darkness crackled and thudded.

She knew the hidden tunnels, from when they'd escaped to Asanai. She dived down, winding up towards the topmost floor. Every time the foundation shook, she slanted sideways and hung onto the wall, waiting before continuing to scale up the steps as quickly as possible.

The Moonbearer and the Dawnbringer had once ruled Nava together. Complementing each other, the dark and the light, one who could steal, one who pulled. Maintaining balance with the Dragons, their counterparts.

Now, the Dragons were dead. It was all blown apart.

Her footsteps were quick and light, breathing ragged, trying to stay silent as she reached the hall that held the balcony. Her heart pounded in her ears.

The space was already swirling with ink, like a void, his

form in the centre. His eyes, when they fixed on her, sent that familiar fear lighting up her entire system.

The Dawnbringer had told her she contained all the light she needed to destroy him. But she didn't want to summon forth any light. She wanted to surge forward and meet him with his own darkness.

'You've thrown the entire world out of balance,' Shadow said. 'Again and again.'

'You've come to save the world, child?' he said.

'No. You stole my entire life from me. I want you to pay for it.'

'I gave you everything. You just weren't strong enough.' And then he sent darkness lashing towards her.

A rough hand yanked her back, fast as lightning. She nearly lost balance.

'Stay back, Shadow,' hissed a voice in her ear. 'Don't go any closer.'

Scarlet.

'Let go of me,' Shadow said, straining free.

'No.'

'I'm so close. I've never been this close.'

'To defeating him? You don't even know how.'

'I do know,' she said. 'When the Dawnbringer put me down, all those years ago, she did it with all the light of Nava. And you were the one who suspected I could absorb other elements. You were right. All of that light is *still inside me.*'

'How can you summon all that power?' Scarlet asked.

'If you awaken me again,' Shadow replied. 'If you bring forth the Soldier. Together, we can kill him.'

Shadow waited for the surprise, the victorious relief.

Scarlet stared at her. But then she only frowned sharply. 'I'm not doing that.'

'What?' she said urgently, confused. 'Did you hear me? All

of Nava's light is *inside* me, if you awaken me again, we can—'

'I heard you,' Scarlet said, matter-of-factly. 'I won't do it. It could kill you. I could lose control.' Her tone was certain.

'You don't know that,' Shadow said.

'And the last time the light *went in* you, you were knocked out for who knows how many years.'

'This isn't exactly a science, Scarlet.'

'I won't,' she said. 'I won't do this. There has to be another way.'

This, Shadow had not expected. She had not expected the value of her own life to matter, to be a factor. She hadn't even considered that it could hurt her, kill her.

It baffled her.

But did it even matter, when so much was at stake? She beheld Scarlet's hand – outstretched, palm out, forbidding her from coming closer – and took it between her own.

Scarlet's fingers were tense, rigid. She softened them, folded them together. She drew the hand to her chest. 'You're right,' Shadow said. 'I'm no Soldier now. I'm just Shadow.'

'I know,' said Scarlet stiffly.

'And I'm glad I am.'

'I'm glad, too.'

'So, you have to let *me* try,' she said. 'We have to try. We did it in Asanai – we can do it again.'

'This one thing,' Scarlet said. To Shadow's shock, her eyes were filmy, wet. 'Can't I just have this one thing?'

'Look.' Outside the walls of the palace, a divide had begun down the cliff, all the way across to the sea. Entire sections of land were sinking, drowning, heaving underneath to be replaced by something else. A city of corpses and bones, perhaps. Crow and Yo-han were still caught in the whirlwind of the deadzone, fighting off an entire army of remades. Sae would be somewhere on her own, hiding, or, more probably, taming deadzones and trying to tap into the earth. Saltwater soaking into grass; the sea turning into inky soup. The sky couldn't decide whether to shine or rain or break. The land was in agony, in false rebirth. 'There is no other way.'

The hall was strewn with littered debris from rooms. Loose pieces of clothing, broken vases, papers, pieces of wood furniture. A collection of glass shards of a mirror was swept into one corner, and Shadow saw fragments of her own reflection among them.

'I don't want to die,' Shadow said. 'Do you know that? The universe hasn't burdened me with memory. I remember very little, all of it very distantly, like a series of dreams. Like I'm on the outside, looking in. It haunts me, weighs on me, still, but I don't remember. My mind is free. That's why I don't want to die. No matter what, my body will still fight to live. I won't go easily.'

Scarlet was silent.

'I've always had trouble with memory,' Shadow continued, 'I can't distinguish between real and fake. But there are two so vivid it's like they're scarred into my head: the first is waking up, when the Moonbearer first raised me. And the second is you.'

'Me?' Scarlet said. 'Which memory of me?'

'All,' she said simply. 'All of them.' She turned away from Scarlet. 'One last time. Awaken me.'

'I don't want to hurt you.'

'Believe you won't,' Shadow said. 'Believe that *I* can keep control.'

Silence.

'After all this is over,' Scarlet said, 'I should like you to come to Anje with me.'

'I will,' she replied without hesitation.

The Last Soldier of Nava

A resounding explosion, the hall caving down around them, made them leap apart. Parts of the ceiling collapsed; debris sprinkled.

The Moonbearer had caught wind of them. He sent a slash of darkness in between them, so strong that he could barely control it.

Under the Yong of the East. 동쪽의 용 아래. *Under the Daltokki.* 달토끼 아래.

One last time.

Scale. 비늘. *Shard.* 비늘.

'*Out*,' he snarled, veins crawling up his neck, his head. His eyes were turning entirely black, no whites visible. 'I'm bringing it back. I'm going to bring it all back.'

Nine. 아홉.

'The Dawnbringer is here, Father,' Shadow said, softly. 'Did you know that?'

Lost. 죽은.

Those lightless eyes shifted to her. 'She's dead.'

Rusted. 녹슨.

'She's alive. She survived, and she did what you couldn't. Lived in the new age. Had a family. While you spent centuries manifesting this dark power, trying to reanimate what was already lost, she was forging love.' She pointed at Scarlet. 'She is the product of her love. And so was the Desert Rose.'

Twilight. 어스름.

'Do you think whatever this is, is enough to stop me? I've already slaughtered the *yong*. My strength grows by the second.'

He struck out against her, and incredibly, it was thick, viscous, like a mould she was passing through that coagulated around her. The pressure of it sickened her, choked her out; the iron-grip of it around her. He held the strength of two Dragons in him. She squirmed in his twisted grasp that closed around her vision as the image of the handler, of him, in front of her grew fainter and fainter. She struggled to breathe – to climb out.

Scarlet whispered: *Moon.* 달.

Shadow let her in; the Soldier gasped to life.

Where she would try desperately to hold onto herself, this time, she gave herself over.

She felt her handler's steady hand, the firm control.

THE LIGHT, pressed the handler, but the Soldier could hardly see. CALL FORTH THE LIGHT.

The handler's voice faded away, dissipated quietly into nothing. The presence dwindled.

And then there was only the dark, and in the dark, there was only her and him.

You're too late, he said. *Give in.*

Give in.

But the Soldier would not give in. The Soldier – Shadow – felt something rising within her, something new, something strange, and she reached down, grabbing hold.

For the first time, she had no handler. There was nothing but herself. There was the anger, sure, but there was something smaller, newer, more solid. Determined.

'You're wrong,' the Soldier – Shadow – said. 'We're not too late.'

'You don't have enough light,' he snarled.

I do, Shadow thought, then there was a sensation that she couldn't – had never felt before, one that she could hardly describe – a slow sloughing off, like her body was being cleaved in two, but not painfully; in a way that felt like easing a burden, lifting off a load, a separation; and she gave herself over to it, head tipping back and closing her eyes just as a light so bright as to be blinding erupted in the distance. But it wasn't so distant, it was her, from her, so close she could feel its heat, but so far it drenched everything, erupting from her palms, channelled at her fingertips.

And then nothing at all but whiteness, like a heavy, blanketing cloak, everywhere.

Chapter 36

She woke to the sensation of water dripping gently onto her face.

Rain?

She opened her eyes slowly, blinking.

A girl's face loomed above her.

She wasn't sure to whom this face belonged. It was an arresting face, a regal face, and it was streaked with tears, eyes bloodshot. *Don't cry*, she thought; and a strange, familiar ache stirred in her.

'Shadow,' the girl said, and embraced her tightly, stricken with relief.

Sha-dow. Was that her name? She tried to get a sense of her extremities, how they felt. She was propped up against a tree. There was a dark-haired boy standing beside them. The ground was damp, though it wasn't raining, and the scene around her was devastating. Trees uprooted and grounds overturned, as if a storm had just cycled through. The remnants of a palace, with one side blown out.

The landscape was changed. The landscape was always changing, though – she knew this.

The Last Soldier of Nava

Puddles seeped beside her, collecting in the uneven grass. Her body ached; her heart burned in her chest, as if asking for an out. Her blood pumped as low and as sluggishly as the sky – verging on downpour – commanded it.

'Who are you?' she whispered.

The girl stilled in her embrace; and then pulled back, searching her face.

She wished she could remember.

Then the girl exchanged a quiet glance with the dark-haired boy. 'My name is Iseul,' she said.

The boy knelt, too. 'Mine is Jae-sung.'

She tried to sit up more, but her stiff bones protested. 'Then what's my name? I . . . don't remember.'

'It can be anything you like,' Iseul said, softly. 'It's not important.'

Sha-dow, Sha-dow.

'I know someone who can help you,' Iseul said. 'Who can bring your memories back.'

'Who?' the boy asked her.

'The Dawnbringer.'

'The Dawnbringer's *alive?*'

Iseul nodded. A stunned silence. And then –

'Does she even want her memories back?' Jae-sung said.

Iseul glared at him but turned back. 'Do you?'

She looked again at all the destruction. It seemed too unpleasant to want to remember, what had happened in this place. Why the beautiful girl cried before her, and the boy looked defeated.

But still.

She would like to remember it.

'Yes,' she said. 'I can already . . .' *remember.*

'What?' Iseul said.

'Just . . . feelings,' she answered. 'It feels familiar.'

The girl nodded. After a long moment, she got to her feet, reaching down a hand. 'Can you stand?'

She took the hand, got painfully to her feet.

'The deadzones have closed,' Jae-sang said. 'The land is settled, for now. Even with both Dragons dead.'

'I don't know how,' Iseul said.

The boy exhaled. 'Me neither. For all we know, the storms could still be at bay. There's still so much work to do.'

'It's all right.'

Then both of them looked towards the sea.

Standing out in the distance, overlooking the ocean, stood a white-haired boy with his back to them.

'I know he's wronged you,' Jae-sung said, turning back. 'But he can still help. We can strip him of his royal title, have him mend relations with Asanai by reaching out to his sister. Show mercy on him.' He looked at both of them, as if trying to gauge their feelings, though she didn't even know who the boy was or what had happened.

'Don't ask us for mercy,' Iseul said. 'We're your equals. And he's my brother, too – I care for him, still.' She paused. 'He has blood on his hands. But – we all do.'

A silence.

It began to rain, lightly. She didn't know what these names meant, these details; she wanted to help, too, but she couldn't. She tried hard to will her memories back, but only frustration unfurled. They flickered at the edge of her consciousness; they would return soon, but not right now. Right now they were nothing but murky outlines in the distance of her mind. And then as the water dripped down, pattering across the back of her hands, each drop hit like a sharp cry for help, and in this water, she saw everything she shouldn't, plagued by images overwhelming her senses.

The Last Soldier of Nava

She fell to her knees. Iseul started to her, alarmed, but Shadow only held up her face to the sky, eyes closed.

'The rain calls out to me,' she said, and there was wetness on her face, though she wasn't sure from what.

Slowly, Iseul knelt.

'I think that's the Dragon,' she said gently. 'The death of its body and its ashes becoming dirt, becoming water, becoming rain and sky. All one circle, and you always felt it – but you must feel it most now.' Then she, too, looked at the sky. The boy followed. 'It's frightening, because of its scope, but it's beautiful, too. Isn't it?'

She looked down at her hands. Hands that had once been smaller and lighter and dust, hands that might have once been fragments coalescing into this whole, once soil and sapling and seed. These hands never lied. They told only the truth.

Acknowledgements

Readers are often kept in the dark about how a book comes into creation, so I want to illuminate the steps that went into this one. Thank you to everyone who worked on it: Ajebowale Roberts for originally believing in the story's potential; Chloe Gough for her amazing editing and oversight; Jason Lyon for his incredible cover and character artwork; Sarah Foster for the cover design; Fran Fabriczki for copyediting; Indigo Griffiths and Angelica Bowden-Jones for publicity and marketing; and Emily Chan for production. Thank you to my agent Allegra Martschenko, who always knows what I'm trying to do in my writing even when I'm not sure myself. Thanks sincerely to every early reader who championed the book.

My writing is possible because of the teachers who helped me in high school and the brilliant peers I met at Kenyon and YoungArts who opened my eyes to the talent and ambition of young writers. Thanks to my university friends for their support, especially Natalia (remember when you saw my deal announcement before me? That's what I get for sleeping in). To Alicia, who has been here since the start of this book's journey in Paris. To Philip, who came near the end of the

Yejin Suh

journey (but just in time). To my childhood friends Kayla, Bella, Jenna, Matea, and Ashley, who remind me how fun life is outside of fiction. To my family for their sacrifices and unconditional encouragement of my dreams. And finally – saving the best for last – thanks to my dog Gatsby, who understands me as I do him.